GENE℞ATIONS

Those Who Don't Know History . . . May Live to See Tomorrow

KENNY SARGENT

GENERATIONS: *Those Who Don't Know History ... May Live to See Tomorrow*
© 2018 by Kenny Sargent

ISBN: 978-1-94429-806-7

Cover and Interior Design by Niddy Griddy Design, Inc.
Cover Photos: iStock and Shutterstock—Used by permission

LCCN: 2018949505
Printed in the United States of America
1 2 3 4 5 6 7 8 9 10 Printing/Year 22 21 20 19 18

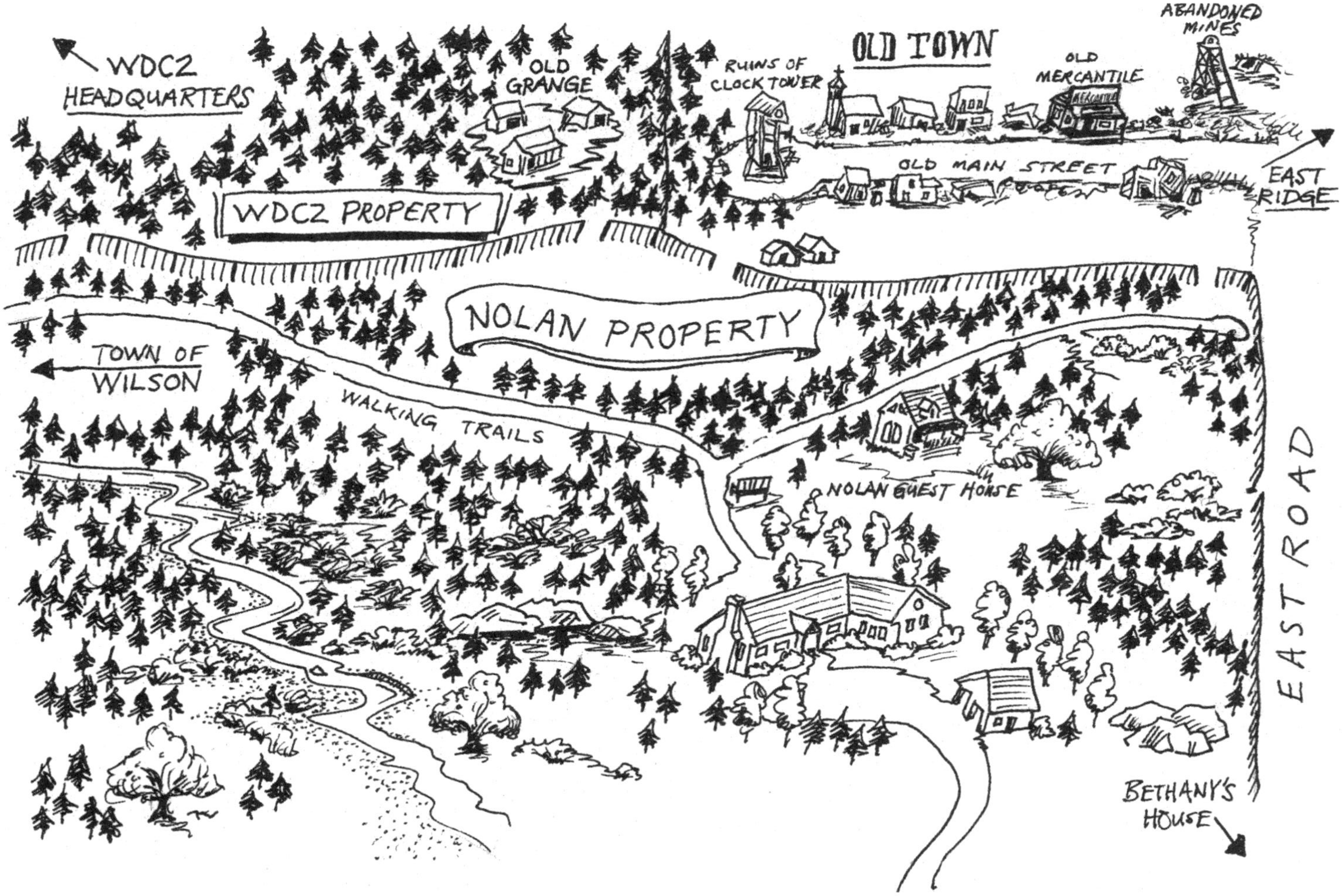

WDCZ HEADQUARTERS
OLD GRANGE
RUINS OF CLOCK TOWER
OLD TOWN
OLD MERCANTILE
ABANDONED MINES
OLD MAIN STREET
EAST RIDGE
WDCZ PROPERTY
NOLAN PROPERTY
TOWN OF WILSON
WALKING TRAILS
NOLAN GUEST HOUSE
EAST ROAD
BETHANY'S HOUSE

The GENERATIONS

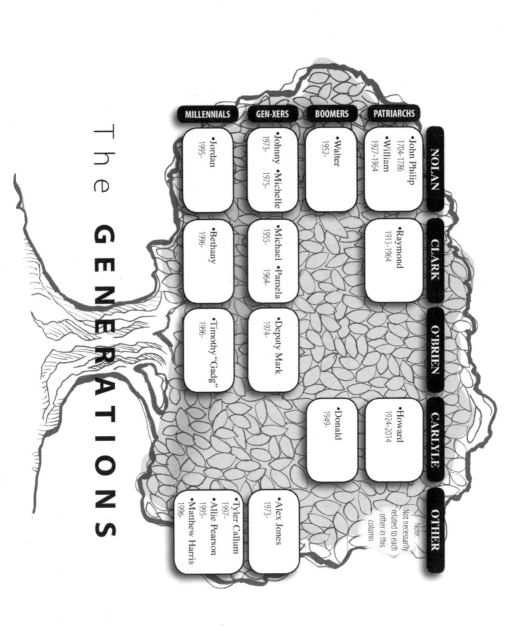

	NOLAN	CLARK	O'BRIEN	CARLYLE	OTHER
PATRIARCHS	• John Philip 1704-1786 • William 1927-1964	• Raymond 1913-1964		• Howard 1924-2014	
BOOMERS	• Walter 1952-			• Donald 1949-	• Alex Jones 1973-
GEN-XERS	• Johnny 1973- • Michelle 1975-	• Michael 1955- • Pamela 1964-	• Deputy Mark 1974-		
MILLENNIALS	• Jordan 1995-	• Bethany 1996-	• Timothy "Gadg" 1996-		• Tyler Callum 1997- • Allie Pearson 1995- • Matthew Harris 1996-

Note:
Not necessarily
related to each
other in this
column

Lovingly dedicated to Father, Son, and Holy Spirit—
for calling me out of darkness and loving me in the Secret Place.

"I am my Beloved's, and He is mine."

Contents

Part Two: Jericho

Part Three: The Promised Land

·

May this copy of God's Holy Writ ever be unto thou and this family as a testimony that "His faithfulness is unto all generations." (Psalm 119)

John Philip Nolan
Northampton, Massachusetts
June, 1754

PART ONE

Jordan

Chapter 1

Plan B

Thursday, April 23, 1964, 11:30 p.m.
Hallway outside the research lab of Carlyle Enterprises, Wilson, CO

"This is definitely illegal," whispered William.

"I know," said Ray. "But it's right."

The moon shone through the glass door and cast the words "Research Lab" backward onto the wall across the narrow hallway. Flashlights hung from their belts as the heavens shined a questioning spotlight on their activities.

Normally in lab coats, William Nolan and Raymond Clark wore all black. The hallway was so unadorned that William had hardly noticed it the last six years. Now at midnight, surrounded by silence that could be felt, it looked ominous.

Three minutes passed and the quiet deepened. Tiny clicks were the only sounds as William worked the lock. "How can I get this open if I can't even hold my hands steady?"

Fifteen years his senior, Ray spoke with a calm as eerie as the sterile hallway. "We're past the point of no return. Get it done."

William's hands stopped shaking and the pick found its mark. The lab door creaked open. "Eight hours ago we could have done that with a key," said William with a grim smile.

"I never thought we'd have to steal our own work," said Ray. He nodded toward the inside of the lab. "Collect what we need from here. I'll meet you at the rendezvous point." He turned back down the hall.

William swallowed hard. "You sure you have to do that?"

Ray turned around and said nothing. Moonlight shined on his eyes like headlight beams reflecting off black ice.

William pressed his lips together and gave a nod. "It just seemed a lot different when we planned it in my living room."

"Stay with the program. You know the stakes." Ray gave him a smile, then crept down the hall.

William stared as his best friend rounded the corner toward the executive offices.

We may live through this night after all.

●●●

His lungs screamed for oxygen. Twenty minutes after he and Ray had split up, William found himself dodging tree limbs and skirting rock formations east of the research lab. The mountain air of Wilson, Colorado, compounded the problem. Worse still, he looked down at a body lean enough to belong to a runner, but only because he'd spent years poring over test tubes with half-eaten fast food getting cold within arm's reach.

He forced himself to think through his part of Plan A. He had to trust Ray with the rest. His mind stopped on his final task.

Ask Katherine and Walter to take me back...

Gasping for air, William stumbled up to the nearest pine tree. His eyes glossed over as a wave of longing flooded his heart. Two weeks ago, the thought would not have come up, much less been entertained. But so much had happened. For the first time in his life, he was truly living. As his breath calmed, he gave in to the yearning and allowed the emotions to wash over him.

Oh, Katherine, I'm so sorry.

A scientist by trade, his training compelled him to analyze the feelings as they came. William shook his head as he identified a mixture of love laced with nostalgia. He forced the clinical thoughts to stand down and let himself simply feel.

Oh, Walter.

Except from a distance, he had not seen his son in five years. If only they could make it through this night...

I'm going home.

●●●

BOOM!

The crack of a rifle shot reverberated through the forest. William leaned his head against the trunk of the tree as the bottom fell out of his stomach and a crushing darkness dragged his eyelids shut in one slow blink. That sound could mean only one thing.

They were switching to Plan B.

Plan A was bad enough: secrecy; covert accumulation of evidence; the danger of finding themselves chained to a cement block at the bottom of Wilson's Creek; powerful people as lifelong enemies—even if it worked.

Plan B was horrible.

It wasn't much of a plan at all. It was more like a desperate hope for a miracle wrapped in huge leaps of logic.

Forcing his eyes open and pushing his newly awakened feelings down, William spurred his mind into gear.

Should he go back and check on Ray?

Even though he knew in his gut that it was a futile exercise, William worked through the possibilities line by line in his head. Sixty seconds later the conclusion was obvious.

Plan B was the only option.

William slammed his fist against the tree. He wanted to feel. To love. To belong. Plan B didn't include any of those things.

He was amazed at how crazy life had become in the last few days for him to even consider, much less adopt, a "plan" so absurd.

He was a dead man. Soon.

Ray was a dead man—maybe already.

Their families were in grave danger, and that wasn't even the worst part.

His stomach felt like a clenching vise as he thought of the thousands of people who would soon suffer. He punched the tree again. There was nothing he could do about that now.

He took off running. The odd sensation of a bundle wrapped in green felt and tucked under his right arm reminded him of the next move. Though it was a death march, he still had to work Plan B.

The pursuit was within earshot. He had to hide the bundle in exactly the right spot. They'd spent several nights putting all the pieces in place. The smallest light broke through his frustration as he thought about the possibility, however remote, that his son might come to know the truth.

A second gunshot rocked him from his musings. William adjusted his course to get farther from the sound. He stumbled to the edge of his own property.

Except for the last two nights, he had not set foot near this place for five years. Tonight, he would do so again only in stealth.

Is this really happening in Wilson?

In 1964, the people of Wilson left their keys in their cars. In addition, two gunshots wouldn't even earn glances out of windows in Western Colorado.

Continuing around the perimeter of his property, William came to the remains of Old Town. Started as a copper mining settlement in the late 1800s, several now-abandoned buildings still stood along Old Main Street. His great-grandfather had been one of Wilson's founders and was rewarded with twenty acres near the edge of the original town. An abandoned house still stood on Nolan property. William sneaked through the fence and made his way up to the porch.

He stepped on a creaking floorboard and a shudder coursed through him. William opened the door to the cellar and looked down into the darkness. To his knowledge, only three people in Wilson knew of this secret.

He paused for a moment and tried to breathe. His heart rate steadied. Turning around, he looked out across the property toward the main house. No lights were on, yet he longed to walk up and pour out his heart.

I won't see them again.

To do so would mean death for them. Besides the people who would soon suffer, this was the most heart-wrenching part of Plan B: the survival of his family depended on his silence.

He turned back to the cellar door and recalibrated his thinking to the remaining items in Plan B.

With one more glance at the main house, he descended the steps and spent the next three minutes carefully disposing of his bundle.

●●●

William still wanted to *feel*.

Being on his property again only fanned the flame. Several realizations slammed him like waves on a beach:

I can be a good husband.
I can be a good father.
I can love.

I can feel.

I can live!

As he picked his way through the forest, he dared to hope. He didn't know for certain they'd switched to Plan B. It was time to find out for sure. He had to check on Ray. Several minutes later, William spotted him leaning with his back against a tree. He sucked in a breath.

Stopping to listen for the sounds of pursuit, he tiptoed around trees and ducked under branches to get closer. Peeking around one last tree, he looked down at Ray.

A bullet had found its mark. Plan A was dead. Ray Clark would soon follow. And so would he.

William squeezed his eyes shut as hot tears pounded on the inside of his eyelids, forcing their way out. With two fierce swipes of his hand, he cleared his vision. He knelt down and reached out toward Ray. His hand shook as he tried to remove the blood-soaked handkerchief Ray had pressed to his side.

Ray shook his head. "Don't bother." He punched the words in between gasps of air.

William looked away.

"Look at me!" Ray forced the words out in a commanding whisper.

William's face contorted as images of his wife and son flashed through his mind. Eyes still stinging, he looked down at his friend.

Ray directed his gaze like a laser into William's soul. "You masterminded this. You know it's the only choice left." His voice lowered to an almost inaudible whisper. "You can do it."

William sighed. "Option 3?"

"I think it's the best option. Don't you?" Ray labored to get the words out.

William looked down at the wound and back up at Ray. He nodded. A fresh tear pooled in the corner of his eye. "You're an incredible man, Ray. I'll miss you."

"Not for long you won't," said Ray with a deadly matter-of-factness. His body shook with pain and labored breathing, but his eyes were placid.

William stared at him for a few seconds. Gradually, as he beheld the icy calm of his dying friend, a steely change that reflected in the moonlight came across his countenance. His nod was resolute.

Ray managed a pain-wracked smile. "Get it done, William. I'll be waiting for you on the other side." He handed over a cigar box that William hadn't noticed before.

There was no mistaking it. Hacienda Grande. Dominican Republic. High-quality imported Spanish cedar with a tasteful blend of blue, red, and white trim—along with a picture of a large hacienda surrounded by a lush plantation.

"A little present from The Man," said Ray quietly.

"Just couldn't leave without delegating one more assignment?" William unlatched the box. He pulled several folded pages from his pockets and added them to the pile.

"You need another task for your list." Ray grimaced out a chuckling reply as William reclasped the lid. "Turn it over," said Ray.

William turned the box bottom up as Ray reached into his bloody side with his index finger. William cringed at the pain that registered on Ray's face.

Ray took his finger, now drenched in his own blood, and scrawled a short message on the bottom of the cigar box. "That should help."

"If it ever sees the light of day," said William.

Ray nodded, and a moment later he said, "My letter won't. It will never get there."

"What do you mean?"

Ray coughed some blood.

"You don't think he betrayed us?" asked William.

For the first time that evening, a tremor crossed the face of Ray Clark. Not fear, but sadness. "How else could they have known about tonight?"

"I thought he was with us."

"So did I," said Ray. "Work the plan. This is the last chance." His voice was barely audible. "You're a good man, William." He let out one more breath and was gone.

"Thank you," William whispered, "for everything."

He placed his hand over the back of Ray's hand, picked it up, and used it to scratch his own face as hard as he could. Four trails of blood from his cheek to his neck sprang to the surface. He then stuck his hand under the handkerchief, pulled out some of Ray's blood, and smeared it on his own clothes.

Crack. A twig. Two hundred yards away.

Go, William. Now!

He flung his hat toward Ray's dead hand, grabbed the cigar box, and ran with all his might.

"Get him!" yelled a voice.

The night erupted. William felt air puff past his face as a bullet whizzed by and blew off a chunk from a nearby tree. Up to that point, William had only felt the danger secondhand. A wildness came into his eyes. Adrenaline surged through him. A branch from a passing pine sliced across his cheek, but he hardly noticed.

A sense of déjà vu came over him as he sprinted back toward Old Town. His property lay to his right, but he didn't head for it. Instead, he passed the clock tower, ran straight down the sidewalk of what was once Main Street, and made for the Old Mercantile.

Ducking behind the building, William looped around, doubled back and made his way toward his property. He could hear the pursuit reaching Old Town. He found the gate closest to the ridge on the eastern side of Nolan property and sneaked through the rock outcroppings back to the abandoned house. The cellar was his starting point this time instead of his destination. A few minutes later, the last assignment from his boss was complete. Had it not been for the danger to their families, he could have escaped.

One more task on his list. William closed his eyes and prayed. This one really did need a miracle.

Plan B didn't include escape.

Chapter 2

Birth of a Stigma

Friday, April 24, 1964, 1:30 a.m.
William Nolan's apartment, town of Wilson, CO

With his .22 caliber in hand, William sat patiently at the kitchen table and waited. He had a magazine spread open before him, but his mind refused to focus on the words.

Oh, God.

He switched to praying out loud because it might be his last chance. "I just have one more request. Will You do a miracle?"

Any minute now.

The kitchen door crashed open. Three men burst in and fanned out across the room. "Freeze," barked one as all three raised their guns. "Put your hands in the air."

William did as he was told. He let go of the gun, being sure to touch it with his whole hand and all his fingers as he laid it down on the table.

Everything hinged on this moment.

The first man strolled up to the table. He looked down at the blood on William's shirt and face. "You realize you've done us a favor, don't you?"

William's heart sped. "You'll never make it stick." He bluffed with all he had.

"You're not nearly as smart as they say," the intruder took his time. "Not only will it stick, but you are going to die knowing that your family will bear the stigma of your misdeeds for years to come." He smirked and picked up William's gun with a gloved hand. "How does that make you feel?"

Tears escaped from both of William's eyes simultaneously. Relief flooded him.

Smiling, but misunderstanding, the man gave a satisfied nod.

The impossible had just happened.

Plan B worked.

Tears streamed now.

Our families are safe.

Like a cat toying with a mouse, the man walked around the table.

William's peace mingled with pain for the thousands of people who would soon suffer. He had failed them. He closed his eyes and used the grief to make himself look as beaten as possible.

A calmness flooded his soul. He had wasted most of his thirty-seven years, but gratitude filled his heart for a few short days well lived.

Lord, please remember Walter. Will You make a way for the truth to come out?

This time he didn't even hear the shot.

Local Researcher Kills Coworker, Takes Own Life

William Nolan, 37, of Wilson, Colorado, shot and killed a coworker, Raymond Clark, who also hailed from Wilson. Witnesses close to the men said that a conflict between them had escalated rapidly in the last few days, culminating with Nolan shooting Clark in the forested area behind Carlyle Enterprises' Research Lab. Nolan was also found dead later in his apartment of a gunshot wound to the head. A Smith and Wesson bearing his fingerprints lay on the floor next to him. The police have ruled it a suicide.

Howard Carlyle, CEO of Carlyle Enterprises, made the following statement: "We are deeply saddened by the news. Our sincerest condolences to the Clark family in this most difficult time."

From an article in *Old Town News,* local newspaper of Wilson County
Friday, April 24, 1964

No.	Entry Date	Name	Age	Issue Date	Impact
1	1-1-1965	Raymond Clark	52	4-24-1964	Murdered
2	1-1-1965	William Nolan	37	4-24-1964	Murdered

Chapter 3

Dreams and Nightmares

Present Day
Saturday, May 10, 6:07 a.m.
Peak Vista Hotel, Colorado Springs, CO

Jordan blasted awake from a vivid dream, snatched up his smartphone, and voice-launched a new diary entry with the day less than five seconds old.

Strange Dream

Standing before a bridge that has word "Wilson" inscribed across top

Can't see where it goes

In my hand a pen, and I'm signing away life savings to buy the bridge

Filled with more joy than I've ever experienced in my life

Wow!

His smile threatened to split his face—a rare occurrence in the last several years.

What was that about?

He took a moment to get his bearings. It was 6:08 a.m. and he was already in fourth gear. His best friend still slept in the other bed.

He looked over the entry to see how it read. For many, voice recognition technology could be hilarious or annoying, as it didn't always interpret the words correctly. For Jordan, it was personal. His future depended on his ability to articulate clearly. His diary entry was off by one word.

Unacceptable.

Three seconds later, what he barely lacked in diction, he made up for with technological savvy. Using nothing but his voice, he corrected the slight error and looked it over.

He nodded at the screen. Nine minutes past six, and he was already racking up the geek points.

Even at the groggy two-minute mark of the day, Jordan was highly articulate. His future demanded it. An undergraduate degree from Harvard and a law degree from Yale were dreams for some, and wishful thinking for most. For Jordan, they were stepping stones. State government and national government were mile markers on the road to the United Nations.

His surroundings came into focus.

Where am I?

He was in a hotel room in Colorado Springs. Recollection crashed in and pulled his face into a mask of determination.

This is it.

All of it hinged on this day.

Today he could write his ticket. It was the final hurdle on the journey to escape his hometown of Wilson, Colorado. To get out of Wilson, he had to receive the Senator's Internship. To receive the Senator's Internship, he had to win the final round. To win the final round, he had to get six of eleven judges to vote for him. To get six judges to vote for him only had one obstacle: Matthew Harris.

Dark clouds rolled across his mind as the dream faded.

Matthew.

Jordan's thoughts snapped unbidden to elementary school. Everything had looked so big. The play structure was huge. The twin fields for flag football and soccer were larger than life. His heart was open, and he was ready.

Until the first day of school.

It started when a group of parents, led by Matthew Harris's father, forbade their children to play with "that Nolan boy."

Long before he knew what a synonym was, Jordan realized that the Nolan name represented something dark and sinister to the community.

Matthew led the cool crowd at school, which meant that most kids shunned Jordan Nolan. To make matters worse, Matthew had an uncle who mentored him in the art of being a bully. When the boys did play with Jordan, they enjoyed a game called "Nineteen-sixty-four" in which Jordan was cast as Raymond Clark while they played William Nolan. Their favorite part of the game was pinning Jordan to the ground on his back, holding his limbs down and covering his mouth. Then Matthew jabbed his finger over and over into Jordan's chest while he struggled to breathe.

Memories flung him back to that playground. Panic seized his gut and a screaming, helpless rage exploded red across his mind as he gasped for breath.

Waiting longer than he should have, Matthew instructed the other boys to release him. Jordan lay, panting for air as Matthew said, "Okay, class, the history lesson is over." Turning to smirk at Jordan, he concluded with, "We'll pick it up again tomorrow."

Jordan clutched the comforter with an iron grip. The hotel room came back into focus. Even with his eyes open, red still hovered around the edges of his thoughts. His heart pounded against the back of his ribs. Several deep breaths and a long drink of water steadied his pulse.

The memories didn't usually hit him like that anymore.

He had survived that first year thanks to the kindness of an eight-year-old girl. After one such occasion, the boys had pushed Jordan facedown and left him crying in the dirt. When he pulled himself into a sitting position, his head swam with horror and he searched for something—anything—to ease the pain.

He didn't have to look far. A young girl made her way across the yard and knelt next to him. She put the palm of one small hand on his cheek and wiped his tears away with the other. For a second he thought she was an angel. Then he realized she was a classmate—and not just any classmate, but the daughter of one of the men who did not allow their kids to play with him.

"Bethany?" He blinked through a blur of tears.

"Yes, it's me." Her voice was so melodic, it sounded like singing. "My Daddy told me you're going to make it."

"Your daddy hates me and my family," said Jordan.

"Not that daddy—my Heavenly Daddy. He told me you're going to be okay." She stood, offered her hand, and lifted him up. They faced each other for a few seconds and she gave him a tender smile, turned, and walked away.

Jordan never forgot that day.

The following week, a new family moved into the community. Young

Timothy O'Brien became fast friends with Jordan, despite Matthew and his gang. It didn't hurt that their dads had been best buds in college, or that Timothy's father had come back from the big city to be an officer in the Wilson Police Department. Matthew still kept a wary eye on them, but Jordan began to grow physically. With the start of the next year, the threat of torture had passed.

The rivalry, however, had just begun.

In junior high, Matthew missed two words in a row at the regional spelling bee and suffered a humiliating loss that sent Jordan to nationals. Ironically, the national competition that year had been in Washington, DC.

Five years had done nothing but ratchet up the intensity between the two. Today, they would face off again.

One debate.

The winner would go to DC. Harris vs. Nolan.

Matthew was a Harris. That meant money and honor.

Jordan was a Nolan.

Great-grandson of a murderer.

Grandson of a one-armed construction superintendent.

Son of a state football star.

Nolan: many things to many people. To Jordan himself, it was a scarlet letter branded on his chest like a modern-day Hester Prynne.

He would wipe it out.

To do so, he had to get out of Wilson.

● ● ●

The last straw came two years ago. Jordan and his father had spent many hours with an eleven-inch leather spheroid holding their relationship together. Jordan enjoyed football, but his father, head coach at a local high school, lived for it. The fateful day came in July before his junior year.

Jordan walked to the door of his dad's home office and looked around the room. Football paraphernalia covered every open section of wall space. With papers strewn in front of him, Johnny leaned back in a rocking desk chair, propped his feet on the desk, and worked a wad of bubble gum in his cheek. Forehead creased, he pored over a clipboard. He shook his head and mumbled about something that wasn't going to work.

Jordan stepped in cautiously. "Dad, I've come to a decision."

"Oh yeah, what's that?" asked Johnny, still looking down at his clipboard.

Jordan opened his mouth and closed it again.

Johnny flipped a page over the back of the clipboard and held it in place with one hand. Under the red brim of his cap he skimmed the second page. "What is it, son?"

Jordan took a deep breath and blurted out, "I'm not going to play football in the fall."

Johnny's head jerked up and his feet hit the floor. "What?"

Jordan took a step back. "I'm going to devote my energies to speech and debate. If I'm going to become an attorney—"

"Don't be ridiculous," Johnny cut him off and sat back down. "You're just getting to the place where it's starting to pay off."

"My heart's not in it, Dad. It's not what I want."

Johnny stared hard at his son. "I cannot believe I'm hearing *this*."

"And why is *that*?" Anger pushed Jordan's fear into the background.

"Oh, let's see," Johnny said, "How about my *starting quarterback* decides to quit the summer before his junior year, after going eight and three as a sophomore? No reason."

"How about 'your *firstborn son* decides to follow *his* passion?'" Jordan fired back.

"You just can't take it." The cords of Johnny's neck grew taut.

Jordan's face flushed. "That's garbage and you know it."

"Speech and debate," Johnny's voice dripped scorn. "What a sissy sport. I can't believe I ever let your mom talk me into it. In fact, it's not even a *sport*."

Jordan started for the door but turned back and blasted, "You're right. It's not a *sport*. It's the makings of a *career*. It's a future. Hopefully in a place far from *here*."

"What do you know about a career?" Johnny waved him off and snatched up his clipboard. "Shut the door."

Jordan slammed the door. As he did, a door in his heart slammed at the same time. Now, almost two years later, his ticket out of Wilson dangled in front of him like a carrot in the shape of the Washington Monument.

Losing wasn't an option.

That reminder brought him back to the present. He pressed the side buttons on his phone and lifted it to his mouth.

Last Minute Notes on the Big Day

Stay calm

You know his case and you know your case

If you draw AFFIRMATIVE go with the ethics of living donor transplantation case

If you draw NEGATIVE choose the human dignity value or personal freedom value based on his opening speech

Do not use sarcasm—it's counterproductive

Go for the jugular in the cross-examination—be respectful but attack without mercy

In the final speech go for the heart of the judges

You can do this!

He threw back the covers and headed for the shower with a fist pump. With the day only seven minutes old, the dream was already a distant memory.

Dear Doctor,

Enclosed is a clinical sample of a remarkable new sedative soon to be released by Hampden Pharmaceuticals. The drug is called XD and will be marketed under various over-the-counter brand names. Completely nontoxic...

Summer 1964—Hampden Pharmaceuticals letter to 130,000 doctors worldwide announcing the forthcoming release of XD.

No.	Entry Date	Name	Age	Issue Date	Impact
77	8-7-1965	Elliot Spencer	0	7-16-1965	Right arm birth defect
78	8-18-1965	Lawrence Kahn	0	7-21-1965	Stillborn

Chapter 4

Going Nowhere

Saturday, May 10, 8:05 a.m.
Peak Vista Hotel Café, Colorado Springs, CO

"Can you believe it?" Allison Pearson spoke over the hubbub of a hotel café full of young people dressed like attorneys. Her cheek quivered. "The last hurrah."

Bethany reached across the table and took Allie's hands in her own. "No. I can barely remember a time without it."

"Six years," said Allie, blinking away the mist. "We're such nerds."

Bethany stared for several seconds into Allie's eyes before responding with a melodic voice that would be heard in both the broadcasting and storytelling finals today. "Good friends, great memories, real skills. Who needs to be cool?" She smiled. "Plus, you look rather fetching in that power suit."

Allie's eyes twinkled.

The final day of the Forensic Communicators League National Tournament would be underway soon. The press of the crowded café forced them to lean in closer to hear one another. Their friendship provided a sanctuary for them in the din of rising excitement.

"I've got to give your mom a hug if I see her," said Allie. "Did she end up making it?"

Bethany's faced tightened.

"I'm sorry, Beth. I know how much she would have wanted to be here." Allie had the singular privilege of using a nickname for Bethany. "Any update?"

Bethany let out a long exhale and shook her head. "It's crazy. They've tried every test they can think of."

"How about I come out and stay with you this summer to help out?" Allie suggested. "I'm sure you'll be super busy with all you're doing."

"More than you know," replied Bethany. "My dad is heading up the committee for the 50th Anniversary Celebration in August."

Allie raised an eyebrow. "The Wonder Drug?"

Bethany nodded. "It's a horrible time for it really, but my mom wants him to. She doesn't want him worrying the summer away."

"How about I check with my folks?" said Allie.

Bethany's chin trembled. She closed her eyes and gave a nod. "I'd like that."

Still holding hands in the midst of the noisy crowd, Allie gave her a look that communicated a decade of friendship without a single word.

Bethany forced a smile. "You're not helping. I have to tell a story at nine thirty that is supposed to make people laugh."

Allie grinned and gently pulled her hands free, reaching over to smooth a crease in Bethany's suit. "Speaking of fetching"—she paused and let her words hang in the air—"how about that debate final?"

Bethany smirked.

"Who would've believed it would all come down to one debate for the whole thing? I wish I could've been a fly on the wall this year," said Allie.

Bethany smiled. "I've been more than a fly."

Allie's eyes lit up. She had known Matthew and Jordan since childhood and was no stranger to their rivalry. "I wanna hear all about it. Tell me!"

Bethany chuckled. "Remember five years ago?"

"The spelling bee final?"

Bethany nodded. "Matthew's been wanting to get even ever since."

"Ooh, sounds juicy! I love it!" Allie had qualified to speak in the dramatic and humorous finals later that day.

"More like tiring," Bethany sighed. "I just want them to grow up—or at least tolerate one another."

"I don't think today is going to help with that," said Allie.

"That's for sure. However, at least one of them will be out of Wilson for a while. That will be a relief." Bethany stared into the distance and a shadow crossed her face.

"Sooooo, who do you want ... to lose?" Allie asked with a wink.

Bethany frowned. "Neither. It's too bad they both can't go."

"Oh come on, Beth, don't tell me you haven't given it a thought ever."

● ● ●

Deep in conversation and close to the buffet table, the girls were unaware of Jordan scooping food onto his plate. Their conversation had arrested his attention, and he slowed to a deliberate pace, examining each item as if this championship breakfast would have to last him for weeks.

Bethany responded, "Matthew is out of the question. He's a Harris, after all."

Jordan breathed easier. Bethany was far too down-to-earth for a Harris. He wasn't so sure Allie thought the same.

"Jordan is more complicated." Bethany paused. "He's very handsome, very bright, and an extremely gifted communicator. Also, he's relentless when in pursuit of something."

Jordan's chest threatened to puff out of his dapper suit. He chose three pieces of bacon with such care that it looked like he was playing a game of *Operation* and didn't want the buzzer to go off. His smile faded as Bethany continued.

"He's also out of the question for two reasons."

"What?" said Allie, trying to keep her voice low.

"First, you know my dad would never allow it."

"April 1964?"

"You got it. My great-grandfather Ray was murdered by William Nolan, who committed suicide later that night. For some reason, my dad takes that personally. I love him dearly, but this is one subject that almost makes him grow fangs. Jordan is guilty by association just because of his last name."

Jordan ground his teeth as he was reminded again that he could never quite break free of the Nolan Stigma. He had to get to Washington. Out of the corner of his eye, he saw Matthew enter the café.

"What's the second reason?" asked Allie.

"He's going nowhere," answered Bethany.

"Jordan?" Allie sounded surprised.

He almost dropped his entire plate into the bacon dish. Fumbling it twice, he managed to hold onto it without making a scene.

His mind reeled as he hunched over the buffet table. If he won the Senator's

Internship, Jordan had an extremely bright future ahead of him. He certainly would become an excellent attorney, and could even become a senator himself someday.

Just as Bethany started to respond, Matthew strode up from a different direction and caused the burning question to go unanswered.

Meanwhile, Jordan snatched up two more pieces of bacon and hustled to the end of the buffet table to get silverware. Clenching his jaw, he grabbed three napkins.

How dare she say I'm "going nowhere"?

"Good morning, ladies." Matthew's smile was as big as his ego. Jordan was far enough away now to escape the danger of getting caught eavesdropping, but Matthew's voice was strong and resonant—easy to hear, even in a crowd. Some other competitors stopped their conversations and looked up. *Everybody* knew what today meant.

"Good morning, Matthew." Allie didn't have to force her smile. Bethany responded with a slight nod.

"You going to watch the final?" he asked.

"Of course!" responded Allie.

Bethany's reply held a touch of sarcasm, "Wouldn't miss it."

"Payback time." Matthew's voice got lower and rougher.

Jordan chose that moment to approach the group. "Good morning, all." He addressed each one with a focused gaze. "Miss Pearson." He cocked his head. "Miss Clark." He narrowed his eyes. "Mr. Harris." For the last eighteen months, Jordan had practiced addressing his associates in the same way he would as an attorney—by their surnames. The noise died down as the café realized that they might get a preview of tonight's festivities. "I couldn't help hearing that you intend to finally pay me back that five bucks I gave you in grade school."

A hint of crimson crept up above Matthew's perfectly pressed collar. He reached into his wallet and pulled out a twenty-dollar bill. The room got even quieter as more people tuned into the pregame show. "I wasn't aware I hadn't paid you back." Matthew slapped the twenty down on the table. "Today I will—with interest."

A low murmur went around the room.

Bethany sighed.

"Awesome." Jordan pulled out his phone, pretending to be oblivious to Matthew's jab. "I could use the money to buy this slick new knowledge consolidation app I've been wanting. It combines a dictionary, historical documents, an atlas, and many other things. You should try it."

"I'm sorry you had to wait ten years to get twenty bucks, but it doesn't surprise me," Matthew fired back. "Why would I want that app? Maybe to make sure you weren't going to mix two definitions tonight?"

Allie smirked. A few quiet "oohs" could be heard around the room.

Jordan started to walk away, then turned and glanced at Bethany before addressing Matthew. "I just want to make sure you know how to *spell* Washington."

Thursday—The Association of Medical Professionals honored Howard Carlyle of Wilson Drug and Compounding Center as the medical community's "Man of the Century" for his outstanding contributions to humanity. This summer marks the 35th anniversary of the release of Amitolin— better known as the Wonder Drug.

The Wall Street Journal, May 7, 1999.

Chapter 5

Beware of the Nolans

Saturday, May 10, 6:15 p.m.
Hospital room at Denver Adventist, Denver, CO

Donald Carlyle sat in a hospital room in Denver, waiting for his father, the Man of the Century, to die. Fifteen years ago, the medical community had bestowed the honor upon Howard Carlyle after he had brought Amitolin, better known as the Wonder Drug, to the human race. The crowds were long gone as Donald and his father awaited the inevitable in the stark cleanliness of room 415 at Denver Adventist.

The heart rate seemed dangerously slow, with an odd rhythm that Donald knew could not be right. He looked down at his father, his thoughts a jumbled mix of emotions.

Sadness? Some.

Relief? Yes.

Anger? Not really—not in this context, anyway.

Any minute now, Howard Carlyle would die. Amitolin—his Wonder Drug—would live on. The father had made a significant contribution to the human race.

Following in his footsteps, the son could not say the same about himself. Donald now ran the empire known as WDC2—Wilson Drug and Compounding Center—headquartered in Wilson, Colorado. Howard had made his mark. Now Donald, having lived in his father's shadow for most of his life, tried to keep things afloat.

Howard had possessed boundless energy and significant popularity. As chairman of the board, he had held the reins of WDC2 until well into his eighties. Even in the last five years, he had exerted considerable influence over the company's direction.

Donald had been in executive leadership at WDC2 for the past seventeen years. He took over as CEO at age fifty-five—a position he'd held for the last ten of those years. He was ready for his father's influence to be gone.

Howard opened his eyes and Donald could tell it took a lot of effort.

"Son, I asked the staff to step out for a while. Listen closely. Maybe you can get this one right." He paused for several laborious breaths.

Ouch.

Even at the very end it still hurt. Donald brushed aside the pain and leaned closer. Howard's final message was imminent.

Slowly, he pushed out the words. "Beware ... of the ... Nolans."

Donald's jaw dropped.

The sustained tone of a flatline filled the air. Hospital staff rushed in and brushed Donald back as the room erupted in a buzz of activity. As if from a distance, he heard "Clear!" a few times. The line stayed flat.

Donald staggered out into the hall and somehow found his way to the waiting area. He flopped into a chair as his mind replayed the last few minutes over and over.

Seriously? Those were the last words of the Man of the Century?

Donald had expected some grief. He'd expected a mixture of several emotions. He had not expected to leave puzzled.

●●●

Thirty minutes later and many miles from Denver, a quiet gentleman pushed the off button and set the cordless phone back into its cradle. Sitting down in his desk chair, he buried his head in his hands. Tears upon tears, but not for the dead man, flowed until a small puddle pooled on his desk. The quiet of the house was his only comfort.

He dried his eyes and tried to stand up. His elbows hadn't left the desk before another wave slammed him and forced his head back down. Sobs racked his whole frame. Many minutes passed as he emptied and re-emptied the pent-up reservoir.

Howard Carlyle is dead.

He lifted his head and looked out the huge window at Wilson's Creek winding its lazy course past his river cabin. His arms shook as he pushed himself to an upright sitting position. He stared at the slow-moving water.

Howard Carlyle is dead.

Who could he talk to? Who would understand?

He reached for pen and paper. It was time to write a letter to two of his oldest friends.

Never mind that they'd been dead for fifty years.

Over-the-counter sales make up two thirds of all revenue from XD. Therefore, we must resist efforts to force XD to require a prescription. "Completely nontoxic" should, however, be amended to "very low toxicity" as the worldwide marketing efforts of several manufacturers prepare to launch.

Internal memo, Hampden Pharmaceuticals, January 1966

No.	Entry Date	Name	Age	Issue Date	Impact
535	9-15-1968	Allejandra Martinez	0	8-20-1968	Stillborn
536	9-17-1968	Jonathan Simpkins	0	5-22-1968	Congenital heart disease
537	9-17-1968	Theresa Simpkins	27	5-31-1968	Ongoing peripheral neuritis

Chapter 6

Final Round

Saturday, May 10, 6:25 p.m.
Purple Mountain Community Church, Colorado Springs, CO

"Welcome, ladies and gentlemen!" The rich baritone voice of Senator Smith boomed through the microphone, filling the packed sanctuary.

The crowd responded with warm appreciation.

"Seeing this wonderful group of young people"—he waved his hand toward the rows of competitors seated before him—"gives me great hope for the future!"

Jordan organized his papers one more time in an effort to look purposeful. He and Matthew sat opposite each other behind the podium where Senator Smith spoke.

Stay in control.

"Because I believe in the next generation"—Senator Smith looked down at them as if trying to look each one in the eye—"last September, I introduced the Senator's Internship award. My goal was to stimulate interest in different forms of communication in the state of Colorado and provide an opportunity for a few young communicators to experience politics and our nation's Capitol up-close and personal. This was supposed to be a Colorado thing. Little did I know, one of those forms of communication would culminate in the final round of a national competition!"

Jordan put his finger on the touch ID of his phone to wake it up. Butterflies flew every which way on the inside. He looked up at the ceiling to appear thoughtful. In truth, he used his peripheral vision to scope out where his dad sat in the auditorium. In a hall of nearly fifteen hundred people, Jordan felt all the energy compress down to a single seat on the left side near the large doors leading to the foyer.

What's he thinking?

The senator put his hand over one side of his mouth, cocked his head as if he were telling a secret, and added, "But I do love a good competition!"

Glancing across at Matthew and back down, Jordan swiped through his notes one more time.

"In three months," the senator continued, "I will be taking four rising young leaders to Washington with me for an intense, one-year internship as a part of my staff. Three of the four spots are awarded by merit. The fourth spot I reserve as a wild-card pick that I will choose myself later this summer. I did not know that the speech and debate national tournament was going to be held in Colorado this year, and I couldn't believe it when I was told yesterday that the issue was still undecided."

A fresh wave of nervous energy swirled through Jordan's stomach as he thought about DC. To keep his mind from spiraling out of control, he picked up a pen and wrote out his thoughts in his notebook.

Don't go there. Take care of business first.

The senator paused to look over each shoulder and survey the two competitors. Turning back to the mic, his volume increased a few decibels as he said, "I am even more amazed that the two finalists both herald from the wonderful town of Wilson, Colorado."

Cheers broke out across the auditorium.

"Everybody knows Wilson, do they not? Fifty years ago, a small drug company brought Amitolin, better known as the Wonder Drug, to the market. Millions of people have benefited from this great gift to mankind." Many in the crowd nodded.

Jordan forced a plastic smile, acknowledged the senator's glance, and looked back at his phone in front of him.

The only place I want to see Wilson from is the rearview mirror.

Suddenly, unexpected and unwanted, the dream from this morning rushed back into his thoughts and hit him with fresh impact.

Not now!

Jordan tried to distract himself.

Senator Smith continued with his speech.

More thoughts bombarded Jordan.

What if the dream means I have to stay in Wilson?

He clamped down hard on a brief flash of panic as his mind kicked into analytic mode. He wrote furiously on the pad next to him.

1. I don't believe in this stuff anyway
   A. Church is boring and God is irrelevant
   B. I am going somewhere that is neither boring nor irrelevant
   C. A + B does not equal C (staying in Wilson)

2. The dream doesn't necessarily mean you have to stay in Wilson
   A. Joy had flooded me
   B. Staying in Wilson would not be joyful
   C. A + B does not equal C (staying in Wilson)

He looked up at the ceiling and then back down at his notebook

3. Those first two points are fundamentally incompatible
   A. Either I don't believe in God, and dreams by extension
   B. Or the dream might have some significance for my life

He nearly pressed the pen through the page.

4. No, they are <u>not</u> incompatible. If the goal is to GET OUT OF WILSON, <u>either works</u>

Jordan looked over his notes and relaxed as Senator Smith neared the end of his introduction.

"This August, shortly before the internship starts, I will be privileged to represent the United States government, and the State of Colorado, as we honor Wilson Drug and Compounding Center at the 50th Anniversary Celebration of the Wonder Drug. In the meantime, one of these two fine young leaders will put Wilson, Colorado, on the map once again!"

The crowd erupted.

"Please welcome my chief of staff, Jeffrey Kingston, to join me on the stage for the final instructions."

The audience responded with a cordial, but impatient, welcome.

● ● ●

As Jeffrey Kingston laid out the final instructions, Bethany sat ten rows back within the Colorado contingent next to Jordan's best friend, Timothy "Gadg" O'Brien. Allie sat next to him on the opposite side. Even though she now hailed from California, she had lived in Colorado long enough to be considered part of the home team.

From October to April, competitors from different speech clubs within the states battled it out with each other. Then in May, at nationals, these same clubs banded together against the other states. Occasionally, a final debate round at nationals included competitors from the same state. Once in a great while, this happened in the state hosting the national tournament.

Never had it happened with two competitors from the same hometown with a "write your own ticket" opportunity like the Senator's Internship on the line.

Bethany glanced at Gadg as he stared up at the stage and took in the atmosphere. The light riggings were set to cast a purplish glow on the podium where the competitors would speak. An unapologetic techno-geek to the core, Gadg made Jordan's solid grasp of technology look amateur by comparison. He possessed a photographic memory, an inquisitiveness that almost matched Jordan's, and a way with electronic devices that made some people think the technology actually feared him. Sometimes he would ask to take a look at something, and a device that had been misbehaving would start working again. That phenomenon had led to the nickname "Gadget," which had evolved to "Gadg," and was used so universally that some people didn't know his name was Timothy. Though introverted, Bethany knew him to be a loyal friend who, once he felt safe, could let out a dry sense of humor. Just now, he seemed caught up in the excitement of his best friend's dream.

"Representing the affirmative position," Jeffrey Kingston raised his voice and angled to one side, "from Wilson, Colorado, ... Jordan Nolan!"

Allie elbowed Gadg in the ribs and pointed to the stage. Her smile lit up their entire section. "Gadg, there he is!"

Bethany watched the exchange. She'd seen it before: Gadg's cheeks reddening, Allie beaming. Last year, Gadg had confided to her that Allie was way out of his league and that he had long since dismissed any romantic thoughts toward her. The fact he was much more in tune with actual devices than women's devices, put just a hint of a playful spark in Allie's demeanor toward him.

Looking up at the stage, Gadg let go of the rest of his reserve and smiled big.

"Look at you," said Bethany. His smile was contagious.

"What?" asked Gadg.

"We don't normally see you like this," Allie said, raising her eyebrows with a mischievous grin.

Gadg turned to Bethany. "If she doesn't win either the dramatic or humorous final, I'm going to file a complaint."

Bethany shot Allie a sideways smirk and said, "I agree."

The applause died down for Jordan as Jeffrey Kingston continued, "And representing the negative position, also from Wilson, Colorado, ... Matthew Harris!"

Another huge cheer from the audience. Many of the same people who had applauded Jordan did the same for Matthew. Allie brightened.

Bethany's face went flat as she watched her friend.

What does she see in him?

Jeffrey announced, "Whichever competitor receives at least six ballots in his favor will win the championship, *and* ... the Senator's Internship!"

The audience gave a swelling cheer.

"If, for some reason, the champion cannot or will not attend the internship, the runner-up will be invited as the alternate."

The whole audience, including Bethany, saw Jordan and Matthew cast a brief glance at each other. A low murmur rippled over the pews. There was no way that would happen. Only an autopsy would keep the winner from DC.

Jeffrey Kingston smiled. "I see you all know the stakes. Without further ado, let's see who wants it most!"

San Diego, CA

Many hometown fans from Wilson, Colorado, who made the road trip to San Diego, held their collective breath as Johnny Nolan, first team all-American wide receiver, lay unmoving on the grass of Jack Murphy Stadium. A huge, and highly controversial, helmet-to-helmet hit from longtime-rival, Alex Jones, flattened Nolan in the second quarter of the Holiday Bowl.

Nolan, strapped carefully to a stretcher and carted off to an ambulance, had been projected by many NFL analysts to be selected in the first five picks of the 1996 NFL draft, which is to be held April 20–21 at Madison Square Garden.

Team physician, Thomas Stillman, had this to report:

"It's still too early to tell conclusively, but the injury to Johnny Nolan's neck appears to be very serious. It is likely that multiple surgeries and many months of physical therapy will be required just to allow him to walk again. I regret to announce that this is almost certainly the end of a promising football career. Our thoughts and prayers are with him."

From the *Wilson Gazette*, December, 30, 1995

Chapter 7

Final Speech

Saturday, May 10, 7:15 p.m.
Purple Mountain Community Church, Colorado Springs, CO

Matthew finished his final speech. It was solid, but at best, he had drawn even. He stepped down from the podium, turned back to his table, and looked sideways at Jordan with a glare that was hidden from the audience.

Jordan looked back in acknowledgment of a formidable, but defeated foe. He adjusted his tie and stood up. His suit glistened a blue so dark it made his eyes look like the ocean under a full moon at midnight. He felt like a bloody, sweat-covered gladiator, with a sword stuck to his hand and a lion lying dead at his feet. This was the arena and he was home.

He stepped up to the podium as if saluting a Caesar of old. Scanning the crowd, Jordan smiled. They were with him. The internship was his for the taking. He took in the moment and prepared to begin.

Out of the corner of his eye, he saw one of the side entrance doors open. Johnny Nolan walked out.

Jordan's face flushed as the last two years came flooding into the present. He stared at the door.

It's bad enough he doesn't want me to go.

Five seconds passed. A current of restlessness shivered through the audience.

Jordan peered down at his notes. They looked incoherent. He turned a page, aimlessly. The warmth of the overhead lights suddenly distilled down into a bead of sweat on his forehead that snapped him back into the present. His eyes widened.

A stab of panic shot through him so hard that he nearly collapsed. Mercifully, he stayed on his feet.

How long have I been like this?

He looked back at the audience and saw uncertainty. He dared not look at the judges. He rearranged his notebook, scrambling for something—anything—to try to redirect his thoughts. Jordan closed his eyes. The theater inside his head was laced with red. He gripped the podium like a life preserver and clamped down on any shred of emotion inside him. It only took a second and a half, but he bundled it all into a rage that turned him to steel.

He opened his eyes and then his mouth. What came out was a torrent of passion against the various injustices in the medical community that kept people from receiving a transplant. He was back. His voice rang out strong and true. Enough, it seemed, to erase what had just happened.

Almost.

Three minutes later, it was over. The crowd applauded loudly, but it was more from shock than enthusiasm. Jordan and Matthew shook hands and Jordan could see the slightest uptick of a smirk on Matthew's face.

The judges scooped up their notes and ballots and headed for the room where they would decide his fate. Jordan ground his teeth as he turned back to his table.

If I lose because of that, I'll never forgive him.

● ● ●

The awards ceremony continued its march toward the pronouncement of doom. Jordan's stomach squirmed as the emcee announced the results of the other events. Bethany had finished fourth in broadcasting and second in storytelling. Gadg didn't have to file a complaint, as Allie had won the title in dramatic interpretation and finished sixth in humorous. Of course, they saved the announcement of the debate finals until the end.

Jordan's friends smiled at him. Some hugged him or put a hand on his shoulder. They tried their best, but not even his most staunch supporters could banish the uncertainty. Debate rounds were a zero-sum game: one winner, one loser.

The crowd set the tone with gusto as Senator Smith was invited back to the stage. Who better to preside over the announcement of the final event than the benefactor of the internship himself? He invited the last sixteen debate competitors to join him on the stage. As they filed up the stairs, Jordan glanced over at the section by the side doors. The seat next to his mother was still empty.

A spray of disgust mixed with the anxiety churning inside produced a toxic cauldron of desperation. Washington wasn't far away enough, and he couldn't get there fast enough.

Jordan stared straight ahead, above the back row of the audience. The countdown began. Senator Smith took his time. Sixteen. Eight. Four. At last, only the two finalists remained on the stage. In most tournaments, just prior to the announcement, the last two competitors would hug one another as a show of friendship and solidarity. Matthew and Jordan didn't even look at each other.

"On a six-five decision..."

Senator Smith paused. Jordan's heartbeat pulsed through the side of his neck.

"In second place ... from Wilson, Colorado, ... Matthew Harris!"

The crowd erupted. Senator Smith shouted the announcement of the champion, but was drowned out by the noise. Jordan's emotions splattered like a smoothie exploding out of a blender when the speed got cranked up too fast. At the same time, his mind shut down like a pinball machine going tilt. Somehow, he got through the next few minutes on autopilot.

He was on his way to DC.

In just two short years, sales of Amitolin have skyrocketed. Hailed on three continents as remarkably effective in combating flu-like symptoms, many are calling it the "Wonder Drug" as Hampden Pharmaceuticals prepares a massive global marketing campaign.

Time Magazine, from an article entitled "The Wonder Drug," November 1966

Commission

Monday, May 12, 11:00 a.m.
Executive office of Donald Carlyle at WDC2 headquarters,
Wilson, CO

Back in his large, luxurious office, Donald took a long draw from a cigar and stared down at the *Wall Street Journal*. Most of the front page was dedicated to the memory of his father and the Wonder Drug. He finished reading the second page, which featured a prominent photo of himself alongside an article discussing the future of WDC2.

He had spent most of yesterday, and would spend most of the week, fielding calls and answering the press. The funeral was scheduled for Saturday. People would come from everywhere. For a fleeting instant, he wondered if he could get out of it. He banished the thought out of a mixture of pragmatism and respect. Of course not.

In the last thirty-six hours, his shock had diminished and given way to relief. He thought hard about his father's final message. Even in his nineties, Howard Carlyle was not one to waste words. It had to mean something.

Beware of the Nolans.

Donald could not imagine the Nolan family being much of a problem. Many in the town still held some residue of bitterness about the murder of Raymond Clark in 1964. Not-so-small Colorado towns like Wilson didn't forget easily. Johnny Nolan's rise as a state football star had caused the hearts of some people to turn to a more favorable view of the Nolans—at least for a while.

Donald smirked to himself.

Nothing heals like winning.

His smirk widened into a smile. Saturday had been a big day for Johnny's son. Jordan now held a one-way ticket out of Wilson, thanks to the national debate final.

Good for him.

Donald's thoughts found their way back to the Old Town Café a few weeks prior. He had been meeting with some community leaders about the renovation of Old Town, which he had recently sold back to the Town of Wilson. Just before he got up to leave, Donald heard one of the town hard-liners, related by blood to the Clark family, make a crack about Jordan's dad. The whole table laughed, acknowledging the son seated in the booth behind them.

Jordan's face pinched. Donald walked over to his booth. "May I sit down?"

"Oh, Mr. Carlyle!" Jordan smashed his thighs on the underside of the table in his effort to stand up quickly. "Ouch!"

"Don't get up." Donald Carlyle held up his hand and chuckled. "It's much too painful."

Face flushed, Jordan sat back down. "I'm sorry, sir. I didn't expect you to come over. Please sit down."

Mr. Carlyle slid into the booth across from him. Several heads in the café turned to stare. "Actually, I'm sorry, Jordan."

"You're sorry, sir?"

"I am. I know what it feels like."

Jordan looked back at him.

"I'm not saying I know a stigma like you do," Donald continued, "but I do know what it's like, for good or bad, to live in the shadow of an ancestor."

"Yes, sir, I imagine you would. What was it like?"

"What was it like living in the same house with the 'Man of the Century'?" Donald smiled and shook his head. "What do you think?"

Jordan stroked his chin and nodded. "Probably something like living in the same house with a football star."

Donald stood up to leave and offered his hand. "Yes, probably something like that. Good luck, Jordan."

A knock on his office door brought Donald back to the present moment.

He looked down at the newspaper in front of him as his father's last words echoed again in his head.

Beware of the Nolans.

His face hardened as he thought about the next meeting. Regardless of how he felt about Jordan, Donald knew he needed to find the meaning of his father's message. Setting down his cigar, he said, "Come in and close the door."

●●●

Alex Jones, head of security at WDC2, stepped into the room. All he could see was polished mahogany, leather, and cigar smoke. Theoretically, this was an office. Practically, it was more like a den combined with a modern-day version of a medieval throne room. High-backed chair; dark, hardwood desk; impressive fireplace. Needless to say, the smoke alarm was turned off in this room.

"Welcome back," came Donald Carlyle's voice from behind the mahogany.

"Thank you, sir," said Alex. His voice sounded like pieces of sandpaper rubbing together. Last week, he had traveled back east to meet with the security team of Hampden Pharmaceuticals. He waited for Donald to say what was on his mind.

A quick glance at the desk revealed a newspaper with a large photo on the open page. The picture showed a man, smiling and holding a blue and red pill between his thumb and forefinger. The face behind the desk wasn't holding a pill and wasn't smiling. "I've got a job for you," Donald said at length.

Alex chanced another quick look at the paper. The headline read: "Big Shoes to Fill." He tried to listen while his curiosity about the article and the death of Howard Carlyle fought for control of his thoughts. "Mr. Carlyle, you know I'm swamped. Are we talking beyond what's already on my plate?"

"We are. Just between you and me, we're talking ten grand more onto your plate."

Alex's eyes got wide. "Seriously?"

"Besides the money, I think you might find this one interesting for other reasons." Donald took another long pull from his cigar. "I don't need to remind you, since this is all you talked about last week with Hampden, but the 50th Anniversary Celebration takes place this August at the fairgrounds."

"No sir, you don't. August 16th is etched in blood on the calendar." One more glance at the article revealed the subtitle: "With the Man of the Century Gone, Can Donald Carlyle be WDC2's Man of the Hour?"

Donald drummed his fingers on the mahogany next to the paper. "For multiple reasons, it's imperative for the celebration to go smoothly and *predictably*." Alex felt the scrutiny as Donald looked him over.

"Forgive me for asking, but is there some concern that it might not?"

"Good question. Not necessarily. However, I received a cryptic message from my father on his deathbed."

"I'm sorry for your loss."

"Thank you. It was time."

Whoa. Alex glanced around the room and then down at his feet. "So, what was the message?"

"My father told me to beware of the Nolans."

Alex's head shot up. He tried to suppress a grin. "Really?"

Donald nodded. "Those were his last words—verbatim."

Alex could no longer conceal his interest.

"I thought that might get your attention," Donald returned his smile.

"It does. Of course, so does ten thousand bucks. What do you need from me?"

"That was all he said. I don't have any idea what it means—or what, if anything, I should be concerned about." One more long tug on the cigar. Donald exhaled and a rich layer of smoke curled upward. "Let me put it real simple. I need you to make sure there's nothing I need to *beware* of."

Dear William and Ray,

The Man is dead.

Even though I cried more than I ever have, I wasn't sad. How can you be sad when you're out from under someone's thumb? He was the only other one that really knew the truth. Sometimes we would look at one another and a small bit of knowing would pass between us.

He knew what we did.

I knew what we did.

He never came right out and said it, but every so often he would remind me that he owned me. As for my material needs he made sure I was comfortable - house, job, river cabin, pension. I would want for nothing in life.

Nothing, that is, except peace.

Occasionally, he would ask me a question such as "Are you comfortable?" or "Do you need anything?" The soft, quiet edge to his tone chilled me. Yes, one step out of line, and I would disappear. Do you know what it's like to live in fear for 50 years? It might as well have been ten lifetimes.

Now he's gone.

He's gone, and I'm contemplating the unthinkable. There's no way I would ever come right out and say it, but I may drop some hints. If I do, I think you'll be pleased with whom I choose.

He reminds me so much of you, William

Chapter 9

Watch Your Back

Sunday, May 18, 11:10 a.m.
Outside Nolan guest house, Wilson, CO

With his favorite mug in one hand and a stack of envelopes addressed to him in the other, Jordan walked the seventy-five yard path toward the guest house. His emotions were all over the map as he swung from elation to exhaustion, from decompression to disgust.

He sat down on the handcrafted bench, made by his grandpa Walter. He set his mug down on one of the armrests. All around him was a stunning Colorado day that he didn't even notice.

Setting the envelopes on the bench next to him, Jordan stared past the guest house at the remains of Old Town. Several buildings sat opposite Nolan property on land that was now owned by the Town of Wilson. Looking past an abandoned house where he had played as a youngster, he surveyed the other buildings that lined Old Main Street.

I live next door to a ghost town.

To the left of Main Street, just inside the forest, on WDC2 property that had not been sold to the town, he could see the hollowed out shell of the old grange.

Why are those buildings still standing?

He recalled something about a dispute over ownership that had kept the process mired in a legal battle, making it easier to just leave things as they were.

I don't really know Wilson's history.

He was so disconnected from his normal focus that he zoned out for a few seconds before it hit him:

Who cares? Good riddance!

He looked at his coffee mug and saw the word "Washington." In an instant, his thoughts flashed back to his father walking out of the auditorium during the debate final. He snatched up his phone, engaged the diary app, and launched into a tirade.

Got Away with One

YOU ARE AN IDIOT!!!
What were you thinking? Letting him get under your skin like that
I can't believe he would do that right at that moment
What difference does it make when he did it? You need to be above those kinds of minor distractions
Minor?
Yes, all he did was get up and leave the room. You don't even know why. What's such a big deal about that?
Nothing
Then why does it bug you?
The timing was horrible
So?
It nearly cost me the internship
No, it didn't. You nearly cost you the internship
Does he even care?

Jordan took a breath.

Wow, am I actually going?

His phone vibrated, alerting him to a text message. No name came up on the screen, but when he glanced over it, he recognized the number immediately.

Matthew.

You got lucky. You better watch your back. This isn't over until you're on the plane. You may have some surprises this summer.

What a jerk.

Jordan pressed his lips together. He appreciated Matthew's reminder: it wasn't over. Jordan's strategy this summer was to dot every i, cross every t, and play it squeaky clean.

He touched his finger to the screen and launched the new app Gadg had whipped up for him last week. He gave a grin as the words "Internship Ticker" came up, displaying a simple counter ticking down in real time:

98 days, 20 hours, 34 minutes, 27 seconds
98 days, 20 hours, 34 minutes, 26 seconds
98 days, 20 hours, 34 minutes, 25 seconds

He could endure one last summer in Wilson.

● ● ●

Jordan set his phone down next to the stack of envelopes and tasted his coffee for the first time. A spark of life came into his eyes and softened the angry lines leftover from his diary entry.

No way.

He cocked his head, smiling at his mug. He had long been a student of a curious phenomenon which he and Gadg had nicknamed "The Jackpot Cup." A jackpot cup only happened when all the coffee stars aligned, and it tasted *perfect*.

Strong, yet smooth.

Bold, not burnt.

Not too hot or too cold.

Just the right amount of half-and-half, milk, or cream.

A beautiful blend of flavor, color, temperature, and texture, coupled with a mug that one enjoys holding and enjoys looking at.

He and Gadg had gone on a quest to systematize the making of the jackpot cup, but so far, the process had proved elusive. Using the same ingredients in the same quantities, with the same timing and the same equipment would often produce a wide spectrum of cup quality, ranging from jackpot to just mediocre. Their quest had caused the general level of their coffee making to go from average to excellent, and turned them both into indisputable coffee snobs. On any given day, Jordan and Gadg held two of the ten best cups of coffee in the region. The jackpot cup however—that special something that still seemed to happen only once in a while—remained a mystery that refused to be pinned down.

Today, with his emotions going every which way, the surprise of the jackpot cup made for a welcome friend.

He took another sip, set the mug down, and reached for his phone. He launched the Facebook app and the taste of his coffee went sour as he read.

You've got to be kidding.

He snatched up the envelopes, grabbed the mug, and marched to the guest house.

Tonight, they pushed him over the edge. One comment too many about his father. He punched one in the face. Three of them grabbed him and pinned him back against a table. One flashed a knife and stabbed him under the arm near the shoulder. Normally reserved, Walter Nolan went into a frenzy. Mugs went flying. Glass broke everywhere. The whole place reeked of beer. Bleeding profusely, he used his good arm to beat the tar out of the other three. He's one of the toughest men I know. He kicked the last one so hard I heard something crack. The police came and the paramedics got to work. The rest of the customers looked like they were in shock.

Will this town ever forget?

From the diary of a local barmaid at Old Town Bar
Wilson, CO. June, 1974

No.	Entry Date	Name	Age	Issue Date	Impact
6956	6-2-1974	Terrance Clement	7	4-16-1974	Died from complications related to 4th kidney surgery
6957	6-24-1974	Walter Nolan	22	6-22-1974	Lost use of left arm in bar fight

Chapter 10

Milk

**Sunday, May 18, 11:25 a.m.
Nolan guest house, Wilson, CO**

"In here, Jordan." Grandpa Walter's deep voice seemed far away as the sound ricocheted through a labyrinth of metal, wood, cloth, and clutter in a "garage" that combined several layers of amateur auto mechanic sediment with two attic's worth of stuff, spanning several decades of accumulation.

This part of the guest house was never shown to guests.

In fact, the Nolan guest house wasn't a guest house at all, but rather, the residence of Jordan's grandfather, Walter Nolan. Widower for five years and retired for two, Grandpa Walter still had a solid build for a sixty-two-year-old.

Jordan set his half-empty coffee mug and the stack of letters on the kitchen bar. Still holding his phone, he turned as Grandpa came out of the garage, wiping his hands on a work rag that he stuffed into the front pocket of his overalls. Jordan could feel the strength in Walter's upper body and right arm as he pulled him close for a hug. Grandpa's left arm hung limp as he released Jordan and stared at him.

"What's wrong?" he asked.

The combined space of the living room, dining room, and kitchen shared two large windows that overlooked the back few acres of Nolan property, as well as the remains of Old Town. With his good arm, Walter invited Jordan to sit on one of the stools at the bar.

"Do you want to tell me about it?"

Grandpa Walter was the only person, with the possible exception of Gadg, who Jordan ever let his guard down in front of. "I was having the best debate of my career. Matthew Harris was giving it all he had, and I had him by the throat going into the final speech. Then my dad got up and *left*." He spat the last word. "The first time in two years he condescends to attend, and he walks out right before my closing speech."

Grandpa nodded with the understanding of a grandparent who appreciates when a grandchild takes time to be with him.

"I nearly blew the whole thing in the next ninety seconds. It was horrible," Jordan turned to face Grandpa. "And now, to make matters worse," he showed Walter his dad's Facebook post, "I just learned that dad wants to do this *blessing ceremony* thing next weekend. A treasure hunt? Seriously? Why can't he just do a thirty-minute graduation ceremony and be done with it? I'm not sure I can stomach it."

"Your mom was going to talk to you about it. I guess she hasn't yet." Walter looked apologetic.

Jordan didn't miss a beat. "Grandpa, blessing ceremonies are *lame*! I've watched my dad's life from the back row of a church for as long as I can remember. What's it ever done for him?" Jordan continued with an argument that was well rehearsed. "Ninety-eight days and I'm out of here. I'm done with him. I'm done with Wilson, and no offense to you," he paused, "but I'm done with all that the Nolan name represents."

Grandpa turned to the window, his countenance darkening with a mix of pain and understanding. His left arm had hung limp for forty years because his last name was Nolan.

Jordan was too preoccupied to notice the reaction. He took a sip from his mug and grimaced. His jackpot cup had become dreadful with the significant drop in temperature of both coffee and mood.

I wonder if attitude has anything to do with a jackpot cup?

He walked over to the coffee pot with his mug to "give it a charger," which consisted of pouring hot coffee over the cold to give it the heat it needed to be drinkable again. Jordan knew Grandpa wouldn't have any half-and-half so he turned to the fridge and over his shoulder he asked, "Do you have any milk?"

Grandpa looked back at him. A tear rolled down the face of the solid brick of a man.

Jordan glanced back at him before opening the fridge and did a sharp double take. Setting his mug down, he walked back to the bar and sat next to his grandfather. "I'm sorry, Grandpa. What did I say?"

Walter looked back out the window.

Jordan waited before Grandpa faced him again, his normally strong voice cracked with emotion, "It was fifty-five years ago in a kitchen seventy-five yards from this one, when a little boy dropped his milk and received from his father a slap across his face in return."

Jordan's eyes and mouth opened in tandem.

Grandpa continued, "I can still feel the warmth on my leg as I peed my pants. I was seven years old."

Jordan gave a slow blink. He didn't say a word as shame washed over him.

"I never told that to anyone," Grandpa sighed. "Growing up, my mother told me about a tradition in the Nolan family where the father sets up a treasure hunt for his son that culminates with a blessing ceremony." Grandpa's jaw quivered.

Jordan lifted his elbow and swiped his head across his sleeve.

"My father had spotted a hymnal open to the song 'Let the Circle Be Unbroken.' The title angered him and he threw the book against the wall. That's when I dropped my milk." Both of Grandpa's eyes filled with tears.

"After my father slapped me, my mother saw the wet spot on my pants and the look on my face, and said she'd had enough. She kicked him out of the house that day. He left with only a box of books and a suitcase." Grandpa wiped his eyes and straightened.

"Five years later, we learned he was dead. Killed a man and then killed himself. I've lived my whole life wondering what I did wrong. Why was I the one who didn't get the blessing?"

Jordan stared at his grandfather.

"I understand how you feel about your dad and our name," Grandpa continued. "Believe it or not, he felt terrible about leaving your final speech. He told me he had some kind of stomach pain and spent most of the evening in the bathroom. He asked me on the way home how he could begin to rebuild bridges with you. The idea for the blessing ceremony didn't come from him. I suggested it. We've spent this whole week working on it together. Fifty-five years later, I still long for that ceremony. I still long for that treasure hunt. Most of all, I still long for the blessing of my father." Wistful, Grandpa gazed out the window.

Jordan put his arms around his grandfather and the door of his heart cracked open.

When their hug ended, Grandpa stood up, turned to face Jordan, and said, "I know you think blessing ceremonies are lame, but would you consider doing it for me?"

Denial. Cover-up. Sleight of hand. Reluctant admission. Settlement.

Eighteen months after it could no longer be contained, in a repeat eerily reminiscent of the Thalidomide debacle, Hampden Pharmaceuticals has agreed to a $50 million settlement for the victims of the side effects of XD.

Time Magazine, **from an article entitled, "Thalidomide Reprised," June 1970**

Chapter 11

Summer School

Sunday, May 18, 11:50 a.m.
Outside Nolan guest house, Wilson, CO

Jordan sat back down on the bench outside the guest house. He took a few deep breaths to steady his roller-coaster emotions. For lack of anything better to do, he reached for the stack of envelopes and opened a few of them, each containing a card or a note congratulating him on his achievement and upcoming graduation. He grabbed the second to last one and looked it over.

That's strange.

It was letter-sized, typed, and had no return address. It was probably another college trying to entice him to attend after the internship. His stock had risen significantly in the last week and universities were begging for him. He tore it open. It had the appearance of a form letter.

> Dear Mr. Nolan,
>
> Congratulations on your wonderful victory! Winning something on that scale is truly an achievement that will stay with you the rest of your life. It also affords you the opportunity to study at any school you'd like to attend. That is a tremendous honor.
>
> Have you decided what your major will be? Whatever it is, you may want to also consider a minor in history. It's a great choice for an aspiring political leader.

There is something special about you. You're intelligent, ambitious, level-headed, and driven. As such, it would be unthinkable for you to squander your time off. How would you like to enroll in summer school?

Jordan grimaced. *How lame.*

As he set the letter aside, his eye caught the next sentence.

What?

Frowning, he snatched it back up and stared at the headline.

If you decide to attend, your first course will be...

History of Wilson 101

Here are some excerpts from selected lessons:

"As you have undoubtedly heard, tragedy has struck the research department of Carlyle Enterprises. One of our employees killed his fellow researcher and then went on to commit suicide. In light of these events, we respectfully ask to be released from our contract to research the drug XD. As we were still early in the research process, there had been no significant findings. If this is acceptable, we will refund any money already paid to us."

Letter from Howard Carlyle to Hampden Pharmaceuticals after the deaths of Ray Clark and William Nolan, April 27, 1964

"Due to the recent and tragic loss of two team members, management has determined that the research department of Carlyle Enterprises will be disbanded, effective immediately. The lab will be repurposed, and positions will be found elsewhere in the organization for the remaining personnel."

Internal memo from Howard Carlyle to the staff of Carlyle Enterprises, early May, 1964

"Carlyle Enterprises, Inc., of Wilson, Colorado, has announced that its name will be changed to Wilson Drug and Compounding Center, or WDC2. This change will be effective July 1."

The Wall Street Journal, May 18, 1964

The above represents a sample of the many subjects offered. Enrollment is by invitation only. This is a limited-time offer. Act now to enjoy a unique, highly customized study opportunity. It's best if you don't speak of this communication.

P.S. Your father posted on Facebook about the treasure hunt and blessing ceremony this weekend. Perhaps you'll find more treasure, and a greater blessing, than either of you expect.

What in the world?

Jordan's jaw hung open as he pored over the paper. He read it through two more times. It was the weirdest letter he'd ever received.

Could this be real?

He reached for his phone to send a text to Gadg. When he pushed the Messages button, the text from Matthew was still open.

> **You may have some surprises this summer**

A wave of skepticism rolled over Jordan. He started to ball his hand into a fist, with the letter still in it. As the letter began to crumple, he stopped.

Is Matthew really that clever?

Jordan looked toward Old Town and spoke his thoughts aloud, "If this is a hoax, it's extremely elaborate." Cynicism drained as his face hardened into resolve. Something told him this wasn't a joke.

I need to check this out.

Jordan pressed the creases out of the letter, folded it in three parts, and stuffed it back into the envelope. He grabbed his phone and the other letters, and stood. Curling his finger around the handle of his mug, he flicked his wrist and launched the remaining coffee onto the ground.

"Hampden Pharmaceuticals has been a great partner of ours ever since the release of Amitolin in 1964. XD is a truly unfortunate situation for both the victims and the company."

Interview with Howard Carlyle, CEO of WDC2, commenting on the $50 million XD settlement, June 1970

Chapter 12

Allies

Tuesday, May 20, 12:30 p.m.
O'Toole's Irish Pub and Smokehouse, Denver, CO

A young man in his late thirties, dressed in a navy blue suit, looked across the booth at Donald Carlyle and chuckled inwardly. Powerful people, even those he didn't think highly of, had the luxury of playing it cool. That was fine with him. Even at his age, he was becoming a master at this game. The more they underestimated him, the better.

Mr. Carlyle rolled a large, unlit cigar between his thumb and forefinger. The residue of two Black and Tans and a plate of great Irish food sat disregarded on the table. O'Toole's was one of the few restaurants in the area that still allowed their patrons to smoke.

"This career you've chosen," Donald paused, "you know what you need, don't you?"

The young man did know, but he didn't want Mr. Carlyle to know how well he knew. He offered a deferential smile and a nod. "Allies." He also knew where this line of questioning was going. Mr. Carlyle wanted something.

Donald nodded back, pleased at the opportunity to bestow his wisdom on a young protégé. He fingered his cigar some more and said, "You know we are in talks with Hampden, don't you?"

Hampden Pharmaceuticals, who originally helped market the Wonder Drug, had been one of the world's largest drug companies for several decades. Earlier this year, they'd begun discussing the possibility of acquiring WDC2.

"Yes, sir, I had heard something about it." Technically, that was true. Two members of Hampden's executive team had contacted him directly, but Donald didn't need to know that. "It doesn't surprise me. I assume this is a good thing?"

"Very good," said Donald. "It represents a serious influx of capital and a much-needed boost to the community of Wilson."

The young man suppressed a laugh at how Donald neglected to mention that he himself would make a killing on the deal. On the outside, he remained grave and attentive as he said, "Wow, that *is* a good thing." He paused a moment and decided to play it naive, "Sir, why are you telling me this?"

"Because you're right about allies," said Donald. "They can help you get things done and get you where you want to go."

The young man gave an easy smile helped along by the thought that he preferred competent allies. All he said out loud was, "How can I help?"

"The 50th Anniversary Celebration of the Wonder Drug is coming up in August. If the talks continue as they have, we'd like to make the announcement after the senator's keynote."

"That sounds great. What do you need from me?"

"My father told me there is a family that I need to beware of."

"A family, sir?"

"Yes, and I think you'll get a kick out of this one. Guess who it is?"

"I have no idea."

"Nolan."

A smile. "As in Jordan Nolan?"

"The same."

The younger man sat back and contemplated. "Do you know why?"

"No clue," said Donald.

"How serious are you about this being a threat?"

Donald reached inside his suit jacket and pulled out an envelope with a small stack of hundred-dollar bills. "Quite."

The younger man glanced in multiple directions, pulled the envelope across the table, and examined the contents. "Of course, I can't be personally involved."

"Of course. What kind of help are you thinking of getting for me?" asked Donald.

"Depends on your need and budget," said the young man.

"This is short-term and important. Make it happen."

"Yes, sir. The party I have in mind is known for delivery," he paused. "And cost."

"And secrecy, I hope."

The younger man nodded. "What constitutes success?"

"The deal goes off without a hitch at the celebration."

"Much of that depends on you, sir. I can't be responsible entirely."

"Understood. Just make sure that no threats emerge."

"Will you remember this in the future when I come calling?"

Donald pulled out a gold-plated cigar cutter, sliced the tip off a 50-ring Hacienda Grande, and lit up. "If allies are your goal, *that* is a good question."

"Sir," the young man narrowed his eyes, "*allies* are not my goal. They are only a *means* to my goal."

Mr. Carlyle smiled. "I can work with that."

It was the best of drugs, it was the worst of drugs.

Both swept the medical world in 1964.

Amitolin and XD. One became a wonder drug. One became a byword for corporate greed.

One company, one season, two drugs.

Fifteen years later we peer into Hampden Pharmaceuticals' incredible and tumultuous rise to the top of the drug industry.

Time Magazine, article entitled "A Tale of Two Drugs," August, 1979

Chapter 13

Questions

Friday, May 23, 4:00 p.m.
Jordan's room, Wilson, CO

Jordan pored over his desktop screen. His phone and the summer school letter sat on each side of his keyboard. Within arm's reach, a mug of coffee cooled to room temperature next to a half-eaten sandwich. His cousin sat on the couch opposite his bed and looked through an old photo album.

Gadg poked his head into Jordan's room. "Tyler!" He stepped in with a big smile, walked over, and gave him an affectionate, but street-savvy handclasp. "I didn't know you were coming. It's great to see you. Are you here for the treasure hunt?"

Jordan glanced over and cringed.

Tyler smiled back up at Gadg and said, "Nah, that's just a bonus. I'm here for a scholarship."

"Oh, I see. Spending the summer with your Uncle Johnny?"

"Yes. There's a wealth of experience under this roof."

"Yeah, there sure is," Jordan piped up without taking his eyes off the screen.

Gadg mouthed the words, "Good for you." Jordan put his head down quickly, pretending he didn't see the exchange. Gadg walked over and clapped a hand on his shoulder. "Hey buddy, I got the weekend off. I'll be ready to go tomorrow morning. You said you had something you wanted me to look at?"

Still staring at the screen, Jordan scooped up the summer school letter and lifted it over his shoulder.

Gadg took it and scanned the page, a slight hum escaping his lips. "This is the strangest letter I've ever seen." He held it out to Tyler, who stood up to take it.

"Tell me about it," said Jordan. "I almost dismissed it out of hand last weekend. I had just received a text from Matthew and thought he might be trying to bait me into poking my head into some areas that could get me in trouble. If there's any reason I can't go to Washington, he gets to take my place."

Gadg pulled his fist to his lips in a pose that reminded Jordan of the famous statue called *The Thinker*.

"It could, you know," he said.

Jordan leaned back.

"Could what?" asked Tyler, handing the letter back to Gadg.

"Get me in trouble," said Jordan.

"Why?"

"At a minimum," said Gadg, "this letter hints at a connection between WDC2 and XD."

Jordan whistled between his teeth.

"I don't get it," said Tyler. "I thought XD was called the 'Wonder Drug.'"

"No," said Gadg. "There were two different drugs released by Hampden Pharmaceuticals in 1964—Amitolin and XD. Amitolin became known as the Wonder Drug. It thrust this town, and Howard Carlyle, onto the world's stage. Mr. Carlyle was even named the 'Man of the Century' in 1999 by the pharmaceutical community."

"In contrast to the Wonder Drug," Jordan added, "nobody in the medical community wants to be within a hundred miles of XD. It was pushed to market with a lot of hype but without fully understanding the side effects. There are 15,000 documented cases of birth defects, stillbirths, and a host of other symptoms. Have you ever heard of Thalidomide? XD was cut from the same cloth. If it hadn't been for the Wonder Drug, Hampden Pharmaceuticals would never have survived."

Tyler pushed out an exaggerated breath.

"That's not the worst of it, though," said Jordan.

They looked at him.

"Do you see the progression in this letter? Carlyle Enterprises asks to be released from a contract, disbands the research department, and then changes the company name—all in less than a month." Jordan sniffed. "Can you smell the insinuation?" He locked eyes with Gadg.

Tyler glanced between them.

"A cover-up," said Gadg.

"You got it."

Gadg continued, "These are serious allegations. You think they're true?"

"No idea. There's not a lot on the Internet about Carlyle Enterprises, but I did confirm that it was the precursor to WDC2, and that the name was changed in 1964."

"True or not, we should keep this quiet. The subject matter is toxic," said Gadg.

"Totally agree." Jordan took a sip from his mug. His face contorted. "So is this coffee. Let's go."

I realize that the Town of Wilson owns a portion of Old Town. Like many others in Wilson, I much prefer Old Town in its pristine state. It is my desire to leave Old Town as Old Town—not to excavate, disrupt, or turn it into a tourist trap. Obviously, the town is free to do what it wishes with what it owns, but so am I. If the town chooses to move forward with the restoration of Old Town, I will choose to move WDC2 to another city.

Open letter from Howard Carlyle, President and CEO of WDC2, to the Wilson Town Council, September, 1998

Chapter 14

Promise Me

Friday, May 23, 6:15 p.m.
Clark home, Wilson, CO

Bethany closed her eyes and savored the sound, as the electric kettle dinged a pleasant B-flat. With one trip to the store, and one trip to the hall closet, the old-school shrill of their previous tea kettle was never heard again in the Clark household.

"I'm home!" Mr. Clark's voice boomed through the back door as he set his briefcase next to the wall and hung up his keys.

"Daddy!" Bethany's smile lit up the kitchen as she started the first syllable on F and ended on D in perfect harmony with the kettle's B-flat.

Michael Clark's face shone at the way Bethany sang her greeting like an elegant doorbell. He clasped his hands in front of him and gave a slight bow. "Excuse me, miss, I'm looking for a little girl named Bethany Clark."

"I'm sorry, sir," Bethany played along, "but there are no *little girls* here by that name. There is, however, a grown woman with that name. Would you like to speak with her?" Bethany sidled up to her dad and nuzzled under his arm.

"There will always be a little girl with that name to me." He gave her a squeeze.

"Your little girl happens to be *eighteen* years old."

"It's your birthday?" asked Mr. Clark separating from her hug and opening his eyes wide.

"Da-ddy." Bethany rolled her eyes as another minor third slipped off her tongue—this time the B-flat down to a G.

Mr. Clark smirked. He got up from the table and walked toward the door with his back turned to Bethany as he fished something out of his briefcase.

In most ways, Bethany was growing up fast. She liked to reserve this part of her life—her relationship with her dad—to pretend she was still a little girl.

"Happy birthday, sweetheart." Standing six foot four, Mr. Clark possessed a smile as big as he was. He handed the present to her as she sat down at the table and stirred some sugar into her mother's tea.

Face lit up, Bethany received the package. Wrapped in pink paper with a white lace bow, the box was about three-inches long, three-inches wide, and two-inches high. She took her time, opening it with dramatic fanfare. She put a hand over her mouth.

Glinting up at her was a beautiful necklace with the words, "Daddy's Girl" engraved in delicate script on a pendant hanging from a chain. The kitchen light sparkled off the gold. Bethany set the box aside, stood, and threw her arms around her dad in a fierce hug.

When she stepped away, Mr. Clark said, "Why don't you put it on?"

Bethany turned to face the mirror that decorated the far wall of the kitchen. The chain was just the right length so that the pendant rested with elegant precision just below her neckline.

Mr. Clark looked hard at his daughter. "Promise me you'll wait for my blessing?"

Bethany arched an eyebrow and turned back to him. "Of course I will."

"My baby's eighteen. When did I get old?"

She pushed down the previous thought about why he would bring this up now. Fingering the pendant, she chose to take him at face value. Her countenance radiated affection for him.

"I'm not clueless," continued Mr. Clark. "I know this is first for your Heavenly Father. I'll settle for second."

Bethany tilted her head and gave him an I-have-you-wrapped-around-my-little-finger smile. "Is this real?"

Mr. Clark cocked his head in response.

"We can't afford this."

"Well, if we're going to lose the house, I figured we might as well lose it in style."

Bethany turned serious. "Are we really going to lose the house?"

"Sorry, bad joke." He sighed. "I don't know, sweetheart. That all depends on whether the doctors can figure out what's going on."

"What about this latest round of tests?" asked Bethany.

"Inconclusive."

"Again?" Bethany sighed.

"I'm afraid so. Still no closer to a diagnosis." The smile tried to stay, but the life went out of his eyes. "Let's go check on her."

Bethany picked up the cup of tea and followed Mr. Clark into the living room. Her mother lay propped up on a sofa, staring out the large front windows. When they entered the room, she glanced up with a weary smile.

Bethany's eyes filled with mist. She set the tea on the end table, reached down, and wrapped both arms around her mother's neck. "Oh, Mama." Bethany held on. When the embrace ended, she said, "Look what Daddy got me!"

"It's lovely, Bethany. And true."

Mr. Clark beamed.

Pamela tried bravely to keep her smile and hold back a sigh, but enough of it slipped out. She looked back out the window.

Bethany bit her lip.

Oh, God. What is this?

The night was too special to focus on the ever-present elephant in the room. She needed a change of subject.

"Mom, did you hear about Jordan?" Bethany asked.

"I did, sweetheart. That's a wonderful achievement."

"That final round was amazing. I wish you could have seen it. I've watched debate for several years now, and I've never seen anything like that."

Mr. Clark stiffened.

Bethany glanced at him and remembered her conversation with Allie. Her dad was about to grow fangs.

"That's quite an accomplishment for young Mr. Nolan." His tone sounded like his stiff jaw.

"Daddy, Jordan is not his great-grandfather."

Anger flashed through his eyes, but he brought it back under control. "I know."

What is his problem?

"So, did he win the internship?" asked Mr. Clark.

"Yes, he did. The whole club is proud of him."

Mr. Clark looked away. "Is he going to Washington, then?"

Why do you want to know?

"You don't have to worry about it," said Bethany.

"Don't I?" Mr. Clark snapped back. "You look awfully excited."

"Oh, Daddy," Bethany almost sang the words as she shook her head. "Jordan and I are just friends."

A few seconds passed and Mr. Clark seemed to breathe easier. After a moment, he smiled.

Bethany fingered her new necklace.

"Do you still promise?" he asked.

"Yes, Daddy. I promise."

● ● ●

Bethany found herself once more, curled up in a ball on her bed. The cool night air wafted from window to window through her room. She had taken off the necklace and now held it in front of her.

Daddy's Girl. He was right—her Heavenly Father came first.

Daddy.

Her thoughts drifted back to her mom.

"I'm all yours, Daddy, but what's it going to take?" She cried out again for God to put His finger on what was wrong with her mom and to lead them to a solution.

As sleep overtook her, Bethany again felt the cool night air against the dampness of her pillow.

Chapter 15

The Hunt

**Saturday, May 24, 8:30 a.m.
Jordan's room, Wilson, CO**

Jordan awoke refreshed.

He looked past Tyler, sleeping on the floor, and Gadg, sleeping on the couch, to behold a gorgeous late-May Colorado morning. The words of Grandpa Walter rested on his heart.

"I know you think blessing ceremonies are lame, but would you consider doing it for me?"

Looking up at the ceiling, Jordan whispered, "Yes, for you, I will." He didn't want to do a treasure hunt—especially one that might take three days, but when he thought of his Grandpa, living with decades of pain, three days didn't seem like much.

Johnny, Michelle, and Walter had tried their best to come up with a treasure hunt difficult enough to challenge the boys. They'd given them three days to solve the clues and bring the treasure back to the blessing ceremony, which would be held on the evening of Memorial Day. A large group of friends and family were invited.

Jordan dreaded that part, but it was still a couple days away so he pushed it out of his mind. With Gadg here to help, he wasn't too concerned about solving the clues. Two weeks had passed since his victory at nationals. He took a deep breath and tried to exhale the last eight months of pent-up pressure.

He wasn't even that angry with his dad right now. It was hard to stay mad on a day like this, with so few pressures weighing on him and the promise of Washington ahead. He continued to stare at the ceiling.

My dad is trying.

Fair enough. Jordan could concede that today.

●●●

After breakfast, Johnny gave instructions, along with the first clue, to his son and his two companions. Outside, the weather was even more beautiful than it had looked from Jordan's bedroom. Few places on earth had sky as blue as Colorado.

For the hiding of the clues, Johnny and Walter had a lot with which to work. Jordan's family lived on twenty acres of western Colorado land, which featured several types of trees, jutted rock outcroppings, and even a lazy stream that was an offshoot of Wilson's creek. Treasure, and clues, could be hidden anywhere.

The boys approached the most impressive cluster of rocks and boulders on Nolan property. When Jordan read the first clue, he knew at once that this would be the place. He caught up with Gadg and Tyler and unfolded the clue once again. The paper and the script both looked old. A nice touch.

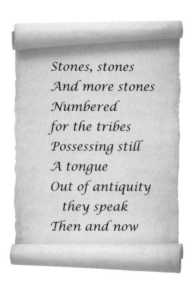

Stones, stones
And more stones
Numbered
for the tribes
Possessing still
A tongue
Out of antiquity
they speak
Then and now

"*Antiquity*," said Tyler. "Wow, big word for a football coach."

"You mean big word for an English teacher. I'm sure my mom helped with the clues."

Looking at Tyler, Jordan smiled at the memories they shared. Besides being his cousin, Tyler had been a freshmen wide receiver on Jordan's team two years ago—before Jordan had quit football. Tyler's family had moved away that summer, forcing him to transfer schools. With his senior season coming up in the fall, there was a chance he could get a scholarship if he had a big year.

Jordan's dad had been a Division 1 All American wide receiver before an injury in his final collegiate game had ended his career. Tyler had moved in with the Nolans to be mentored by Johnny throughout the summer and his senior year, and Johnny was plenty glad to have him back. Tyler was a simple young man who loved God, football, and food, the order of which depended on the timing of his last meal. Jordan didn't expect much help from Tyler in solving the clues, but he had always felt a unique bond between them. Shaking himself free from the memories, Jordan asked, "Numbered for the tribes?"

Tyler glanced at Gadg.

Jordan's eyes narrowed. "Oh, I get it. The twelve tribes that crossed the Jordan River. Very funny. It hasn't been *that* long."

Tyler looked up into one of the trees.

"Okay, so it's been a while," Jordan grimaced as if the words had the texture of something slimy. He glanced down at the paper and then back up at the rocks. Several large boulders, at least eight-feet high, stood as sentinels, with a peppering of smaller boulders scattered around them.

The boys walked to the other side of the formation and stood thirty yards from the fence, which marked the eastern edge of Nolan property. Looking back at the boulders, they spotted the answer at once. The flat surface of one of the largest rocks had twelve small stones stacked against it in three neat rows of four.

They returned to the base of the boulder, and tried to get their fingers in between the stones. Some of the gaps were big enough to get a hand into, but they found nothing. They looked again at the clue in Jordan's hand.

"This has to be the first part," said Tyler.

"Agreed," said Jordan. "What are we missing?"

"Possessing still a tongue. Possessing still a tongue," Tyler repeated, mulling it over.

"We know they are trying to be clever. In what sense could a pile of rocks have a tongue?" Jordan walked back toward the fence and turned to scope out the formation from another angle. He shook his head with a smirk.

Clever, Dad.

He motioned for Gadg and Tyler to join him at his vantage point.

A few seconds later, Gadg's eyes lit up, "Is that a face?"

Jordan nodded with a chuckle. Tyler caught up and followed his gaze. From this distance, there was no mistaking that the stones had been stacked in such a way as to create two crevices for eyes, one for a nose, and a long seam between the bottom two rows, which slightly resembled lips, pursed in a tight smile.

"All right. Where's the tongue?" said Jordan.

They hurried back over to the stones and went to work on the seam, checking for any areas that gave way to the touch. Sure enough, an eight-inch section of rock, previously undetected, had been broken or somehow cut by Johnny and Walter. Jordan pulled out the pieces of rock to reveal the contents. He found the unmistakable shape of a mug wrapped in newspaper.

Jordan worked his way through the wrapping and pulled out the coolest coffee mug any of them had ever seen.

"Wow," said Gadg. "Serious jackpot cup potential."

"No doubt," said Jordan.

On one side was a deep blue sky, with a tasteful mix of white and red, surrounding a master shot of Washington DC, which included the Washington Monument on a gorgeous fall day. Turning the mug around, the picture blended perfectly into a night shot that featured a stunning gleam of the monument, shining on the water in the moonlight.

The material was double-walled glass, made to retain the heat of the coffee without scalding the hand, even after being pulled from the microwave. It had just the right balance of density to give it a solid feel without being too heavy. And it was as big as a vat. It could hold a good twenty ounces.

"That had to be at least seventy-five bucks," said Gadg.

As Jordan stared at it, his face shone a reflective thoughtfulness. Without taking his eyes from the mug, he said, "He's never supported my dream. He's hated the thought of Washington ever since I first started talking about it. He's never forgiven me for giving up football."

Tyler opened his mouth and then closed it.

"What?" said Jordan.

"Don't take this the wrong way," said Tyler. "I'm totally stoked for you." He pointed at the picture on Jordan's mug. "But have you ever thought about it from his perspective?"

"Thought about what?"

"We had a shot at the state championship."

Jordan looked away, glancing again at the mug. Finally, he pulled a rolled-up piece of paper from the inside, and read aloud:

> What do you get when you cross Perry Mason with the first Psalm?
> An attorney with a solid, unshakable foundation. Where you're going you need stability.
> The promise is still true. Look to the foundations.

Chapter 16

Something's Not Right

Saturday, May 24, 11:25 a.m.
East side of Nolan property, Wilson, CO

Jordan reflected on the clue, and even more, the word choice.

Attorney.

I can't remember my dad ever using that word.

He gave a quick shake of his head. "Okay, let's get to it. Who has Bible software on their phone?"

Tyler was already launching it. He held out his phone so they could read over Psalm 1.

"He shall be like a tree..." Jordan read aloud over Tyler's shoulder. "Obviously, it might have to do with a tree."

"Almost seems too obvious," said Gadg. "Especially if he's trying to make it challenging."

Tyler still held the phone as he tried to work out the clue.

Gadg rested his fist on his chin. Absently, he looked past the screen toward the large, flat rock that the twelve stones leaned against. His left eyebrow lifted. "What's that?" He pointed to the bottom right-hand portion of the boulder.

"Is that the Nolan family crest?" asked Tyler.

"The *what?*" Jordan replied.

"The Nolan crest," Tyler returned. "Remember yesterday when you were heads down on your computer? I was reading through an old photo album that Grandpa found in the attic above his garage. Last night, after we got home from coffee and dinner, I asked your dad about a few things in it. Do you see how the swords cross in front of the shield? That's definitely it."

The friends moved in closer. Jordan used his hand to wipe a layer of dust from the face of the boulder. The color could not be discerned, but the image was a three-inch version of an angular shield with two swords crossed in front of it. The crest appeared to have been clearly but crudely carved into the face of the rock. Underneath was an arrow about four inches in length that pointed northward along the face of the boulder from left to right.

"That looks old," said Tyler. "Dude, it's obvious they put a lot into this, but that's over the top."

Jordan furrowed his brow and took two steps back. "So my dad showed you *this* crest just yesterday?"

"Yep, he sure did. We talked about a lot of different things. The crest was on one of the pages in the album."

"Did he point it out, or just mention it in passing?"

"I pointed at it and asked him what it was."

"So, just to be clear"—Jordan paused—"did it seem that my dad intended, in any way, to point it out to you?"

"When you put it that way, I'd have to say no."

"Interesting."

"You forgot to say, 'No further questions,'" said Gadg in a dry deadpan.

Jordan smiled and pushed him in the shoulder.

"What's the deal?" asked Tyler.

"I'm not sure," said Jordan. "I guess I just thought his reaction would've somehow tipped you off that this was something to pay attention to."

"Maybe he was trying to keep it hidden since he knew we'd find it soon enough?"

"Yeah, maybe."

Gadg squinted in the late-morning sunlight as he stared at Jordan. "Where does it lead?" he asked.

They looked to the right and tried to follow the path of the arrow with their eyes. There were too many potential objects for them to easily discern the destination.

Jordan fished his phone out of his pocket. "Check this out." He swiped his right index finger a couple times and pressed the screen. "Once a presenter, always a presenter."

"Is that a laser pointer?" asked Tyler. "How'd you get that in a phone?"

Jordan gave Tyler a pat on the shoulder. "You don't think Gadg is limited to stuff that normal people have, do you? He tests all his dad's toys for the police force. And sometimes he shares." Jordan placed the phone against the face of the rock and oriented it parallel to the arrow. He tapped the screen, and thirty yards away, a small red dot danced between branches of a large thicket. "Ugh," he said.

"Quercus gambelii," said Gadg with a frown.

"What?" said Tyler.

"Scrub oak," said Jordan.

"I'll check it out," said Tyler. He ran to the thicket and tried to find a way in.

"It's probably a red herring," said Jordan. "Aren't we looking for a tree?"

"Here it is!" Tyler yelled from inside. Jordan shook his head with a smile, got up from his squatting position, and shot a glance at his best friend.

"I thought you said this was going to be lame," said Gadg as they walked toward Tyler.

"I'm sure the ceremony will be intolerable," replied Jordan. "But this isn't too bad."

Around the back side of the thicket was another flat-faced rock. They squeezed in between the rock and the scrub oak, and were rewarded with another Nolan family crest.

"The red dot hit it straight on," said Tyler.

Jordan weaseled his way to a position directly in front of the boulder. Gingerly, he ran his hand over the dusty face and brought it back, pressing the dust particles between his thumb and two fingers. He then traced the outline of the crest with the pad of his middle finger.

This doesn't make sense.

Gadg studied him.

With six inches between the thicket and the boulder, the right-to-left arrow had a clean shot. "That's gotta be it," said Tyler as he pointed with eager impatience.

There was no mistaking the destination object this time. About forty-five yards away stood a large, sprawling oak tree—one of three on their property. Now sixty-feet high, it had stood sentinel on Nolan property for well over a century, with roots so deep it had defied many a storm.

Jordan looked at Gadg again with the slightest squint of his eyes. Bending down, he lined up the laser pointer and took aim at the base of the tree, about eight feet off the ground.

Tyler hustled to the thick trunk of the massive oak. It had several crags and notches that could easily hold the next clue, but none of them were in the immediate vicinity of the red dot. Higher up the tree, the trunk split into four major branches. Tyler yelled back to Jordan, "Are you sure you have it lined up?"

"I think so," he called back. "Gadg, does this look right to you?"

For answer, Gadg leaned in, looked closely, and nodded.

"Okay, c'mon over and check it out," said Tyler. "I'll switch with you." Sprinting back and squeezing into the thicket, he took the phone and lined up the laser pointer along the orientation of the arrow.

When Jordan reached the tree and saw the red dot, he tilted his head, pressing his lips together.

That's odd.

The last arrow had lined up so perfectly with the destination symbol that he expected this to do the same.

Tyler yelled to him from his crouched position, "Try that crag about a foot below and to the left of where the dot is."

Jordan asked Gadg to give him a boost and reached inside. The hole yielded nothing except dusty residue. Using the laser dot as a center point, Jordan felt around in a circle to see if there were any other places where a clue might be hidden. Nothing.

When Gadg released him, Jordan took a few steps back and surveyed the tree. The red dot, hovering about eight feet off the ground, was positioned squarely in the center of the trunk.

"Still need me to do this?" asked Tyler.

"No, come on over," said Jordan. From fifteen feet away, all three of the hunters scanned the base of the tree for anything that might contain the clue. They tried three other possibilities with no success.

Jordan turned to Gadg. "What type of tree is this?"

"Quercus macrocarpa," said Gadg, "commonly known as the bur oak."

Jordan shook his head with a pained expression. "I should have known."

"Should have known what?" said Tyler.

"What do you get when you cross Perry Mason with the first Psalm?"

Gadg's face took on the same expression.

Jordan turned to Tyler. "Perry Mason was an attorney played by Raymond Burr. I don't think my mom helped with this one. My dad's humor always comes with a side of corn."

"So, this is it," said Tyler. "Nice." He squeezed his hand into a fist.

"It would appear so," said Jordan. With arms crossed, he stared at the oak. His voice was quiet when he spoke again, "Would you guys please hoist me up one more time? I want to check something out."

Gadg and Tyler held his feet as Jordan made his way even higher up the trunk. They switched from underhand to overhand as his feet got to shoulder level. Using one of the appendages that sprouted from the trunk, Jordan scurried up to where the branches separated. He paused for a moment to catch his breath. Inside the largest of the four branches, at the base of where the trunk split, there was a dark opening. He removed several handfuls of dead leaves, raining debris as he attempted to get deeper into the opening.

Probably a dead end.

One last time, Jordan jammed his hand in as far as it would go. It came to rest on something that felt like a paper bag. He pulled it out and studied it. Folded like a lunch sack, one side displayed a worn, but nicely drawn version of the Nolan crest. He opened it and found a scroll with a tie around it.

"I got it," he said over his shoulder. Hand over hand, with the paper sack between his teeth, he jimmied himself out away from the trunk, hung for a second, and dropped to the ground. The sack dropped from his mouth. A moment later, he fished out the clue and unrolled it.

"Helvetica," remarked Gadg, under his breath.

Jordan smiled. *Geek point.*

"You can tell the font just by looking at it? Dude, you *really* are a geek," said Tyler. He tilted his head back and laughed. "Nice variety from your dad though." He turned to Jordan. "This is pretty cool."

I wonder.

Jordan scratched his head behind his ear, and held up the clue so they could all read it.

> *My dear son,*
> *Congratulations on solving your second clue. I realize I can't make up for the past, but I can give you some words to live by going forward. I won't be around to give counsel and support, so I pray these words will bring hope and comfort in the difficult days that are ahead of you.*

Jordan rolled his eyes. Any remaining sentiment related to the mug was gone.

Seriously?

Jordan fought to push the feelings aside. He breathed deeper.

Okay. Remember Grandpa.

> *Choose your friends and choose them wisely.*
>
> *The last few weeks have shown me the value of a dear friend. I would not be where I am without his support and encouragement.*
>
> *Remember these three things:*
>
> *1. Comrades are critical—good ones lift you up; bad ones bring you down (remember Psalm 1).*
>
> *2. You can choose who they are.*
>
> *3. God will help you if you ask Him.*
>
> *There is no such thing as an old friend in a short time. However, depending on what you go through together, a great friend can be forged over a brief period.*

Jordan put his hand on Gadg's shoulder.

> *This then is your next clue:*
> *"Old Town time my hands reveal*
> *Handclasp of friends, deepest bonds to feel*
> *Ere sun's last light come Saturday night*
> *Will long cast shadow of substance real"*
> *With love, Dad*

Jordan frowned.

"What are you thinking?" asked Gadg.

"Something's not right. Why would my dad use the Nolan crest to point the way to the clue? Wouldn't the clue itself be enough?"

"Also," said Gadg, picking up the line of questioning, "why would the first arrow point directly at the crest, and the next arrow miss it by five feet?"

"Yes, I was wondering that too," said Jordan. "Also, why does he think my days are going to be so difficult? Who is the friend that has so profoundly impacted him in the last few weeks?"

"But this has to be your dad," said Gadg. "A bur oak? Psalm 1?"

"I know. That's totally his style, but the tone sounds different." Jordan exhaled and squeezed his lips together. "I guess I'm just confused."

"Maybe in their attempt to be challenging, they've gotten overly cryptic, or didn't fully think through the clues," said Gadg.

"Maybe," murmured Jordan.

"Guys," said Tyler. "Think about it. It's amazing what was put into this treasure hunt. This is totally cool."

Jordan cracked into a smile that caused his shoulders to drop a full inch. He took a deep breath and let it out slowly. "I've missed you, Tyler." He gave him a fist bump. "This year's been so intense, I've forgotten how to think like that."

"Now you're talking," said Tyler. "I'm hungry."

"We still have plenty of time," said Jordan. "Why don't we go into town? We need to do some research, and I want to try out this new mug."

"Won't you get better coffee at home?" asked Tyler.

"Depends on what you mean by better," said Gadg with a wink. "Bethany works at Old Town Café."

Chapter 17

Back in the Arena

**Saturday, May 24, 11:55 a.m.
A few blocks from Old Town Café, Wilson, CO**

Walking down the sidewalk, Jordan noted that the Town of Wilson tried hard to provide a downtown area that was both quaint and functional. Well-maintained restroom facilities were one of the many efforts that made Wilson an attractive community.

For anyone whose name isn't Nolan, that is.

Tyler had stopped to use one of the restrooms. Jordan waited until he was out of earshot, faced Gadg, and said, "Do you think I'm going nowhere in life?"

Gadg scanned his friend's face and took his time forming a question in response, "Where did that come from?"

"Bethany thinks I am," Jordan blurted. "I mean ..." his eyes darted back and forth as he searched for something to cover his tracks.

Gadg put a hand on his shoulder and offered him a lifeline, "I've been your best friend for years. Do you think I don't know how you feel about her?"

Jordan hung his head. "No."

"What's wrong with having an interest in Bethany? She's a fantastic girl."

"Only that she'll never be mine," Jordan said miserably. He then told Gadg what he'd overheard in Bethany's conversation with Allie.

"Well," said Gadg, "those are two serious obstacles." Tyler emerged from the restroom as Gadg finished, "So, when has that ever stopped you?"

● ● ●

Hidden from view, in the commons area of Wilson's Main Street, Alex sat on a bench surrounded by a rich assortment of vegetation, walking paths, and a gazebo.

The picture in his hand had faded with the years, but the memory had not.

He held the photo up in the late-morning light. Two friends with big smiles looked back at him. One had his arm around the other. He flipped the picture to see the inscription on the back.

Dear Alex,
Thanks for being a great friend.
Love,
Michelle

He looked up as Jordan entered the Old Town Café across the street. Reaching for his cell phone, he exhaled a blast of blue smoke and flung away a cigarette butt with an angry snap of his middle finger.

Alex hated Jordan Nolan for one main reason: he should never have been born.

● ● ●

The Old Town Café sat in the heart of Wilson's central business district. Named after the ghost town a couple miles away, the café provided a quaint atmosphere of cozy booths, surrounded by photos that chronicled the history of Wilson. To stimulate a family atmosphere, the tables were covered with white butcher paper, and a cup of crayons perched next to the ketchup and hot sauce.

Seated at a side booth, Jordan took one of the crayons, drew a large square near the edge of the table, and wrote the words "REFILL ZONE." He plopped his new mug proudly in the center, then unfolded the clue and studied it.

Tyler smiled. "So, besides coffee, why did you want to come here?"

Gadg smirked.

"For two reasons," responded Jordan. "First, I'm hungry."

Tyler's face said he had no problem with that. Food was his love language.

"Second, and more importantly, I wanted to discuss the clue with you guys in a place where we could look at some photos of Old Town."

Gadg looked sideways at him.

"What?" said Jordan.

"Nothing," said Gadg.

Jordan hid his face in the clue again as he caught Bethany's approach out of the corner of his eye. She had worked in the café the past two summers, and had just started up again after nationals.

"Good afternoon, gentlemen," said Bethany, in her made-for-broadcasting voice. She looked down at Jordan's mug in the refill zone. "Nice."

Gadg chuckled.

Jordan tried, and almost succeeded, in portraying the cool, bored look. He didn't lift his eyes from the clue.

Easy, Jordan.

"Hey, Bethany," said Gadg. "You know Jordan's cousin, Tyler, don't you?"

"I think we've seen each other before," said Tyler, extending his hand across the corner of the table. "Good to meet you."

"Likewise," said Bethany. She shot a glance at Jordan before giving Tyler her attention. "Are you visiting?"

"I'm spending the summer with my Uncle Johnny. I'm a wide receiver. I'm trying to get a scholarship to a Division 1 school."

Bethany nodded. "That's great, Tyler. Anywhere in particular you'd like to go?"

"*Some*where," Jordan said the word slowly, speaking for the first time "... in the SEC or PAC-12." Looking up, he said to Bethany, "Oh, hello, Miss Clark."

"Hello, Jordan." Bethany turned back to him and narrowed her eyes. "Is that right, Tyler?" She asked without looking away from Jordan. "*Somewhere* ... in one of those two conferences?"

Tyler opened his mouth to speak, but Jordan interrupted before he could. "Well, he doesn't want to go to some school in the middle of *nowhere*. Do you, Tyler?"

Tyler's mouth was still open as Bethany responded, "No indeed. No one learning from Johnny Nolan would be content to go *nowhere*, would they?"

The normally reserved Gadg burst out laughing. He gave Bethany a fist bump.

Tyler's mouth remained open as he glanced back and forth between the other three, confused.

Bethany and Jordan looked at each other. "Touché," said Jordan.

Bethany looked over Jordan's shoulder at the piece of paper in his hand.

"What's that?" she asked.

"My dad set up this treasure hunt thing for me this weekend. Gadg and Tyler are helping. We've got to get it solved by Monday." Jordan showed the clue to Bethany.

Her eyes lit up as she read it.

"Wasn't there a clock tower in Old Town?" Jordan continued. "I was hoping you could direct me to any photos that might have the clock in them."

"Of course," she said with enthusiasm. "I love puzzles!"

"That's what I said!" returned Tyler. "But Jordan's been all weird this last half-hour."

"Not weird," said Gadg. "In serious thought. Some things about this treasure hunt don't seem to add up."

"What do you mean?" said Bethany in a more serious tone.

"I'm not sure," Jordan replied. "This clue seems somehow inconsistent with the others. Can you show me some pictures?"

"How about I start with the ones your dad was looking at the other day?" she smiled in response.

"He was here?"

"Sure was. Follow me."

Jordan and the others followed Bethany to a wall that held several shots of Old Town, as well as Nolan property, from different angles and in different time periods.

Jordan looked up and spotted a black-and-white photo from the perspective of Old Main Street looking west. He saw the clock tower at the end of the street and the old grange about a hundred yards past it in the distance. The tower was twenty-feet high with a gazebo-like structure on top, allowing the sun's evening rays to shine through the enclosure.

"Bingo," said Jordan. The enclosure that housed the clock was still intact, but the clock itself had long since been removed. "We've got to get back there this evening."

"What are you thinking?" asked Bethany. "Ere sun's last light?"

"Yes," said Jordan. He snatched his phone from his pocket, engaged the microphone, and asked what time the sun would set tonight in Wilson.

"Sunset will be at 8:13 p.m., Mountain Daylight Time," his phone responded in the perfect British accent Jordan had chosen for the voice character.

"Do we need to have somebody up on that platform at 8:13?" asked Tyler.

"Or multiple people in a handshake?" asked Bethany, looking up from the clue. "Handclasp of friends?"

"Shouldn't you be taking orders, Miss Clark?" said Jordan with a smile.

"Yes, I probably should, Mister Nolan," Bethany fired back in a tone that mimicked the voice character on Jordan's phone. She intoned in a flawless accent, "I am sorry. I have been too busy answering inquiries regarding Old Town for a group of *boys* that came into the establishment."

Gadg laughed again.

Jordan chuckled and responded to Tyler's question, "Yes, I think we need at least one of us on that platform by 8:13."

●●●

The tinkling sound of the front door opening signaled that more patrons had arrived. Bethany turned to leave as Jordan's face froze.

Matthew entered the café, followed by a rock of a man in a black leather jacket. Even in his forties, Alex Jones still looked like a defensive back: six foot two with hardly an ounce of fat on him; slick, black hair and dark eyes.

"Hello, Bethany," said Matthew as he walked up, ignoring the three guys. "Can I get a table for two?"

"You may," replied Bethany. She said the syllables as a tritone for maximum dissonance, and then walked to the counter, where a pitcher of ice water sat next to a stack of plastic cups.

Matthew's text flashed through Jordan's mind like a popup.

You got lucky.

"Hello, Jordan. Hello, Gadg." He looked each of them in the eye. "Who's this?" He turned to face Tyler with an outstretched hand. "Name's Matthew Harris."

"Tyler Callum," said Tyler, shaking Matthew's hand. "I'm Jordan's cousin. I'm here for the summer to spend some time with my uncle. I'm a wide receiver."

Jordan's arms stiffened at his sides as he sneaked a glance at Matthew. *He'd better not go there.*

"Is that so?" Matthew said. "Well then, let me introduce you to *my* uncle, Alex Jones. He's the head of security at WDC2. He might be a better one for you to spend time with this summer, as he *finished* his football career."

Jordan's heart ignited. "Yeah, he sure did. While he was finishing his career, my dad got *married* and started a family. Didn't he, Mr. *Jones?*" Jordan stabbed the last word.

Alex shot back a look of venom. "You better watch yourself, young man."

"Why is that, sir?"

"A lot can happen in a summer. Don't you agree?"

"Are you asking in your official role as head of security at WDC2? I'm sure the town—and Mr. Carlyle—would be very interested in what you're thinking right now. Wouldn't *you* agree?"

Alex's face hardened into a mask of steel, but he said nothing.

Jordan's heart pounded into his chest, as he was suddenly launched back into the arena with a sword in his hand and unfinished business to attend to. His dad wouldn't be getting up out of his seat this time to distract him. There would be no accusation that he'd gotten lucky. Jordan wheeled on Matthew and thrust his words like an icy dagger, "Did you bring him along to keep you company *at home* this fall, or to pay him for his services?"

Matthew's neck flamed crimson. His face shook, but he kept quiet. Lifting his chin, he turned and strode toward their table. Over his shoulder, he tried for a comeback, "I'm sure we'll see you around."

● ● ●

"What was *that*?" asked Tyler as they walked out of the café.

Jordan's heart hammered like a hard-rock song as he took determined strides down the sidewalk. Gadg and Tyler had to hustle to keep up.

Tyler bit his lip. Neither spoke as they continued walking.

Jordan stopped in front of the same restroom as before. He faced Gadg, abruptly. "What?"

Gadg let a few seconds pass and brought his voice down to a calm whisper. "Are you sure that's the best way?"

Jordan's chest collapsed as he exhaled. He hung his head. "No. It's not." His face flushed. "I'm such an idiot. How am I ever going to be an attorney if I can't control myself?"

Gadg put a hand on his shoulder. "Come on. Let's check out the clock tower. We can meet in the café later."

Jordan wiped his forehead with the back of his arm. "Okay."

Tyler brought his voice down as well. "I didn't know it was that bad. I'm sorry." He paused. "For what it's worth, that was amazing."

"Thanks, Tyler, but it's really not. Gadg is right. You can win a battle and still lose the war. I'm afraid that exchange might make some things worse."

Old Town Café

Saturday, May 24, 7:15 p.m.
Old Town Café, Wilson, CO

"How are you doing?" Gadg took the menu from Tyler and stuffed it back behind the crayons and condiments.

They'd spent half an hour checking out the clock tower and familiarizing themselves with what remained of Old Main Street. Jordan hadn't seen it up close since he was a kid. Since they had to wait until eight o'clock for the next clue, they decided to split up for the afternoon and reconvene at the café later that evening. Jordan had spent much of that time at the Wilson County Library and Historical Building, digging through more information on the town's history.

"I'm doing okay." Jordan ran a hand through his hair. "I've never looked into it before." He showed Gadg an article on his phone.

Local Researcher Kills Coworker, Takes Own Life

William Nolan, 37, of Wilson, Colorado, shot and killed a coworker, Raymond Clark, who also hailed from Wilson. Witnesses close to the men said that a conflict between them had escalated rapidly in the last few days, culminating with Nolan shooting Clark in the forested area behind Carlyle Enterprises' Research Lab. Nolan was also found dead later in his apartment of a gunshot wound to the head. A Smith and Wesson bearing his fingerprints lay on the floor next to him. The police have ruled it a suicide.

Howard Carlyle, CEO of Carlyle Enterprises, made the following statement: "We are deeply saddened by the news. Our sincerest condolences to the Clark family in this most difficult time."

"I'm sorry, Jordan," said Gadg.

"I don't think about it much." Jordan took a sip from his new mug, straightened up, and gave a tight-lipped smile. "I should have known I would bump into this. If you're going to look into Wilson's history, you can't miss it."

"So," Gadg said, redirecting the conversation, "are we considering summer school?"

Jordan raised an eyebrow and pulled up another article. "This is interesting. Did you know that WDC2 bought all the land right up to the edge of Old Town in the midsixties? They tried to buy Old Town as well, but the Town of Wilson wouldn't sell."

"Why is that interesting?" asked Gadg.

"Look at this." Jordan turned his phone. "Even though he didn't own the property, Howard Carlyle threw his weight around, threatening to move WDC2 to another city if the Town of Wilson insisted on restoring and renovating Old Town."

"Hmm," said Gadg. "That is curious."

"I agree. He sent an open letter to the City Council, saying that he preferred Old Town in its 'pristine state.'" Jordan made air quotes.

"Pristine, or *unsearched*?" asked Gadg.

Jordan nodded. "That's what I'd like to know."

"Is that why it still looks like a ghost town?" asked Tyler.

"Yes," said Jordan. "It was clearly more important to the Town of Wilson to have the revenue from WDC2 than to have Old Town as a historical site. Since there's not much over there besides WDC2 and our property, Old Town just sat there much the same as it was in the sixties, which was much the same as it was in the twenties. It wasn't until earlier this year that Donald Carlyle, Howard's son, finally gave WDC2's consent to the renovation of Old Town."

"So why now?" asked Tyler.

"Two reasons, I think. First, Howard Carlyle, the one who didn't want it renovated, died earlier this month."

"Spite?" asked Gadg.

"Possibly," said Jordan. "I have a feeling that not all was well in that relationship."

"What was the other reason?" asked Tyler.

"PR," said Gadg.

"You got it," Jordan agreed. "WDC2 has been in financial difficulty ever since that fiasco a couple years ago with the US Center for Disease Control.

They were accused of improper compounding. There was an outbreak of meningitis, and as a result, Donald Carlyle, as CEO, was in the hot seat. I think he would be thrilled to have WDC2, and himself, getting some good press again. I wouldn't be surprised if he's preparing the company to be sold."

"Do you know him?" asked Tyler.

"Donald? Just a little. He introduced himself to me right over there," Jordan pointed to another table. "He overheard someone make a rude comment about my family. He told me he's lived his whole life in the shadow of Howard Carlyle, 'Man of the Century.'" More air quotes. "It's like he has nowhere to go but down."

Tyler asked, "Is that what it's felt like for you?"

"Somewhat," Jordan's face darkened a shade as he continued, "I've lived my whole life under two shadows: a football star for a father, and a suicidal murderer for a great-grandfather. It's been a weird mix of fame and stigma— like half the town loves us, and half can't stand us."

"Why did your family never leave?" asked Tyler.

"Good question. The simplest answer is that, back when it was really bad, they couldn't leave for financial reasons. When it was only moderately bad, inertia kept them here." Jordan looked up and forced down a smile as Bethany arrived with the food. He knew that her father, Michael Clark, was squarely, and immovably, in the stigma camp.

But Bethany isn't.

They'd both played up the banter earlier, but he knew Bethany had at least one real reason for thinking he was going nowhere.

What could it be?

She stood close enough that he felt a slight tremble.

"What time is it?" asked Tyler.

Gadg used one of the six ways he could get the time at any given moment. "It's 7:25."

"We've got about thirty minutes," said Jordan.

"For the clue?" asked Bethany, her eyes brightening at the mention of the puzzle.

"Yes, we've got to be up in Old Town by about ten after eight for the sunset," Gadg replied.

Tyler put his hands out, palms facing up, and asked the group if he could pray for the meal. Bethany smiled. Jordan grimaced, but put one hand in Tyler's anyway. Bethany stood right next to him, and his heart sped up a beat or two. He didn't dare reach for her hand, so he did his best to look indifferent, absently glancing up at an old analog clock behind Tyler that showed the time as 7:26.

Suddenly, he sprang up out of his seat, banging his thigh on the underside of the tabletop. He yelped, and every one of the twelve or so other people in the café looked up at him. Bethany put a hand to her mouth and squeezed her jaw to keep from laughing. Jordan's face was still scrunched up in pain as he pulled out his wallet and threw two twenties on the table. With a groan and bad grammar, he said, "We gotta go, *now*."

"But the food just got here," Tyler squalled as the aroma of his loaded half-pound Wilson burger wafted just inches from his nose. "Why do we have to go now?"

"Handclasp of friends, ere sun's last light," said Jordan. "We have ten minutes. We have to be in position when the big and small hands of the clock *touch each other* before sunset—at 7:37."

Chapter 19

Ere Sun's Last Light

Saturday, May 24, 7:35 p.m.
The East Road to Old Town, Wilson, CO

Gutless, Jordan's endearing truck, spewed rocks from the back tires as Gadg dug fingernail imprints into the vinyl headrest in an effort to remain inside the vehicle.

Nearly totaled three times, Grandpa's old Chevy S10 had been a fixture in Jordan's life since he was fifteen. Dull orange, the truck was plastered with a big Band-Aid sticker on the hood, where a deer had jumped in front of him on one of Wilson's many back roads. The truck barely survived. The deer, unfortunately, didn't.

Back on the road again, they soon noticed that the truck had lost much of what little power it had once possessed. Gadg had dubbed it "Gutless Deersbane"—and the name stuck.

Jordan's driving, more than the speed, kept gravel spewing and Gadg clutching the seat. With his foot rammed to the floor, Jordan coaxed Gutless down Wilson's East Road. Sandwiched between Nolan property and a ridge that marked the eastern edge of Wilson County, the East Road had the lowest traffic of any road maintained by the county.

For most people in Wilson, Old Town was old news. Because Howard Carlyle had threatened to take WDC2 and its revenue to another city if Old Town was renovated, this corner of Wilson County stayed frozen in time.

"Okay, listen up." Jordan jerked his head around. "We have two minutes, three at the most. Tyler, you run down the street and find a way up the clock tower. Be careful. Once you've climbed up, get centered and put your arm in the position of the minute hand at 7:37 p.m. Gadg, follow behind and align him to the photo we saw in the café."

"I didn't get a good look at it," replied Gadg. "I was checking out a different picture when Matthew walked in."

"Here's my phone," Jordan handed it back over his head. "I took one today. Use the analog setting on the clock to know exactly when the moment is. I'm not sure how precise this will be, but I want to get as close as possible." He reached out his hand again. "Give me your phone and call me when it's time. I don't think I'll be able to hear you from up on the ridge. It's a few hundred yards, at least."

Jordan turned to Tyler. "T minus five seconds."

Tyler's hand rested on the door handle as a smile lit up his face. They'd practiced this a few times last summer, just for fun.

Jordan yanked the e-brake, spun Gutless around in a cloud of dust, and skidded the rear wheels in a motion that flung Tyler into a full sprint down Old Main Street. Jordan burst from the driver's side door and scrambled up the ridge, dodging rocks and ducking under tree limbs. At first, he had no idea how far up he needed to go. One minute remained. He tried his best to use the shadows from other abandoned buildings, but they were either too short, or too close to the ridge to be of much use as a guide.

Gadg called him. "Tyler's in place."

"Have him put both hands in the air for a moment," Jordan held Gadg's phone to his ear. "Ugh, it's farther up than I thought. Hold on." He sprinted up the hill to the huge shadow cast by Tyler's frame. "Okay, now, have him put his arms in position." He paused for several breaths. "Good. I see it." More heavy breathing. "Stand by, let me get a picture." Due to the length of the shadow, Tyler's arm covered a sizable stretch of ground in multiple directions. Jordan snapped a few photos. "That's good. Come on up, gentlemen."

● ● ●

Gadg clicked off Jordan's phone and started up the length of Main Street toward the ridge. As they walked, Tyler asked, "Gadg, what's going on?"

"What do you mean?"

"You guys are speaking a language with your eyes that I don't get."

"That would be the result of hundreds of hours together in the academic version of a foxhole."

"With your mouths, too."

"I'm sorry, Tyler. It feels like we can read each other's thoughts sometimes."

"And what are you reading right now?"

"What are you talking about?"

"Ever since that last clue, Jordan's got something on his mind."

"I know he does," Gadg glanced up the street. "I just don't know what it is yet. I'm not sure he does either. The pieces just don't fit."

●●●

Five minutes later, Tyler and Gadg joined Jordan halfway up the ridge. He glanced up and down a few times, studying the photos and trying to orient the shadow from his picture with the blank terrain in front of him.

"Tyler, would you mind walking up about fifty yards? I'll direct you as you get close," said Jordan.

Tyler trotted ahead, with Jordan aiming him like a guided missile.

"That's good," said Jordan, satisfied that Tyler was in place. "What do you see?"

"Nothing," replied Tyler.

"That's what I thought." Turning to Gadg, he said, "Will you go up and confirm?"

A moment later, Gadg called to Jordan, "Tyler's right. There's no sign of any disturbance of the ground. It's definitely not here."

They came back down as Jordan surveyed the area in a broad swath. "I don't know how much light we have left, but let's spread out and search the area. Keep an eye out for something with a surface that could have the Nolan crest on it."

"Like that," said Gadg, pointing to a group of rocks about fifty feet away.

"Yes, like that," said Jordan. He went down the hill a few yards and aligned his approach to mimic a shadow from the clock tower. Much like those on Nolan property, several boulders of various shapes and sizes clustered into a community.

Their search took all of thirty seconds. "No way," said Gadg as he looked through an opening between two large rocks in the front. "There it is."

Chiseled into the face of the boulder, a small, dusty, faded version of the

Nolan crest sat roughly two feet off the ground. Just below it, the signature arrow pointed downward.

"Sweet!" said Tyler. He bounded over to the rock and peered at the arrow. "Looks like we're gonna need a shovel, though. The ground is hard."

The nagging feeling that something didn't belong kept tugging at Jordan. *The clue is not where it should be.*

Jordan surveyed the area. "Gadg, what day of the year would cause the shadow from the clock tower to hit this point before sundown?"

"What are you thinking?" said Gadg.

"It's possible they put it up here earlier—say, last weekend—and didn't account for the rotation of the earth," said Jordan.

"Or maybe we're misinterpreting the clue," said Gadg. "We're assuming that 'handclasp of friends' and 'ere sun's last light' represent the last time before sundown that the hour hand and the minute hand touch, or rather, would touch, if the clock was still there."

"True," said Jordan. "But the crest is right here." He pointed to the boulder. "Assuming we're correct, can you figure it out?"

Gadg was already heads down on his phone.

"Wait, you're serious?" said Tyler.

"Just watch the magic happen," Jordan whispered in Tyler's ear.

Ten minutes later, after using nothing but his brain and his phone, Gadg declared, "You were right. It's April 25th."

Tyler shook his head. "Wow."

"Really?" said Jordan. "That's a month ago." His forehead creased as he cocked his head and stared at the face of the rock. He slid the palm of his hand over the crest and wiped away a layer of dirt.

"No idea why," said Gadg, "but it's true. Maybe they miscalculated."

Jordan's fingers brushed the outline of the carving. It was totally smooth. Turning away, he did a double take, glancing back at the crest. His eyes and mouth opened wide. "It can't be," he whispered to himself, transfixed.

Gadg and Tyler blurted simultaneously, "What?"

Jordan lifted his eyes and his face shone in wonder. "Let's go back to the old oak tree. You're not going to believe this."

Chapter 20

Much Time

Saturday, May 24, 8:20 p.m.
Nolan property, in front of large oak tree, Wilson, CO

They sprinted and slipped down the hill, ignored Jordan's truck parked at the bottom of the ridge, and jumped the fence onto Nolan property. A moment later, they stood panting in front of the bur oak where they'd discovered the last clue. Jordan reached into his pocket, pulled out the summer school letter, and reread it.

"Perhaps you'll find more treasure, and a greater blessing than either of you expect," he read the final words aloud. "I didn't think that was meant to be literal."

"Are you thinking what I think you're thinking?" said Gadg.

Still wide-eyed, Jordan could only nod.

"Would somebody please let me onto the bus?" asked Tyler, eagerly. "What's going on?"

Jordan pulled out his phone and aimed the laser pointer at a spot about eight feet up the trunk of the tree. "This is where we *expected* to find the clue." Lifting his arm, he aimed five feet higher, where the tree split into its four main branches. "Up there," he continued, "is where we *found* it." His tone quieted almost to a whisper and turned deadly serious. "What I'm saying, Tyler, is this: my dad did not put the clue up there."

Tyler stared. "Then who did?"

"No one," Jordan replied.

Even Gadg didn't get that one. He turned to Jordan.

"Then how did it get there?" asked Tyler.

"Time."—Jordan paused—"and a lot of it."

It clicked for Gadg, and he smiled. "We just stepped into the shoes of one of your ancestors."

Jordan nodded. Turning to Tyler again, he pointed his laser back to the spot where they'd expected the clue to be. "That"—he paused again—"is where the clue was *fifty* years ago. It was put there by *William* Nolan."

"What?" Tyler stood awestruck. "Are you telling me that we are on two treasure hunts, from different generations, at the same time?"

"Unbelievably, yes!" replied Jordan with rising eagerness.

"Why April 25th?" asked Gadg.

Jordan tapped his screen a couple times to turn off the laser pointer and showed them one of the articles he'd found in his research earlier: "William Nolan died early on the morning of Friday, April 24th, 1964. The first Saturday after his death was April 25th. He had previously set up a treasure hunt for my grandpa."

"This is incredible!" said Tyler, glancing at each of them. "So, where's your dad's clue?"

Jordan's smile lit up his face. "I don't know, but this just got *way* more interesting."

"May I see the clue again?" asked Gadg.

Jordan handed it over.

"Check this out." He motioned to Jordan with his head. "Does this sound like a suicidal murderer?"

Jordan leaned over Gadg's shoulder and focused intently. "I can't imagine what it means, but it sure doesn't sound like a murderer."

"What about the line about him not being around?" asked Tyler. "That does sound a bit like a suicide note."

Gadg quoted it from memory. "'I won't be around to give counsel and support, so I pray these words will bring hope and comfort in the difficult days that are ahead of you.' I don't know"—Gadg shook his head—"that doesn't sound like someone about to kill himself."

"I thought it was my dad saying he wouldn't be in DC with me," said Jordan. "Now I can only assume it means William knew something was going to happen. It must be related to the events in the letter I received."

"I agree," said Gadg.

"Two things I know at this point," continued Jordan. "First, it's important that we keep this between us."

Tyler interjected, "Shouldn't we go get Grandpa? After all, this treasure hunt was made for him."

Jordan thought for a moment, looked each of them in the eye, and said, "I would ask you guys to trust me on this one. I don't think we should mention it to him just yet. I have multiple reasons, but the main one I'll share is this: there's no guarantee we'll be able to get to the end of this treasure hunt, fifty years after it was put in place. I think we should follow it as far as we can, and based on what we find, we can decide how best to proceed. It doesn't sound like something I want Grandpa to get mixed up in."

Tyler and Gadg glanced at each other and eventually nodded.

"What's the second thing you know?" asked Tyler.

Jordan smiled with a twinkle in his eye. "It's time to enroll in summer school."

Unexpected Encounter

Saturday, May 24, 9:45 p.m.
Kitchen of Nolan home, Wilson, CO

Jordan and Gadg were to provide the snacks and the decoy. Tyler would get the tools from the garage. Jordan's mom was busy cleaning the kitchen, along with Grandpa, as the two boys went about re-dirtying it. Jordan lined up some bread slices on a cutting board when Johnny, dressed in a gray sweatshirt with a big U on it, walked toward the door to the garage.

Gadg fired a look Jordan's way.

"Uhh, Dad"—Jordan stalled—"I have to say, I'm impressed with this treasure hunt."

Probably not for the reasons you think, though.

Johnny's hand was on the doorknob. Turning back to the kitchen, he looked at his son. "Really? I'm pumped you guys are taking this so seriously. I'm not good at this stuff, you know."

"Mr. Nolan," Gadg said with a diversionary smile, "this is great. Please don't give us any hints. It may take us all weekend, but we want to solve it ourselves."

Nice work, Gadg. All the time and space we need.

"I agree. I've never been on a more challenging quest," said Jordan, "with the possible exception of the internship, of course." Without warning, Bethany's face flashed into his mind.

Yeah, that too.

Johnny adjusted his cap. "I was afraid you might think this whole thing was lame."

Grandpa coughed and stared into the rafters while drying a plate.

Jordan shot him a glance.

"I didn't want this to be just another thing," Johnny continued, "so I did something I've never thought to do. I asked God to help me make it more interesting."

Jordan quickly refocused on the sandwich. "That's cool," he said, looking at the whipped pattern of a newly-opened jar of mayonnaise.

"Really?" Gadg asked.

"Jordan got his quick mind from his mom." Johnny looked at his wife. "I knew I'd need help to make this challenging for you guys."

Gadg's bottom lip stuck out a bit as he nodded thoughtfully. "It would appear that He has answered that prayer. This is fascinating."

Don't push your luck, buddy.

Johnny gave a satisfied nod. "Well, that's great."

Jordan layered a slab of ham on the bread.

"I just hope it doesn't end up being *too* challenging," said Johnny.

"I agree," said Jordan. He looked at Grandpa and thought of the obvious affection for him in the clue from William. "That would be *most* disappointing."

● ● ●

Gutless sat parked at a strange angle where they'd left him at the base of the ridge. Jordan made a mental note to bring the truck back home after they tried to dig up the next clue. Donning sweatshirts, the three sneaked away with the tools Tyler had stashed.

The excitement of the day remained. By 10:15, the boys had started up the base of the ridge toward the rock they'd found earlier.

"Hello, gentlemen." The voice was a deep rumble, unexpected and yet unmistakable.

Jordan inhaled sharply and his pulse skyrocketed. He tightened his grip on the shovel.

A moonlit shadow emerged from behind a tree, confirming the presence of Alex Jones. Matthew followed behind him.

Tyler and Gadg stayed silent, but their eyes were wide, glowing orbs in the moonlight.

"What's going on, boys?" asked Alex, looking at the shovels. "We saw your truck out here, so we thought we'd stop and say hello. Nice parking job, by the way."

"You *saw* my truck?" Jordan's voice came out sharp. His pulse hammered the inside of his neck. "That's an interesting way to put it."

"Not nearly as interesting as three boys hiking the ridge wearing dark clothes and carrying shovels. What do you think, Matthew?" Alex looked at his nephew. "They're not planning to do any digging on county land, are they?"

Matthew shook his head. "No, they wouldn't do that."

Multiple thoughts sprang into Jordan's mind in an instant. First, there was no way they were going farther right now. Second, he didn't know how, or when, they would have another chance to investigate. Third, he was seriously beginning to wonder what was up with Alex. Still fighting off the initial fright, he fired back a snarky, "What do you want?"

A limb from a nearby tree blocked enough of the moon to cover Alex's face with a dark claw. "Maybe you need to remember your little tantrum today. I am head of WDC2 security, after all."

"We're not on WDC2 property."

"That's true, but when people carry shovels *near* company property, I make it my business."

"I'm sure you do. Especially when it happens to be those with last names that start with N. For your information, we're closer to Nolan property than WDC2 property."

A cord tightened on Alex's neck.

Jordan tried for casual.

What is he really doing here?

An awkward five seconds passed. Gadg stood stone-still. Tyler fidgeted.

"Beautiful evening, isn't it?" said Jordan, looking around.

"What a crock," said Matthew. He turned to his uncle. "Are you just going to let him do this?" He took a step toward Jordan, but Alex held him back.

Jordan's heartbeat steadied to a mix of adrenaline and anger. He leveled his gaze at Matthew. "Mr. Harris, this behavior is beneath even *you*. Following us around after dark? This isn't elementary school. It would probably be more subtle if you just broke both my legs and got it over with." He turned to Gadg. "Would you mind taping this? I think your dad—not to mention Mr. Jones' boss—would be interested in this discussion."

Gadg pulled his phone out and started recording.

"Say hello to Deputy O'Brien, gentlemen," said Jordan.

The three boys began their retreat toward the truck.

"Goodbye, Jordan," said Alex in a voice aimed at the camera. "It is indeed a beautiful evening. Too bad you won't be able to see it from *higher up* the ridge. Gadg, make sure you get the shovels in the video if you choose to show it to your dad. I imagine he'd find them especially interesting."

They reached the truck, threw the shovels in the back, and climbed into the cab. Alex and Matthew followed them down. A few seconds later, both doors opened as Jordan realized he had left his keys on the rack at home. They grabbed the shovels from the bed and started the short walk back to Nolan property.

Alex and Matthew laughed, and Matthew piped up, "Is the camera still rolling, Gadg? Keep that up and you could send it in as an audition for the Darwin Awards."

Chapter 22

Brief and Debrief

Saturday, May 24, 10:35 p.m.
Jordan's room, Wilson, CO

"Sorry, guys. That was dumb." Jordan spoke in hushed tones to the others as they huddled in his bedroom.

"Not really," replied Gadg. "But it was unexpected, unrehearsed, and unwinnable."

"Unwinnable?" asked Tyler.

"Yeah, what could he say or do to salvage that situation?"

"I could've remembered my keys," said Jordan, disgusted.

"Yeah, that would've helped." Gadg winked at him.

Jordan punched him in the shoulder. "You know what I appreciate about you? I act like a total idiot and you manage to paint it in a pleasant way."

Gadg looked him in the eye. "Bro, cut yourself some slack. That was an honest mistake on a bizarre day. Not to mention we'd just been scared spitless. I nearly jumped out of my skin."

"Me, too," said Tyler. "That was freaky."

The muscles on Jordan's face relaxed. "You're right."

"What I don't understand," continued Tyler, "is how that guy Alex knew to be there. And even more important, *why* would he be there?"

"Great questions," said Gadg.

"I'm not sure what the box top looks like," said Jordan, "but the puzzle pieces are interesting. First, I get a cryptic 'summer school' letter that all but suggests a link between WDC2 and the drug XD. Second, we find a fifty-year-old clue from a suicidal murderer that sounds decidedly out of character. And now it would appear we're being followed by Alex Jones. None of it makes any sense."

"Do you think it's just him?" asked Gadg.

"What do you mean?" asked Jordan.

"Would Alex do this on his own?"

"Well, he does hate our family." Jordan turned to Tyler. "My mom and Alex were good friends in college, but then she chose my dad over him. He's had it out for us ever since."

"True," said Gadg, lowering his voice. "But it still doesn't change the question. Why is he interested in this?" He let it hang in the air as the stillness entered the conversation like a fourth person.

Jordan stared at Gadg. Something in his friend's gaze caused him to look at things with fresh eyes. "Starting from scratch, let's assume for a moment that the insinuations in the summer school letter are true."

Gadg flipped his fingers in a motion for him to keep going.

"Alex is dangerous enough on his own," Jordan continued.

"Yes, he is," said Gadg. "But did you see how he held Matthew back?"

"What do you make of it?"

"I don't like it," said Gadg. "Who's calling the shots here?"

"I don't know," said Jordan, "but if the summer school letter is legit, this could easily go beyond Alex."

Gadg nodded.

"How are we going to get to the clue?" asked Tyler.

"We absolutely must not lead them to the digging spot," said Jordan.

"We could wait," said Tyler.

Jordan shook his head. "Three issues. First, we don't want to give them any chance in daylight of finding what we found today. Second, we don't even know if the treasure still exists. If it does, I want to have it by Monday. And third, we can assume there's more to this than a fun little treasure hunt. We're in summer school, gentlemen."

"Roger that," said Gadg.

"So, what do we do?" asked Tyler.

Jordan pondered for a long moment. "From this moment forward, we assume we are being followed." He went to the window and looked out. The normally cozy forest seemed to be guarded by black silhouettes. He closed the curtains and turned back to the others. "Okay, here's the plan."

● ● ●

"That's right, Mr. Carlyle." Speaking into his cell phone, Alex watched Matthew walk away from the car. "They were on their way to the ridge with shovels in their hands."

"Shovels?"

"Yes, sir."

"Where were they going?" asked Donald.

"I don't know, sir. They never made it up the ridge."

"And why is that?"

Alex looked away, even though there was no one else in his car.

"Never mind," said Donald. "What have they been up to?"

Alex breathed easier. "I'm not sure. Reading. Looking at the Old Town photos in Old Town Café. And then"—he paused for effect—"they jumped in that old beater and raced out of town. We found it parked at the base of the ridge."

"We?"

"Matthew's been with me."

"Your nephew?"

"Yes, sir."

"Does he know anything?"

"Not really. He just wants to find a way to Washington, that's all."

"Listen up, Jones. I did *not* give you permission to tell anybody about this."

Alex remained silent.

"Think about how this will look if anybody finds out." Donald's voice got louder in Alex's ear. "I'm paying you to see if there's anything I need to be concerned about. I'm also paying you for secrecy. Does the word *discretion* mean anything to you?"

Chapter 23

The Clue on the Ridge

Sunday, May 25, 3:30 a.m.
Eastern ridge, Wilson, CO

Leaning on his shovel, Jordan peered down between two trees from high on the ridge. It had taken him an hour and a half to go the long way around. Adrenaline and exhaustion fought for the upper hand. So far, fatigue had a slight edge. If he'd calculated correctly, the location of the next clue should be about a hundred yards below him. Thankfully, there was some moonlight, as he didn't want to use a flashlight for fear of giving away his location. There was still the risk that he wasn't in as good a position as he thought.

> I'm on final approach.

He texted Gadg while trying to conceal any light from his phone.

> I'll let you know when I'm in position.

> Roger that.

Gadg texted back.

> **We're standing by.**

Jordan could see the remains of Old Town in the moonlight.

Who are you, William Nolan?

Jordan shook his head to snap his thoughts back into the present. His eyes darted to and fro, scanning the ridge. If Alex got hold of the clue, the whole thing was shot.

He found it vaguely comforting that Gadg and Tyler were a few hundred feet away. Straining to hear any noise that didn't fit with the normal night sounds of a semi-forested ridge, he crept down the hill.

The wind kicked up just a bit, causing him to shiver.

You have one shot at this.

There it was. Even in the moonlight, the rock outcropping from earlier was obvious. Jordan sneaked up to it, walked around the nearest boulder, and scrunched down in the spot where he planned to dig. There was just enough moonlight by which to see. He ran his hand over the Nolan crest and the arrow pointing down toward his feet. It was smooth and faded. A knowing smile stole back the upper hand as Jordan's weariness gave way to excitement.

Unbelievable. Fifty years old.

He fit the Bluetooth earpiece into his ear and turned it almost all the way down. He didn't want to risk being heard, so he sent a text to Gadg that read:

> **Phase 1 complete.**

● ● ●

Gadg and Tyler had also crept down to a spot several hundred feet south of Jordan's position, but not so far that it couldn't have been a possible destination earlier when Alex intercepted them.

Gadg called Jordan's phone. They'd ensured that the ringer was off. He could tell by the soft breathing that Jordan was listening. "Initiating phase two," said Gadg, quietly. He stayed on the call.

They strolled noisily into a cluster of trees. Tyler wore Jordan's varsity jacket, and pulled a baseball cap down almost over his eyes.

"I think this might be it." Tyler played a recording of Jordan's voice.

"I agree," whispered Gadg. "Let's get it and get back home."

They began to dig.

● ● ●

Through the earpiece, Jordan could hear the sounds of breathing, and shovels creasing the earth. He pushed the mute button to make sure no sounds from his end would get to Gadg. Three minutes passed.

"There it is," whispered Gadg.

Jordan could picture Gadg pulling out the crumpled sack they had staged as a prop when they were in the kitchen.

"We've got it," said Gadg. "Let's get out of here."

"Well, well, what have we here?" Jordan heard a deep gravelly voice in his ear.

I knew it.

"Go," hissed Gadg. Jordan could hear them running with all their might.

Leaving his earpiece on mute, Jordan turned the volume all the way up. As soon as he heard Gadg and Tyler running, he attacked the ground with his shovel.

"Get 'em!" Jordan heard Alex say, fiercely. He assumed he'd brought Matthew with him.

Jordan knew from earlier that the ground would be hard.

You idiot.

Why hadn't he brought an additional tool, such as a pickaxe, or at least a large screwdriver? Too late. He'd have to make do with the shovel. Jordan shook his head at his progress. Compounding the problem, he had no idea how deep he would have to dig—or if there was even anything here.

"They're gaining on us," Jordan heard Gadg say to Tyler.

Slowly but surely, Jordan made headway. The ground was a softer after he got a couple inches down.

He heard Gadg continue his conversation with his decoy. "Jordan, you take it. You're a faster runner. Get it back to your house. It's the only chance."

Jordan smiled as he thought of Gadg.

He's a sharp cookie.

No time to think of that now. Back to business.

"Hi, guys," Jordan heard Gadg greet Alex and someone else whom he assumed was Matthew.

"You stay with him, I'll get Jordan," Alex growled.

"Hello, Matthew," Gadg said through heavy breathing.

"Hello, Gadg. I knew you were an early riser, but this is a bit ridiculous, don't you think?"

"The early bird gets the worm," he panted. "What are *you* doing here?"

"The early cat gets the *bird*," replied Matthew.

Even with the night chill, sweat covered Jordan's forehead and dripped onto his face. Gadg and Tyler were doing great. Even so, Jordan knew his time was limited. He was about fourteen inches below the surface.

"I'm going to check on Jordan," said Gadg. Jordan could hear the sounds of air pushing past Gadg as he jogged south. Matthew stayed with him easily.

"Why do you have an earpiece in your ear?" asked Matthew.

Uh-oh.

"I'm a geek," replied Gadg, without missing a beat. "I always have an earpiece in my ear."

"Wait a minute!" Matthew's voice was sharp. "There were three of you earlier."

Jordan could still hear Gadg's breathing.

"Alex!" This time, he heard the yell even without the earpiece. "Come back! It's a decoy!"

"Jordan," Gadg said as he ran, "the game is up. You've got three minutes—maybe four at the most."

● ● ●

Jordan was sixteen inches into the earth. He thought about running away to come back at another time, but the hole would be obvious. It was now or never. Thirty seconds passed ... sixty ... ninety.

Come on. Come ON!

Alex would be coming back his way at top speed at any moment.

His next stroke hit something. He dropped his shovel and furiously scraped away dirt with his hands. A rock. Jordan pounded his fists once onto the dirt beside the hole. The rock was about seven inches in diameter. Another forty-five seconds passed as he wedged it out. He shook his head. Standing up, he plunged the shovel one more time. Bingo. That had to be metal. He dropped again to his knees and scooped away dirt with his hands. A few moments later, he produced a small, round tin that looked like it had once held hard candy. The now-dented label had a vintage look that was not twenty-first century.

A thrill shot through him at the same time his insides screamed for him to hurry.

Hands sweaty and shaking, he pried open the tin with the tips of his fingernails. Inside was a single, folded piece of old paper. He plucked it out, yanked off his right shoe, and stuffed the paper down into the toe. He then slipped his foot back into his shoe, scraped some dirt into the tin, and closed the lid.

Alex broke into view, seventy-five yards away on a dead sprint.

Jordan stuffed the tin in his pocket, picked up the shovel, and ran. It wasn't two seconds before the shovel smashed the edge of the rock and was wrenched from his hand.

He yelped.

Breathing hard, he ran back toward the town. Almost before he'd started, he knew it was futile. Alex used to be a Division 1 defensive back.

Fear gripped him.

It only took a few seconds for Alex to catch him. He chased him down, wrapped him around the waist and slammed him to the ground.

Jordan felt his bones crunch together.

"Give it to me," Alex didn't wait for Jordan's response. Holding him to the ground with one hand, he used the other to reach into his pocket and pull out the old candy tin.

Alex let go of Jordan to open the lid. Jordan scrambled away and took off as fast as he could down the hill. Most of his body hurt. He was surprised he wasn't seriously injured. It had been two years since he'd taken any kind of a serious hit. Seconds later, he heard an angry curse. Inside his head, a blur of red sliced across his consciousness. Suddenly, he was in elementary school again, on the playground of terror. Adrenaline kicked him into a gear he didn't know he had.

Even so, he wasn't sure he could make it back to the truck.

Just before he reached the bottom of the ridge, Alex caught up to him. This time he dove, tripping Jordan up by the feet. Jordan stumbled, splayed forward, and rolled to a stop on his back.

Alex got up and walked toward where Jordan lay, sprawled on the ground.

He reached down, grabbed him by the collar, and jammed a finger into his chest.

Memory flooded back, and Jordan's mind swam in a sea of red.

"Where is it?" snarled Alex.

"Where is what?" Jordan's voice sounded eight years old.

"Whatever was in that thing." Alex gripped Jordan's sweatshirt just under the neck with both hands.

Gadg strolled into view, holding his phone in front of him. There was no sign of Tyler.

"You try that recording trick again Gadg—I'll make you eat that phone," Alex hissed.

"What was that, Mr. Jones?" asked Gadg. "Could you speak up? I don't think my *dad* could quite hear you."

Alex looked back, sharply.

Gadg pointed the phone at him, revealing a Skype call.

"What's going on here?" The face and voice of Deputy O'Brien came from Gadg's phone as he walked toward them.

Alex turned away to hide his face. He released Jordan and took off up the slope. In three seconds, he rounded a tree and was out of sight. Matthew had been watching from a distance. Hearing Deputy O'Brien's voice, he slipped behind a tree and followed quietly after Alex.

"Thanks, Dad," Gadg spoke loudly to the trees. "Would you mind staying on the line?" He then walked over to Jordan and reached down with one hand. "Let's go."

Quick Thinking

Sunday, May 25, 4:17 a.m.
Jordan's room, Wilson, CO

Jordan tiptoed with Gadg back into his bedroom as the last residue of red disappeared from his mind.

"Don't step on Tyler," whispered Gadg.

Still in his clothes, Tyler lay, dead-to-the-world on a mat next to the closet.

"I won't."

"I texted him that we'd meet him here," said Gadg. "Guess he couldn't stay awake." He turned to Jordan. "You all right?"

"I'm exhausted, but okay," said Jordan. He laid a hand on Gadg's shoulder. "Thanks."

Gadg nodded.

Jordan sank down onto his bed. "That was some quick thinking, getting your dad on the call. I'm surprised he hasn't shown up here already."

"He won't," Gadg said.

Jordan took off his sweatshirt. "Why?"

"He's asleep."

"You sure? He must be concerned about us," Jordan threw his sweatshirt between Tyler and the closet.

"It's fine. I never spoke to him."

"What?" Jordan jerked his head around.

Gadg shrugged. "Just some clips I put together with my dad's voice a few weeks ago. I didn't think I would ever actually *need* one."

"Let me get this straight. That was taped? Your dad knows nothing about this?"

Gadg gave a pursed grin.

Jordan smiled for the first time in hours. "I take it back. That wasn't quick thinking ... that was brilliance."

"So, did you find it?" asked Gadg.

"It was in a 1960's candy tin, which Alex took."

Gadg let out a sigh. His face looked pained.

Jordan's face didn't look pained at all.

"*What?*" said Gadg.

"I said it was in the tin that he took," Jordan paused. "I didn't say it was in the tin *when* he took it. Thanks to you, he didn't get that far."

Gadg's face lit up. "You still have it?"

Jordan couldn't keep his grin from blossoming into a huge but tired smile. He pulled off his right shoe and emptied it onto his bed. A small, folded, fifty-year-old piece of paper dropped onto the blanket.

"Now *that* was brilliance," said Gadg.

With dark circles under their eyes, they looked at each other, knowing that sleep, even at 4:30 a.m., was not going to happen just yet.

> My dear son, if you are reading this, you're almost there. It took me 37 years to learn, and I've known it just a little—and only for a few days.
>
> Humility.
>
> Blessed are the meek; for they shall inherit the earth.
>
> It's one of the first lessons, and one of the final lessons.
>
> Humility.

Sometimes after you've humbled
yourself, you need to go even lower.

This then is your final clue:

Old Town homes in a cluster of three

The southernmost, stands, separate
you see

Enter in and go low, far as you can
measure

Lower still to find the treasure

"I can't wait to tackle this, but I'm brain-dead, Gadg. Let's talk this through in a few hours."

Gadg stepped around Tyler, plopped himself down on the couch opposite Jordan's bed, and grabbed the blanket that was draped over the back. He had slept on this couch so many times it was form-fitted to his fetal position when he curled up. He was asleep in fifteen seconds.

Jordan knew he would soon follow into slumber. He read over the clue a couple more times, and then stashed it in between the mattress and the box spring. He spread out on top of the blanket. His last thought as sleep took him was that he should take off his other shoe.

Chapter 25

Why Now?

**Monday, May 26, 12:30 p.m.
Nolan home, Wilson, CO**

Sunday came and went with no more than a headache to show for it. Half of Monday proved no better. They had solved two more of Johnny's clues, including the original Perry Mason clue. One of the other bur oaks on Nolan property had held the answer. But the real treasure—Jordan *knew* it was out there—still seemed miles away. He reviewed his diary entry from the day before.

Why is all this happening now?

Why would I get the weird summer school letter now?
Why would Alex be following me at 3:30 a.m.?
Why would he be willing to rough me up to see what we found?

Why now?
Has anything else happened recently?

The treasure hunt?

No. Not by itself. Why would a family graduation ceremony cause such a fuss?

National championship?
No. Many people will be glad to see me go, and the others are excited for me.

The death of Howard Carlyle?
That's it. It has to be. But why?

What does Howard Carlyle's death have to do with me?

Stuck.

The family and a few friends had started to gather for the blessing ceremony. At this point, only sandwiches and chips graced the tables. The real festivities—and the real food—came later. Gadg's dad, Deputy Mark O'Brien, would be the grill master. Barbecue. Jordan's favorite.

But right now he didn't feel like eating anything. Jordan excused himself to make it look like he needed to use the restroom. Sitting on the edge of the bathtub, he stared at a towel on the back of the door. The last twelve hours had been disheartening. Fruitless. The blessing ceremony was just a few hours away, and even though he held William's last clue in his hand, Jordan grew more pessimistic about their chances of solving it.

He wasn't too concerned with the challenge of completing his dad's hunt, but he drug his feet. To the adults, it looked like he needed time to solve Johnny's last clue. In reality, he was stalling. He did need time, but not for his dad. What he needed was a big break. Perhaps even a miracle.

He remembered Grandpa sharing his heart about the glass of milk, the look in his eyes, the longing.

Even more than that, though, he knew something was up—something big enough for Alex Jones to risk getting in serious trouble for beating him up. Thanks to Gadg, it hadn't come to that.

We're so close.

He stood and looked at himself in the mirror. His shoulders were tight.

He tried to loosen them, to rub the knots out of them. But social acceptability dictated that one could only stay in the bathroom for so long. He had to get back to his friends and the hunt.

He glanced down at the clue in his hand.

Humility.

He'd never given it much thought.

I'm surrounded by stuff that doesn't make sense.

Jordan studied the clue. William Nolan called to him from fifty years ago.

Okay, Great-grandfather, I'll try.

He closed his eyes, turned his face to heaven, and opened his mouth. No sound came out, and the realization hit him.

I haven't prayed in two years.

Prior to that, he had prayed and read the Bible on the coattails of his parents' faith. He closed his eyes again.

"God, I don't know how to do humility. I don't really even know what it is. All I know is that I want to give my grandfather the "blessing" that he longs for, whatever that means. I don't know how to do it. It feels so close, and yet it might as well be the moon if I can't decipher that clue, or if the treasure is no longer there."

He paused for a moment.

"Oh, and God, to be honest, I want to find this treasure because I'm insanely curious about this whole thing."

Hmm.

Was this what a genuine prayer felt like? It seemed honest. He decided to just put it out there for God—raw and straight up.

"If You're for real, I need Your help. Will You help me find William's treasure?"

Chapter 26

A Father's Blessing

Monday, May 26, 3:15 p.m.
Upstairs library/attic of Nolan guest house, Wilson, CO

Jordan liked this room.

Filled with books and mystery, and more than its share of junk, the "library" was little more than a large attic. Cluttered in the same decades of strata that layered Grandpa's garage below, the room carried an aura of mystery.

Jordan had never directed his curiosity toward the library before because his pain and loathing of anything related to the Nolan name had been stronger than his desire to unearth any hidden secrets.

The attic was blessed with an ancient table with worn edges—smooth and pleasant to run a hand over. Four comfortable chairs surrounded it. Two possibly sixties, probably seventies, dreadful-to-look-at-but-delightful-to-read-by lamps bathed the room in a soft glow. Jordan had carved out this area as the only clutter-free space in the whole room.

For lack of anything better to do, they'd set out to find his dad's treasure. The final clue had proved to be quite simple, and ten minutes of searching had produced a large, pirate-looking treasure box. They posted Gadg as a lookout, while Jordan and Tyler sneaked the box into the attic. They didn't want the others to realize they'd finished the hunt. From Jordan's perspective, they were decidedly *not* finished.

They plopped the old treasure box down on the attic table.

"Bro," said Tyler, his face full of admiration, "you gotta admit, your dad's done this treasure hunt up right."

Jordan grew quiet. Several thoughts passed through his mind. His conversation with Grandpa Walter, his father walking out on the last debate round, the clue, the cool DC mug that made him wonder if he'd ever had a jackpot cup without it.

"Dare I say"—Gadg looked at Jordan and paused for effect—"not lame after all?"

"Oh, there's still time. We haven't hit the 'blessing ceremony' yet," Jordan said with air quotes.

"What do you say we get this bad boy open?" said Tyler.

Jordan reached down to open the latch and realized it had a four-digit combination padlock they hadn't noticed before. "Ugh," he said.

"Where's the clue?" asked Gadg.

"I think it's underneath," said Tyler.

They retrieved the clue, and Tyler and Gadg zeroed in on it. They didn't notice when Jordan slipped away from the table. Gadg was about to open his mouth when a popping sound ended their need to study the clue.

Jordan smirked as he set down a pair of bolt cutters. "I'm tired of figuring stuff out." Pulling off the now-destroyed lock, Jordan unlatched the box and lifted the lid.

The inside was spacious, but Johnny and Walter had filled it with packing peanuts. Jordan removed handfuls of them, careful not to throw anything away. At bottom, he found what looked like a marble pouch. Next to it nestled a sleek, rectangular box, wrapped in celebratory paper. A full-sized envelope was attached to it by a ribbon.

Gadg gave Jordan a wry smile.

Jordan held up the box and smiled back. There was no question what it was.

"Tools," they said in unison.

Gadg and Jordan were both tool guys-but in twenty-first-century style. This was no toy. This thing would get loads of use in the coming months, both at home and in DC.

Wow, thanks, Dad.

Setting aside the wrapped box, Jordan opened the pouch. He peered at the contents and then poured a bunch of silver coins onto the old, wooden table.

Tyler just stood and stared. Ten seconds later Gadg said, "That'll be $964.88, if we use last Friday's spot price."

"Dude, seriously?" said Tyler, gaping at Gadg. He turned to Jordan, "Is he for real?"

"Don't get me started," said Jordan.

"You ready?" asked Gadg as he handed him the package.

Jordan slid the ribbon back like he was removing a hoodie. Setting the envelope to the side, he took his time pulling the wrapping paper off the signature white box. The familiar elegance of a shrink-wrapped, fully-loaded laptop shined under the soft light of the seventies lamps.

He blinked hard.

Gadg handed him the envelope.

"Three days ago, I dreaded this moment," Jordan looked at the envelope in his hand. "Now, I don't know what to think."

"You think too much, man," said Tyler. "He loves you. Just read it."

Jordan opened the envelope, pulled out a single sheet of thick paper that resembled parchment, and began to read.

> Dear Jordan,
>
> You know I'm not so good with words. Most of my life has been lived holding a football and not a pen. You probably guessed your mom helped with the clues. (The good ones and the writing are hers.) I may not be that great with words, but I can recognize a great son.
>
> I noticed it on the night you won the tournament. As I sat in the audience, I sensed something I hadn't felt since my college days. I smelled battle. Two warriors standing eye to eye. I had no idea that what I had called a "sissy sport" carried that element. Even with my untrained view, I could tell you dominated. I feel terrible about leaving when I did, but I'm so glad you still pulled it out.
>
> I don't know if you'll understand this, but when your grandpa first told me about this idea for a "blessing ceremony," I thought it was a stupid idea. But the more he talked to me about it, the more I realized he was right. You are worth it. I've been so angry with you for quitting the football team. But God showed me recently that this has a lot to do with me. I've been bitter for years about what happened to end my career, and I had hoped you might carry it forward.
>
> Jordan, I'm sorry. I ask you to forgive me. Please

receive these gifts knowing that I fully support your chosen career path. I'm so proud of you.

Love, Dad

● ● ●

I need to think.

Time was running out on the quest to find William's treasure before the ceremony. Jordan had asked Gadg and Tyler to meet him at Old Town Café for one last brainstorming session.

He needed to concentrate, but his dad's letter kept pulling his mind in a different direction.

He walked the dirt path toward downtown Wilson. It was hard to stay angry in the face of genuine apologies and heartfelt gifts. He thought back over the last two years. His anger didn't have the same zip to it anymore. Why? What had drained the venom out of his memories?

Humility.

That was it. His dad had come back to him in humility. A desire to reconcile. A willingness to support. Evidence that he believed in him.

He stopped and leaned back against a large tree.

A wave of clarity broke in on Jordan. He saw three generations of fathers that preceded him: his great-grandfather's tender clues, his grandfather's request for him to do the blessing ceremony, his dad's sincere apology. Were all these humility? Yes, they had to be.

He thought of his last name.

Nolan. Maybe not so bad after all.

Another flash of clarity sharpened his mind. He closed his eyes with a scrunched face.

What about you, Jordan?

A giant thumb pressed down on his heart. He faced the tree.

"I'm sorry," he whispered to God, the tree, and no one in particular.

A mist clouded his eyes. The pressure in his chest didn't let up.

What?

For the third time in five minutes, he saw with a heightened sense of clarity.

Leaning his head against the tree, he fought with himself. The weight on his heart bore down. Finally, when he could take it no longer, he blurted, "Okay, I forgive him."

Chapter 27

A Purposeful Accident

Monday, May 26, 4:30 p.m.
Old Town Café, Wilson, CO

Gadg pored over a pair of aerial photos of Wilson.

Jordan joined him in the round booth in the back corner of the café. "Let's get to it. We've got maybe two hours." He gave a quick glance about the room.

It was a good choice. No windows too close. Easy view of the front door. Surrounded by pictures of the town, which represented many different time periods. He spotted a photo of Old Main Street from when it wasn't even Old Town.

The guys had already ordered a couple of sodas. Tyler waited for the rest of his order so he could pound down a truckload of fries with a trough of ketchup.

"Remind me of the clue," he said.

Jordan fished the old piece of paper out of his pocket and handed it to him.

"Old Town homes in a cluster of three," Tyler read aloud, "The southernmost, stands, separate you see. Enter in and go low, far as you can measure, lower still to find the treasure."

"Here's Nolan property," Gadg traced one of the aerial photos with his finger. "Here's the road we took to the ridge the other night. This is Old Main Street, to the north of your property. Here's the old grange. Do you see this area between the grange and the clock tower? Somewhere in here is the boundary of WDC2 property."

Jordan nodded as he got oriented. "Where did you get these?"

"I printed them off at the station. They were taken last year. There's Gutless parked in your driveway."

Jordan smiled. "Where's the cluster of three homes?"

"I'm not sure," said Gadg. "That's what I've been spending the last twenty minutes trying to figure out."

"It's not here," said Jordan.

Gadg looked up at him.

"These photos are forty-nine years too *new*."

"You're right," said Gadg. He brought his palm to his forehead. "We need an older shot."

"There's one over there," Jordan gave a slight tilt of his head and directed his eyes toward a picture of Old Town, taken from the ridge in the 1950s.

"Was Old Town called Old Town in the fifties?" asked Tyler.

"Yes," said Gadg. "The town's heyday, prior to the Wonder Drug, was in the 1920s."

The bell above the front door jingled.

Quick as a video game, Gadg stashed the photos beneath the table. Tyler saw him and snatched the clue, pulling it down beside him onto the seat in the booth.

Jordan laughed out loud.

"What are you doing?" asked Tyler.

"Don't turn around," said Jordan. "Laugh."

"Laugh?" asked Tyler.

"Do it now."

Tyler laughed. Gadg joined them.

"We're just having a good ole time," Jordan whispered, forcing a huge smile.

"What's up with this?" said Tyler.

"That's hilarious," boomed Jordan. Some of the other customers looked over at their table.

Gadg smiled big in return and whispered, "Don't look now, but Alex is here."

"Is Matthew with him?" whispered Tyler.

"That's so cool!" said Gadg, raising his voice. He then wiped his mouth with his arm and whispered, "Yeah." His eyes turned dark. "I've had just about enough of him."

Matthew and Alex took a seat at a table about thirty feet from them.

"They see us?" asked Tyler.

Jordan brought the volume back down to a normal level. "I'm sure they do. Let's pretend we don't see them and that we're focused on a fun conversation. Keep smiling and make gestures with your arms."

Tyler played along like he was telling the group a football story. "This can't be a coincidence."

"I agree," said Jordan.

"What do we do?" asked Tyler.

"Unless we want to leave empty-handed, we need to be discreet. Let's try and get a good look at that picture on the wall to see if we can locate the cluster of three homes near Old Town."

"We could come back later," suggested Tyler.

"Negative," said Jordan. "If we want any chance of finding the treasure before the ceremony, it's now or never."

Gadg continued, "Neither of us can do anything without raising suspicion. It's going to have to be you, Tyler."

"What do I do?"

"During the chaos"—Jordan smiled—"you take a picture."

"Chaos?" Tyler smiled big and easy and sat back in the booth. "Dude, I like it." He dug his phone from his pocket. "What are you gonna do?"

"Just follow my lead," said Jordan.

A moment later, Bethany walked over to their table and set a large basket of fries between the sodas.

Tyler cast a longing glance at the large pile of cut-potatoes and grease.

Bethany set a pitcher of ice water down and pulled out her pad. "You ready to order, Jordan?"

"We've had a change of plans, Miss Clark," said Jordan. "Will you do me a favor?"

Bethany cocked her head. "Maybe. You've got a look in your eyes."

"Just play along, okay?"

Bethany stared at him. Her voice reached almost as low as her alto would take her, "Play along with *what*?"

Jordan just smiled.

"I've got to go wait on that table. Don't do anything I wouldn't approve of." She grabbed the pitcher, turned, and walked over to the table where Alex and Matthew sat.

"Hello, Bethany," said Matthew. "Great to see you again."

"Hello, Matthew. Hello, Mr. Jones."

"Bethany," Alex nodded. His voice sounded like crushed glass and too many cigarettes.

Bethany reached over and filled Alex's glass with ice water. She then leaned forward to tip the pitcher over Matthew's glass. At just that moment, Jordan walked by and stumbled. The side of his hip smashed into her, causing her to lose her balance. All the water from the pitcher sloshed into Matthew's glass, and drove the entire combination—glass, water, and ice—straight into his lap.

"Hey, watch it," Bethany and Matthew blurted in unison as Jordan sprawled onto the floor.

Alex whirled on him, "You idiot!"

People from tables all over the café stared at the scene. Several stood to get a better view. Matthew flayed his arms and grabbed for napkins. Bethany turned to him, "I'm so sorry." She made a fuss of grabbing some napkins and trying to keep the remaining water from pouring onto him.

Gadg walked over to help Jordan up.

Tyler snapped a couple shots of the Old Town photo, stashed his phone back in his pocket, and strolled to the restroom.

Jordan got up and dusted himself off. "I'm sorry, guys."

Three pairs of eyes glared at him.

Bethany put her hands on her hips, and her gaze smoldered.

"I'm sorry, Miss Clark." As he turned his head toward the front door, he gave her an almost imperceptible wink.

● ● ●

Matthew stumbled out of the booth. On his way to the restroom, he stared down a young boy who giggled at him. In the bathroom, he did his best to dry himself off. The mirror reflected back a gargoyle caricature of his face. He held onto the sink to steady himself.

That's the last time he gets the best of me.

On his way back to his seat, Matthew walked by the booth that Jordan, Gadg, and Tyler had just vacated. He stopped.

A full order of French fries sat, uneaten on the table.

Why would a football player leave his fries?

He studied the scene.

Hmm.

As he turned away, something on the seat caught his eye. He reached down and picked up an old piece of paper. As he unfolded it, a huge smile spread across his face.

Chapter 28

End of the Line

Monday, May 26, 5:05 p.m.
Northern fence of Nolan property, Wilson, CO

"Where is it?" asked Jordan.

Gadg held his phone in one hand and the aerial printout in the other. "Right where we're standing," he said.

Jordan cringed. He and Tyler looked around, and saw nothing but grass and scrub oak. The northern fence that bordered Nolan property stood forty feet away.

"Here are the three Old Town homes in the 1950s photo," Gadg pointed. "The aerial shot from last year only has those two on the other side of the fence. The southernmost home should be right here on your property."

"My great-grandmother must have had it taken down." Jordan stared into the distance. He turned his face away from Gadg and Tyler.

Tyler put his arm around Jordan's shoulder. Gadg looked down at his shoes and then back up.

There was nothing here.

Jordan glanced at his phone. It was just after 5:00 p.m., and fifty people waited for them back at the house. He was out of time. He walked over to the fence with a sigh, not ready to face the crowd yet. Gadg sat down on a grassy knoll and looked up into the sky. Tyler pulled out his phone.

Jordan had never thought much about how close Nolan property was to Old Town. He leaned on the fence. The abandoned grange looked like a hollowed-out gourd a few hundred yards to his left. Straight ahead was the clock tower. It seems like a year, rather than two days, since Tyler had stood on it to achieve the 7:37 p.m. shadow. Jordan scanned the rest of Old Main Street. It amazed him how untouched it had remained.

He waved for the others to join him. Gadg and Tyler trudged over and leaned against the fence next to him.

Without turning his face from Old Town, Jordan said, "Gadg, why does Main Street look the same as it did fifty years ago?"

"Howard Carlyle," said Gadg in a monotone.

"Pristine indeed," Jordan said, sarcastically. He slammed his hand down on a fence post. "Guys, I can't help but believe we are within a quarter-mile of something big."

Tyler's stomach growled. Looking at the two abandoned houses, he said, "Where would they keep food?"

"They didn't have electricity yet," said Gadg. "Probably a root cellar."

A board creaked behind the house on their right.

All three turned toward the sound.

"Who's there?" yelled Jordan. He jumped the fence. Tyler did the same while Gadg climbed over. Jordan ran to the far side of the house in time to see Matthew duck behind some scrub oak.

"What do you think you're doing?"

Matthew spun to face them, cheeks turning red. "Nothing."

"I've had just about enough of this. What have you been up to these last three days?" demanded Jordan.

Matthew's hand went into his pocket. "None of your business."

"None of my business?" Jordan was hot. "That's one of the dumbest things you've ever said. You harass us at all hours, showing up out of nowhere in the most unexpected places. That thug of an uncle of yours assaults me, and now you have the gall to tell me it's *none of my business*?"

Standing next to Jordan, Tyler felt around in his pockets, getting visibly agitated.

"What?" said Jordan, facing him.

Tyler's expression grew pained.

"Looking for this?" Matthew gave a smile and pulled his hand from his pocket. He held out William's last clue. "You want to talk about dumb, Mr. *Nolan*? Leaving this in a public place." Matthew shook his head. "Looks like you're coming up empty—again."

A switch flipped on Gadg's face. From a reservoir unknown to Jordan, he launched a verbal assault. "I'm not sure what you mean by 'again,' Matthew. Last time I checked, 'again' implies something with a precedent. You keep talking like Jordan's a loser, but you're 0 for 2 against him when it's really counted."

Matthew's face went red. "Shut up, Gadg. Jordan knows what I mean. I'm speaking of the trough that is his life."

"The more you open your mouth," Gadg shot back, "the more idiotic you sound. Besides, you still look like you peed your pants."

Matthew maintained eye contact as his face went a shade darker. The ice water hadn't fully dried. He spun on his heel and strode off down the dirt sidewalk of Old Main Street.

Jordan looked at Gadg. He'd never seen him like this before.

What a great friend.

A moment later, the gravity of the situation crashed in on him. Matthew had the clue. Jordan's exhale deflated his entire body.

"I'm sorry," said Tyler.

"It's not your fault," said Jordan. "We don't need the clue anymore. We know what it says. The only remaining possibility, which is still a long shot, lies below ground over there." Jordan pointed to where the third abandoned house should have been. "Even if, by some miracle, the treasure still exists, it will require a serious excavation effort to get to it. No way that's going to happen today."

Jordan ran a hand through his hair and then squeezed it into a fist. He scrunched up his face, waved his hand in a disgusted dismissal of Old Town, and walked away.

The quest, at least for today, was a failure.

●●●

"That's right, Mr. Carlyle," said Alex. He sat behind the wheel with the engine off. "They came up empty."

"Still no idea what they were looking for?" Donald asked through the phone.

"Well, we have an old note, presumably from William Nolan, that says it's a treasure." From a picture on his phone, Alex read the clue to Mr. Carlyle.

"If it was written by William, this clue is not *meant* for Jordan."

"What do you mean?"

Alex heard the sigh through the phone. "Do you really believe that William Nolan set up a treasure hunt for his great-grandson and called him 'my dear son' in the clue?"

He couldn't think of anything to say.

"Jones," exasperation threaded through Donald's tone, "*think* about it. My father told me to beware of the Nolans. Jordan and his friends have now gone beyond a family graduation ceremony and are tracking something that is fifty years old from an ex-employee of my company. Doesn't that cause alarm bells to go off?"

"You're right, sir." Alex paused. He wanted to say something that didn't sound stupid. "Well, at least they didn't find anything." He winced.

"You're talking like that's some sort of accomplishment." The pause was long and painful. Alex could hear the man's breath getting heavier. "I assumed I needed to beware of the Nolans here and now. But what if my father was warning me of something *out of the past* that could somehow reach into the present? This is *not* good news."

Alex kept silent.

"Whatever they're looking for is probably still out there."

"Understood."

"*Find* it, Jones."

"Yes, sir."

"I assume you're being discreet about this," Donald continued, "especially when you're not on WDC2 property."

Probably best not to mention tackling Jordan on the ridge.

"Yes, I am," Alex said as the Call Ended message appeared. He gripped the phone in his fist and then threw it against the passenger door. Turning the key, he slammed the gear shift into drive and pounded on the gas pedal.

He thinks I'm an idiot.

Chapter 29

Two Sanctuaries, Two Secrets

Monday, May 26, 5:20 p.m.
Upstairs library/attic of Nolan guest house, Wilson, CO

The boys gathered again in the sanctuary of Grandpa's attic. Gadg looked out the back window toward Old Town. He shook his head and turned back to the others.

Jordan leaned against the wall, his expression as morose as the lamps. Even the shrink-wrapped laptop in front of him just sat there. Relentless inquisitiveness only went so far. It had to be coupled with hope, and right now, there wasn't much. He didn't have the stomach to face the blessing ceremony in such a dismal mood, so he just sat and stared.

To come this far and come up empty.

Tyler had wormed his way through the clutter to one of the bookshelves in the far back corner. He felt like an archaeologist on a dig, or a trail-blazer hacking his way through the jungle with a machete. His removal of some clutter allowed certain books to see the light of day for the first time in decades. Jordan had always hated anything to do with Nolan family history, so Tyler had kept his interest in the family to himself. Whenever he visited Uncle Johnny, he studied items on the walls and bookshelves of their main house. Today was his first shot at the attic.

Jordan still made no move to head back to the house for the ceremony, so Tyler decided to do a bit of exploring. He wasn't a bibliophile like Jordan, except to the extent that the books contained pictures. A wide receiver by training, Tyler processed life through the eyes.

And the stomach.

His failure to obtain any food at the café began to gnaw at him. They wouldn't be here much longer, as Jordan could only delay the inevitable for so long. Tyler tried to lose himself in something interesting.

Several minutes passed. His expedition through the clutter produced two old photo albums. Their covers looked more tired, but not as hideous as the lampshades, so he guessed they might be fifties or early sixties. He stood up. The clutter was high enough in places for Tyler to set one of the photo albums face up, and look through it without sitting down.

He turned the pages and recognized some of the photos from this property.

"Huh!" Tyler exclaimed.

"What?" asked Gadg with some alarm.

Tyler leaned in to look closer.

"Tyler, what is it?" repeated Gadg.

"I've not helped even once with this treasure hunt," Tyler spoke from between the legs of an overturned chair that sat atop a pile of furniture. "I feel like such an idiot because of the clue Matthew found."

Jordan remained zoned out in the direction of the lamps.

Gadg was about to open his mouth when Tyler stepped around the corner, sauntered over to Jordan, and served the open photo album to him like an entree at a five-star restaurant.

"Might this be of interest?"

Jordan took a few seconds to shake off his dismayed lethargy. His countenance registered shock, as if a glass of ice water had been thrown in his face. His eyes lifted, and his jaw dropped. His voice cracked. "Tyler, you're amazing! Let's go."

● ● ●

"You call her," Jordan said to Gadg as they hustled from the guest house back toward Old Town. "I think I'm in hot water right now."

"Call Bethany Clark," Gadg spoke into his phone. In a few seconds, he held his fist up to his mouth to suppress a smile. "Yeah, he's here. Wanna talk to him?"

Jordan shook his head and waved his hands in front of his face.

Gadg laughed. "Listen, Bethany, we're in kind of a hurry. Can you tell me if you've seen Alex and Matthew recently?" Gadg pressed his lips together. "Yes, unfortunately, we know that all too well. Have you seen them since?" Gadg smiled and nodded. "I can't talk about it right now. Maybe soon. Thanks again." He hung up. "They're back at the café."

"Perfect. I just got a text from my dad. He and mom are wondering where we are." Jordan stopped at the same grassy mound Gadg had lain on thirty minutes ago.

"You're serious?" asked Gadg.

"I can't believe we didn't think of it before."

"We got kind of distracted," said Gadg.

"No kidding," said Jordan, bristling at the thought of Matthew.

"So we were right on top of it?" asked Tyler. He stood, beaming.

"According to the picture you showed me," said Jordan. He put his hand on Tyler's shoulder. "You alluded to the desire to be helpful," he held out a shovel he had grabbed on the way out of grandpa's garage and matched Tyler's smile. "Care to do the honors?"

"Nice," said Tyler, dryly. "You ever do a hard day's work?"

"I used to do two-a-days in ninety-five-degree heat. Does that count?"

"Ugh, don't remind me. August will be here all too soon." Johnny Nolan's twice-daily football practices were legendary. Tyler grabbed the shovel and slammed it into the side of the mound. A few minutes later, they had scraped away five decades of overgrowth to reveal a root cellar that had once sat opposite the southernmost home.

They stared at one another for several seconds.

Jordan took off for the guest house and returned with the same bolt cutters he'd used to crack open his dad's treasure box. They made quick work of the rusted lock, and the door opened upward.

Jordan stepped down six stairs and back in time several decades. He pulled out his phone and launched the flashlight. Held up by timber beams, the cellar had enough height for them to walk without stooping. It was fifteen feet long and ten feet wide with wooden shelves lining the sides.

Still all smiles, Tyler stepped down with Gadg following him.

"Wow, is this like, from the fifties?" said Tyler.

Jordan shook his head. "I think it's much older. The house was abandoned by then."

Gadg panned his head around and took it all in.

Jordan pointed to the opposite end. "There's the door that once led to the house."

"Probably the basement," said Gadg.

"I agree," said Jordan. "Remember the clue? I'm guessing the basement was as low as you could go in the house, and this cellar is lower than that."

All three looked at each other.

"So, where is it?" asked Tyler.

Jordan turned this way and that with his flashlight. The three spread out to scan the room.

Jordan stooped down near the shelves on the north side.

"Guys." His voice said it all. With a jerk of the head, he indicated for Gadg and Tyler to join him. They rushed over and knelt to look under the bottom shelf.

"Is that a handle?" asked Tyler.

Jordan reached under the shelves and pulled. A small trap door in the northern wall, maybe two feet high, swung open to reveal absolute blackness.

Gadg looked at Jordan. "You know what this could mean, don't you?"

Jordan stared into the void. His face was a mix of excitement and shock as he processed the implications. "For better or worse, nothing will be the same again." He pointed his flashlight into the hole. All thoughts of the blessing ceremony fled away as an old bundle, wrapped in green felt, saw the light for the first time in fifty years.

Chapter 30

A Grandson's Blessing

**Monday, May 26, 6:30 p.m.
Great room of Nolan house, Wilson, CO**

Late by a half-hour, they'd ducked, dodged, and stalled with some cryptic texts and a careful lookout.

"Okay, guys"—Jordan looked both ways as they approached the main house from the rear—"let's meet in my room at 10:00 p.m."

"What for?" asked Tyler.

"A history lesson." Jordan gripped his dad's treasure box tighter under one arm and gave a fist pump with the other. "We've got a lot to talk about." His mouth stopped just short of a full-on grin. "First things first, though." Just outside the screen door, he turned to Gadg, "Would you mind getting this on film?"

Gadg nodded and pulled out his phone. His face turned sober and watchful. He looked up at Jordan. "Be careful how you play this."

"What do you mean?" asked Jordan.

He glanced at the treasure box under Jordan's arm. "Not everything is safe for public consumption."

"Understood."

Gadg smiled again and pulled open the screen door. "Welcome home, Mr. *Nolan*."

Jordan pushed open the back door and burst into the party. Some fifty pairs of curious eyes turned to him.

One by one, the guests smiled or nodded as they spotted the treasure box under his arm. Some whispered not-so-quiet variations of *finally*.

Phone camera rolling, Gadg followed Jordan into the room and panned out to get a master shot, while Tyler perched to the side in order to get a good view of the proceedings.

Jordan scanned the room until he saw his grandfather out of the corner of his eye. He forced down his smile like a Texas Hold'em card shark holding pocket aces.

The gathering hushed as Jordan strode to the center of the room, and with obvious ceremony, plopped the box down on the large rectangular coffee table. He looked around for another face. He had to do it. He couldn't move on to the fun part yet. His arms hung to his sides as he stared at his father.

Johnny broke free from a conversation and walked up to him. They stood eighteen inches from one another, and neither spoke. Ambient noise drifted from other parts of the house, but in the great room, all was quiet.

Johnny's slightly off-center chin, reconfigured by a vicious hit in high school, quivered as he broke the silence in a hushed tone. "I'm sorry, son."

Jordan forced his arms to hang at his sides even though his heart screamed to put up his defenses. Out of nowhere, the clarity from his encounter with God at the tree slammed him with a fresh wave of understanding. His cheeks flared, and he couldn't maintain eye contact. His normally sure voice held a stammer when he spoke, "I'm sorry, too. I didn't give a second thought to *your* feelings. You—no, *we*—had a shot at a state championship, and I treated it like it was *nothing*." His shoulders hunched as he glanced back at his dad.

Johnny reached out and pulled him in. The hug was manly yet tender. Tears dropped onto his dad's shoulder. His upper body heaved. The room was silent.

He cried and cried.

When the embrace ended, Jordan wiped his cheeks with his palms. Awareness of his situation dawned on him, and he lowered his head. It felt as if eyes from everywhere were stripping his heart bare. Before he could dwell on it, Walter stepped up and engulfed him in a one-armed hug that felt like a vise grip of pure affection.

Johnny took the floor. "Dear family and friends"—his voice was still recovering, but his years as a coach added strength to his tone—"thank you for coming to show your support. We are here to celebrate the graduation of our son, Jordan, and to pray a blessing over him as he prepares for his next adventure."

Jordan sat down in Johnny's football chair, which was swiveled away from the seventy-inch TV on the main wall. Family and friends gathered around him, or bowed their heads where they were seated. He chanced a look around just before the prayers started. There were several present from his speech and debate club, many family members, some townspeople, former teammates, and even a few people he didn't know or hardly recognized.

Is that Jeffrey Kingston? In my house?

Blood rushed to his face as he tried to push aside the embarrassment. This was much to handle for someone who'd prayed only twice in two years. He closed his eyes, as much to block out the surroundings, as prayers of blessing came from various guests who laid their hands on his shoulders. Walter prayed a heartfelt blessing over his grandson. Gadg methodically rounded the gathering in a semicircle to continue the documentary.

Johnny prayed last. "Lord, You know the mistakes I've made. You know how sorry I am. I thank You for my dear son. I'm asking for Your blessing on this young man. It says in Your Word that *'The blessing of the Lord makes one rich, and He adds no sorrow with it.'* I ask for that 'no-sorrow blessing' on my son." He paused for a moment. "And Lord, I ask even for things that seem impossible to become possible. In Jesus' name, Amen." Johnny hefted Jordan up like a fellow player on the football field and held him by the shoulders at arm's length. One more hug and it was over.

Jordan blinked hard. The lingering embarrassment was still there, but it was overshadowed by a new feeling.

What is it?

Healing. That's what it was. There was a bit of healing.

People began to rise from their seats to head to the kitchen for refreshments. Before they could get far, Jordan straightened and pulled himself together. He looked at the treasure box as a fire kindled in his belly. He stepped over to the table and turned to the gathering.

"Dear family and friends…" Borrowing his dad's phrase, he snapped the guests to attention with a voice fresh from the national debate championship. He was back in his element.

Surprised, folks settled back into their seats as Jordan drew every gaze to him. Even Jeffrey Kingston, standing by the cordless phone on the wall, peered intently at him. "Please indulge me for a few moments while I tell you a story." Jordan's tone carried a wonder that softened the atmosphere and readied the group to listen to his tale.

"As some of you may know, I have not looked forward to this day. In fact, just eight days ago, I told my grandfather that blessing ceremonies are *lame*."

Grandpa nodded. Johnny's arms crossed his body and his belly expanded a couple times as he held laughter behind a grin.

Jordan glanced at his dad with the warmth of new forgiveness. "He's laughing because he literally said the same thing. So"—Jordan paused to pull his audience even closer—"if both father and son thought this would be lame, you might wonder—why are we having it?"

Some nodded.

"First, I'd like to honor the one who *really* had the idea, and the heart, for this ceremony—my Grandpa Walter." Jordan stepped back and clapped his hands, gathering the room in an impromptu ovation.

As the clapping went on around him, Grandpa waved it off with an embarrassed dismissal.

Jordan stepped behind the treasure box and planted both feet. "The other reason it *wasn't* lame"—his words jerked the guests to the edge of their seats— "is because the past has punched a hole in space and time to change the guest of honor at this ceremony."

Johnny shot a quizzical look at Michelle.

Grandpa's eyes widened.

Jordan released the latch and pulled back the lid with a creak. He reached into the box and yanked out a bundle wrapped in green felt.

Johnny studied it, blinking, his expression confused.

With a flourish of his whole left arm, Jordan threw the top layer of felt to one side, switched hands, and flung the second layer to the other side. Green felt now draped down from his left hand with an ancient book perched atop his palm. Like a maître d' holding out the chef's special, he presented the group with a genuine, 1733 King James Bible.

Amazement cradled the group in its soft embrace. Nobody spoke.

Jordan gently peeled back the front cover. "Ladies and gentlemen, may I present to you, all the way from Massachusetts, the patriarch of the Nolan family, John Philip Nolan." It wasn't Bethany-level quality, but his English accent was serviceable as he read aloud from a barely legible, handwritten letter on the inside cover.

My Dear Son,

In the second chapter of the book of Judges, it records "...and there arose another generation after them, which knew not the LORD, nor yet the works which He had done for Israel." After the same fashion, I forsook the God of my fathers and did follow the gods of money, drink, and pleasure. Thy mother would hath had every right to seek a dissolution of our marriage. However, she chose to remain and to pray.

Thirteen years ago, when thou wert still a young lad, I met a man named Jonathan Edwards, who spake of a God Who hateth sin. I was cut to the heart, and God used this man to awaken the nearly dead embers of my childhood faith. Mr. Edwards, a true spiritual father, presented me with my own 1733 Edition Bible which hath become to me as important as my daily bread.

Then, just two years ago, there was great concern that I might not live. My health was ebbing quickly from an illness that doctors could not diagnose. I was sure I had reached my last few days. I remember it vividly: Standing behind the barn, I cried out to the LORD. I said, "God, I'm not ready to die. I desire to be here to serve Thy purposes and this family. If Thou wilt bring me through this, Thou canst have all the boys of the Nolan family."

Needless to say, I doth now stand here, healthy and strong. I see thy coming of age with my own eyes, and my heart is filled with gratitude. I present thee this day, the very Bible given to me by Mr. Edwards himself. Go forward with my blessing, and as Psalm 119 says, may this copy of God's Holy Writ ever be unto thee and this family, as a testimony that "His faithfulness is unto all generations."

John Philip Nolan, 1754
Northampton, Mass.

Shock silenced the gathering.

Jordan's face lit up with a grand smile. "Friends, our patriarch started a tradition that day." He turned the book around to show the group. "The next few pages are full of letters from Nolan fathers to Nolan sons, carrying on the tradition started by John Philip. Here finishes the 1700s." He held the Bible in one hand and pointed to the page. "Here ends the 1800s." He flipped to the bottom of the fourth page. "And here"—he turned to a page which also included some introductory text about the Bible—"is the blessing from Kenneth Nolan to William Nolan in 1945."

The room held its collective breath. Jordan zeroed in, "Grandpa, would you join me?" He motioned to his dad's chair.

Grandpa stood and hobbled on shaky legs to the blessing seat. He sat, and Jordan knelt in front of him, holding out the Bible. Walter's fingers trembled as he reached out and took it. His rough hand cradled it as if it was a newborn baby. Gadg maneuvered closer and zoomed in to capture Walter's face—and the Bible in his lap—up close and personal. Even Jeffrey Kingston seemed breathless with anticipation.

Walter paused as if reluctant to proceed. Finally, with great effort and trembling in his right hand, he turned the page against the weight of fifty-five years holding it back. As he read silently, the tears flowed.

All pretense at dignified reserve was gone. Eyes everywhere were wet. The room was breathless, wishing they could hear the words on the page. Jordan gave a nod to Tyler, who disappeared into the kitchen. Johnny and Michelle each put a hand on Walter's two broad shoulders.

My dear son,

The events of the last few days have been unusual in the extreme. Never in my 37 years could I have imagined a scenario so difficult that I could not think of any course of action that even began to make sense.

As you and your mother are painfully aware, I've not been in the habit of praying or asking God for anything—much less help. As I've been agonizing over these present difficulties, I went to the closet looking for an old photograph of you both. When I reached into the box my hand fell on this old Bible.

I had forgotten all about it. I opened the cover and saw the first blessing of our old patriarch, John Philip Nolan.

His words cut to my heart as he told God that He could have all the boys of the Nolan family.

I fell down to my knees. Like a soldier who is dying on the battlefield, I looked up to heaven. Through the first tears I'd shed in my adult life, I said, "God, is it still true?" An arrow from heaven pierced my heart as the still, small Voice whispered "Yes, it's still true. You are a Nolan boy."

At that moment, Plan A and Plan B began to take shape in my mind. After days of agonizing, I knew the answer: I had to do what was right. Too many lives—many more than just mine and yours, are at stake. If you are alive and reading this, and myself or my coworker has been implicated as a criminal, you can know that it was Plan B.

Be extremely careful who you share this with. You are not safe as long as anyone suspects you know anything about what we've been involved with.

I shouldn't be doing this at all—it's far too dangerous— but I can't bear the thought of you living a lifetime with only the memory of my abuse and the stigma of what people might think of me and our family. I'm so sorry for what I've been and done. Please know that I love you with all my heart, and you have my blessing. I wish I could reach out and hold you, and bring you a new glass of milk. Please tell your mother that the circle will be unbroken, and that I'll see you on the other side.

With all my heart,

William Nolan,
Wilson, Colorado
April 20, 1964

Walter's shaking hand covered much of the page, which Jordan noticed had included a postscript. His eyes were a blur of moisture as he looked up.

Tyler stepped out of the way after his mission to the kitchen, and Jordan knelt before Walter with a glass of milk in his hand.

Tears fell from both eyes and slipped onto Walter's cheeks. Fifty-five years of pent-up pain were unleashed in a gushing torrent.

Grandpa was undone.

Many in the room turned their faces away or stole quietly for the other rooms. Only the immediate family, and Gadg, at Jordan's signal, stayed close.

Setting aside the milk, Jordan slid the open Bible out from under Walter's good hand and set it on the table. He then turned to him and put both arms around him. Walter's body shook as fresh waves of grief washed over him.

The rest of the family sensed what was happening, and left Jordan and Walter alone. When he could finally speak, Walter said, "I don't know how to thank you. What do you say when a dream comes true that you never even dared to dream?"

"I'd say that His faithfulness is unto all generations," answered Jordan.

"Really? How interesting."

"Grandpa,"—Jordan lowered his voice and darted a glance in either direction—"that letter hints at much more than just a blessing for you, don't you think?"

Walter blinked again. "It would appear so. But I'll deal with that later. For now"—he reached for the Bible and settled back into the enveloping leather—"I just want to bask in the glow of my father's blessing."

Chapter 31

R3

Monday, May 26, 10:15 p.m.
Jordan's room, Wilson, CO

With blinds closed, Jordan's desk lamp cast shadows onto the closet. Leaning on their forearms, the boys knelt on three sides of Jordan's bed and spoke in hushed tones.

"That was incredible," said Tyler. "Great job!"

"I don't think that was me," said Jordan. "What happened tonight had been in the works for many years. I was just along for the ride. I'll never look at that verse the same way again."

"At least you're looking at it," joked Tyler. "That's an improvement."

"Very funny."

"Generations. Who would have thought?" said Gadg.

"How many is it from you back to John Philip?" asked Tyler.

"I'm not sure," said Jordan. "I didn't get a chance to count. When we left, Grandpa had the Bible open on the coffee table and was still reading. I'm guessing it was about thirteen."

"Are you proud to be a Nolan?" asked Tyler.

"Maybe," Jordan said with a sigh. "I'll settle for not-completely-disgusted at this point."

"Another improvement." Tyler chuckled. "What's next? You gonna want to stay in Wilson now?"

"Don't push your luck."

"Guys"—Gadg lowered his voice even further—"can I say it again? That letter didn't sound like a suicidal murderer."

"It sure didn't," agreed Jordan. "The whole thing sounded calculated. Not to mention, the tone was quite tender."

Gadg pulled up his phone and navigated to a point in the video where a shot over Walter's shoulder gave a clear view of William's letter. He froze the image and turned the screen so the other two could see. "Don't forget the connection between real life and Plan B—whatever that is," said Gadg. He read:

"If you are alive and reading this, and myself or my coworker has been implicated as a criminal, you can know that it was Plan B."

Jordan stared at the words. "There's no question that the prevailing narrative is that William Nolan killed Ray Clark, and then killed himself."

Gadg pointed at the phone in his hand. "This doesn't come right out and say it, but it sure hints that the narrative may not be the truth."

"He didn't kill him," said Tyler. His honest face was so matter-of-fact that Jordan and Gadg both sat, gaping at him.

"What?" they said in unison.

Tyler didn't flinch. He looked them both in the eyes, back and forth.

Gears turned and circuits blew as eighteen years of programming was put to the test. They pondered for a long moment.

"Dude," Jordan said finally, landing a soft punch on Tyler's shoulder, "thank you for helping us see the obvious. That's it exactly."

"So, then, what *did* happen?" pressed Tyler.

"*That's* what we've got to figure out," said Jordan.

Gadg yawned. "Agreed. But let's start tomorrow." He got up to leave. "This has been, like, a hundred-hour weekend. I'm totally fried."

●●●

Jordan felt like he'd slept for five minutes. In truth, it had been seven hours. He popped awake at 5:30 a.m. and couldn't get back to sleep. He stared at the ceiling as Tyler sawed logs on the floor next to the closet.

How could I be awake at this hour?

Today wasn't a big day, per se, but he did have a lunch meeting with Jeffrey Kingston at the Old Town Café at noon.

That must be why he was here last night.

Having visited the two other winners, Mr. Kingston was on the last leg of a tour that would formally offer the internship to the qualifiers and outline all the details they would need to take care of before heading to DC.

Nine days ago, everything had been clear. Except that he was staring at the ceiling, Jordan didn't know which way was up. He took his time trying to unravel the knot of tangled thoughts in his brain.

Trying to make sense of this

I've been on spin-cycle for three days
What do I feel now?
Tired?
Surprisingly, not really
Is this what peace feels like?

I still have many questions:

Is everything I've ever known about my great-grandfather a total lie?
What in the world are Plan A and Plan B?
What lives are, or were, at stake?
What's the danger?
What do I do next?

Jordan continued to stare at the ceiling. He thought of the postscript that Grandpa had covered with his hand last night. Pressed for time, and needing to get to the ceremony, they'd only skimmed the letters enough to know the basics. He needed a closer look and considered getting up right away.

I doubt Grandpa is awake.

Thirty minutes went by. He had plenty to think through, so he decided to take it slow.

For lack of anything better to do at the moment, he reached again for his phone to check his email. For the second time in two days, the past reached into the present to rock his world.

Dear Jordan,

Congratulations on passing History of Wilson 101 with flying colors! It took you all of ten days to complete the course. Perhaps you are ready for a bigger challenge. Next up in the series is History of Wilson 201.

Because of the challenging nature of the subject matter, the course has a prerequisite:

Accounting 101

Here's an excerpt from one of the lessons:

No.	Entry Date	Name	Age	Issue Date	Impact
1	1-1-1965	Raymond Clark	52	4-24-1964	Murdered
2	1-1-1965	William Nolan	37	4-24-1964	Murdered

Once again, enrollment is by invitation only. Act now to enjoy an accounting course unlike any other.

This path will likely not take you through Washington, DC. Are you sure you want to travel it?

You hold Pandora's Box in your hand. Are you sure you want to unlock it?

Don't bother replying to this email. The account will be deleted by the time you read it. It's best if you don't speak of this communication. I'm sorry I didn't introduce myself last time. I had to know if you were serious.

You can call me R3.

PART TWO
Jericho

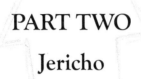

Chapter 32

Something Else Is Not Right

Tuesday, May 27, 6:55 a.m.
Nolan great room, Wilson, CO

Trying to keep his footfalls silent, Jordan hurried into the great room.

He could feel his pulse throbbing through the hand that held his phone—and the email from R3.

The treasure box from the night before, still containing his laptop and the silver coins, had not moved. Everyone had been too wrung-out from the excitement of the evening to worry about cleaning up.

Even now, Jordan didn't give much thought to his own gifts. He sank into the football chair and clutched the armrest with one hand as his insides revved up again. He took a deep breath and forced himself to reread the email. Was this some kind of joke?

He launched a diary entry.

> **R3 Email**
>
> A ledger with entries for murdered people?
> That's creepy
>
> What does it mean?

A cover-up? A conspiracy? A morbid fascination with death?
Who would have such a ledger?

Somebody named "R3" - that's who
Why not? This whole thing is bizarre

Could it be true?
William Nolan was murdered?

It says the internship is at risk
Am I ready for this?

Jordan shook his head and took another deep breath as his internal RPMs began to slow. He pocketed his phone and walked into the kitchen.

How am I ever going to be a lawyer if I freak out about everything?

He gave that a moment's pause.

"No, that's wrong," Jordan spoke out loud with a closing argument tone. "Some unusual things are happening in rapid succession. I'm just trying to get my bearings."

He leaned on the counter and rubbed his forehead.

Slow down. One thing at a time.

The answer came immediately.

Coffee.

That was the need of the moment.

A few minutes later, he took his first sip from his favorite new DC mug. A whimsical smile lit up his face. He couldn't decide if he was happier with his dad for the mug, or himself for the coffee. Not jackpot, but he could easily make money selling it.

At least one thing was right with the world.

The clock on the microwave read 7:03 a.m. The house was quiet.

Is everybody still asleep?

It was unusual to have no activity at this hour, but it had been a hectic weekend.

Balancing his almost-overflowing mug, and determined not to hurry back to the problems he needed to tackle, Jordan slowed his approach into the great room. He froze.

The old Bible lay unopened near the corner of the coffee table. Two of its sides were perfectly aligned to the edges of the table. The rest of the room was in disarray, causing the precision to stand out.

He took a couple steps back, set his mug on the kitchen bar, and looked around. His senses jumped to high alert, and he didn't know why.

Quiet permeated the room.

A slight breeze from outside caused the screen door to bounce an inch from closure.

He walked softly to it.

The inside door, mostly glass with several inches of trim around the sides, was not quite closed.

The wind caused the screen door to bounce again with the tiniest *whap* sound.

He looked back at the table from a different angle. The Bible just lay there in razor-sharp alignment with the edges of the table.

Jordan's spine tingled, and he reached for his phone to record a video. Five minutes later, still in his sweatshirt and gym shorts, he put on his black "attorney gloves" and reached for the Bible. His coffee would just have to go cold. Gadg needed to see this right now.

● ● ●

A half-hour later, Jordan sat in a room that was over-the-top geek.

Gadg had spent five years and a bunch of his consulting money to blend technology, ergonomics, and organizational efficiency with a coolness factor that could turn NORAD generals into jealous schoolboys.

One side of the room looked like a command center. The other was a forensics lab. Around the edges, neatly placed in containers that would make a homeschool mom drool were various tools and toys that his dad allowed him to prototype on behalf of the police department. In turn, Gadg would pass on a steady stream of feedback, making Deputy O'Brien the most tech-savvy officer in the whole department.

The pièce de résistance was a loaded coffee bar in one corner, which Gadg had decked out to look 80 percent avant-garde and 20 percent slot machine. He wanted a constant reminder of their quest for the Jackpot Cup. The coffee bar was surrounded by several tall bookcases, filled floor-to-ceiling with books, and fronted by two tables with three chairs each. The whole atmosphere whispered a call to study that pulled one into contemplative thoughtfulness. Jordan put the finishing touches on a breakfast blend that would give them a jolt of much-needed caffeine.

Back in the command center, lights flashed as Gadg leaned back in a chair that was so ergonomically efficient, it practically came with its own chiropractor. Setting down the mugs, Jordan couldn't help but smile as the sound from his own recording came through the speakers, filling the room with such clarity that the soft screen door *whap* sounded just like it had thirty minutes ago in person.

The Nolan great room filled three of the huge monitors.

"Gadg, take a look at this," Jordan's voice came through four surround-sound speakers. The camera panned around the room, showing the general disarray, the Bible on the coffee table, and finally, the door. "I can't put my finger on it, but something is not right." Jordan was no professional, but he knew the principles of videography well enough to get the job done. The camera started with a panoramic master shot and moved through the room to capture the relevant details.

With a pen, which alternated between his twirling fingers, and sticking out of his mouth like a cigar, Gadg leaned back and let it all soak in.

Jordan had worked with him long enough to instinctively know the cadence of their communication when Gadg was in his element. Most of the time, Jordan set the pace and took the lead in their friendship.

But in this room, Gadg was the master.

He blended so seamlessly into the fabric of his console that the line between man and machine blurred almost to unrecognizability. Jordan waited for an internal vibe to proceed before he said, "I'm probably just being paranoid, but this is weird."

Gadg pushed a couple buttons on Jordan's phone, and the email from R3 filled the center screen. Gadg read and reread it three times. He then pulled out his own phone and cued up the video he'd shot last night during the blessing ceremony. He shuffled the screens so his video from last night took center stage, while Jordan's video and the email from R3 played supporting roles.

"I think that email rules out paranoia," said Gadg.

"I'm just trying to keep the ground from shaking."

Gadg nodded. "I understand. This is crazy. And the implications..."

"There!" said Jordan.

Gadg stopped talking and froze the screen. The shot angled down over Walter's shoulder and captured the Bible, open in his hands.

"Can you zoom in?"

Gadg didn't even look up. He zoomed in. The resolution was so high that the faded grain of the old paper was visible.

The room's overhead lighting bathed them in a radiance that was perfect to read by—bright but with a golden hue that softened any strain on the eyes. Jordan put his gloves back on and opened the old Bible to the letter from William. Gadg took one look at it, and his fingers flew into action.

"What?" said Jordan, forgetting his normal rule in this room: do not question the master.

Gadg ignored him. He switched off the soft lights and flipped on two fluorescent bulbs that gave the room a more clinical feel. He then grabbed his phone from the side table, held it over the Bible, and snapped a still image of the letter. On screen, Gadg pulled it up side-by-side with the video image from last night. "Look at that," he said.

"What?" asked Jordan again.

Gadg zoomed in so far on both images that the crack between the pages came clearly into view on both screens.

"Is that what I think it is?" said Jordan.

In answer, Gadg zoomed even further. A one-inch pine needle rested in between the pages of the still photo Gadg had just taken. It was distinctly absent from last night's shot.

"Did you open this at all?" asked Gadg.

"No."

"Then how did a pine needle get between these pages?"

"My grandpa?"

"It's possible, but I'm inclined to agree with you—something isn't right."

Jordan exhaled audibly. "So, let me get this straight. We find a two-and-a-half-century old Bible that's been hidden for fifty years, and within twelve hours, I receive an explosive email, and now you're suggesting somebody broke into my house?"

Gadg nodded.

"What is going on here?" Jordan took a long breath. "Why not just take the Bible? Why set it down so impeccably aligned with the corner of the table? Who would do that? It's almost like they wanted it to be noticed."

"I have no idea. I'm just observing at this point."

"Do you think it's Alex?" said Jordan.

"I hope so."

Jordan did a double take. "You *hope* so?"

"At least he's a known enemy," Gadg looked down from the monitors. "Does this seem like his style?"

"No, it doesn't." Jordan took a sip of coffee. "It's one thing to intimidate us, but it's quite another for the head of security at WDC2 to go breaking and entering."

Gadg spun around, stood up, and walked a few paces to his forensics lab. He pulled on a pair of latex gloves and snapped them tight. He lifted a surgical mask over his head and fitted it to his mouth. Switching on a bright lamp, he pulled the extensible arm close to the table. "Let me see that thing," came his muffled voice.

Jordan, still wearing his black gloves, set the Bible under the light.

Gadg went to work.

A few minutes later, Jordan declared, "We should get back to my place so we can look for fingerprints."

"You won't find any."

"What makes you so sure?"

Gadg pulled the mask off his mouth and let it dangle under his chin. He looked up at Jordan and announced, "Yours weren't the only leather gloves to touch this thing since yesterday."

Chapter 33

Something to Be Aware Of

**Tuesday, May 27, 9:05 a.m.
WDC2 headquarters, Wilson, CO**

A small, wiry man walked around Donald Carlyle's desk and spread a series of printouts before him. The little guest made no move to leave.

Donald rolled his shoulders in an attempt to create more room. *Nobody* was allowed on this side of the desk, especially not a four-foot eleven-inch wisp of a man, standing twelve inches away from him, deep in his personal space.

The small man still didn't move. "As you can see from this, William Nolan was concerned that something he was involved in would endanger his family."

Donald took a drag from his cigar and guided the exhalation, as discreetly as possible, toward his guest.

The small man remained unflinching.

Donald turned his focus to the printouts. "How did you get these?"

His guest stared across the room, ignoring him like it was a stupid question.

Donald didn't like what he saw any more than he liked how he felt. "Look at that paragraph there"—he pointed—"lives at stake, Plans A and B ... what were they up to?"

"I don't know."

Donald tried to take it slow. At least this was progress. Here was something tangible in front of him instead of a cryptic message from a dying father, or the empty promises of Alex Jones. "Tell your boss you need a raise," he said, forcing a smile.

"As far as my *employer* is concerned, I don't exist."

A patch of crimson emerged behind Donald's ear. This conversation was not going his way. Trying to salvage something, he looked again at the printouts and said, "I think I have a problem."

The small man returned to the front of the desk, grabbed an attaché case, and headed for the door. He turned back to Donald and said, "As long as you don't become *my* problem, you have nothing to worry about."

● ● ●

Alex Jones walked down the hall leading to Donald Carlyle's executive office. A little man who reminded him of the kicker for his college football team strode toward him. Alex's first thought was that he could break him in half.

Until the man looked up at him.

Alex swallowed hard. He rounded the last turn and entered the corner office. With one more look over his shoulder, he said to Donald, "Who was *that*?"

"It doesn't matter," said Mr. Carlyle. The tone was all business and terse with anger.

"You wanted to see me, sir?"

"What am I paying you for?"

"Excuse me?"

"When are you planning on delivering anything of *value*?"

"As soon as I can," Alex was confused. "Why do you ask?"

"Do you even know what those boys were looking for?"

"Not exactly, but I'm closing in."

Donald's chuckle oozed scorn. "You're two steps behind, Jones. Not one, but *two*."

"Sir, I don't know what you're—"

"Save it." Donald waved his cigar and a few ashes flew off. "It was a *Bible* they were looking for. A very old one. And not only looking for, but *found*. Do you see these pages?"

Alex stepped over to the desk as Donald handed him a couple of printouts. He opened his mouth and closed it again. He flipped from sheet to sheet in a way that almost ripped the paper. In a much quieter voice, he finally muttered, "Where did you get these?"

Donald ignored the question and popped the cigar back into the corner of his mouth. His words came out like a gangster, "Why am I seeing these, but not from you?"

Alex winced. "I don't know, sir. May I ask where you got them?"

"You don't think I'm going to leave something this important in only *your* hands, do you?"

Alex looked away.

Donald continued, "Now, pay attention. I don't like the implications of this. There's nothing inherently incriminating in these pages, however, this hints that there is something more out there. Wouldn't you agree?

"Yes, sir, I would."

Donald studied the photocopies on his desk. Without looking up he said, "How about you *find* it this time."

●●●

As Alex left the office, Donald pushed a speed dial number on his phone.

"Mr. Carlyle," an easy voice spoke into the phone, "how are you, sir?"

Donald launched right in. "You told me the party you had in mind was known for delivery. You didn't tell me he was as tall as an eleven-year-old and known for *presumption*."

The tone came back contrite. "Sir, I'm sorry if he came across a bit much. You wanted delivery. Isaac Molencki always delivers, but he does so on his own terms."

"He had the audacity to walk in here as if he owned the place, looking over my shoulder like I owed him something."

"Yes, sir, that would be him. Let me ask you this, though,"—the sound of the voice indicated that the speaker already knew the answer—"did he deliver?"

Donald ground his back teeth. "Yes. I just don't like him or his methods."

"Without meaning to be sarcastic in the slightest," the voice came back, "does that really matter?"

"I'm the customer," said Donald. His voice rose almost an entire octave. "I expect to be treated as such."

"I understand, sir. Do you want me to call him off?"

Donald looked again at the printouts and ground his cigar butt into an ashtray. "No, I don't."

Chapter 34

The Answer Is No

Tuesday, May 27, 2:15 p.m.
Old Town Café, Wilson, CO

Jordan finally had a chance to look over the postscript following William's beautiful letter to Grandpa Walter. Finishing up a late lunch, he spent a few minutes perusing a photo he had taken after Gadg had concluded his forensic examination of the old Bible.

He was starting to feel a strange but wonderful connection to his great-grandpa.

P.S. "A man plans his way, but the Lord directs his steps." Life's journey is a search for truth and a walk of faith. "Faith is the substance of things hoped for and the evidence of things not seen." "Faith works through love." Love God. Love People. Love Truth. Love is the key.

Here are some Scriptures that will help guide you on your quest:

2 Corinthians 8:7

Mark 12:38

John 3:16

1 John 3:1

Leviticus 19:18

Song of Solomon 1:3

Romans 13:8

Isaiah 61:8

1 John 3:18

Psalm 119:132

Deuteronomy 10:19

2 Corinthians 8:24

Matthew 5:46

Amos 5:15

Jordan smiled at the image on his phone.

Thank You, Lord.

Over the last few days, he had experienced some of the things that his great-grandfather had mentioned in the postscript: faith, love, God's direction. He had even received a direct answer to a specific prayer.

Wow.

Still looking over the postscript, Jordan opened a Bible app on his phone and read through some of the Scriptures listed by William. He didn't know what to make of them. Some made perfect sense. Some were a bit strange. One, from the Song of Solomon, was totally off-the-wall.

He switched off the app as excitement drew him back to his inbox. He reread the email from R3. It all but came out and said that William Nolan had been murdered, contrary to the prevailing narrative in Wilson.

It was time to study.

Jordan stuffed his phone in his pocket, picked up his laptop bag, and headed over to the historical society.

• • •

Jordan crossed the street from the café and entered a hive of activity. The Wilson Colorado Historical Society building connected to the Wilson Public Library, forming a community hub that brought literature, history, and community involvement together under one roof. He looked over the Upcoming Events board. No wonder everyone seemed so busy.

Thursday, July 31—Wilson Community Center
Community Meeting: "Restoring Old Town"

Saturday, August 16—Wilson County Fairgrounds
"The Wonder Drug: Celebrating Fifty Years!"

Jordan walked up to the information desk. Bethany had her back turned as she pored over a smattering of newspaper clippings and old photographs.

He couldn't get a certain phrase out of his head. He'd heard it with his own ears.

"Very handsome."

Jordan took a deep breath. The other phrases were never far behind.

"He's out of the question for two reasons."

"My dad would never allow it."

"He's going nowhere."

Jordan tried to shake the words out of his head.

Oh well. She's still my friend.

"Hello, Miss Clark."

Bethany spun around and shot him with laser eyes.

Jordan gulped. "You're not still upset about the café thing, are you?"

Bethany seethed. "I seem to remember saying something like, 'Don't do anything I wouldn't approve of.'"

Jordan stood, guilt warming his cheeks. His eyes darted back and forth, searching for anything that could salvage the situation. A sudden twinkle came into his eye, "So . . . what part of dumping a pitcher of ice water on Matthew Harris do you not approve of?"

Bethany forced her lips together. Her cheeks twitched and the corners of her lips turned upward. Finally, she could hold it in no longer and burst out laughing.

Jordan's smile reached to the far edges of his face.

What a beautiful laugh.

Realizing she was in a library, she put her hand over her mouth and struggled to suppress any further chuckling. When it was safe to pull her hand away, she said, "I can't believe you did that."

"I know. I need to be more careful." Jordan's eyes danced. "You never know when you might trip."

"Clearly," said Bethany. Her tone was dry. "By the way, it's been a couple weeks since the tournament. Has it sunk in yet?"

"Believe it or not, a lot has happened in that time. Especially in the last twenty-four hours. I've not had much time to think about it."

Bethany narrowed her eyes. "Really?"

"Maybe later," he said, acknowledging her unspoken questions. "What are you doing here?"

"Helping my dad. He's got a lot on his plate."

"I heard he's running the whole historical society now. How does he find the time between work and caring for your mom?"

"He doesn't. That's why I'm here. He agreed to do the 50th Anniversary Celebration before my mom got sick."

Jordan sighed. "I'm sorry, Bethany. Any news at all?"

Bethany looked pained. "None. It's aggravating."

Jordan paused. He opened his mouth, then looked away.

"What is it?" Bethany asked.

His normal self-confidence was gone as he tentatively offered, "This may be hard to believe, Bethany, but I've prayed recently." He glanced back at her. "It's crazy, I know. But even more than that, I've received a *real* answer."

Bethany's eyebrows rose.

"I don't know what I'm doing. I'm just asking for stuff. It's clumsy and inarticulate, but I'm trying."

Bethany cocked her head, waiting.

"I've never offered this before, but would you like me to ask God to show you what it is?"

"I would," Bethany answered with dead sincerity. "Go for it."

"Now?" gaped Jordan.

"Yes, why not?"

He grimaced. He could talk in front of thousands of people with ease, but to pray in a public place was another matter. Anxiety flooded his gut as he and

Bethany bowed their heads. "Okay, here goes. Dear Lord, I'm still not very good at this. Would You please show Bethany and her family what is going on with Mrs. Clark? And if it's not asking too much, could You do it before I leave? In Jesus' name, amen."

"Amen," said a deep voice.

Jordan's eyes flew open. "Mr. Clark!"

"Bethany, will you excuse us?"

Bethany pinched her lips. She whirled around and said over her shoulder, "Thank you, Jordan."

Michael Clark did not need a shadow to pass over his countenance. "Hello, Jordan," he said, slowly. "Congratulations on your recent victory. When do you leave for Washington?"

Ouch.

He strove to be as polite as he could. "Well, sir, I leave in late-August."

Mr. Clark nodded. "What brings you to the historical society? I'm sure it wasn't to see Bethany."

Double ouch.

Jordan knew it was futile, but he decided to play it out anyway. "Mr. Clark, would you consider allowing me to be a part of your team this summer? I know you're swamped, and there's a lot I could help you with."

"I don't think that would be appropriate," replied Mr. Clark.

Jordan fought back the heat rising up the back of his neck. "Sir, may I ask you why? You know my research and communication skills. I could be an asset to your team."

"Jordan," replied Mr. Clark with thinly veiled scorn, "we are responsible for collecting and preserving the history and legacy of our town. Unfortunately, your family's part in that story is like a black smear across an otherwise beautiful painting."

Jordan's mind flashed back to the letter from William in the Bible.

"I had to do what was right. Too many lives are at stake."

His eyes blazed. "Sir, with all due respect, you don't know what you're talking about."

Mr. Clark's eyes remained cold. "Oh really? Tell that to the community. I don't have time for this. The answer is no. Excuse me." He strode away.

Jordan stood in stunned immobility and rage. His heart galvanized. Pandora's Box or not—this was not right.

Chapter 35

The Currency of Washington, DC

Monday, June 23, 12:00 p.m.
Patio outside a 16th Street Mall café, Denver, CO

Seated at a Denver café on the sidewalk near the 16th Street Mall, Jordan looked up from under the awning at a sky that was bright and clear. No surprise there. Most non-natives had no idea that Denver boasted over three hundred sunny days per year.

The weather in his dream that morning had been almost identical.

Twice in six weeks, this time with even more clarity, Jordan awoke from a striking dream about a bright Colorado day. In the dream, he stood before a bridge with the word "Wilson" emblazoned across the top. He could not tell where the bridge went, or why he was so interested in it.

A huge smile had lit his face.

Pen in hand, he signed away all he possessed to buy the bridge.

Even now at a downtown café, the dream remained clear in his mind. He was no longer about to burst with joy, but a pleasant peace had settled over him and accompanied him all the way from Wilson.

Jordan forced himself to think. He was still new at this whole God thing, but come on—the same dream twice?

That had to mean something.

● ● ●

"I'm sorry I'm late, Jordan," Jeffrey Kingston flashed a million-dollar smile and extended his hand.

Play it cool, Jordan. Stay calm.

It was not easy to do. A man whom he respected and wanted to emulate stood three feet away. Jordan took a deep breath, stood, and shook his hand.

"So, Mr. Nolan, it's been a few weeks since we last talked," said Jeffrey, sitting down, "has it become real yet?"

Jordan smiled. Besides the incredible peace he'd felt all day, he *most certainly* was going to DC. It was strange not feeling the animosity for his dad that had been driving the *need* to get out of Wilson, but his recent altercations with Mr. Clark and Mr. Jones had served as an alternative fuel. Four weeks of futile searching on the supposed summer-school thing had rekindled in him an excitement about the internship.

"I'm so glad to see that," said Jeffrey, reading Jordan's smile.

"It feels surreal, Mr. Kingston. I'm going to Washington! It feels like the opportunity of a lifetime."

"That's because it is. Eighteen months ago, I was skeptical when Senator Smith first pitched the idea to us, but it grew on me. Your counterparts are excited as well."

"Has the senator's pick been chosen?"

"Not yet," said Jeffrey. "the senator doesn't seem to be in a hurry on this one. However, if you can keep a secret, I think he's leaning toward a young lady from Fort Collins."

"Excellent," said Jordan.

It won't be Matthew.

"Jordan, I've seen some real promise in you. What you did in that debate tournament, especially the final round, was impressive."

"Thank you, sir."

"I mean more than just congratulations. You have a bright future ahead of you."

Jordan beamed on the inside and listened intently.

"I'd like to make you a proposition," continued Jeffrey. "How would you like to be personally mentored by me?"

Jordan's eyes lit up. "Do you mean it, sir?"

"Of course. The senator's internship is an excellent opportunity in and of itself, but being mentored by the chief of staff of a US senator,"—he paused, letting the words hang—"what do you think?"

Out of nowhere, Jordan felt the slightest twinge of fear, deep in his gut. He tried to push it aside. "Mr. Kingston, I know I am not yet the savviest DC native, so the prospect of this appeals to me. However, may I ask you a question? Why would you do this?"

The warmth of Jeffrey's smile reached across the table. "Like the senator, I believe in the next generation, and you are a living representation that I could help shape."

Jordan couldn't believe his good fortune. The nibble of unease pressed farther into the back of his mind.

"Part of the reason I offer this is your first lesson." Jeffrey continued, "What is the *currency* of Washington DC?

"I don't know, sir. You tell me."

Jeffrey reeled him in. "Allies."

●●●

"Thanks so much for the meal and for taking the time to meet with me," said Matthew.

"You're welcome," Jeffrey Kingston's smile was grand. "I was quite impressed with you this year."

They walked from the downtown restaurant and stood on a small bridge overlooking Cherry Creek. Several buildings from Denver's small skyline became silhouettes as the setting sun fought a losing battle against the backdrop of the Rocky Mountains.

Matthew lowered his gaze. "I don't know how you could be impressed. I couldn't get the job done."

"I know you're disappointed. But remember, there are usually multiple paths to reaching one's objective."

Matthew looked up at Jeffrey. "What are you saying, sir?"

"Your uncle is Alex Jones, is he not?"

"Um," Matthew searched for context, "yes, sir, he is. How did you know? Why do you ask?"

Jeffrey chuckled. "Let's just say I'm paid to know a lot of things. The reason I ask is because I know what you're trying to do, but your uncle is not going to help you get it done."

Confusion clouded Matthew's face. "What do you mean?"

"I believe you said something to Jordan Nolan such as, 'It's not over until you're on the plane.'"

Matthew's eyes widened and his stomach twisted. "How could you possibly know *that*?"

Jeffrey reassured him with a smile. "I told you, it's my business to know a lot of things. Don't worry, I know what it's like to have goals of my own."

Matthew gripped the railing to keep his hands from shaking. He looked at the buildings around them. Somehow they seemed bigger this evening.

"I appreciate what Mr. Jones is trying to do," Jeffrey continued, "but he is not going to be the answer, either for Mr. Carlyle or for you."

Matthew kept his gaze forward.

"There are multiple parties interested in the little town of Wilson this summer. I'm assuming Mr. Jones told you about Howard Carlyle's last words?"

Matthew nodded. "Beware of the Nolans."

"That's right," Jeffrey's tone was smooth, "but Donald is not the only one with a vested interest in the 50th Anniversary Celebration this August."

Matthew swallowed. *How much does this guy know?* "Who else is?" he finally asked.

Jeffrey just smiled.

"Whose side are you on?" asked Matthew.

"The senator's, of course." Jeffrey's smile covered the bottom half of his face. "My role, however, puts me in a position to help and be helped by a number of interested parties, including you."

Matthew looked hard at the man. "Are you saying you could help me get the wildcard?"

"The wildcard, or ..." Jeffrey trailed off as he leaned on the railing of the bridge and looked out over the water. He lowered his voice, "... or you could go as the *qualifier*."

"You mean ...," Matthew's voice came out with a squeak as he struggled to keep from sounding like a twelve-year-old. He stopped and spoke again in a tone much deeper, "You mean that I would get to go, and Jordan wouldn't?"

"If the winner can't go," Jeffrey paused, "who gets to?"

"The runner-up." Matthew's face brightened.

"Much can happen in the course of a summer, wouldn't you say?"

"Well, yes, I guess it could."

"I can't guarantee anything, of course. It's still Senator Smith's decision,"

Jeffrey's face warmed, "but he does trust his right-hand man a great deal."

"You would put in a good word for me?"

"I come from DC, Mr. Harris. Do you know how we do things in that town?"

"I scratch your back, you scratch mine?" asked Matthew.

"I wouldn't put it quite so crassly." Jeffrey's voice got even smoother, "Let's just say we remember our friends." A ten-passenger, black limousine with heavily tinted windows pulled to a stop behind them. Jeffrey continued to look out over the water as if the vehicle didn't exist. "Would you like to be friends, Matthew?"

Matthew glanced at the limo and back to the senator's aide. He put his hands in his pockets to hide their shaking. His voice carried the tiniest waver as he said, "I think I would."

Jeffrey cocked his head and studied him. The setting sun glinted off the water, reflecting in his eyes. "Good." He nodded. "I look forward to being friends with you." He turned and opened the limo door. "Matthew Harris," he motioned him into one of the rear seats. "Meet Isaac Molencki."

Chapter 36

Hot Tears, Icy Rage

Friday, July 11, 2:45 p.m.
Wilson County Historical Society Building, Wilson, CO

Bethany walked up to her dad's office at the historical society and leaned against the door frame. "Hi, Daddy!"

Head down in a pile of paperwork, Michael Clark's face brightened as he looked up. "Hi, sweetheart."

She glowed. "You look like you could use a break."

He set his pen aside and leaned back in his chair. "You're right. What's on your mind?"

She stepped over to the desk, pulled a chair around to his side, and sat down. She twirled her necklace, wrapping it once around her pinky. "Daddy, tell me a story."

He sat up straight and spoke in a soothing tone, "In the great, green room, there was a telephone..."

"Da-ddy," Bethany rolled a minor third and made a face. "I'm eighteen, not five."

"Just teasing, darling. What would you like to hear?"

Her face turned serious. "Will you tell me about your grandpa? I mean the real story—the story behind the reason you don't care for Jordan Nolan?"

His smile wavered. "Why would you want to know that?"

"I have to know. Tell me the truth, will you?"

"Are you sure you're ready?"

"I am," she kept her voice even by force of will, "I've heard plenty around town. I think it's time I got the straight scoop from you."

Mr. Clark reached into his desk drawer and pulled out a laser pointer. He aimed it at a spot left-of-center on a huge Colorado map that covered most of the office wall. His eyes blurred out of focus and his tone turned wistful as he began to narrate in third person.

"Right there," the pointer hovered over a blue line, "is where an eight-year-old boy stood, many years ago."

As she listened, Bethany was reminded that her storytelling gift hadn't developed in a vacuum.

"A big man called 'Pappy Ray' put his big hand over Little Mikey's small one. Together, they held a fly rod. Pappy Ray's big hand covered Little Mikey's with a strong and tender grip, and Little Mikey felt the motion of the cast. The early-morning mist of the Upper Arkansas River twirled about the hidden cove that had become the most special place on earth to Little Mikey."

Nearly a national champion storyteller herself, Bethany knew better than to interrupt.

"Even though it was still cold," Mr. Clark spoke to the map, "Mikey was warm on the inside. That three-day weekend in late-March of 1964 was heaven-on-earth to an eight-year-old boy. Little Mikey Clark had learned to fish, and learned a bit about manhood as well, from the greatest man on earth."

Mr. Clark pinched his fingers at the bridge of his nose and squinted. "Four weeks later, Pappy Ray was dead. Murdered. Murdered by a coworker and supposed 'friend.'" He sighed.

Bethany's chin gave a slight tic as she pressed her lips together. She'd known some of the story, but she'd never felt it.

"Little Mikey stood at the gravesite and experienced a slice of hell-on-earth as something died inside him. At the grocery store, a week later, he looked down an aisle and saw twelve-year-old Walter Nolan and his mother, looking down at some soup. Mikey's mother practically yanked his arm off in her haste to evacuate the store. Hot tears burned his eyes as she told him 'that boy' was the son of the one who had killed Pappy Ray."

"Hot tears cooled to icy rage in the years that followed. Ebbing and flowing in intensity, his anger at the Nolan family resurfaced when Johnny Nolan started making headlines as a football star in the early nineties. Various people came to the defense of the Nolans, as if winning football games somehow made up for murder."

His voice trailed off as he took a breath before continuing, "But Little Mikey never forgot the spring of 1964."

"I'm sorry, Daddy."

Mr. Clark continued to stare at the map on the wall.

"So," Bethany tried to tread carefully, "what does this have to do with Jordan?"

Mr. Clark snapped out of his musings and his eyes flashed at her. He pushed backed his chair with a screech, stood, and filled the office with his towering six-foot-four frame.

Bethany gulped.

He turned away, it seemed to her, so as not to lash out or strike her.

Eyes full of mist, she got up and hurried to the door while his back was turned. She still didn't know what, if anything, her dad had directly against Jordan. It didn't matter.

Sitting down at the information desk, she brushed away an angry tear. There was more to her feelings than she'd realized. She peered over the top of her computer as Jordan walked up to speak to Mr. Everett. She sighed. *Put it out of your mind, Bethany. It's never going to happen.*

● ● ●

Jordan threw down his pen. He scrunched up his face and rubbed his forehead. He had studied until his brains almost fell out, and though he was convinced of William Nolan's innocence, the lawyer in him said the case was becoming unwinnable.

For the hundredth time, he looked over a digital picture of the letter from William. He was convinced the postscript contained a clue, but he couldn't figure it out.

Everything had seemed so different a few weeks ago—so full of promise.

He decided to persevere through the weekend. If he was no closer, he'd call it quits and turn his attention to Washington.

A realization hit him. He smacked his forehead.

What am I thinking? I haven't even prayed about this at all.

He looked up at the ceiling of the library. Under his breath, he said, "Lord, You helped me once before. Would You consider doing it again?" He realized he was still not good at this prayer thing as he almost ended with, "Sincerely, Jordan."

Mr. Everett walked by with a few books in his hand. Jordan stood and followed him a few paces. "Mr. Everett, can you help me?"

The librarian had the keenest, yet heaviest eyes of anyone Jordan had ever met. "What can I do for you, Jordan?"

"Have you lived in Wilson your whole life?"

"Much of it. I moved here in my twenties."

"I'm trying to do some research on a company called Carlyle Enterprises," said Jordan.

Something flickered deep in the eyes of the old man. He thought for a moment. "I think I remember hearing something about it during my tenure at WDC2."

"You worked at WDC2?"

"Of course," Mr. Everett gave a weary smile. "So has almost every other adult in this county. What are you trying to find out?"

"Anything, I guess. I can barely find any references to it." Jordan continued, "I think it might have been a company my great-grandfather worked for."

"I think it was a company owned by Howard Carlyle prior to WDC2."

"Mr. Everett," Jordan lowered his voice as the summer school letter crept back into his mind, "was it really just some *company*? Or was it the predecessor to WDC2?"

"I know this building pretty well, but I don't think there's much in it about that. However, I can keep an eye out if you'd like."

Jordan put on his attorney face.

That's no answer.

All he said out loud was, "That'd be great. Thank you, sir."

●●●

Feeling skittish, Jordan walked up to the information desk where Bethany sat, working. Ever since that wonderful time of laughing and praying with her, followed by that awful conversation with her dad, Jordan sensed he was being repelled by an invisible shield.

What he wanted was a tractor beam.

"That was weird," said Jordan, trying for a casual demeanor.

"What was?" Bethany was in one of her usual positions—eyes glued to the computer screen. What was unusual was that she didn't look up.

"Have you ever heard of a company called Carlyle Enterprises?"

Bethany stared at the screen. "I don't think so. Why do you ask?"

"I can't seem to find out much about it."

"Okay?"

"Our great-grandfathers worked there."

Bethany looked up for the first time. Her eyes turned a shade darker as she glanced toward her dad's office. "What?" Her tone had an uncharacteristic sharpness to it.

"I just spoke to Mr. Everett."

"And?" she twirled her fingers as if to say, "get on with it."

He tried to keep things light. This was not going well. "He said he'd heard of it when he was with WDC2, but he didn't think the library had much information about it. He said he'd look, though."

"He told you our great-grandfathers worked there?" asked Bethany.

"No, he didn't," Jordan looked past her at a map of Wilson County, hanging on the wall. "There's not much on the Internet about it, either. I saw a reference to it in the report about their deaths." He decided now was not the time to mention the summer school letter—or R3.

A darker cloud passed over her countenance. She turned back to the computer. "Jordan, I really don't have time for this."

He winced, crossing his arms as some color appeared under his cheekbones. "Of course you don't, Miss Clark."

Bethany glanced up at him. Her expression was flat. Normally it sounded cool when he called her that. Right now, it sounded weak and presumptuous. Why the sudden hostility? Taking a breath, Jordan said, "If you happen to see anything, I'd appreciate it if you'd hold it for me." Turning around, he blinked, balling his fists as he walked away.

Chapter 37

Creepy Eyes

Friday, July 11, 6:50 p.m.
Wilson County Historical Society Building, Wilson, CO

Bethany looked up as her dad burst from his office and pulled his bag over his shoulder. The tearful reminiscence, followed by the angry response to her question, had been replaced by an amped-up urgency as he hurried to make it to a meeting in Colorado Springs. Bethany barely had time to react as he threw her the keys and rushed out the main door.

"I'm sorry, sweetheart. I'll talk to you later," he said on the way out. She snagged the keys on one hop off the information desk and smiled at the good catch. Even though it was quick, her burden lifted slightly with his apology.

Mr. Everett had already left, which meant she would have to lock up tonight.

Now, at nearly 7:00 p.m., and with the 50th Anniversary Celebration only a month away, Bethany stared at a task list that seemed to have a life of its own. Over the next two hours, she finished several items as the last students and community members bid her goodnight and left the building.

Ugh.

Fatigue clawed at her as she locked the front door and turned off all the main lights. Besides the after-hours lighting, her dad's office was the only other light still on. She rounded the information desk and entered the room.

Yuck. What a mess.

His desk looked like a three-year-old had used it for a play date with a copy machine. Nothing new there. He wasn't known for his organizational skills in the best of times, but this intense season had dragged his office down to new lows of disarray.

Plodding around in a weary daze, Bethany touched it up just enough so that it didn't look awful. Last of all, she grabbed a folder off the desk and walked over to a tan file cabinet that took an already ugly wall and kicked it while it was down. The renovation that had linked the historical society building with the library hadn't touched this room. Bethany had characterized it as "seventies ugly."

Opening the top drawer of the left-hand file cabinet, she scanned the tabs and realized she'd chosen the wrong drawer.

Not that she could be totally sure; her dad's "system" consisted of stuffing folders into cabinets with the loosest possible link to the alphabet.

She sighed. Unfocused, Bethany started to push the drawer closed, but paused as something caught her eye.

What was that?

She pulled the drawer back open. A frayed and bleached tab with a faded capital "C" peeked out from behind several newer folders. It was so worn that it curled in on itself. The letter "C" jumped out at her. She peeled forward the tab that blocked her view and gulped.

Carlyle Enterprises.

Her conversation with Jordan flashed across her mind, and she sighed again.

He didn't deserve that.

Fresh from her dad's story—and response—Bethany had been stomping out embers in her heart when Jordan walked up to the desk. Even as she began to reconsider her assessment that he was "going nowhere," she realized it was a lost cause. Jordan would never be hers.

His words came back to her. *"Our great-grandfathers worked there."* In her understated way, she had bitten his head off. She stared at a wall that was a color she couldn't identify.

Somewhere between beige and tan.

She looked back down at the folder.

I should apologize.

She ran her thumb along the curled edge of the tab. The sound was crisp, and the texture was rough. The old folder was faded. She scanned the other tabs that filled the drawer. Not a single one even came close to the age of the one she held.

Her fingers trembled as she tugged the file out from between its neighbors.

She was suddenly aware of a quiet that could be felt. A sense of foreboding slithered up her back and settled around her throat.

●●●

She stood, skimming through several articles related to Carlyle Enterprises and the deaths of her great-grandfather and William Nolan.

"Excuse me, miss," a dry, low voice called to her from outside the office.

Bethany's heart slammed into her throat. The file folder flew out of her hand. Old newspaper clippings floated down like a snow globe.

"I'll be right there," she choked, still facing the file cabinets. She stalled, knowing that she would look like a ghost if she tried to greet the man now. She fought hard to will her pulse down to a manageable level.

She had locked the main doors thirty minutes ago.

The thought that a man had been inside the building with her for a half-hour caused a shiver worse than a spider creeping up her back.

Breathe.

She shivered again. Bethany had once done an after-midnight Internet search for "creepy eyes" and gotten a serious case of the willies. This was far worse. She tried again to slow her breathing. She scooped up the articles and set the folder on her dad's desk. Knowing she couldn't wait forever, Bethany said a quick prayer and walked out of the office to the information desk.

She looked *down* at a man in his mid-forties who was as tall as a fifth-grader but built like someone in Special Forces. His dress was professional—button-up shirt open at the neck and a contrasting sport coat. He pulled a curious set of brown leather gloves off his hands, one finger at a time, and stuffed them in his pockets. Satisfied, he looked up at her.

Her pulse surged again.

Nothing in his eyes resembled fifth grade. The sockets were deep and cavernous. The huge irises, with a brown so dark it was indistinguishable from the pupil, consumed most of his eyeballs. The bit of white that did show was bright and reflected an eerie contrast from the dim after-hours lighting above them. Her midnight Internet search had nothing on this guy, and it was only 9:30 p.m.

"I'm sorry, sir, we're closed." Bethany somehow kept her voice even.

"You are? I'm sorry. I assumed you were open, as the front door was unlocked," said the man.

Weird. She was sure she'd locked it.

Bethany pulled herself together. "That's strange. Well, what can I do for you?"

"I'm looking for some information."

Bethany gave a nervous laugh. "Looks like you're in the right place." She pointed upward. An Old-West vintage sign that read "Information Desk" hung down from the ceiling.

Without looking up, he smiled back at her from the nose down. His eyes remained locked on hers. "What's your name?"

Why does he want to know my name?

"I'm ... I'm Bethany."

"Hello, *Bethany*. It sounds beautiful the way you say it." He stuck out his hand. "Isaac Molencki. I'm an investigative journalist in town to research a story about the Wonder Drug in preparation for the 50th Anniversary Celebration."

She hesitated. After an awkward three seconds, her politeness won out. She shook his hand. "Nice to meet you."

He gripped her hand a second or two longer than was comfortable. "I'll be in and out, here and there throughout the summer doing my research," he continued.

Terrific.

"Do you mind if I ask you a few questions?"

Another shiver. "Actually, Mr. Molencki, we're closed now, and I should be getting home. Could I ask you to come back later? I'd be happy to talk to you at another time."

"Of course." His eyes never left hers. "Well, it's nice to make your acquaintance." He smiled again. "Just wanted you to know I'm in town."

Bethany forced a smile in return.

"Goodbye for now, *Bethany*." He turned and walked down the hall, past the restrooms toward one of the side exits. He pushed the bar open and disappeared onto the sidewalk. The door clicked shut.

Bethany let out a long exhale. She looked down and noticed that she was gripping the counter with both hands. She turned back to her dad's office as the conversation repeated in her mind. She stepped back inside and sat down at the desk. Her pulse felt like the driving beat of a modern worship song.

Slow down. Breathe.

She glanced at the folder.

What a bizarre day this was. First Jordan, then the file cabinet, then the smallest, creepiest man on planet Earth. She grabbed her backpack off one of the wall hooks, stuffed the folder into it, and hoisted it over her shoulder. She walked to the front entrance and pulled on the handle.

Her hand flew over her mouth.

The door was locked.

● ● ●

As the moon rose high into the night sky, Isaac Molencki leaned on the railing of the fifth-floor balcony, gazing out over the town of Wilson. He'd checked into the hotel yesterday after being gone five weeks on another job. His only other visit to Wilson had been in late-May when he sneaked into a house and made some copies from an old Bible to bring them to the customer.

Donald Carlyle. *Pathetic.*

He knew the type: someone who rose to his position on the achievements of others. Isaac would put up with him only because he was paid to do so. Back for the duration of the summer, this job was so simple it almost didn't count. It was more like a vacation.

Or so he had thought.

The moonlight glinted off his darkened eyes.

He'd seen a face today—a face that threatened.

Nobody ever threatened him. Nobody. Ever.

Memories flooded back, unbidden, unwanted.

Memories of the last day he'd been vulnerable.

Memories of the last day he'd been one of the good guys.

Memories of the day he vowed he'd never be hurt again.

The name wasn't exactly the same, but it was close.

Bethany.

A twisting thrust from a salt dagger carved the wound afresh. It might as well have been yesterday.

Elizabeth.

The only one he'd ever loved. The only one who had ever loved him. The only one who didn't mind his height. The only one who knew the horror of where he'd come from. He'd shared everything with her.

Several years of criminal forensics training had included two courses in graphology. Opening the letter that day, it only took two words for him to *know*. The handwriting betrayed a sadness not present in the fifty previous letters with the same introduction.

Dear Isaac,

This has been the most difficult decision of my life. I'll get right to the point. I've decided to marry Charles. I've wrestled and wrestled these last two weeks, and the answer has finally become clear.

I'm sorry.

I've enjoyed every moment we've had together. Thank you for everything. I wish you the best in your future endeavors.

Sincerely,
Elizabeth

Sincerely?

Eighteen months later, and the answer was "*sincerely?*"

He gripped the railing as memories from a few years ago declared war. Eighteen months of pouring out his heart. Eighteen months of receiving—he thought—a heart poured out in return.

Sincerely.

He'd crossed a line that day. He knew what his "future endeavors" would include. It would start with Charles, the man who beat him—a tragic car accident before their first anniversary.

Isaac chose not to attend the funeral, but he did write a letter to Elizabeth, informing her that he was sincerely sorry.

Chapter 38

$2 + 2 \neq 5$

Saturday, July 12, 11:15 a.m.
Wilson County Historical Society Building, Wilson, CO

"I'm sorry for being a jerk yesterday," said Bethany. "You caught me off guard when you mentioned our great-grandfathers. My dad had just told me the details." A touch of red teased her cheek. *I probably shouldn't say more than that.*

"Your dad doesn't have a *clue.*" Jordan's tone carried no hint of respect.

Her jaw dropped.

"Ray Clark and William Nolan were best friends," he continued.

The apology from five seconds ago became ancient history. Weird ideas were one thing. Openly insulting her dad was quite another. Looking back at her computer, Bethany gathered herself. She sucked in an exaggerated breath through her teeth, gripped the sides of her chair, and prepared to blast him with a serious stink eye. "Now listen here, Mr. Nolan," Bethany began, looking up.

Jordan had walked off and was going through the front doors.

Bethany gasped. She sprang up, rounded the information desk, and hurried after him. She caught up to him on the sidewalk. "Jordan, wait."

He turned around.

She'd seen that look before.

His eyes flamed.

"What are you talking about?" she asked.

He didn't answer.

"Best friends don't kill one another," pressed Bethany.

"You're right, they don't."

A pause.

Bethany clenched her fists. "Jordan, two plus two *cannot* equal five."

"That's true, *Miss Clark*," the spark was back in his tone, "but two plus *three* does equal five." Jordan spun around and strode off.

Now it was Bethany's turn to have some heat as she demanded, "What's that supposed to mean?"

●●●

Eyes bright, Allie said, "Let me hear the whole thing, especially the part about *you-know-who*." She had arrived earlier that day to help the Clark family for the remainder of the summer.

Bethany lay sideways on her bed with her head resting against her hand, which was propped up by her elbow. She stuffed her diary back under the mattress.

Allie leaned against some pillows on the loft bed across the room and folded her arms behind her neck.

Bethany relayed her last two conversations with Jordan.

"What an arrogant jerk," said Allie. Trained as an actress, she could shift emotions in an instant.

"I wonder," said Bethany.

"What's to wonder?"

"Well, I was upset at first, but I've been thinking about it for a few hours. Let me ask you a question. Have you ever known Jordan Nolan to be wrong about something? I mean, *really* wrong in regards to something he has spent time looking into?"

"No, I haven't." Allie had another split-second change. "Especially not in his choice of who he *likes*."

Bethany huffed. "Can you be serious? You're worse than a tabloid."

"Am I?" Allie milked it.

"Yes, as a matter of fact, you are. Don't you remember the thing I told you?"

"Oh, it's *the* thing, is it?" Allie made air quotes. "I seem to remember you told me *two* things."

Bethany buried her face into her mattress and shook her head.

"Could it be that our young Mr. Nolan may not be *'going nowhere'* after all?" asked Allie.

Bethany pulled a pillow from beside her and fired it sidearm across the room. Thanks to what happened with their great-grandfathers, it didn't matter if he was going nowhere or not.

Allie lifted her arms just in time to catch the pillow in front of her face. She pulled it down and peeked over. It was clear she had an enormous smile hidden behind the pillow.

"Just answer the question," said Bethany. Her cheeks were rosy.

"Okay," said Allie. She threw the pillow aside and flipped back to serious mode. "Jordan's a bit smug for his own good sometimes, but he's no dummy."

"Agreed," said Bethany, relieved at the shift in the conversation.

"Then what did he mean?"

"That's what I've been trying to figure out," said Bethany. "I let him know that my dad had just told me the details about Ray and William, but he practically spat the words back to me that *my dad didn't have a clue.*"

"Jordan said that?"

Bethany nodded. "His tone indicated that he wasn't thinking too highly of my dad. I'm most upset at him for that, but I'm trying to keep an open mind. I can understand his feelings. After all, my dad has taken this out on him personally before."

"He's fed up with the stigma," said Allie.

"For sure," said Bethany, "but that's not what's bugging me. After that, he said that William and Ray were *best friends.*"

"Seriously? That's ridiculous."

"Yes, that's when I told him that two plus two cannot equal five."

"Huh?"

"Obviously, he agreed that best friends don't kill each other," said Bethany.

"It hasn't been that long since I moved to California, Beth. I know the history: 1964, two men worked together, one killed the other and then killed himself." Allie paused. "I'm not a math whiz, but that does not *add up* to the two men being best friends."

"Tell me about it," said Bethany. "Then Jordan got all cryptic, saying, 'but two plus *three* does equal five.' It also hasn't been that long since I took algebra. It can only mean one thing."

"What's that?"

"He's challenging one of the assumptions I'm using to set up the problem."

"But which one?"

Bethany stared up at the ceiling and then tilted her head to look Allie in the eye.

"No," said Allie. "No way."

"I agree, but I can't think of anything else that makes sense."

"He—you—can*not* be asserting *that*."

"I'm not." Bethany paused. "But Jordan might be."

"Beth, that's crazy. Everyone knows the history. William Nolan murdered Ray Clark. End of story."

"Unless everyone—including my dad, and us—really *don't* have a clue."

"That kind of talk could get you in real trouble in this town—and this house for that matter."

"I know," said Bethany, "which is why you and I are going to keep real quiet about my new course of study."

Allie brightened. "What might that be? History?"

"No," Bethany said with a grin. "Math."

Chapter 39

The Key

Saturday, July 12, 3:30 p.m.
Upstairs library/attic of Nolan guest house, Wilson, CO

Maybe this is nothing after all.

Jordan was half-tempted to disregard the email from R3 as a hoax if not for the fact that the summer school letter had been correct, and that somebody had broken into his house to take pictures from the old Bible.

"Pandora's Box," R3 had called it. It didn't feel like Pandora's Box. It felt like a dead end.

Who is R3?

Was William Nolan really murdered?

Jordan sighed.

Come Monday, I'm done with this.

The seventies lamps were his only company. As ugly as they were, Jordan was beginning to feel at home with them. They cast a cozy radiance and gave off a hum that he found comforting.

He had spread everything out on the old attic table—the clues, the Bible, his research, and printouts of the communications from R3. His laptop sat open in front of him, while a great cup of coffee grew cold six inches from his hand. The only sip he'd taken from it was to chase down a couple of ibuprofen.

In ninety minutes, the Nolan grill would fire up and begin churning out some serious meat. Today's cookout would include some regulars, such as Gadg and his father, Deputy O'Brien, but mostly it would be overrun by a herd of hungry football players in town for Johnny's annual camp. Jordan reached for two more headache relievers.

Despite the throbbing in his temples, something continued to nag at his subconscious.

Like a general bent over a field map, Jordan scanned his research. He settled on the postscript of William's message to Grandpa Walter. He had looked at it several times in the last few weeks.

> P.S. "A man plans his way, but the Lord directs his steps." Life's journey is a search for truth and a walk of faith. "Faith is the substance of things hoped for and the evidence of things not seen." "Faith works through love." Love God. Love People. Love Truth. Love is the key.
>
> Here are some Scriptures that will help guide you on your quest:
>
> 2 Corinthians 8:7
> Mark 12:38
> John 3:16
> 1 John 3:1
> Leviticus 19:18
>
> Song of Solomon 1:3
> Romans 13:8
> Isaiah 61:8
>
> 1 John 3:18
> Psalm 119:132
> Deuteronomy 10:19
> 2 Corinthians 8:24
> Matthew 5:46
> Amos 5:15

Jordan turned the pages as if they were made of tissue. Taking his time, he flipped to each of the Scriptures and typed them into a spreadsheet. He had gone through all of them over the last few weeks, but it was time for a more systematic approach. It was a laborious process that he could have shortened with online tools, but he wanted to be sure he had exactly the right text. He stared at the screen and voice-launched his diary app without looking at his phone.

William's Postscript

Okay, something about this still bugs me
What is it?

Obviously, there's some good wisdom here
Is there any rhyme or reason?
Any coherent theme?

None that I can see

That verse about the scribes makes no sense to me
Song of Solomon?
The virgins love thee?
That is bizarre.

Who would give that scripture as guidance to his son?
In what sense would this guide Grandpa Walter on his quest?
For that matter, what quest?
Life?

Lord, what am I missing?

Jordan got quiet. The attic was so still that even the smallest of noises could be heard. He stared. He listened. He stared and listened. His thoughts drifted back to the message from R3.

You hold Pandora's Box in your hand. Are you sure you want to unlock it?

Leaving the spreadsheet open on his computer screen, Jordan launched a web browser on his phone.

Unlock? Isn't the phrase usually "open Pandora's Box"?

He did an Internet search. Pandora had strict instructions from Zeus not to *open* the box. He snatched up the printout of the email from R3.

"Unlock" is underlined.

Jordan lifted his eyes and spoke to the seventies lamps; "Why would R3 ask if I wanted to *unlock* it?" He rubbed his chin. "It could be just a figure of speech or a misquote of the idiom."

The lamps just sat there, humming their support.

"No, I agree. That doesn't seem likely. He seems way too clear on the details."

A crack of light shone in his understanding.

"To unlock something, you must have a key. Is it possible I have the key right in front of me?" He looked back at the postscript and expanded his diary entry.

Love is the key.

Wait a minute
Is that "k" a little darker?
Yes
Is that just an accident?

Are there others?
Yes
There are four total:

plan<u>s</u>
s<u>e</u>arch
evid<u>e</u>nce
<u>k</u>ey

S-E-E-K
That *cannot* be an accident!

Do the words that contain the darker letters have any significance?
Plans, search, evidence, key

Interesting words in light of the contents of William's
letter

Okay, this might be a stretch, but here goes...

Could this be a clue to help find some kind of evidence?
Evidence of what?
Plans A and B?
Maybe

The darker letters say to seek
Seek for what?
Love
Each of the Scriptures has the word love somewhere
in it

Maybe love is the key to more than just navigating life
That might make sense
Some of the Scriptures are pretty strange
Maybe they are strange because their main purpose
isn't to communicate wisdom

Seek for love
Love is the key
Keys unlock things
What do they unlock?
The truth about William Nolan
Yes, but according to R3, they also unlock Pandora's
Box

Whoa

In the spreadsheet, Jordan clicked on the word "love" in each verse and
underlined it.

Is that a word count?

Using his finger, Jordan counted how many words in each Scripture it took to get to the word "love."

He looked up at the lamps and apologized as if they were looking down on him. "I know. I lose a geek point for that. Don't tell Gadg."

He could have done it with a formula, but he had a headache and didn't care.

Okay, so I have a list of numbers

21, 14, 4, 5, 18, 20, 8, 5, 7, 18, 1, 14, 4, 5

So?

Jordan took a couple steps back and cleared a path so he could pace.

Back and forth.

Back and forth.

He stopped to lean on one of the shelves and spotted an open word puzzle book with a pen in between the pages. Jordan had loved these kinds of books ever since he was ten years old. He had scattered them all throughout the house over the years.

Mom got me my first one of these.

Michelle Nolan had realized at an early age that Jordan possessed a strong gift with words. That realization had been the catalyst that led her to look into speech and debate, even though she had no background in competitive speaking.

Something about the book caught his eye, and he looked closer.

He gasped out loud and turned to the lamps.

"It's a cryptogram!"

He lurched back to his computer for another look. One minute later, after counting with his fingers like a kindergartner, he slammed his hand down on the table.

"Yes!"

Lukewarm coffee spilled over the edge of his mug, but he didn't care.

Looking up at the lamps, he said, "Do you see this?" He gestured at the screen. "I've got to show this to Gadg!"

Snapping his computer shut, Jordan snatched up the old Bible. "Thank You, Lord," he blurted as he got up and weaved his way back through the junk toward the door.

Chapter 40

Learning to Read

Saturday, July 12, 5:45 p.m.
Driveway in front of Nolan home, Wilson, CO

The final day of Johnny Nolan's football camp was always a hit.

After a hard week of practice, the boys were ready to eat. Many of them, especially those from outside Wilson, only knew Johnny as an all-American wide receiver.

The Nolan Stigma meant nothing to them.

The afternoon consisted of an informal football lesson on the Nolan blacktop, followed by an evening of medium-rare, grass-fed rib-eye steaks, and a heaping mound of fried, thick-cut bacon. The men, young and old, would pile bacon on top of their steak and feast with a knife in one hand and fork in the other.

It was western Colorado's version of a filet mignon.

They would chase down the meat with fiercely cold soda. Nothing green was allowed at the table. Wilson wasn't known for its vegetarians.

Deputy O'Brien would be the grill master. Friends since college, he and Johnny had enjoyed dozens of cookouts—really cook-*offs*—together. After several years, Johnny had finally conceded that his friend was undisputed lord of the grill.

Wearing a frayed apron, Deputy O'Brien also sported a four-inch-high trucker cap that featured a dead possum and a message about the merits of roadkill for supper. His smile was dorky, and he looked un-deputy-like.

Jordan, seated in a lawn chair, looked at Gadg, who rolled his eyes.

In the afternoon breeze, Gadg's hair was as tall as his dad's cap. In a story about Moses, he could play the bush. Somehow it looked alarming and yet perfect on him. He was a golden retriever with big hair—and he could fix *anything*.

Johnny was in his element. Linebackers, defensive backs, and wide receivers clustered around him on the large, circular blacktop in front of the Nolan house.

Ever since Johnny had asked for his forgiveness, it had been hard for Jordan to stay mad at him. He wasn't ready for buddy-buddy, but his respect level had increased. With his headache now a distant memory, he turned to Gadg and said in an excited whisper, "Check this out." He handed over the old Bible, open to the postscript. "Notice that the Scriptures are in groups of five, three, and six, with spaces in between."

"Yeah, I wondered about that," said Gadg.

"Notice also how there are a few letters that are darker than the others."

Gadg raised an eyebrow.

Jordan handed him his phone, open to the diary entry from earlier.

"Are you serious?" Gadg read through Jordan's hypotheses, handed the phone back, and lifted the Bible from his lap to confirm. "Now we're getting somewhere."

Jordan pressed his lips together to keep a smile from spreading. He handed over his computer.

Gadg set the Bible down next to the chair and looked at the spreadsheet. "These are the Scriptures in those groups, correct?" It was more of a rhetorical statement than a question.

"Yes."

Gadg read through them. "Even though the word *love* is underlined, I agree with your assessment—they don't seem to have a coherent theme."

"Click on the next sheet."

Gadg clicked on the next tab. The count for the position of the word *love* was next to each verse. He turned to Jordan. "This is that list of numbers in your diary entry?" Another statement phrased as a question.

"Yes. Each number represents a position in the verse and a corresponding position in the alphabet. Notice the word *love* is the twenty-first word in the first verse. The twenty-first letter in the alphabet is *U*."

"I got it," said Gadg. He clicked on the next sheet. "Unbelievable. Does that say, '*Under the Grande*'?"

"If we put spaces between the fifth and sixth letters and the eighth and ninth letters—just like the spaces between the words—it sure does. What are the odds of that being a coincidence?" Jordan tried to keep his voice down.

"Infinitesimal," said Gadg. He stared at the screen in wonder. Numbers, and number patterns, had always fascinated him.

"How infinitesimal?" asked Jordan.

Gadg gave a mock frown. "You realize that's a dumb question, don't you? That's like asking how close we are to a star as if we're going to make travel plans."

Jordan smiled. "I know. I just wanted to make sure."

Gadg lowered his voice again. "In terms of odds, there's *no way* that's an accident."

"I agree." Jordan lowered his voice even further. "So, are we back in school?" His eyebrows lifted in a playful arch.

"Finally," said Gadg. "I was beginning to lose hope."

"Me, too. Shall we go tomorrow?"

"We can't," said Gadg. "They've been setting up for that mountain bike race that starts Monday. The Grande bridge is part of the course."

"Ugh. I leave for DC on Wednesday."

"That's right. I forgot. Is this for the preliminary meet-and-greet?"

"Yes." Jordan sighed. "I was looking forward to it, but I won't be back until Saturday."

"Sunday it is, then."

"Before dawn," said Jordan. "I'll touch base with you sometime this week to firm up the specifics."

Gadg nodded. "Try not to think about it too much."

"Yeah, right."

● ● ●

"Hey Jordan," called Johnny, "can you come here for a sec?"

Jordan grimaced and pried himself out of the lawn chair. It was true he could throw. To stay in shape, he had switched to Ultimate when he'd quit football, but it had only been two years since he'd thrown seventeen touchdown passes as a sophomore. Johnny underhanded the football to him as he approached.

"Okay, defensive backs, line up in the formation I just went over," instructed Johnny. "Jordan, you line up as quarterback. Tyler, line up in the slot to his right. Okay, don't anybody move." Off to one side, Johnny addressed the group, "Guys, remember, wide receivers take the playbook and put meat on the bone."

One of the players pounded his chest, making noises like a gorilla.

"Meat," said another in a low voice.

The boys laughed and looked toward the grill.

"Hang in there, gentlemen," said Johnny. "This is a final summary, and it's important. The first step is for the quarterback and receiver to be so in sync that they *see* the same thing when they look out over the defense. You must understand this first as a *reading* lesson. You're learning to read the defense. Defense, your job, of course, is to read the formation, and the quarterback. Either way, it's reading first, execution next." Johnny addressed Tyler specifically, "You need six yards for a first down and are planning to run a quick slant. Based on the formation you see, how many steps would you take before you cut?"

Tyler studied the defense and responded, "Three?"

"What do you guys think? Do you agree?" asked Johnny.

One of the others replied, "At least that, maybe four or five because of that linebacker."

"I agree," said Johnny. "I'd go with four and not as sharp of a cut left."

Several of the guys nodded, including Tyler.

"What's the key to a good cut?"

Tyler answered, "Giving no indication whatsoever that the cut is coming. It's a whole-body shift in an instant."

"Everybody agree?" asked Johnny.

"Definitely," replied one of the defensive backs. "If you can do it right, it's brutal to defend."

"It gives us an advantage," said one of the receivers, smugly.

"That's why *we* have to be *better athletes*," said another of the defenders. More laughs.

"Another question, very basic"—Johnny turned to Jordan—"and this is equally true in Ultimate Frisbee: *where* do you want to throw the pass?"

Before Jordan could answer, a thought flashed across his mind.

I'm not angry anymore.

His mouth opened with a generosity of tone that surprised him, "It's critical to throw it where the receiver *will be*, which is usually *not* where he already is." He sounded more like a debate champion than a football player. "It's especially true in Ultimate because the disc stays in the air so long."

Johnny smiled.

Jordan felt the football in his hand as he looked at his dad. He couldn't remember the last time he'd held one.

"Yep, there's nothing like catching a perfectly thrown ball on the dead run," chimed in one of the other receivers. "It's one of the greatest feelings on earth."

"Sometimes the throw has to be made even before the wide receiver cuts," agreed Tyler.

Blinking, Johnny turned to the other receivers and spoke as if he were forcing his voice to stay steady. "If he were going to run an out pattern against this defense, where should you throw it?"

"Just inside the right sideline about eight yards down the field," said Jordan with a grin.

Johnny looked at him.

Jordan felt the approval.

"Show me," said Johnny.

"Go, Tyler," said Jordan. Tyler took off straight at one of the defensive backs and cut hard right. He hauled in Jordan's pass with one foot touching the blacktop and sprawled onto the lawn. Growing up together, they'd made that same play a hundred times.

One of the receivers yelled to Jordan, "Dude, where you been the last two years?"

Jordan stood erect, straightened an invisible tie around his neck, and launched into a high-volume parody of himself. "The ethics of living donor transplantation. In this speech we will explore whether it is ethical for a living person to donate an organ."

Several of the guys groaned.

"Come and get 'em," called Deputy O'Brien in a thick Colorado drawl, which he used only during these kinds of outings.

The herd stampeded to the picnic table beside the grill.

"Nice throw, son," said Johnny, approaching him.

Jordan grinned and said, "I don't think I missed my calling."

"I agree," said Johnny, "but it's still fun to watch."

"You agree?" asked Jordan.

"I do." Johnny held out a fist.

Jordan fist-bumped his dad as Tyler and Gadg walked over. Gadg held the Bible and Jordan's computer.

"Uncle Johnny," said Tyler, "do you ever get angry with Alex Jones?"

Johnny paused. "I've had to forgive him many times over the years. Old anger can flame up quickly."

Jordan and Gadg exchanged glances. Jordan opened his mouth to speak, but thought better of it.

Looking at Tyler, Johnny didn't notice.

"Do you ever want to get him back?" Tyler continued.

"Usually not." Johnny got a glint in his eye. "Though I wouldn't mind one more game." He put his arm around Tyler's shoulder and turned toward the table. "This is going to be a great year for you. You've worked so hard this week. I'm proud of you. You ready for a steak?"

Jordan had expected an internal reaction, but none came.

Good for him.

Gadg waited until they were out of earshot. "You were about to tell him, weren't you?"

"About Alex? Yeah, I was," said Jordan.

"Why didn't you?"

"I didn't think it would help us. Have you spoken with your dad?"

"Only in generalities. He doesn't know the specifics."

"I'd almost given up," said Jordan. "Besides, we haven't had much pursuit or surveillance since that first week."

"I know." Gadg looked down at the old Bible and handed it back. "But that could change in a hurry. Be careful."

Chapter 41

DC

Wednesday, July 16, 9:30 p.m. EDT
The front room in the home of Senator Smith, Washington, DC

Jordan tried to play it cool. He sat on a couch with two other young leaders in the open front room of the spacious Washington DC home of Senator James Dakota Smith.

I cannot believe I'm here.

In May, Jamie Hamilton from Thornton had been announced as the champion of the "Sword of the Mighty Pen" writing competition, which featured more than a thousand aspiring wordsmiths. A couple days later, Scott Sprague of Highlands Ranch was awarded the media spot on the team with his captivating presentation, "Politics in the Electronic Age." Jordan, of course, had earned his ticket by virtue of his narrow victory in the winner-take-all debate against Matthew Harris.

The senator, having grown up in Montana, was big on hospitality. He insisted on having the group stay at his home rather than a hotel, and he had enlisted the help of some staff members to provide the hour-by-hour support that such an endeavor required. Jeffrey Kingston and two other aides, Linda and Tony, rounded out the group in the senator's living room.

"Much business in this town gets done in settings like this," said the senator. "Even at this hour."

Jordan noticed the tremor in his hand as he touched his phone, 9:30 p.m.

Seven-thirty back in Wilson. I need to call Gadg soon.

"Have you chosen your "Senator's Pick" yet?" asked Jamie.

"Well, I *had*. In fact, we'd extended the invitation to a young lady from Fort Collins, but it turns out she is moving with her family to Malaysia."

The kids looked at each other.

"Yes"—the senator nodded in response to their unspoken question—"I've made my next pick." He looked over at Jeffrey.

"We plan to make the call to invite him later this week," said Jeffrey.

"Him?" said Jordan.

"Yes, *him*." Jeffrey raised his eyebrows with a hint of a smile. "We can let you know who it is on Friday before you leave. Don't worry, Mr. Nolan, I'm sure you won't mind our choice."

Jordan's face reddened a touch as he let out a breath he didn't know he'd been holding. The others chuckled. Jamie, it seemed, though respectful, could be a spitfire if it suited her purpose. "You sure you don't want to invite Matthew Harris?" she said to Mr. Kingston. "Might be an entertaining year." Scott and Jamie were aware of what had happened at the debate final.

Jeffrey smiled. "It would not be good press for the senator if one of the interns killed another."

Laughs all around. Jordan's hand wasn't shaking anymore. The senator and his crew did have a gift for hospitality. Jordan relaxed back into his seat. As discreetly as he could, he flipped over to the internship ticker on his phone.

39 days, 12 hours, 25 minutes, 50 seconds
39 days, 12 hours, 25 minutes, 49 seconds
39 days, 12 hours, 25 minutes, 48 seconds

This will be a great year.

"I'm sure you're wearied by your travels," the senator spoke up. "It comes with the territory. I trust you all feel welcome."

"We do, sir," said Scott. "This is—beyond exaggeration—the most incredible privilege of my life."

Jordan and Jamie glanced at one another and nodded their agreement.

The senator gave a big Montana grin. "I should have done this years ago. You might as well know that Washington can wear you down and suck the life from you. But looking at your faces reminds me why I do this."

The three grinned.

"We're so glad you're here with us and settled into your rooms. Boys"—

the senator turned to Scott and Jordan—"Tony will be in the room down the hall from yours. Jamie, Linda will have the room next to yours on the upstairs wing. Don't hesitate to let either of them know if you need something. My wife will be back tomorrow, but in the meantime, please make yourselves at home. I would encourage you to get some sleep—if you can." He turned to head up the stairs. "We've got a big day ahead of us tomorrow. Jeffrey will be here at 8:00 a.m. to pick you up. So for now, I bid you goodnight."

"Goodnight, sir," they replied in unison.

A few minutes and a few instructions later, Jeffrey said goodnight and left the room.

● ● ●

"Gadg, this place is amazing! I can't believe I'm really here."

The sound quality of Jordan's voice coming through the earpiece was good enough to suit his purposes. He clicked on the recorder. He would hear only Jordan's side of the conversation, but he hoped that would be sufficient. In the last few weeks, young Mr. Nolan had been busy researching the history of Wilson. It might be nothing, but the Wonder Drug celebration was only a few weeks away, and he needed some answers. Jordan spent a few minutes catching Gadg up on what had happened so far on his trip.

This is probably a waste of time.

He reached for the button to stop the recording and hesitated.

"Are we still on for Sunday morning?" Jordan paused to listen and then continued, "Yes, I'm thinking 4:45."

Wait.

"Are you sure we're reading the clue right? I still feel like I'm making this stuff up. A cryptic message from fifty years ago that tells us—we think—to look under the Puente Grande bridge for evidence of a crime we're not even sure happened? Sounds far-fetched to me."

Jordan listened for a minute.

"Okay, thanks, Gadg. I just wanted you to tell me I'm not crazy." Thirty seconds of only Jordan's breathing went by. "Is it possible we could exonerate William Nolan?"

Oh, there's a lot more to it than that, young man.

"I'm trying not to get my hopes up. Even as awesome as this place is, I'd rather be back in Wilson right now. Let's talk through the specifics."

The next three minutes filled in many of the details.

"I'll see you Sunday," Jordan continued. "We'll head up the river bank to the bridge just before five." The conversation switched to something about coffee.

Interesting.

A few minutes later he clicked off the recorder.

Jordan's won't be the only call to Wilson tonight.

He dialed the number for Isaac Molencki.

Chapter 42

Under the Grande

Sunday, July 20, 4:57 a.m.
On the banks of the East River, Wilson, CO

Jordan and Gadg picked their way between trees as they crept down the river bank.

Spanning the river several hundred yards downstream from where Wilson's Creek met Colorado's larger East River, the "Grande"—as the locals called it—was the only possible structure within a hundred miles that could be the answer to the clue. Built in the late fifties, the underside of the Puente Grande Bridge contained dozens of places that could hide a box of evidence.

Grey was the only distinguishable color in the predawn. The soft *slish* of the river and their gentle footsteps were the only sounds. The sun would rise in fifteen minutes at 5:12 a.m.

Jordan whispered, "I've always looked down my nose at conspiracy theorists and people who found hidden puzzles in ordinary events or documents." He looked over at Gadg. "Now I am one."

Gadg gave the slightest smirk as he continued to zigzag through the trees.

"I don't think I'll mention this when I get back to DC," Jordan mused.

● ● ●

"You have got to be kidding," said Jordan, enunciating every syllable except the last. They rounded the final bend and stood, gaping. On both sides of the river, even at the water level, a six-foot fence barred the way to the underside of the bridge. Construction orange was everywhere.

Gadg circled round and walked up the causeway.

"What does that sign say?" asked Jordan.

"Under construction. Keep out," Gadg called back.

"Seriously?" Jordan crossed his arms.

Gadg read the public notice. A corps of engineers had been commissioned to study the safety level of the aging structure. He walked back down to the river's edge.

"Climb it?" suggested Jordan.

Gadg looked pained. "My dad's on the police force, and you're going to Washington. Not sure that's a good idea."

"There must be a way. Who authorized this—Department of Transportation?" asked Jordan, his voice rising in pitch.

Gadg nodded.

"I'm guessing Mr. Olson will head that up," said Jordan.

"Probably," said Gadg. "I saw him the other day. He was driving a new truck."

Jordan paused. "Mr. Olson?"

"Chevy Silverado, midnight blue, fully-loaded. MSRP $49,500. Gorgeous."

Jordan's mouth dropped open. "Doesn't that strike you as odd?"

"Why?" Gadg looked at the fence again. "You don't think..." His voice trailed off.

"Would Mr. Olson be able to afford that on his own?" Jordan asked. "He just went through a divorce."

"So, who bought it?" asked Gadg.

Jordan grabbed the fence and shook it. His whole face scrunched up as he wrapped his fingers around the chain links. "I cannot believe this." Face clouded in mist, he turned and stared up the river. "Are we too late?"

Gadg waited a full minute and then put his hand on Jordan's shoulder. His voice remained soft and calm. "Who do you think it is?"

"Whoever paid somebody to break into my house." Jordan clipped the words. "They're looking at the same clues we are. Somebody must have figured it out and cordoned off the area to ensure that nobody but them would find anything."

"I agree with you about cordoning off the area," said Gadg. "However, I don't think somebody figured it out."

Jordan looked sideways at him, angry tears held in check.

"It's possible," said Gadg, "but not likely. I think it's much more likely that someone stole the information from us."

"What? How?"

"I don't know. But remember your house was broken into—on the same night we found the Bible. Have you told anyone this week?"

"No. The only time I even spoke about it was with you."

A dark cloud passed over Gadg's face. "Jordan, where were you when you called me?"

The same cloud spread to Jordan. "I was in the home of Senator Smith. What are you saying?"

"This could be much worse than we thought. If I'm right," Gadg continued, "these people have some serious resources and powerful connections—enough to influence the DOT at a moment's notice."

"In Wilson, that kind of clout only exists in a few places."

"True enough," said Gadg, "but who says it's limited to this town?"

Jordan's eyes grew round. "You don't mean that Senator Smith is somehow tied into all this?"

"I don't know," said Gadg. "But I do know that somebody, somehow, learned about 'under the Grande' and got here first."

"What's going on here, Gadg?"

"We can answer that question later. Right now, we better go. Let's see if there's another way."

Jordan heaved a heavy breath, made a show of letting go of the fence, and spun on his heels. He strode off without another word.

● ● ●

As they made their way up the bank, Gadg caught a glimpse of a slight movement across the river. A small figure pulled his head behind a tree and out of sight.

Stolen Glances and Hard-Earned Information

Friday, July 25, 3:30 p.m.
Wilson County Historical Society Building, Wilson, CO

From her perch at the information desk, Bethany peeked over the edge of an old newspaper clipping to steal a glance at Jordan.

A smattering of articles fanned out around his computer with his phone to one side and his DC coffee mug to the other. His laser focus provided a protective shield better than any DO-NOT-DISTURB sign could have.

What is he up to?

Jordan lifted his head and surveyed the historical society, staring at nothing in particular. Even when he looked her way, he didn't really see her. He put his head back down and started typing.

What are you thinking, girl?

Bethany chided herself and tried to focus on the article.

He's been praying.

The words on the page refused to become coherent.

So? What difference does that make?

None.

She sneaked another look over the top of the page.

Jordan lifted his coffee mug to his mouth, and just as the double-walled glass touched his lips, his gaze crested the rim like a sunrise and locked on hers. His grin was so big—and obvious—that it almost spread beyond the sides of the mug.

Bethany blushed like a schoolgirl who'd been caught passing a note.

Jordan took a noisy, exaggerated sip and set his mug down with a thud and a self-satisfied smirk. One second later, his face flipped to all business, and he dropped his head sharply.

"Hello, Bethany," came a voice from behind her.

She sucked in a breath. Her face flushed from both directions as waves of fear and shame collided inside. "Oh! Hi, Daddy," she blurted, fumbling with the article.

Mr. Clark glanced at Jordan and then back to her. "I've got some stuff to take care of, and I need to stop by the clinic. I'll be home after dinner."

"Sounds good."

"You okay?" asked Mr. Clark.

"Yes, I'm fine."

He tilted his head. "I love you, sweetheart."

Recovering just enough, she walked over and squeezed him with a "Daddy's Girl" hug. "I love you, too. I'll see you tonight."

As she rested her head under his chin, she realized that her dad had an unobstructed view of Jordan Nolan.

● ● ●

The engineers continued to study the bridge.

They should have found it by now.

After the disappointment at the Grande, and a couple days of anxious waiting, Jordan realized he couldn't do anything about it. Security at the site had been increased.

Am I missing something?

He prayed about it over and over, and decided to hit the books again. Something big was afoot. He doubled down on his research for another two weeks. Fatigue—the kind bred from intense study—pulled at him. Since finding the clue, the Wilson Public Library had become a home away from home.

Sort of.

A notable exception came when both he and Mr. Clark arrived simultaneously at the two sinks in the men's restroom. That had been the worst forty-five seconds of his life.

Jordan thought back to their conversation in late May. Mr. Clark's harsh comments represented a summary statement of eighteen years of living in

Wilson. This memory, combined with a growing sense that *something* was out there to be found, supplied him with a constant source of fuel to continue his research.

The library connected to the historical society building with an expansive commons area, which interspersed plenty of tables around rows and rows of books. At one end were the offices. In truth, it was not easy to distinguish where the library left off and the historical society began. It didn't matter, though—especially this summer with the 50th Anniversary Celebration coming up in August. Mr. Clark's office sat adjacent to the office of Robert Everett, who could usually be seen behind the information desk.

One more hour and it was time for a break. Usually, Jordan's ability to concentrate so intensely was a great gift.

This was not one of those times.

With printouts of old articles strewn across the table, laptop screen wide open, and phone lying next to his right arm, he heard the words before he sensed the approach.

"Interesting title. Whatcha working on, Jordan?" The voice of Alex Jones was gravelly from too many cigarettes.

Using both hands, Jordan slapped the lid of his laptop shut and snatched up his phone in one motion. He stood and spun away from the voice.

"Hey, watch it!" came the angry voice of Matthew Harris as Jordan's shoulder slammed his chin trying to create some space from Alex. Matthew had been looking over Jordan's other shoulder.

"You watch it!" Jordan fired back. "What do you think you're doing?" His voice was way too loud for a library but he didn't care. The weariness vanished as adrenaline shot through him. His papers lay strewn all over the table. Alex snatched one up and started to read.

"Tragedy—Wilson Man Kills Another, Then Kills Self," Alex read aloud. "Taking an interest in Wilson history, are we?"

Jordan didn't respond.

"Wilson Drug and Compounding Center Honored for Wonder Drug," said Matthew, picking up another sheet.

"Care to tell us what you're working on?" asked Alex.

"No." Jordan's voice dripped scorn.

"Why not?" demanded Alex.

"It's at a tenth-grade reading level. You wouldn't understand."

Alex's smile vanished. "How about we find out without your permission?"

"Why not? First, you follow me around. Next, you tackle me like a bullying schoolboy. What's next? Breaking into my house? Oh wait, you already did that."

A flash of uncertainty registered on Alex's face—come and gone in an instant.

Realization hit Jordan like a bolt from the sky.

He didn't do it.

Jordan's eyes darted back and forth and a shiver chilled his spine.

Someone else is involved in this.

Jordan shot a look at Matthew.

What does he know?

Alex took a couple steps toward him before Jordan snapped back into focus. "Are you operating in your official capacity as head of security at WDC2?"

Alex stopped. His jaw muscles tensed. "You just better watch yourself."

"I'm thinking the same is true for you. We're getting some nice camera angles. I'm sure Mr. Carlyle would enjoy a headline such as 'WDC2 Security Chief Busted for Assault.'"

Alex stepped in close. "He might not, but I would. It might be worth it."

Jordan's neck pulsed.

"Mr. Everett?" Jordan turned his head and called out to the librarian. "Could I ask for your assistance?"

Alex stepped back six inches.

The librarian shuffled over.

"Hello, Mr. Everett," said Alex, politely.

"What's going on here?" asked the librarian.

"Just doing some research," said Matthew.

"*I* was doing research," said Jordan. "But it seems Matthew has decided to become a thug instead of an attorney. Alex is mentoring him."

Alex's face turned to cold steel.

"Gentlemen, I don't care what you do outside this library," said Mr. Everett. "But this is not acceptable here. Got it?"

"Yes, sir," said Matthew.

Still staring at Jordan, Alex gave one slow nod.

"Mr. Nolan?" the librarian directed his question to Jordan.

"Sir, I'm not going to pretend that I had any fault in this. I was using the library for its intended purpose and nothing more."

"That may be, but your words are still inflammatory," said Mr. Everett.

"We'll catch you later, Jordan," said Alex as they turned to leave.

Jordan finally took a breath. As Mr. Everett walked back to his office, he bit down on clenched teeth and swallowed the words before they could come out.

Several people glanced at him, before turning away. A couple of them smirked. From behind the information desk, Bethany offered a sad smile that meant the world at that moment.

Chapter 44

The Game Is Still On

Saturday, July 26, 4:30 p.m.
Upstairs library/attic of Nolan guest house, Wilson, CO

"In here, Grandpa," Jordan directed his voice through the clutter.

He had resisted cleaning up the place because each time he forged through to the table, it felt like entering a sanctuary. The far end of Grandpa's attic had become a sacred place where Jordan met with God.

Grandpa weaved around knotted clusters of stacked furniture and wound through amorphous sections of randomly strewn books—all the time picking his way over piles of unidentifiable stuff and dodging dangling appendages that could bring down piles of junk if disturbed.

"Color looks great," said Jordan. Leaning back in his chair, his favorite mug sat before him with steam curling up in front of his laptop. Picking up the mug like a professional wine taster, he took a definitive sip.

"Jackpot?" asked Grandpa.

Mug still at his lips, Jordan motioned to another seat. Setting the mug down, he said, "You want the truth or do you want your grandson to flatter you?"

Grandpa sat. "Jordan, I'm old school. You could pour water through sawdust, and I'd consider it a decent cup of coffee."

Jordan smiled. "Flattery aside, it's good."

Grandpa lit up.

"I don't get it," Jordan continued. "You really don't care about good coffee, do you?"

Grandpa shook his head.

"So, why have you spent so much time learning about it in the last few weeks?"

"You'll understand when you're a grandparent."

Jordan cocked his head.

"The prospect of seeing my grandson on a near-daily basis, simply by making coffee a certain way..." Grandpa trailed off.

"Oh, I get it." Jordan held up his mug. "My dad sure nailed it on this one. It's a thing of beauty."

"Never thought of a coffee mug as beautiful."

"Let me guess, you could drink it from a tin can and consider it a decent cup."

"I have," Grandpa laughed. "But I think I get the idea. I've got some wrenches downstairs that are nice—some might call them beautiful."

Jordan nodded his approval. "See, there you go. You know I'm a tool guy as well, don't you, Grandpa?"

"I know you are. But yours are them newfangled gizmos made of plastic and smoke. Give me something that could hurt somebody if you don't use it right."

"I've sent some emails that have caused me some serious problems. Sometimes I wish all I had was a broken toe from a wrench I dropped."

"Fair enough," said Grandpa. "Here's to tools." He raised his mug.

Jordan raised his mug in return.

Grandpa leaned back in his chair with a smile that said he'd rather be here than anywhere else in the world. He looked at Jordan with his computer and the old Bible spread open in front of him. "You reading that?"

"Yes, why?"

"I expected you to have some fancy Bible program on your phone that has fifteen different versions: Greek and Hebrew, etc., etc..."

"I do, but you want to know something interesting?"

"What?"

"I feel a curious attachment to God and our family history through this old thing." Jordan lifted a few of the pages. "Thanks so much for letting me borrow it. It's fragile, faded, and smells musty, not to mention it's a hassle to read the King James English. But somehow the father-to-son linkage, generation by generation, connects me to the past. Is that strange?"

"Not to me," said Grandpa. His eyes clouded over. "Now *that* is something worthy to be called beautiful."

Jordan glanced up into the corner of the ceiling and spotted a cobweb. "Grandpa"—he looked over his shoulder and lowered his voice—"can I let you in on secret?"

"You mean your search for the truth about William?"

"Is it that obvious?"

"Only to those up close and personal. Your dad and I have been keeping an eye on you."

"There's something else. I've been reading, actually *reading*, the Bible."

"It'll mess you up," said Grandpa with a twinkle.

Jordan handed over his computer. The screen showed the list of verses related to the "Under the Grande" clue. "Do you see the verse that says, 'For if ye love them that love you?'"

"Yeah?"

"I looked up the passage; here's what it says." Jordan slid the old Bible across the table.

Grandpa read aloud, "'Love your enemies, bless them that curse you, do good to them that hate you, and pray for them which despitefully use you, and persecute you.'" He turned to face Jordan. "Let me guess ... Matthew Harris?"

Jordan nodded.

"You wondering how it's possible to love somebody you hate?"

"I don't hate him."

Grandpa let the words hang in the air.

Jordan's chair squeaked. "Okay, maybe a little."

More silence.

The lamps murmured their faint hum. At this time of day, their color was a cross between one of Grandpa's old ties and baby food with peas in it. Jordan finally blurted, "Okay, maybe a lot."

"Just start by praying for him."

"Okay, I'll try." Jordan took a breath and redirected the conversation. "How have *you* been doing? I mean, since the ceremony?"

Grandpa rested one of his calloused hands on top of Jordan's. "That was the best gift I ever got in my whole life."

Jordan's smile stretched the muscles of his face.

Grandpa flipped to the front page and read from John Philip Nolan, "*Go forward with my blessing, and may this copy of God's Holy Writ ever be unto thou and this family as a testimony that 'His faithfulness is unto all generations.'"* Grandpa sat up straight. "You asked me how I'm doing." He pointed down at the page. "For the first time in my life, I feel like I'm going forward with my father's blessing."

"I'm getting a glimpse of that myself," said Jordan.

"Are you now?"

"Hard to believe, I know," Jordan said with a chuckle.

Grandpa asked, "Where was that verse again?"

"What verse?"

"'His faithfulness is unto all generations.'"

"I think it's Psalm 119, isn't it?" said Jordan.

"Look it up, would you?"

Jordan opened the old Bible and turned to Psalm 119. He couldn't find it in the first few verses so he turned the page. "What's this?"

"You okay?"

"Did you know this was here?" He pointed to the bottom of the page.

"What are you talking about?"

"A second postscript."

Grandpa grimaced. "Jordan, I've been a working man all my life. I don't even know what that is."

"A P.P.S.—it's another P.S. at the end of something written. Look, it's William's handwriting."

"What does it say?" Grandpa drew closer, eyes wide.

P.P.S. Every once in a while you must take a second look - a deeper look. My son, look deeper into the verse. You'll find that love is still the key.

"What does it mean?" asked Grandpa.

Jordan's jaw dropped as he stared at his computer. He leaned closer just to make sure, then bit down on his bottom lip and pumped his fist. "It means the game is still on. We've been looking in the wrong place."

Chapter 45

A Deeper Look

Saturday, July 26, 5:05 p.m.
Upstairs library/attic of Nolan guest house, Wilson, CO

"Gentlemen, check this out," said Jordan.

Gadg and Tyler had made their way back to the old wooden table in the attic.

Jordan switched screens on his laptop, and they studied the copy of the spreadsheet that listed the love Scriptures from William.

"You gonna tell me what this is about?" asked Walter.

"Evidence, Grandpa," said Jordan. "Whatever it was that put Great-grandpa William and Ray Clark in such danger."

"You think there's something out there?"

"You tell us if you agree. Look here." Jordan pointed at his computer screen.

Grandpa read down through the list.

"Here are the Scriptures from William's postscript to you," Jordan continued. "The position of the word *love* in each verse represents a numeric value for a letter of the alphabet. A is 1, B is 2, etc. Strung together, it spells 'Under the Grande.'"

"Really?" Walter leaned in closer. "So you guys checked under the bridge?"

"We tried. It's blocked off so that the Department of Transportation can make sure it's safe."

Grandpa raised an eyebrow.

Jordan frowned. "We're not the only ones looking for it."

"How would anyone even know about it?"

"For starters, somebody broke into our house the night of the blessing ceremony." Jordan told him of their discovery of the pine needle between the pages of the Bible.

"What?" Grandpa's tone took on an edge. "Why didn't you tell us right away?"

Jordan's face reddened. "I'm sorry, Grandpa. I guess I'm still getting used to trusting Nolan men."

Walter relaxed. "You sure the pine needle wasn't there the night before?"

"We have before and after on tape," said Gadg. "Also, we think someone might have overheard a phone call between Jordan and me."

Grandpa turned to face him. "Does your dad know about this?"

"Officially or unofficially?" asked Gadg.

"Does it matter?" asked Grandpa.

"The timing of the CDOT study is curious. Some high-powered people may be involved in this," said Gadg. "Officially, my dad knows nothing."

"And unofficially?"

"Let's just say we've been spending some quality father/son time together." The corner of Gadg's mouth turned upward.

"I see," Grandpa pursed his lips. "Why the hush-hush?"

"Because we really don't have anything yet," said Jordan. "This isn't something to speculate about publicly."

"We also don't want to jeopardize the internship," said Gadg.

"It doesn't make any difference anyway," said Tyler. "The engineers will find it any day, if they haven't already. There's no way we can get to it now."

"Neither can they," said Jordan.

Gadg and Tyler both did a double take.

"It's not there. Look at William's *second* postscript."

"He wrote another?" asked Gadg. "I never saw that."

"That's because it wasn't with the letter," said Jordan. "Guess where it is?"

"No idea," said Tyler.

"Psalm 119," said Jordan.

"'May this copy of God's Holy Writ ever be unto thou and this family as a testimony that '"His faithfulness is unto all generations.""" repeated Gadg from memory.

"You got it. Take a look at this." Jordan turned to Psalm 119 and showed them the P.P.S.

Tyler read aloud, *"Every once in a while you must take a second look—a deeper look. My son, look deeper into the verse. You'll find that love is still the key."*

"That still seems cryptic," said Grandpa. "What's it mean?"

"Take another look at Matthew 5:46. It's the 'love your enemies' passage." Jordan pointed to the second-to-last Scripture on the screen. "What do you see?"

Gadg nodded at the screen as the light went on for him. "Love is still the key. Wow."

Tyler shook his head again. "You guys are geeks. Just tell us."

"The word *love* shows up a second time in the verse," Gadg answered. "It is not only the fourth word, but the seventh as well."

"Cool," said Tyler. "So, what does that mean?"

Jordan took a sip of the coffee he'd heated up while waiting for Gadg and Tyler. He smiled as he slurped. "Let's go to Old Town. We've got to figure out how to get under the *grange*."

●●●

Making their way out of the attic and toward the rear of the property, the boys crossed through an opening in the back fence and walked the three-hundred yards to the grange. Built in the town's heyday over a hundred years ago, the structure was solid—but it gave off a vacant, expansive feel since it no longer possessed its two side doors or the main double doors in front. They circled the outside twice before entering.

"What did they do here?" asked Tyler, standing in the center of the huge open area.

"Weddings. Dances. Community events," said Gadg. He walked the inside perimeter. "It was the Wilson County Events Center of its day."

Jordan blinked a few times. "Gadg, what do you think?"

"About what?"

"Why would a building like this—or a town like Old Town for that matter—remain virtually untouched for fifty years even after it had been abandoned decades before that?"

Gadg pondered the question.

"Let me propose a theory," Jordan continued, "Howard Carlyle threatens to leave Wilson and take WDC2 with him if anything happens to Old Town. This much we know from our research, correct?"

Gadg nodded.

"Either he really liked history..." Jordan paused.

"Or he was hiding something," said Tyler.

"I do believe you're catching on, my boy," Jordan used his best Sherlock Holmes accent.

"It's the only thing that makes any sense," said Gadg.

"Do you think Howard Carlyle was responsible for the deaths of William and Ray?" asked Tyler. Once again, his simple honesty cut right to the quick.

"Whew," Jordan exhaled and glanced at Gadg. "Are we ready to go *there*?"

"You tell me. Here's what I have," said Gadg, addressing them both in a terse style that sounded like bullets.

"Jordan receives a cryptic summer school letter that hints at a cover-up related to the drug XD.

"It pronounces a blessing on a fifty-year-old treasure hunt that leads us, after some altercations with the head of WDC2 security, to a Bible that's two-and-a-half centuries old.

"This Bible contains a letter from William Nolan that speaks of circumstances and plans that challenge the accepted history of Wilson and the Nolan Stigma.

"Then, on the same night that someone breaks into Jordan's house, he receives another summer school email, this time from a person identified as R3, who comes right out and says William was murdered.

"To top it off, a difficult clue in a two-part postscript alludes to a search for plans and evidence by using *love* as a key to unlock the phrase that leads us here.

"The grange, with the rest of Old Town, sits untouched for fifty years because Howard Carlyle threatens to move WDC2 to another city if the Town of Wilson insists on renovating it."

Gadg took a deep breath.

"So, if it looks like a duck and quacks like a duck...?" asked Tyler.

"If the duck was 'Man of the Century' and CEO of a company that has been the livelihood of much of the county for several decades, then we say nothing without hard evidence to implicate the duck," said Jordan. "This is like holding a hand grenade after the pin has been pulled."

"So why didn't Howard just demolish it all?" asked Tyler. "It's on WDC2 property, isn't it?"

"It *was* on WDC2 property," said Gadg. "Donald Carlyle sold a bunch of it to the town recently."

"True enough," said Jordan, "but *Howard* Carlyle didn't. If he had something to hide, especially because of William and Ray, he didn't want to risk the chance of it being found."

Gadg continued, "Based on all we've learned, he feared that a renovation would uncover something incriminating. To make matters worse, the town council has expressed a desire to protect everything because of its historical significance."

"The renovators would be thorough and cautious," said Jordan with a nod. "If there was anything to be found, they would find it. Howard Carlyle knew this and was forced to play his ace in the hole. The town would not risk the loss of revenue brought in by WDC2, so Howard won."

"So Old Town just sat there," said Tyler.

"Remember the letter in the Bible. My great-grandfather William described their circumstances in 1964 as 'unusual in the extreme' and 'impossibly difficult.'"

"Something big was going down," said Tyler.

"Which means something big is hidden," said Gadg.

"Agreed." Jordan looked at them. "So how do we get under this thing?

● ● ●

They fanned out and scouted the open area of the grange. Jordan's face darkened. He scampered out of sight of the doors.

"What is it?" asked Gadg.

"Get over here, guys." Jordan motioned with his hand to pull them into the shadows of the side wall. "I just realized what an idiot I've been."

"What do you mean?" asked Tyler.

Jordan smacked his palm off his forehead. "If Alex or anybody is watching us, we just handed them the clue. Not only that—we *are* on WDC2 property right now."

Gadg grimaced.

"I thought you said it was sold back to the town," said Tyler, sneaking a look over his shoulder.

"I'd forgotten that this grange wasn't part of that," said Gadg. He pointed east. "The WDC2 property line is maybe a hundred yards that way."

They darted toward the back of the building. Though it was still daytime, the light dimmed as they moved toward the rear. A good twenty-five feet beyond the vacant side doorways, they came to a wall that spanned most of the width of the building. On the far right was a short hallway that led to a back room.

Tyler whispered, "Why didn't Howard Carlyle have this torn down if it was still on WDC2 property?"

"Remember," said Jordan, "Howard wasn't the one who sold the other part of the property back to the town. It was his son, Donald. From Howard's perspective, this grange was a part of the whole lot that he wanted to leave untouched."

For no conscious reason, they tiptoed down the hallway as the light became even dimmer. They peeked around the corner at an empty room.

"The scullery," said Gadg.

The windows were boarded up. With the exception of the small light from the hall, it was completely black, even this early in the evening. They pulled out their phones, turned on their flashlights, and looked for any sign of a way under the building.

"There's nothing here," said Tyler.

"Oh, yes there is," said Jordan. His eyes glinted steel. "I just don't know how to get to it yet."

Chapter 46

Bethany the Spy

Tuesday, July 29, 9:00 p.m.
Wilson County Historical Society Building, Wilson, CO

It was Bethany's turn to lock up. Her dad had left to pick up her mom from yet another doctor's appointment. Mr. Everett had worked until 8:30 finishing up some details. After he left, Bethany spent the last fifteen minutes before closing scouring the premises to make sure nobody was in the building. She had no desire to see the small man behind locked doors again.

She shivered.

I wonder what he's up to?

She forced herself to take a breath. By all appearances, Bethany had decided to stay and work late. She did have plenty to do. The 50th Anniversary Celebration was only two weeks away, and for every solution two new problems sprouted and took root.

Her real reason for staying had nothing to do with any of that.

She wanted to study the new map.

As far as historical societies were concerned, donations were the bread and butter. No historical society could function without the help of the locals digging through their old stuff and bringing it forth. Usually, the donor who provided an artifact was well known. This time, however, an intriguing mystery gift had been donated: a map from the early 1920s, detailing a system of underground tunnels in Old Town.

Bethany had lived her entire life in Wilson and never heard a peep about them.

Does anybody even know these exist?

In truth, these kinds of tunnels were scattered all over the state of Colorado under various cities and locations. Howard Carlyle's strange overprotectiveness of WDC2 property had kept everything about Old Town a secret.

Did he even know about these?

Yesterday, the postal service delivered the map via a plain brown box. After opening it, they spread it before them in Mr. Clark's office. Bethany, her dad, and Mr. Everett crowded around and discussed their strategy. As of now, only the three of them knew about the gift.

That would change Thursday at the community meeting.

Mr. Clark insisted on adding an agenda item. He said the community should be allowed to discuss the question of the tunnels prior to the 50th Anniversary Celebration, especially since there were rumors of WDC2 being sold. He told Bethany and Mr. Everett that Donald Carlyle would let him know any day if they had an official offer to purchase the company. The plan was to announce the final decision at the celebration.

In the days since Jordan's unapologetic "two plus three" banter, Bethany had begun paying attention. For the past couple weeks, as she sorted through all kinds of history, she observed with fresh eyes. Doubts about the official narrative clawed at her.

She told her dad none of this.

Besides the map, two things happened that day that caused her insides to churn like laundry on spin cycle. First, she had awoken under a fresh burden for her mother and spent the early morning crying out to God. Around lunchtime, she arrived at work with heavier makeup than usual.

She held it together and had gradually calmed down as the afternoon passed into the evening. Amidst her eagerness to see the map, the minutes plodded by until Mr. Everett left and Bethany could lock the doors at closing time.

Back at the information desk, she clicked on her one unread email before logging off and gasped. Her heart cranked back into spin cycle as the second big thing of the day slammed her.

Dear Bethany,

Seek for two letters from the past
    Small number, don't you think?
Yes, just two, written one after the other
    Link Ray Clark's death and what ails your mother

Many times, the truth lurks below the surface. If you
need a hint, go underground and go northeast. It's best if you
don't speak of this communication. The danger is more than
you know.
Sincerely,
R3

With the place to herself, Bethany plopped down in one of the many study coves and tried to relax. She read the email over and over on her phone.

Spin cycle ratcheted up to agitate as she squeezed the sides of her phone.

Lord, what is this?

She stared at it.

What could this mean?

Where are the two letters?

She got up to pace and read it a few more times.

Who is R3?

Back at the information desk, Bethany looked over her shoulder as she printed the email, folded it, and stuffed it into her pocket. Two days ago, the possibility of going underground and going anywhere would have sounded ridiculous.

Now she knew exactly what it meant.

Stepping into her dad's office, she pulled open the file cabinet to get some alone time with the new map. Hands shaking, she spread it out on her dad's desk and tried to get a sense of the underground layout. It reminded her of the Roman catacombs of the first century—an elaborate system of tunnels that spanned a large portion of Old Town.

She tried to orient herself.

Okay, there's the clock tower.

The grange was near the left side of the map.

Main Street had several places where tunnels crisscrossed underneath.

Where is the northeasternmost point?

Her near-perfect sense of pitch did not extend to her sense of directions. She needed some pictures. She had just retrieved her phone from her pocket when the outer door closed with a loud click.

A surge of freak-out juice shot through her. The tiny man with caverns for eyes filled her imagination. She bit down hard on her lip and stuffed her phone back in her pocket. She grabbed the map off the desk, rolled it in one swift motion, and stashed it back into the cabinet. Reaching for the switch, she clicked off the light and stepped out of her dad's office.

"What are you still doing here?"

Bethany's heart slammed into her ribs.

"Oh, Mr. Everett"—she panted as she tried to buy some time—"you scared me." Her pulse throbbed in her neck.

"You sure you should be doing that?" The librarian pulled down his glasses and peered over the top of them.

"Doing what, sir?" She breathed in little gulps.

"Poking around after hours in your dad's office. Does he know what you're up to?"

"What makes you think I'm *up* to anything?" said Bethany with a slight edge. She was glad for the semi-darkness of the office building after hours.

"Oh, nothing. I just know the celebration is coming up. Like your dad, I have instructions from Mr. Carlyle to make it as smooth as possible. I just want to make sure there's nothing he needs to be aware of."

"That makes sense. Well, I've got to get home. Good night." Bethany walked past him and shuddered.

I didn't miss my calling as a spy.

● ● ●

Bethany wasn't the only one working late tonight.

Seated behind the steering wheel, laptop open to his right, Isaac Molencki had watched her for two hours. Three hidden cameras that he had placed in the library yesterday provided a real-time feed. He was getting good at staying hidden in the library building, even with the doors locked. He smiled at the memory of his first meeting with Bethany.

His focus had primarily been on the Nolan family until now. That was what he was being paid for, and something was brewing. However, that "something" somehow included Bethany Clark.

Fine with me.

After he'd gotten over the initial shock, Isaac liked the idea of staking out someone that resembled a younger version of the former love of his life.

Is it possible they're related?

He didn't think so, but every so often she did something that bore an uncanny resemblance to Elizabeth. Over the last two weeks, even with his focus elsewhere, he grew accustomed to the calm with which Bethany carried herself. But not tonight. Something was bothering her.

In a separate window on his computer screen, he switched from real-time and rolled it back a few minutes.

He pushed pause.

There.

The monitor showed Bethany at the information desk, seated behind her computer. For a fleeting second, now caught on video, her face registered shock.

Something on the screen spooked her.

He inched the tape forward as she went to the printer and pulled off a page. She read over it, folded it, and stashed it in her pocket. She glanced over her shoulder.

What are you up to, Bethany?

He lost track of her when she entered her dad's office. Something in there mattered. He switched back to real time.

The old librarian, Mr. Everett, had walked up and was speaking with Bethany. She ended the conversation and walked past him. Isaac paused the tape again and backed it up a few frames. He stopped just as she walked past the old man.

"You look guilty," Isaac said with a chuckle.

He closed the lid on his laptop. Yes, *something* was definitely up.

We Need to Talk

Wednesday, July 30, 3:15 p.m.
Jordan's room, Wilson, CO

Jordan sat at his desk and sighed. There were only two options. He perused his diary entry once again.

Under the grange options

Option 1: Do nothing and forget the whole thing

Option 2: Walk onto WDC2 property and dig a hole through the floor of the grange

No wonder R3 said this path will likely not take me through DC

Do I want to risk my future for this?
Can something be illegal and still be right?

He pulled up his internship ticker.

25 days, 15 hours, 14 minutes, 17 seconds
25 days, 15 hours, 14 minutes, 16 seconds
25 days, 15 hours, 14 minutes, 15 seconds

Less than four weeks.

No time to be breaking the law.

Jordan stared at the ticker just as an email from Gadg landed in his inbox. To take his mind off the present predicament, he opened it. An ever-so-slight touch of sadness blew through him, there and gone like the wind. Mostly, he was relieved. Jeffrey Kingston had just announced that an eighteen-year-old graduating senior from Fort Collins had been chosen as the senator's wild-card pick.

For the second time in five years, Jordan was going to Washington, and Matthew was staying in Wilson.

Love your enemies.

The verse kept coming to mind at strange places and curious times. Jordan shook his head and repeated the phrase again, "Lord, I ask you to bless Matthew."

Looking back down, he tried to refocus on his work, but he couldn't. "I do want his highest good." Jordan spun around in his desk chair. He said to his closet, "Even if he is a jerk." He looked up. "Lord, please have mercy on him."

He would not do the same to me.

It was true. If Jordan got caught trying to dig his way under the grange, Matthew would laugh all the way to Washington.

He looked again at the diary entry. "Lord, is there no other way?"

● ● ●

His phone buzzed in one hand as he gripped the arm of his desk chair with the other. A name cascaded from the top of the screen and appeared in the banner.

> **Bethany Clark.**

He stood up from his desk and walked over to the couch on the other side of the room. He held his phone as if it were a porcelain doll.

> **Confidential: we need to talk.**

Desire sprayed his insides like an aerosol can with a lighter. He took a deep breath.

> **Can you come by the café?**

He texted back a little too quickly but hoped it came across as suave.

> **Certainly.**

> **Bring Gadg if you can.**

He closed his eyes as his face reddened. His pulse thumped the inside of his neck. Of course she wouldn't want to speak with him alone.

"Dude, you need to *chill*," he spoke aloud to himself. "What are you thinking? Put it out of your mind." He took a few more deep breaths, slower this time.

> **What's this about?**

He texted back. His eyes widened when he read the reply.

> **I need a math lesson.**

Chapter 48

Math Lesson

Wednesday, July 30, 3:45 p.m.
Old Town Café, Wilson, CO

"Jordan, check this out," said Gadg.

Jordan's mind bounced between "love your enemies" and Bethany's last text as he sat down in a booth at the Old Town Café and looked across the street at the library/historical society. The last community meeting before the 50th Anniversary Celebration was on the calendar for tomorrow. "Check what out?" asked Jordan.

Gadg wore stock, black-framed glasses that enlarged his eyes and made them look alarming. His hair was curly, and it wasn't so much long as it was big. Every once in a while, Jordan felt like Gadg just needed a white coat to complete the sixties rocket scientist look. This was one of those times. He cocked his head and looked at Jordan with a funny expression.

"What is with you?" asked Jordan.

Gadg got out his phone, tapped it a few times, and held it in front of Jordan's face.

Jordan watched a picture of himself look back and say, "What is with you?" Raised eyebrows pulled the corners of his mouth upwards into a smile. He leaned closer, peering at Gadg's face. "Where is it?"

Gadg peeled off his glasses and handed them over.

"Wow, I still can't see it," said Jordan, examining them carefully.

"Not it, but them," Gadg used his finger to point out two very small cameras embedded in the frame and a tiny microphone that spread the length of the bridge. Both blended seamlessly into the structure of the glasses.

"Let me guess—new toy from your dad, courtesy of the force?"

Gadg smiled as he put the glasses back on. "I'm demoing three models— glasses, hat, and collared shirt. It has a surprisingly large-capacity hard drive to store the captured video."

"How is it powered? Battery?"

Gadg nodded. "Also tiny—and rechargeable."

"Connectivity?" asked Jordan.

"Bluetooth, Wi-Fi, even cellular. It has a mode that can stream without saving locally. That's what I just showed you. It streamed to my phone. Well, technically, it streamed to a server in the cloud that my phone got it from."

"Serious geek points on that one," Jordan gave him a fist bump.

"What's this about?" Gadg changed the subject. "Your message was cryptic."

"Thanks for coming." Jordan handed over his phone with just a hint of a smile. "Check *this* out."

● ● ●

In the ladies' room, Bethany hid behind the door of the closed stall, pretending to be there for other reasons. Page in hand, she reread the printout of the email from R3.

"Daddy," she held it up as if God needed to be shown what she was talking about, "what do I do with this?"

She stared at one line.

Link Ray Clark's death and what ails your mother.

Questions barraged her mind.

Is this a joke?

Could it be true?

How could those two things be linked?

Who is R3?

Some fifty years later, the message said the answer was in two letters. She had to find them. She also knew she needed help. But who could she tell?

He would be here any minute.

Can I trust him? I mean really trust him?

She folded up the paper and stashed it under her apron in the front pocket of her jeans.

It was time to find out.

● ● ●

"Good afternoon, gentlemen." Bethany walked up and stood over them with a pitcher of ice water in her hand. Across the room, two students from Wilson Community College were the only other patrons.

"Good afternoon, Miss Clark," said Jordan.

"Hi, Bethany," said Gadg.

"Do I need to be concerned about this?" Jordan flipped his fingers toward the pitcher of water.

"I don't see why." Bethany offered her most innocent tone. "I wouldn't do anything you wouldn't *approve of*." She filled Jordan's glass and gave a quick bounce with her eyebrows.

He scooped up a menu as a dash of red appeared on his neck just behind the jaw.

She stifled a smirk.

Focus, Bethany.

"That's not very comforting," said Jordan. Without looking up, he switched to his attorney voice and said, "Miss Clark, I must say, that was a most unusual text I received from you today."

"Tell me about it." She poured a glass for Gadg, set down the pitcher, and pulled a pad from her apron.

"Well, I'm pretty good at math," Jordan spoke to the appetizers as if he were trying to disarm a hostile witness. "Gadg is exceptional. What can we help you with?"

Bethany stood before the limb, debating whether to step onto it. "Can you confirm that two plus two cannot equal five?"

"I think I can. However, two plus *three* does equal five." Jordan peeked at her and changed to a playful tone. "Why do you ask?"

She wiped both hands on her apron. "What do you know about the death of Ray Clark?"

Jordan raised an eyebrow. "I know he was murdered."

"You do? I thought you said he and William were best friends."

"I did."

"I told you the other day that best friends don't murder each other."

"Yes, you did. But that was before our math lesson."

Bethany stopped to think. "Jordan, I think I see what you're getting at, but I can't bring myself to believe it."

"What am I getting at?" asked Jordan.

"Somebody else killed Ray."

"Why is that so hard to believe?"

"At the death scene, signs of a struggle were everywhere. Ray's blood was all over William's clothes. Several long scratches from Ray's fingers were identified on William's cheek and neck. William's hat was found right next to Ray's dead body."

"That's true," said Jordan.

"Don't you find that incriminating?"

"How did Ray actually die?" asked Jordan.

"From a gunshot wound," said Bethany.

"What kind of a gun?"

"I don't know. The articles didn't say."

"Gadg dug it up from the police archives," said Jordan.

She looked at Gadg. "You did? What was it?"

"It was a Winchester *rifle*," said Gadg.

Bethany's brow furrowed. "That doesn't make any sense. Why would there be a hand-to-hand struggle if he was killed with a rifle?"

"Good question," said Jordan.

Bethany looked at Gadg. "Do *you* think it was somebody else?"

"Off the record?"

Bethany nodded.

"Let's just say that certain people might have found it quite convenient if it *appeared* that one of them murdered the other."

"What are you saying?"

"He's saying things are not always as they *appear*," said Jordan.

"Do you have anybody in mind when you guys say 'certain people?'"

Jordan's eyes gave a fraction of a flicker. "We're not sure, so we're not saying much on that point. Let's just say there could be people—powerful people—who may not want the official narrative to change."

You better watch yourself, girl. What would your dad think of this?

Bethany paused.

It doesn't matter. I need to know.

She stepped out on the limb. "Is there any way Ray Clark's death could relate to something in the present day?"

Jordan and Gadg exchanged poker-faced glances. "That is an interesting question, Miss Clark. Will you sit for a moment?" Jordan set his menu down and motioned with an open hand to the other side of the booth.

Gadg scooted over and Bethany took the seat across from Jordan.

"*Bethany*," his voice was quiet and tender, "can I trust you? I mean *really* trust you?"

Her heart ignited. She loved the way he said her name. She loved that he used the same words—her words. She stared back and searched his face.

It was intense, resolute, and honest.

She let out a long, slow breath. Leaning back in the booth, she reached into her jeans pocket and pulled out the folded email from R3.

She set it on the table and slid it toward Jordan. With a smile and lift of her hand, she sawed the tree limb off behind her. "Yes, you can."

● ● ●

Jordan's heart blazed.

The power of her trust rolled over him like a wave. He pushed down a gulp as he reached for the message. The paper made an awkward scraping sound as he fumbled an attempt to unfold it. When he finally got it open, his head looked like an old typewriter going back and forth over the lines. His gaze went vacant as he processed the data. On autopilot, he handed the paper to Gadg.

Gadg stared at it like he was trying to absorb it by osmosis. He then refolded it and set it facedown on the table.

"When?" said Jordan, coming back into the moment.

"I received it last night." Bethany slid it from the table and made it vanish into her pocket.

"We've got to find those letters," said Jordan.

"So, you think it's real?"

"How did you feel when you read it?"

"It's either a sadistic joke," said Bethany, "or—"

"Or it's true," said Jordan. "That was how I felt too."

"Just now?"

"No. When *I* received an email from R3."

"You got one too?"

"And a letter," said Gadg.

"You did?" Bethany's face lit up. "You didn't receive *two* letters, did you?"

"I wish." Jordan smiled and shook his head. "That would have been too easy. I'm not even sure my letter counts as one of the two letters."

"It's a cryptic name. R3. Any idea who it is?" asked Bethany.

Jordan shrugged.

"What did the messages say?"

"Oh, nothing much. They hinted at a cover-up, all but said that William Nolan was murdered, and told me that I hold Pandora's Box in my hand, and that the truth would likely not lead through DC."

"Jordan, what's happening here?"

He sneaked a glance over his shoulder to make sure no one was listening. "Here's where I trust you with all of it." He paused. "The evidence to exonerate my great-grandfather is under the old grange."

Bethany's face went white.

"What is it?"

"Depending on how this conversation went..." Bethany paused.

"You mean, depending on whether you could trust me?"

"Yeah. I came to tell you a second thing," Bethany continued. "We received a mystery gift at the historical society earlier this week." Her eyes darted. "A map of the tunnels under Old Town."

"What?" His whisper was fierce.

She nodded.

"Are you serious? There are tunnels? You don't suppose—"

"I *don't* suppose. I *know*. I saw it."

"Saw what?"

"A tunnel that goes under the grange."

Jordan's mouth dropped open. His face looked like a mainframe computer processing through lines of code. He turned to Gadg. "This thing is bigger than we imagined."

"I know," said Gadg. "It's Pandora's Box."

A shadow passed over Jordan's face.

"What is it?" asked Bethany.

"I was just asking the Lord if there was another way. Why don't I feel better now that there is?"

"Because of the risk," said Bethany. "You go underground, and you really are opening Pandora's Box. If you find that evidence..." she trailed off.

Jordan turned to Gadg.

"Bethany's right," said Gadg. "The risks are real. Finding the evidence might just be the *beginning* of your problems. However, this is an opportunity to clear the Nolan name."

Jordan pulled up the internship ticker, set his phone down, and stared at it. Elbow on the table, he closed his eyes and rubbed his forehead.

After a long moment, Bethany lowered her voice and said, "Jordan, can I trust *you*?"

Even before he opened his eyes, his mind went back to the playground where an eight-year-old girl had wiped away his tears.

If you ask me to walk to the ends of the earth, I'll do it.

"Of course," was all he said out loud. He opened his eyes. "Why do you ask?"

"I need to tell you something." She bit her lip. "I hate the dark. I hate cramped, claustrophobic places. I was kind of hoping ... you know ... you guys might ..."

"Go with you?"

"Yes," Bethany blurted, miserably. "I have to go. I hate it, but I must. I'd feel a whole lot better if I didn't have to go alone."

Using his thumb, Jordan switched off the screen of his phone. He sat up straight and smiled. "If there's any chance we can find out what's wrong with your mother, you're right, we must go."

Bethany looked back with gratitude. A tiny sheen of sweat, like she'd just dodged a bullet, reflected the late afternoon light off her forehead.

"At least we can take our time planning this out," said Jordan.

The color drained again from her face.

His smile receded. "What's the problem?"

"You know that community meeting tomorrow night?"

"Yes, what about it?"

Bethany's face tightened. "Everybody in Wilson is going to learn about the map."

Dear William and Ray,

Will it do any good to say it again?

I'm sorry.

As a form of penance, I've spent my life researching the scope of the damage that I did. I know that sounds morbid, but I didn't have much else to do. It's strange not having a care in the world as far as my physical, material needs. I've never had to worry about even the smallest things.

Let me give you an example. I got a speeding ticket once. Yes, long ago. I went to show up for my court date, and I was told that there was no record that I had ever received one. When I walked out of the courthouse I saw the Man.

He smiled at me.

You see? I've had the dream life - not a material care in the world. Except that it's been a living nightmare.

I've not had to work a single day. The Man made sure I was well taken care of. So what have I done? I've had a hobby. You guessed it - research.

I've spent my life discovering the full extent of my cowardice. I've done it in secret, of course. I could never do this openly. I've collected any article, anecdote, or scrap of anything related to it. The worst part, of course, are those that are still living. Even in this county, there are some that continue to suffer.

Will you forgive me?

Chapter 49

The Catacombs

Thursday, July 31, 3:30 p.m.
Wilson County Historical Society Building, Wilson, CO

Preparations for the 50th Anniversary Celebration and the subsequent restoration of Old Town had kicked into full swing. Things were buzzing in the historical building. The last community meeting open to the public before the celebration would start in a few hours.

Bethany had been working up her courage all afternoon. Tonight was the night. It had to be. Her dad had taken her mom to Denver on a last-minute opportunity to meet with Jeffrey Kingston about the celebration. It was the only time Mr. Kingston could meet. Afterward, Mr. and Mrs. Clark would enjoy some time together before the big push of the final two weeks.

That made this even more difficult.

Okay, Lord. It's now or never. Please help me.

"Mr. Everett," Bethany said. Her voice came out with a bit of a squeak.

Easy girl.

"Yes?" The corners of Mr. Everett's mouth looked pulled down by the weight of the world.

"If I work extra hard this afternoon, can I get off work at 6:45?"

"Tonight? What about the meeting?"

"I was hoping you could let me know if there's anything I need to be aware of."

"Bethany, it's not a good time for this."

"Please, Mr. Everett," Bethany looked pained. "I need to do something for my mother."

That's true enough.

Mr. Everett crossed his arms. He tilted his head and studied her. "You do?"

"Yes, sir, I do."

He relaxed his arms. "Okay, I guess it will be all right."

"Thank you, sir. I owe you one."

Mr. Everett nodded. Bethany turned and walked toward the information desk. She put both hands on the desk and let out a pent-up breath.

Thank you, God.

She sat down, launched a new email, and tried to look busy. Heart still doing rapid-fire, she let some time pass.

One down, one to go.

As the afternoon wore on, Bethany made round trips to and from her dad's office every few minutes. On one of these trips, she opened the cabinet and pulled out the map of Old Town's underground tunnel system. Trying to look harried, she brought it out and set it amidst the papers and photos she had strategically cluttered a table with. She picked up a newspaper article with one hand and an old photo with the other. She held them up as if trying to compare them.

Just then Gadg walked up. "Hi Bethany, you got a sec?"

"Oh, hi Gadg. Sure. What's up?"

From the corner of her eye, she saw Mr. Everett look over from the information desk and see them talking.

The conversation was drowned out by the bustle around them. Bethany held the items out in front of her as Gadg looked over her shoulder. She pointed at the article with the hand holding the photo.

"Thanks, Bethany. That helps."

In truth, it did help. Bethany held the papers at such an angle that Gadg could look just under them and get a highly educational view of the map.

● ● ●

Jordan and Tyler walked down the sidewalk and passed the Old Town Café. Jordan chuckled as Tyler looked with longing at the menu taped on the inside of the glass. They still had not had a chance to share a meal at the café.

Gadg crossed the street and joined them.

"Did you get a look at it?" asked Jordan.

"I sure did. Bethany was very helpful."

"What did you find?"

"You're not going to believe where we start."

● ● ●

Pulling the creaky door shut, Jordan, Tyler, and Gadg stepped back into the abandoned cellar on Nolan property.

"You really think so?" said Jordan.

"I know so," Gadg replied. "I got a great look at the map. There's no doubt."

Jordan walked over to the old shelves, got down on his knees and pulled back the trap door.

Last time, they'd been so preoccupied with finding the treasure that they didn't think much about what might lay beyond it. This time, they shined their phones straight into the hole in the wall. The black abyss both beckoned and repelled them.

"Okay, gentlemen, we've got one shot at this. Bethany assured us that the map would be made known to the community tonight."

"Why is that a problem?" asked Tyler.

"There's no way the town is going to just let the public waltz down into these tunnels," said Gadg.

"Even worse than that," Jordan continued, "it's possible that whoever authorized the fence around the Grande bridge will ask for the tunnels to be sealed immediately. Think about it. Someone knows we're looking for something important. Hidden evidence plus underground tunnels equal a toxic combination for anyone who wants to keep a secret."

"What about Alex?" asked Tyler.

"Good point," said Jordan. "He won't be far behind."

Gadg looked Jordan in the eye. "Some of the tunnels go under WDC2 property."

Jordan looked away. "I know. We've got an hour, maybe an hour and a half." He tapped his foot.

"So, what are we waiting for?" asked Tyler.

The phone buzzed in Jordan's hand. "This is Jordan,"

"Jordan, this is Bethany," she said in a quiet voice.

Gadg chuckled. Even in the dim light of their phones, Jordan's face had brightened more than he had intended. He turned away from the guys and faced the old cellar wall. "Hello, Miss Clark. Where are you?"

"I'm at the store. Did you find it?" No pleasantries.

"Find what?"

"What Gadg was looking for today."

"We just did."

"Where?"

"Where an eighteenth-century treasure was found a few weeks ago," said Jordan, assuming she could be overheard. Yesterday in the café, Jordan and Gadg had told her about the cellar.

"I'll be right there."

The phone went dead. Seven minutes later Bethany peeked her head down into the cellar. "Hi, guys."

In the natural light coming through the cracked opened door, Jordan adjusted his eyes and glanced at Gadg.

Bethany's face, with set jaw and eyes wide, reflected a mixture of determination, bravery, and terror.

"You sure you're up for this?" Jordan asked.

"I don't want to talk about it." Bethany stepped down into the cellar.

Jordan looked at her outfit.

Her blouse was so new it was practically neon. Pleated white shorts just above the knee, colored socks that matched the top, and brand-new white, summer walking shoes completed the look.

Jordan turned to the guys. "If we get lost, or our phones go out, we can just follow Bethany's glow."

"I didn't have time to change." Bethany shuddered. "Let's just go."

Jordan nodded and put his fist in the air. "For my great-grandfather."

Tyler and Gadg reached their fists out and touched Jordan's. They turned and looked at Bethany.

She put her fist up to the others and smiled at Jordan. "For *our* great-grandfathers—and my mom."

Jordan's smile was genuine. "Let's go. Tyler, would you get the door?"

Tyler closed the cellar, and each in turn stooped down and crawled through the trap door into the tunnel. Once inside, they scrambled a few feet, stood up, and closed it behind them.

"Turn off your phones for a second," said Jordan.

They did. It was pitch black. There was simply, and absolutely, no light.

"Creepy," said Jordan, turning his phone back on. "I still can't believe we're starting from here."

Gadg turned his phone on and shined the flashlight up into the ceilings of the underground tunnels. "Guys, look at this."

"What?" said Tyler.

"That's a steel girder," said Gadg.

The others looked at it.

"This has to be one of the most solidly built underground tunnel systems in Colorado," he continued. "They're common in our state, but I didn't know we had any in Wilson."

"Are they safe?" asked Bethany.

"You know how we've had it hammered into our heads by the adults to never go into any of the abandoned mines?" said Gadg.

"Yes," said Jordan. "They're deathtraps."

"I thought the same would hold true for the tunnels," Gadg continued. "But whoever built these built them to last."

"Why didn't we know about them?" asked Bethany.

"Howard Carlyle again?" asked Tyler.

"It's possible," said Jordan, "but I'm guessing he didn't even know about them." He turned to Gadg. "Did you see enough of the map to see any other entrances?"

"There aren't many," said Gadg, shaking his head. "If they've stayed hidden like this one, it's no surprise they've remained secret for so long."

"I hate to think what they were actually used for," offered Bethany, looking around.

"Like what?" asked Tyler.

"Don't think too hard. It won't take you down a good path," said Bethany.

"I'm sure it wasn't to go to the store for groceries," said Jordan.

Tyler grimaced.

"Wilson's history is pretty rough around the edges," said Gadg.

"For the last part of the nineteenth century and the first part of the twentieth, it was rough in the center," said Bethany.

"Let's get going," said Jordan. "Gadg, you on it?"

Gadg looked down at his phone, tapped it a few times and started off.

Chapter 50

Answers and Questions

Thursday, July 31, 7:40 p.m.
Clark home, Wilson, CO

It was time to get some answers.

The one called the mole stepped in the back door of the Clark home and pulled it closed behind him. It was still broad daylight but tempered with the golden glow of a summer evening in Colorado.

He could feel the gentle squish of well-worn leather against his hand as he released the door handle. He smiled and shook his head. More communities should be like Wilson. Ranch style homes. Welcome mats.

These people don't even lock their doors.

His biggest risk was being too careless. It had taken all of thirty minutes to plan.

Bethany's schedule had her working all afternoon and evening. Her dad was in Denver meeting with Jeffrey Kingston about the senator's final logistics for the 50th Anniversary Celebration. He had taken his wife with him to spend a couple nights in Denver. Apparently she had some illness, and this was a chance to get away and rest. Mr. Everett would facilitate the community meeting at the historical society in his absence. Down to the last three weeks before the celebration, and it was divide-and-conquer with all the tasks that needed to be done.

With Bethany's mother gone for two days, Allie had some time off. Isaac chuckled. Matthew Harris would keep her occupied tonight at a fancy restaurant.

He strolled into Bethany's bedroom. A little high-tech surveillance earlier in the week had yielded the important fact that Bethany kept a diary stashed under her mattress near the head of the bed.

The penmanship was a beautiful, flowing script.

He knew he didn't have much time, but even so, he wanted to see if there was an entry from July 11th or 12th—somewhere around the night he had freaked her out in the library after the doors were locked. He flipped past a few pages that looked interesting.

There it is.

This particular entry looked different somehow. The ink was pressed harder into the page and the letters looked edgier and more ragged.

He smiled.

She's afraid.

He took his time to read through it.

> *July 11 – Lord, I was scared out of my socks tonight.*
> *I just met the creepiest man I've ever seen in my life.*
> *A half-hour after I locked the doors at work, a man*
> *– ALONE INSIDE THE BUILDING WITH ME*
> *– asks me for information. It may have just been*
> *the dim lighting, but his eyes looked like pictures of*
> *Crater Lake at night. It was ominous.*
>
> *I have no idea what he's really here for. Something*
> *doesn't seem right.*
>
> *Lord, I'm sorry. I told two lies tonight. I told him*
> *it was nice to meet him. I also told him that I'd be*
> *glad to talk to him later. I know I was trying to be*
> *polite, but that wasn't the slightest bit true. Is it too*
> *much to ask to never see him again for the rest of*
> *my life?*
>
> *I don't know when I will, but I have this nagging*
> *feeling it will be a time and place I don't expect.*
> *Daddy, I'm in Your hands. Please protect me.*

Satisfied, he nodded at the page. Good. There was nothing wrong with enjoying one's job.

His gloves fit like another layer of skin. He could leaf through pages with abandon, almost better than he could with bare hands. He continued with several entries that mentioned Jordan Nolan. Bethany thought he was going nowhere in life.

Or did she? One curious line caught his attention.

Lord, I need You to help me put this out of my mind.

Hmmm. She's conflicted.

He liked when the job called for interesting twists. Making sure Jordan didn't find anything incriminating against WDC2 or Donald Carlyle was the main gig. How about a little drama on the side?

He looked at his watch.

Okay, back to business.

It was time to see if there was anything worth seeing. In the last few days, Bethany considered possibilities she'd previously dismissed. It was clear that Jordan, and his friend Gadg, did not buy the official report about Ray Clark's death. The pace of the entries picked up speed as he approached the present day.

July 29 – Daddy, this day was insane. I don't know where to start. I guess I'll start with Mom. What's wrong with her? Will You not see my tears? What's it going to take to make her well? Please, God, will You not hear my cry? Daddy, I'm all Yours.

The ink was now dry, but it wasn't dry yesterday when it was written. A smear sliced across the page and blurred the last few words. The mole paused. His heart pounded as thoughts he hadn't had in years forced their way into his mind. He was a little boy cowering in his room.

No!

He turned the page so fiercely that a small rip appeared near the spine. He exhaled to calm himself.

This was ridiculous.

Former Special Forces and undercover cop, he was a contract guy with ice in his veins. Yet an eighteen-year-old girl had gotten under his skin twice since he'd been here. He pinched his gloved fingers and gently pulled the torn part of the page until it was smooth and wouldn't be noticed.

In the diary, Bethany switched gears.

> *July 29 (continued) – Now comes the weird part. First, we received a map of the tunnels under Old Town. I had no idea they even existed. Then, to top it off, I receive the most cryptic email of my entire life. The message claims that the death of Ray Clark and my mother's illness are somehow related – that I need to search for and find a couple letters.*

Bethany did not put the text of the email into her diary.

> *I've got to talk to Jordan about this.*

Hmmm. Now we're getting somewhere.

> *July 30 – Spoke to Jordan (and Gadg) this evening. He is convinced the evidence to exonerate his great-grandfather is hidden under the old grange. I told him about the map and that one of the tunnels goes under the grange. Then I gave him the bad news – the map will be discussed at the community meeting tomorrow night. He said he'd call me tomorrow. He wouldn't say what he was thinking, but based on our conversation I'm guessing they're going after it. Daddy, is it possible that the answers for both of us are under Old Town? Oh my gosh, does it have to be underground? The message said to go underground and go northeast. I can't even think about it. Lord, You know I hate dark, tight places. Why are You doing this to me? You know I have to do this. Oh Daddy, help me.*

It was time to go. The night was young and there was still much to do. Bethany's desk was immaculate.

Perfect.

He set her diary down so the edges were precisely aligned with one of the front corners of the desk.

Thanks for sharing your thoughts, Bethany.

Opening the window, he climbed over the ledge, slid the window shut, and slipped out into the evening. The mole was going underground.

● ● ●

Donald stood on the veranda outside his office holding a glass of red wine and a cigar. Blowing out the remains of a long drag, he looked over the sprawling WDC2 campus and brooded. He needed answers. It seemed the only place he got any was from Isaac Molencki—a little twerp who unnerved him.

He looked down as his phone lit up. *Speak of the devil.* He answered on the first ring. "Donald Carlyle."

"Mr. Carlyle, Isaac Molencki here."

"Mr. Molencki, how are you?"

"That's the wrong question. Listen up."

Blue smoke choked him up as his cheeks blotched into uneven patterns on the lower half of his face.

Who does this weasel think he is?

All he said out loud was, "I'm listening."

"You got somebody at the community meeting?"

"Of course. What do you need?"

"That's a better question. I need a couple things. Here's the situation."

● ● ●

"This is Alex."

"Jones," Donald Carlyle's voice sounded like a blender struggling to chop large pieces of food. "Where are you?"

"Old Town Café. Why?"

"That figures. Find a couple guys and get ready."

"What's up?"

"What do you think?"

"They found something?"

"They *may* have found something, or at least they're on their way."

"What is it?"

"Jones, why am I always bringing you information and not the other way around?"

Alex bit down to keep from firing back. "Sir, what are you talking about?"

Donald explained what he had learned from the small man about the catacombs and the map.

"You think there's something down there?"

"Don't ask stupid questions. Whatever it is, we don't want them to find it. Is that understood?"

Alex squeezed his phone as he fought to keep his voice steady. "Absolutely."

"Any threat needs to be contained. I will not have this jeopardized. This is your last chance. Do you follow?"

"Yes, sir. I follow."

"Okay, listen up. Here's the deal..."

Chapter 51

2 + 3 = 5

Thursday, July 31, 8:25 p.m.
The tunnels under Old Town, Wilson, CO

Gadg navigated as they picked their way through rubble-strewn passages. Above ground, it seemed the most natural thing in the world to trust Gadg to get them to their destination. Underground, in an oppressive dark beaten back only by the meager light of their phones, Jordan wasn't so sure. He looked down at his own phone.

No signal.

No GPS.

No sense of direction.

I sure hope he knows what he's doing.

He glanced at his friend. Even though Jordan couldn't see much of Gadg's face, what he could see was all business. He nodded to himself. If anybody could get them there, it was Gadg.

Suddenly, they stopped. Gadg turned off his phone and cocked his head.

"Did you hear something?" asked Jordan.

"Shh. Turn off your phones," said Gadg.

All the lights went off. Jordan blinked, opened his eyes wide, and blinked again. It was like looking into a black hole. They stood for a moment, listening.

Gadg turned on his phone again. "Maybe it's nothing," he said.

"Something's going on," said Jordan. "Maybe not down here, but something has been brewing for a while in this town. I can feel it."

"Yeah," said Tyler with a big smile. "We have the chance to rewrite the history books."

"It's way more than that," said Jordan.

"What do you mean?" asked Tyler.

"This isn't just about solving a cold case from fifty years ago. This is present day."

"Why do you think that?" asked Bethany. They circled around Jordan.

Something about her question caused Jordan to do a double take. Because of the dark, he couldn't discern the meaning from looking at her, so he chose to answer the question at face value. "First, Alex has been watching us. Whether on his own or put up to it by someone else, I don't know. Second, he and Matthew tried their best to keep us from finding the clue on the ridge, even at that horrible hour of the morning."

"Don't forget the intimidation at the library," added Gadg.

"I haven't, believe me."

"They know we're looking for something," said Tyler.

"Definitely. But who is it really? As much as Alex hates my dad—and me—there's something about this that doesn't add up. Sneaking around isn't his style. Also, why now?"

Bethany spoke, "Guys, I need to share something with you."

Three heads turned.

Holding her phone under her chin, the light framed her face against the blackness of the catacombs. She had an app that cycled the screen background through various nature shots. A sunshine-laden field of wheat gilded her face as her melodic storytelling voice echoed off the century-old walls. "I thought about telling you this earlier—especially you, Jordan."

He was thankful for the dark that masked his face as his stomach did a back-flip.

"You know my coworker, Mr. Everett at the library? He told me that Mr. Carlyle instructed him to make sure everything went smoothly for the 50th Anniversary Celebration."

"What's wrong with that?" asked Tyler.

"He became suspicious when he saw me leaving my dad's office late at night. He's not normally that way."

"That kind of makes sense," said Jordan. "For obvious reasons, not the least of which is the fact that he is Alex's boss, Donald Carlyle has been on my short list of possibilities."

Gadg nodded. "Don't forget the Grande bridge."

"What about it?" said Bethany.

"Colorado Department of Transportation commissioned a study of it *the same week* we thought the clue was underneath it," said Gadg. "Mr. Olson, who is leading the study, was driving a brand-new Chevy Silverado at the same time."

"You don't think…"—Bethany paused—"he was bribed by Mr. Carlyle?"

Jordan nodded. "It's possible. If Howard Carlyle didn't want Old Town to be renovated because he was hiding something, who would be the most likely person to feel threatened if some clue about the past suddenly surfaced?"

"His son," said Bethany. "But Mr. Carlyle wouldn't commission his own head of security to break into your house, would he?"

"You think that was Alex?" said Tyler, turning to Jordan.

"I don't. When they tried to intimidate me at the library, I accused Alex of breaking into our house. Seeing his reaction, I don't think he did it. However, Gadg did confirm that someone wearing leather gloves touched the Bible after the blessing ceremony."

Bethany's face drained of color, and she took on a ghastly green hue as a moss-filled water scene reflected from under her chin.

"What is it?" asked Jordan. They leaned closer like kids on a camping trip listening to a scary story after the adults were asleep.

"Two weeks ago, I was closing up at the historical society," said Bethany. "I locked the doors, did some other work, and then went into my dad's office. Thirty minutes later, I heard a voice from the information desk saying, 'Excuse me, miss.'"

"I thought you locked the doors." said Jordan.

"I did," Bethany gave a shiver. "This guy was inside the building with me the whole time, and I didn't know it."

"Ewww," said Gadg.

"That's not the worst of it," said Bethany. "He had the spookiest eyes I've ever seen. He was maybe five feet tall and was wearing leather gloves."

Gadg turned to look at Jordan.

"What?" said Bethany.

"I may have seen him," said Gadg. "The morning we went to check out the Grande bridge. A small man stepped behind a tree and disappeared. What was his name?"

"Isaac Molencki," said Bethany. "He said he was in town to do some research related to the fiftieth anniversary of the Wonder Drug. I'm not sure I believed him. He was built more like a soldier than a reporter. I haven't seen him since, but somehow I feel that he is still around."

Each of the guys went silent, processing his thoughts.

"To top it all off," Bethany continued, "don't forget I received a message from R3."

"Do you have it with you?" asked Jordan.

Bethany found the email on her phone and read it aloud.

Dear Bethany,

Seek for two letters from the past
  Small number, don't you think?
Yes, just two, written one after the other
  Link Ray Clark's death and what ails your mother

Many times, the truth lurks below the surface. If you need a hint, go underground and go northeast. It's best if you don't speak of this communication. The danger is more than you know.

Sincerely,

R3

"Guys, I need your help," Bethany continued. "I did not go looking for this. The timing is bad. The implications are worse. The risk to my dad—not to mention myself—is significant. The only reason I'm doing this at all is because of the possibility of finding out what's going on with my mother. I bring it up down here because I need to go northeast."

"I agree," said Gadg. "May I see your phone again?" He sized up the email she had just read.

"Do we know anything more about R3?" asked Tyler.

"I've got one thought," said Bethany. "I'm guessing that whoever donated the map of these tunnels is R3."

"Why do you say that?" asked Jordan.

"Just a hunch," she said. "Did any of you even know these existed before the other day?"

They shook their heads.

"Neither did I," she continued. "This R3 knows a lot, and the timing is curious."

"So let me get this straight," said Jordan. "We have a message from fifty years ago telling us to go under the grange, and a message from the present telling us to go underground and go northeast." He paused. "Am I the only one who thinks this is bizarre?"

"I would too, except for one thing," said Bethany.

"What's that?"

"Because two plus three *must* equal five!" She broke into a grand smile. "This is not a conspiracy theory. What you said before is correct. Something is going on in this town—*right now.*" Her voice punched the last two words. "As much as I'd like to dismiss it, I can't anymore. It's the only reason I'm down in this beastly hole. I know it's true."

Jordan looked at her. A picture of a lightning strike across an otherwise black sky shined from the phone under her chin and lit her face with determination. He held his phone away from his face and took a deep breath.

Wow, she's beautiful.

He kept the phone angled away from his face to hide the heat rising on his cheeks. "Do you believe it?"

Bethany's eyes blazed. "Unfortunately, I do."

"Unfortunately?"

She switched to her most pronounced English accent. "It's terribly inconvenient, Mr. Nolan, having to pursue multiple secrets shrouded in lies and danger. Such a dreadful bother."

Jordan exhaled. The fire in his gaze was rekindled. Any remaining doubts were pushed out of the way.

Gadg coughed. "This way," he said. "It's not northeast, but it moves us close to the grange."

"Let's go there first," said Bethany.

Jordan liked how she said "first."

Chapter 52

The Evidence

Thursday, July 31, 8:40 p.m.
The tunnels under Old Town, Wilson, CO

Two minutes later, Gadg said, "It's on the other side of this wall."

"You are the man!" Tyler said.

Using their hands as much as their eyes, they searched along the wall until they spotted the clear outlines of a door. Jordan reached out to touch it as if it might bite. Trembling, his hands came to rest on a small hole that was just wide enough to insert two fingers.

Except for the trembling in his hands, he didn't move. He just stared at the door.

They all stood still and didn't make a sound.

"Could it really be?" said Jordan in a wistful tone.

"Let's find out," said Bethany.

Jordan pulled hard. Nothing happened. He pushed, and though it was a bit stiff, the door opened on the first try. His heart thumped against his chest as he stepped into the room.

The others followed with their phones out. It appeared to have once been a cellar, perhaps for the kitchen.

"Are we under the grange?" Jordan sounded like a child on Christmas morning.

Gadg pointed to some stairs on the opposite side of the room. "Best as I can tell, those lead to the creepy kitchen area at the back of the grange."

The stairs led up to a door.

"We didn't see a door in that room last time we looked," Tyler pointed out.

"That's true," said Gadg.

"I'll check it," Tyler said as he scampered across the room and ascended the steps.

Jordan hardly heard the discussion.

Is it possible? Could I be ten feet from the end of the Nolan Stigma?

The light of his phone danced on a side wall as he scoured the room.

Tyler was busy with the door. He pulled it open about ten inches. No matter—it would do. Tyler squeezed through it and then poked his head back into the room. "Great job, Gadg. It's creepier than ever, but I'm in the back room of the grange."

Jordan continued his sweep of the room and shined his light up toward Tyler. "Oh!" he blurted.

"What?" Gadg and Bethany said, spinning around.

Jordan rushed over to the steps and laughed out loud. "Love is still the key!" he said. On the front wall, just to the right of the steps, crudely drawn but unmistakably clear, was a faded Nolan crest with a heart around it. An arrow pointed diagonally down to the left at a forty-five-degree angle.

Jordan shined his phone under the stairs to reveal a layer of dirt covering the wood of a high-quality cigar box. He handed his phone to Gadg and reached down to pull it up.

Bethany helped brush aside the dirt, and a Caribbean plantation with the words "Hacienda Grande" stared up at them.

Jordan unlatched it, lifted the lid, and stared down.

With only his head poking into the room, Tyler asked, "What is it?"

Jordan looked up with eyes full of wonder. "Paydirt."

● ● ●

Tyler squeezed back in and hurried down the stairs.

"Gadg, can you give me some light?" said Jordan. His words came out with a squeak.

Gadg held his phone like a reading lamp while Jordan did a speed-read through some of the artifacts.

Bethany did her best to look over his shoulder and keep up. Her eyes were wide and her mouth hung open. She couldn't read the artifacts, but it was clear from her face that she believed they were genuine.

Tyler could stand it no longer. "What did you get?"

"Evidence," Jordan said, head still buried in the papers. "The top item was a memo to Carlyle Enterprises Management on the side effects of XD."

"The drug?" asked Bethany.

"Yes, and you're not going to believe this." He kept reading and went silent.

Bethany gave an excited whisper, "Jordan, we're not going to believe what?"

"Oh, sorry." He looked up and gathered himself. "Here's the scoop: 1964 time frame, Carlyle Enterprises, soon-to-be renamed to Wilson Drug and Compounding Center, has a big deal in the works to sell Amitolin, later called the Wonder Drug, to Hampden Pharmaceuticals. The deal is getting near to closing and the executives of Carlyle Enterprises, especially Howard Carlyle, stand to make a fortune."

"Which they did," answered Gadg.

Bethany nodded.

"At about the same time," continued Jordan, "Hampden Pharmaceuticals is gearing up to release another drug, called XD, to the market." He looked at Bethany, "Our great-grandfathers, researchers at Carlyle Enterprises, were testing for possible side effects of XD. They began to see what XD really was, and brought their concerns to the Carlyle Enterprises leadership."

"Let me guess," said Bethany, "they were told to shut up and stop looking into it."

"You got it. This evidence indicates that they were seriously threatened, and that they and their families would be taken out if they didn't drop it immediately."

"The old Bible alludes to that," said Gadg.

Jordan nodded. "This spells it out. Look." He turned one of the documents toward Gadg.

"If there was evidence, why would Carlyle Enterprises management risk a cover-up?" asked Bethany.

"They may not have known about the evidence. William and Ray were accumulating it in secret," said Gadg.

"Agreed," said Jordan. "Do you remember Plan A and Plan B from the old Bible? It's all here: Plan A was to accumulate enough evidence to go public, quickly and safely."

"How could that be safe?" asked Tyler.

"Safe only because it was public," said Gadg. "The attention would protect them and their families."

"And Plan B?" asked Tyler.

"Remember how the Bible said my great-grandfather dreaded Plan B?" asked Jordan. "One journal entry says it's because he knew two things—#1: in Plan B, both he and Ray were going to die, and #2: one of them could smear his family with the stigma of a crime, cause a rift between the families, and who knows what else."

"You don't mean they planned for one to kill the other?" asked Bethany.

"No, I don't," replied Jordan. "But look at this." He showed her a page in the same handwriting as the page to Walter from the old Bible. "This is the Master Plan. It includes several permutations."

"Dude, in English," said Tyler.

"It's a detailed strategy for Plan A and Plan B. Scenarios, options, possible outcomes, and risks."

Bethany scanned the page. "Looks like they chose Plan B, Option Three."

"What's that?" said Tyler.

"If one of them was killed, and they had opportunity, the other would make it look like he was the murderer," said Bethany.

"Timeout." Tyler shook his head. "Why on earth would anybody do that?"

Bethany read aloud. "Plan B assumes that our families are safe—ONLY if it is our enemies' best interest to keep them alive. These options assume the failure of Plan A and attempt to create a scenario that makes it in their best interest to keep our families safe even if we can't go public with the evidence."

"Which would only be true if those two were dead," said Jordan. "As long as Ray and William were alive, they would be a threat."

"These guys were sharp," said Gadg, peering over Bethany's shoulder. "This looks like a decision tree from a well-written computer program. May I see the box?"

Jordan handed it over and watched as Gadg examined the box while trying to touch it as little as possible.

"Option Three," Bethany continued reading. "This option is the least desirable of the whole plan. If one of us is killed, the other will attempt to make it look like he was the murderer. Two things should happen after this. First, they will come looking for the one that is still alive. The survival of our families depends on him being ready to die willingly. Second, if done well, our enemies will think it best to leave our families alone, rather than risk further scrutiny. This would lead to many undesirable outcomes, such as bad blood between our families, serious emotional harm to our children and grandchildren, and even a possible stigma in the community. Furthermore, it still carries significant risk of failing. In summary, this option should be used only as a last resort."

"That sure seems like what happened," said Jordan. "But technically, we're still speculating."

"No, we're not," said Gadg.

"What are you talking about?" said Jordan and Bethany simultaneously.

Gadg closed the lid, grabbed the box on both sides so as to not allow the contents to fall out, and flipped it ninety degrees to show the bottom to them.

Bethany's free hand flew up and covered her mouth.

"Oh my," said Jordan.

On the bottom of the cigar box, clear as day, even in the dim light of their flashlights, the message "PLAN B" was smeared in cracked, dry blood.

"Wow," said Jordan under his breath. "Whose do you think? Ray?"

"Has to be," answered Gadg.

Bethany looked back to the paper and finished reading. "Risk Level: Very High. This might, quite literally, take a miracle." She looked at the others with tears forming in both eyes. She shook her head and handed over the page.

Jordan read the final words of William Nolan. "Lord, my family patriarch, John Philip Nolan, pronounced a blessing on the old Bible we will hide tomorrow. It said, 'May this copy of God's Holy Writ ever be unto thou and this family as a testimony that "His faithfulness is unto all generations."' In the spirit of that blessing, Ray and I commit all our plans to You. We sincerely hope it doesn't come to the worst, but if it does, will You lead one of our descendants to the Bible, and then ultimately, to the evidence?"

Bethany and Jordan turned to stare at each other, eyes wide. *They* were God's answer to a fifty-year-old prayer.

His voice wobbled as he finished reading, "God, You know we would prefer to live, but ultimately, we don't care what happens to us. Please spare our families."

Eyes full of tears, Bethany smiled at Jordan.

Jordan didn't speak for a good while. When he did, his voice dropped to just above a whisper. "Everybody thinks of my great-grandfather as the worst of the worst in the Nolan family. The truth is exactly opposite. For a few days, he was the brightest light in our family history."

"And my Great-grandpa Ray was not a 'victim' at all"—Bethany made air quotes—"he was a hero."

Jordan nodded. "Two plus three equals five."

"I can see why they wanted Plan A," Tyler broke in. "It's the only plan where they live."

"It's way more than that," replied Gadg.

"What do you mean?"

"It's the only way that thousands of people wouldn't suffer," said Jordan, finishing Gadg's thought. His face was grim. "Here's the sad truth: The Wonder Drug was built on the cover-up of XD and the murder of two good men."

A sound made them jump. All at once, they remembered where they were.

"What was that?" asked Bethany, wiping the tears from her face.

"That was what I thought I heard a few minutes ago," replied Gadg. "Somebody is in the tunnels."

"Who?" asked Tyler.

"Not sure, but I have some ideas," said Gadg. He handed the box back to Jordan and looked over at Bethany.

She gulped.

Jordan took the box, stuffed the pages back into it, and latched the lid. "Let's go."

Reading

Thursday, July 31, 8:51 p.m.
"Smuggler's Cove" (the back room in the old abandoned grange),
Wilson, CO

Last of all, Jordan took Bethany's hand and helped her squeeze through the trapdoor. Gadg finished something on his phone, and they all dusted themselves off in the back of the abandoned grange. This room had been spooky during the day. Just before dark, it was downright creepy.

Gadg used the flashlight on his phone to examine the wall they'd just come through. "Look at this," he said. "No wonder we couldn't see the door. When you pushed it open, Tyler, this seal was broken." He turned from the wall and put his phone against his leg to allow just enough light for them to have a huddled conversation.

"What do we do now?" whispered Tyler.

"We need to get some copies made and get this to Gadg's dad as soon as possible," replied Jordan.

"Definitely not in that order," said Gadg, looking down at his phone.

"What do you mean?" asked Jordan.

"While you were squeezing through, I sent a text to my dad, letting him know what we've found. I asked him if I should take some photos. I just got a text back." Gadg showed the phone to Jordan. "He said that we need to get the actual evidence to him. Copies won't be enough."

"We don't need pictures?" asked Bethany.

"They won't be admissible as evidence," said Gadg. "Jordan's last name presents a problem, and our being tech-savvy is a deal-breaker. We could do some stuff with Photoshop and make it look just as good."

"He's right," said Jordan. "We must get this box back to the police."

"Guys, I'm with you," Bethany said. "I can't wait to see how this plays out."

Jordan looked at her. "What are you saying, Miss Clark?"

"I can't risk being seen with you. Until the police have the evidence in their possession and everything is made public, I can't jeopardize my dad's involvement in the 50th Anniversary Celebration."

"What does that mean?" asked Tyler.

Bethany's eyes twinkled. "Just don't be surprised if you turn around and I'm not there."

"It's dark and creepy back in here," said Jordan.

"I'm a big girl." Her voice sounded like a lullaby.

Jordan pushed down a stab of longing by looking at his phone.

Not sure I'd call you a 'girl' anymore.

He busied himself with a text message. A few seconds later, he looked up. "I just sent a text to my dad, telling him what we've got and where we are. I asked him to come right away."

"I'll text Allie," said Bethany. Her hands flew over the buttons.

Jordan did a double take. "Wait," he turned to Bethany. "You're going to text Allie? You sure that's a good idea?"

"Already sent. Shouldn't I have?"

He looked thoughtful. "I guess it's okay." Suddenly, his face grew taut.

"What is it?" Bethany asked sharply.

"I just realized something. Even though this box is intended for us, in the eyes of the law, we're trespassing and stealing right now."

The others stared at him.

He forced a smile. "As long as we get away, it won't be a problem."

He rounded the corner into the small hallway and crept forward. Gadg and Tyler followed as they entered the cavernous main room. In the descending onset of night, moonlight streamed through the front and side doors like the eye and mouth holes of a giant skull. The silence didn't help. Only a whisper of wind whistled through the vacant doorways.

They took a few steps and stopped.

Two WDC2 security guys entered simultaneously through the side doors.

Jordan's heart rate shot up as a surge of adrenaline hit him like an electric shock.

Gadg shook his head.

Alex Jones, dressed in a black T-shirt with big, white letters spelling "SECURITY," strolled through the front door.

Oh Lord, not now. He bit down as his insides writhed with the injustice.

"Hello, Jordan," said Alex in his gravelly voice.

"Mr. Jones," Jordan said. He cast a brief glance behind him. There was no escape that way. Besides, Bethany was back there, and he couldn't lead them to her. The smooth wood of the cigar box pressed against his palm.

"Whatcha got there?" demanded Alex.

Jordan's eyes darted as he weighed his options. He didn't like any of them. His muscles tightened. If they took the box, he would lose not only the evidence, but likely the internship.

He closed his eyes to say a quick prayer for grace and opened them again.

Alex had taken a few more steps, but was not yet to the center of the hall where the open doors stood to either side. The other two men had taken a few steps and now stood twenty feet from the group.

"Nothing much," replied Jordan. "Just some more history of Wilson."

"Not everybody in this town likes history," said Alex.

"Undoubtedly true," said Jordan. "But I think everyone will be *interested* in this history, whether they *like* it or not."

Alex's eyes turned cold. "It would be a shame if that box never made it back to Nolan property and we weren't able to find out, wouldn't it? You do realize that you are trespassing on WDC2 property."

Jordan sized up the situation. A shaft of light opened in his mind as he saw the position of the three men.

Alex sneered, "You're not ready for history anyway. Why don't you just go back to your little school where Johnny Nolan is teaching you to cut and paste and play with scissors?"

"He is teaching us to *cut*," said Jordan, emphasizing the last word. He shot a quick glance at Tyler.

Tyler gave a smirk but kept his face forward. The quarterback was calling an audible.

Jordan looked back at Alex. "He's also teaching us to *read*. Right, Tyler?"

In response, Tyler took off at a sprint—directly toward Alex. At the last instant, he looked to his right at the open door leading toward Nolan property.

Alex bit and lunged toward that door.

With no indication whatsoever, Tyler cut sharply to his left and sprinted to the other door.

Just before the cut, Jordan launched the cigar box with his practiced Ultimate Frisbee motion toward the left door, away from Nolan property. The box spun clockwise and arced over the top of the left security guy.

Tyler's cut was perfect.

Jordan's throw was on the money.

Tyler caught the cigar box at face level as he burst through the opening.

The thrill on Tyler's face brought a surge of hope to Jordan. A perfect throw caught on the dead run. The odds were still against them, but at least they had a chance.

Alex's old chops came back in a flash. He swore and took off after Tyler. On his way out, he shouted over his left shoulder, "Bring those two to Mr. Carlyle!"

Jordan gave a look to Gadg that asked if they should make a break for it.

One of the men said, "Mr. Carlyle wants to talk to you, Jordan. If you come now, without any trouble, he might not press charges."

Chapter 54

Matthew, Allie, and an Urgent Text

Thursday, July 31, 8:53 p.m.
Chez La Fleur restaurant, Wilson, CO

"I'm glad we were able to do this," said Matthew as he dabbed the corner of his mouth with a napkin. He looked at Allie across the table at Chez La Fleur, one of Wilson's finest restaurants.

"Me, too," she said, eyes shining and decked out in her light summer best. "Thanks so much for inviting me. That was an amazing meal! I've never eaten here before."

"You're welcome, and I agree—it is excellent. I come here often."

"You do? That many, huh?" A cloud darkened Allie's face.

"That many?" asked Matthew. "That many what?"

"Dates."

Matthew let out an easy breath and smiled. "No, nothing like that. My father has an office just a couple blocks away." He pointed out the window. "I'm there all the time, especially late in the evening. This place helps me unwind."

Allie brightened. "That's great that you like to help your dad."

"Yes. I help him out a good bit. Was this place even here before you left for California?"

"It was under construction when we left."

"Well, I'm glad you got to try it. Speaking of California, weren't you in your sister's wedding last summer?"

"Yes, I was. It was a great time."

"Do you have any photos? I'd love to see them."

Allie opened her phone, flipped back a few months in the photo collections, and handed it to Matthew. "Take a look at a few of these."

"Wow, they're good."

"Yes, isn't she beautiful?"

"She is," Matthew nodded. "But she's not the prettiest one in the wedding party."

Allie blushed.

"No, really, that friend of hers next to you is gorgeous."

"What?" Allie shot him a look she'd perfected for the dramatic final speech last May.

"Just teasing," his grin disarmed her. "May I look at a few of these? Maybe you can look at that dessert menu and find something good for us?"

"Certainly," said Allie. She picked up the dessert menu.

Matthew gave a quick glance to ensure she was occupied, and then brought up her text messages. A quick scan led him straight to what he was looking for. There was Bethany's name right at the top with a text that Allie hadn't read yet.

> Urgent and confidential: Jordan Gadg and Tyler about to head back through forest with evidence. If you see Deputy O'Brien send him over quickly. Meet you at house later

Matthew stole another glance at Allie. He'd hoped for something. He'd had no idea he would get *this* lucky.

"Do you like chocolate or what?" she asked, still looking down at the menu.

"Pick three or four things, and I'll help you decide," Matthew stalled. He took a screenshot of the text before emailing it to himself. When he was sure the email had been sent, he deleted the screenshot.

"How about one of these four?" said Allie, attempting to show the menu to him.

"Tell you what," he held the menu back with his hand, "why don't you take a moment and see if you can sort those four in order of my most to least favorite? If you can," he gave his most knowing smile, "I'll take you somewhere even nicer *next time.*"

Her eyes couldn't quite hide her eagerness as she nodded and stared back at the menu.

Matthew swiped and pushed Delete. The text message marked "Urgent" never existed.

In his pocket, he felt the slight vibration of his phone letting him know he'd received the email. "What a great wedding," he said, handing her phone back to her. "So, what's your guess?"

Allie rattled off four desserts.

Not even close.

"That's amazing. How did you know?"

"I guess I can read your thoughts," her eyes twinkled back at him.

Not in your wildest dreams. You couldn't even understand them.

He cocked his head. "Will you excuse me for a moment? I need to use the restroom. Go ahead and order dessert while I'm gone."

Mr. Molencki will want to see this.

Chapter 55

A Clean Hit

Thursday, July 31, 8:59 p.m.
Outside the abandoned grange, Old Town, Wilson, CO

A thrill shot through Tyler. For a wide receiver, catching the ball on the run with daylight was a slice of heaven. The open door dropped two feet to the ground, and Tyler launched from the grange, landed on the surrounding grass, and sprinted the remaining thirty feet toward the forest.

"You better hope I don't catch you, punk," snarled Alex as he burst through the opening.

Tyler looked back sharply. His nostrils flared as excitement flipped to terror. He scraped his arm across a pine tree on the way into the forest, but hardly noticed.

Alex was ten feet behind him, and even though he had lost a step, he had been an extremely fast college football player two decades ago. The trees began to thicken. At fifty yards from the grange, Alex had narrowed the distance to seven feet.

Tyler's football instincts took over. One of Uncle Johnny's lessons came to mind as he focused on three points of contact for ball security, or in this case, cigar box security. Everything rested on his shoulders now. A fumble was out of the question.

Compounding the problem was the fact that he was sprinting in the wrong direction. His choice to go left in the grange meant he was running away from his destination.

It was time to change that.

Flying past a tree with a narrow base, Tyler reached out and used the trunk to fling himself back in the other direction.

Alex blew past the tree, cursed again, and wrenched himself around to continue the pursuit. A guttural, animal-like sound came through the trees.

Tyler's eyes widened, and his heart tried to push his throat out his mouth. All he could do was run. He made a beeline toward Nolan property, but he couldn't shake Alex off his tail. He tried darting this way and that. Useless. Was this what awaited him in NCAA Division 1 football?

Alex again closed the gap to a few feet.

Tyler was in great condition, but he couldn't do this forever. Skirting around a tree, he planted his foot. The earth gave way. His free hand flailed and then touched the ground as his body went diagonal. He barely stayed upright, and the cigar box almost slipped from his grip.

Alex gained two more steps. "I may end your football career—like I did for your uncle," Alex taunted through heavy breath.

Tyler gulped.

One hundred yards to the Nolan property line. Even that didn't mean he was done, he realized. Alex would not stop at the fence.

Seventy-five yards to go. He would be out of the forest in about three seconds. He could see one of the fence gates standing open. With Alex two arm-lengths behind, he didn't think much about it. He needed one more cut. He passed one tree, then another. Not quite yet.

Alex was three feet from him.

Now! At the second to last tree, Tyler planted his left foot, and this time it took. He cut hard to his right and caught a blur of motion to his left.

What was that?

Tyler blasted out of the forest and into the open for the final fifty yards. A half-second later, he heard the unmistakable crunch of a bone crushing hit. Uncle Johnny had come out of nowhere and laid a hit on Alex that was twenty years in the making.

Exhilaration surged through Tyler again. His face lit up. He was going to make it. Uncle Johnny had received Jordan's text. Tyler glanced over his shoulder.

"Go!" shouted Johnny. "Get to Deputy O'Brien ASAP!"

Beaming, Tyler turned his head forward and sprinted toward the Nolan household. The end zone was in sight.

●●●

Johnny had smashed Alex on his left shoulder.

The speed, force, and angle of the collision splayed Alex into a partially forward, partially diagonal, all-the-way painful splat and tumble. Because of the angles involved, it hadn't been dead on. Otherwise, he may not have gotten up.

Johnny had gone down in the process. Rolling to a stop, he picked himself up and faced Alex with certain knowledge that this was not over.

Alex took his time getting up and looked at Johnny with a menacing gleam in his eyes. "You sure you're up for this?" His breath was thick with scorn and the need for oxygen.

Staying just inside the tree line and never taking his eyes from Alex, Johnny circled to his right.

They faced off as Alex closed the gap to where they stood four feet apart. "You're gonna wish you hadn't done that."

Johnny considered a quick-witted response but realized it would do more harm than good. His plan was simple: once Alex attacked, he needed to stay on his feet for three to five seconds.

Alex sprung.

Like an offensive lineman getting flagged for a holding call, Johnny tucked his elbows, grabbed Alex by the word "SECURITY," and stood him up.

Three seconds passed.

Alex would break the hold at any moment.

Johnny looked up and smiled.

A large wrench, held by Walter, crashed down on the head of Alex Jones. He dropped like a 220-pound sack of raw, lean meat. Sprawled out on the forest floor, he lay there, unconscious and unmoving.

Johnny chuckled.

"What?" said Walter.

"I was thinking of Jordan's banter about new-school tools. In this moment, I would much rather have you with that thing than Jordan with a smartphone."

The wrench was a giant affair. With a practiced flip of his one good arm, the business end slapped into Walter's massive palm. Another spin, like a cowboy with a six-shooter, returned the handle to his grip and put a smile on his face. "Old-school," he said in an even deeper voice.

"Thanks, Dad. That was great," said Johnny.

"You're welcome, son."

Alex stirred.

"He'll be up any minute," said Johnny.

"Do we head for the grange or back to the house?"

"The grange," said Johnny. "Let's go see about Jordan. We can make sure Alex isn't really hurt on the way back. I told Tyler to get that box to the deputy."

"I sure hope he does," said Walter. "I'd hate for this to be all for naught. Alex will see this as a declaration of war."

Chapter 56

Wide Receiver

Thursday, July 31, 9:04 p.m.
Outside the back of the Nolan house, Wilson, CO

Isaac Molencki parked his rental car and walked a mile to a spot across the road from the eastern edge of Nolan property. Trees and rock outcroppings between patches of scrub oak shielded him from all but the most prying eyes. The last vestiges of the sun's losing battle with twilight lingered.

Fitting an earpiece into his ear, he spread his thumb and forefinger across the face of his phone to enlarge the photo of the map of the Old Town catacombs. Mr. Carlyle's man at the community meeting, whom Isaac had not met, had sent it to him, along with the message that Bethany was not in attendance.

Interesting.

He smiled at the screen.

"Listen up," the small man said through his phone to the contact Donald Carlyle had made available to him for the evening. "They will be heading for the grange—if it's not too late already. Your job is to scope out the tunnels and make sure they don't get away to the north. Don't get yourself lost down there. I'll forward the map."

As he ended the call, Isaac gave the precise location of an Old Town manhole—on WDC2 property—that provided the northern entrance to the tunnels. He didn't expect much from these back-country buffoons, but he couldn't be everywhere tonight.

Bethany's diary entry, and her voice, kept intruding on his thoughts. *Elizabeth.*

The resemblance was unnerving. He shook his head with a scowl. This girl was getting under his skin.

He forced himself to work through what he had learned from her diary. Bethany needed to go underground and go northeast. It was something about a couple of letters and a link to her mother's illness. He smiled.

I need to find those letters.

He'd planned to catch the boys in the tunnels, or at least make sure they didn't escape that way. Mr. Carlyle had sent some men to cover the grange if they tried to leave above ground.

With Bethany going underground, he could try for two birds with one stone. His smile widened.

She hates the dark.

That could make things interesting.

He studied the map again. There were at least three places he could enter the tunnels. He had just directed Mr. Carlyle's man to the entrance north of Old Main Street.

He swore. The picture of the map wasn't clear enough to positively determine if there was another entrance among the abandoned businesses. Even though that would have been the best entry point, the small man didn't have time to waste on anything that wasn't definitive.

The entrance on Nolan property was farther away from everything, but would be the easiest to come and go from without being seen. Just as he turned to make his way to the hidden entrance, his screen flashed a message from Matthew Harris.

> **URGENT: boys in grange. Going to Jordan's house with evidence.**

"Well done, young man." Isaac nodded and turned to face Nolan property. He stuffed his phone into his pocket and sneaked from tree to tree until he reached the edge of the road. Crossing over, he hopped the fence and said, "That makes my decision real easy."

● ● ●

No touchdown pass had ever felt like this. Even though his lungs screamed for air, exhilaration flooded Tyler's being. Johnny had taken out Alex, the cigar box was still in his hands, and the Nolan home was a minute away. Various thoughts raced through his mind. He settled on the plan of getting inside the house, stashing the box well out of sight, and calling Deputy O'Brien.

He passed the Nolan guest house where Grandpa Walter lived.

Almost there.

Still at full speed, he rounded a rock formation and saw the moving shadow an instant before his feet got tangled in a large branch. The cigar box flew from his hands, skidded, and bounced into the base of a nearby tree. His body flailed past, rolled twice, and sprawled, facedown on a layer of pine needles.

He spat and coughed to get the needles and dirt out of his mouth. His chest heaved. He pounded his fist into the ground, sprang up, and turned to see what had happened. A tiny man stepped out into the open. A five-foot silhouette stood in the glowing moonlight. He recognized him as the man Bethany had spoken of. Tyler's face contorted. He clenched his fists and walked straight at the man.

When he was three feet away, the man said, "You sure you want to do that?"

Tyler stopped.

What a stupid question.

He looked down, full into the moonlit face of one of the smallest men he'd ever seen. Fear shot through his heart like a hot knife.

The eyes of Isaac Molencki reflected the late-July moonlight like a polished 8-ball.

Tyler hesitated.

"Do you enjoy being a wide receiver?"

"What?"

"I asked if you enjoy being a wide receiver."

Tyler blinked. "Yeah, I guess."

"I'm glad to hear it."

Tyler's forehead creased. "Why do you ask?"

The mole never moved. His voice grew even calmer. "Because if you take one step closer to me—or that box—you'll spend the rest of your life in a wheelchair. Now turn around, be thankful you can still walk home, and forget you saw anything."

Chapter 57

Big Girl

Thursday, July 31, 8:55 p.m.
"Smuggler's Cove" (the back room in the old abandoned grange),
Wilson, CO

When Tyler had rounded the corner, Bethany was still undecided on her plan. She debated whether to follow them right then or let them get away while slinking off later. She sneaked up to the corner to listen. The boys were getting farther from her. The growing silence, broken only by the gentle creaking of old wood, permeated the back room with a haunting quality. She turned to look at the opening they'd just come from.

Her heart quailed.

Blackness emerged from the cracked door like a noose. It was like staring into a void. She blew out a big breath, took a couple of steps, and put her ear back up to the cracked door. She could hear no sounds below and realized that the pursuers, whoever they were, had not found the hidden chamber. Not more than a minute later, from the other direction, she heard the unmistakable gravel of the voice of Alex Jones.

Her stomach dropped.

Fear and compassion fought to be the dominant emotion. She could not imagine how the guys would get away with the evidence. At first, she thought they might try to rush back to this room, but she knew they were too smart for that. She prayed a silent prayer and hoped for the best for them.

Oh, Jordan. I'm sorry.

The gravity of her own situation slammed her a moment later. It was only a matter of time before the evidence was found and brought back to whoever was masterminding this. She had to get away unseen and unheard.

What about the message from R3?

The possibility of finding a clue to what ailed her mother nagged at her.

It was bad enough to wait it out here. Bethany clenched her teeth, squeezed back through the trapdoor and pulled it closed behind her. Because they'd just been here, she knew the dimensions of the room. The blackness threatened to swallow her as a jolt of vertigo made her unsteady on the top of the stairs. She flung her hands to the door behind and slid herself down to a sitting position. The silence taunted her.

Big girl, huh?

She wrapped her arms around her legs in what Allie called the "make the bad guys go away" position. Bethany had never thought of it in a literal sense. The worst of it was, she couldn't sing like she had done countless times in the past to brighten up the atmosphere. All she could do was pray quietly and hope that the deathlike silence wasn't broken by either entrance being opened.

Footsteps.

Is that running? Could they get away?

This spot was no good.

She reached into her pocket, switched on her phone, and surveyed her options. She assumed the greater danger would come from the door she was closest to. As soft-footed as she could be, Bethany crept down each step to the bottom of the hidden chamber.

Even the quiet felt old.

She crossed the room to the other entrance and looked up. Another tremor rolled across her heart. Leaning her head against the door, Bethany said a quick prayer.

Should she go back upstairs or make her way through the catacombs?

She would much rather go upstairs, but she would almost certainly be caught.

She hesitated.

The words from R3 whispered to her heart with fresh clarity.

Go underground and go northeast.

Cracking the door a few more inches, she contemplated braving the trek through the catacombs.

I may not get another chance.

Was it worth it? It would be so much easier to go back up the stairs.

Do I have to do it alone?

She heard footsteps in the Smuggler's Cove of the grange. Her stomach was in her throat. The men upstairs would know there had to be a way to get under the building because the companions had just come from it a few minutes before.

She shut off her phone, offered one more quick prayer, and stepped over the line. Squeezing through the opening, she pulled the door closed behind her.

How can it be darker than the room I just came from?

The darkness was so complete that her eyes, and pupils, were wide open with nothing whatsoever to latch onto. A wave of panic overwhelmed her. Her breathing bordered on hyperventilation. Her thoughts were a lightheaded swirl, and her knees shook.

She instinctively closed her eyes to talk to God. A chuckle arose from deep within at how ridiculous it was to close her eyes to pray. It was almost lighter with her eyes closed than open.

Oh, thank You, God. You're with me.

Her breath steadied, and her heart rate slowed a few beats.

Okay, think.

Bethany listened hard to see if the pursuers were anywhere near. Except for the sound of someone trying to get into the room she had just come from, she could hear nothing.

This was good. And eerie.

Hearing nothing of concern in front of her, she pulled out her phone again. She had never been so thankful for light in her whole life.

Okay, that's better. What's next?

Bethany tried to reverse their previous course in her mind. She thought back on a few opportunities in her life to retrace a route from memory. It had not always gone well. Thank God for her phone—at least for the light. She chuckled again as she didn't think the maps feature was going to be of much assistance down here. At least she had a compass on her phone.

First things first. She had to get back to the starting point. She took an immediate right, coming out of the hidden chamber knowing that they had taken a left to enter it. About a half a block later, she took a left, and another half block after that took her back to one of the intersections that they had seen earlier.

I think we went straight here before. She looked behind her and then ahead. *That way would take me back to the Nolan's.*

She looked around again.

I think.

Another turn and she was certain she would be facing the East Ridge if she'd been above ground.

Good. That's northeast now.

She walked another block and assumed she was still facing toward the ridge. The problem with these tunnels was that they weren't straight. This last stretch had been a circuitous back-and-forth, leading in what she assumed was more or less the same direction.

Her heartbeat wasn't so much fast as it was hard. It felt like the driving punch of a steady kick-drum beat. At the next intersection, she stopped.

Bethany launched the compass app. Her eyes widened in alarm.

There's no signal.

"What were you thinking?" she whispered aloud.

Standing at an intersection with four tunnels, she turned this way and that. She headed down a tunnel and turned to her left.

I think this is northeast.

She took another right just ahead and then stared.

I couldn't actually get lost down here, could I?

The tunnel dead-ended forty feet ahead, and unlike some of the other passages, this tunnel had rubble everywhere. Fifteen feet ahead, on the right, was a hole that had been broken out of the tunnel wall. She scanned her options.

Could I, should I, go back and go another way?

She looked down at her phone and the breath exploded from her body. Battery indicator: 2%.

Fear coiled around her neck like a snake. She fought for control. She'd been at work all day and hadn't given a thought to charging her phone.

Her insides wailed, but no sound emerged.

She leaned against the wall of the tunnel, turned the brightness down to the lowest level, and then shut off her phone. Still holding it in her hand, she could almost feel the weight of the precious 2% battery life as the darkness enveloped her. She fought back unseen tears and shivered from the underground chill.

Steady, Bethany. Think. Pray.

A sound.

What was that?

Her heart rate shot to the moon.

Footsteps?

No doubt about it. Coming from the tunnel she had just been facing, footsteps, slowly and methodically, made their way toward the intersection she had just vacated.

She peeked around the corner. A dim light preceded the sound. Her own corridor was still black as a pool of ink. She was exposed where she was, and the footsteps would be here in a moment.

She spun back around and turned her head in various directions, looking for an option—any option—that wasn't horrible. She considered running back the way she came, but she couldn't traverse the distance unseen and unheard. She considered hiding behind the rubble but wasn't sure it would work, and she'd have to use the light to find a good spot. She swiped the back of her hand across her right eye to whisk away a tear.

The phone flew out of her hand.

A half-second after the shock registered, Bethany clenched her fists into tight little balls and fought back a scream of terror and rage that threatened to consume her. Unbelievably, she stayed silent.

The hole in the side wall.

Ignoring her phone for a moment, she felt along the wall of the tunnel as quickly and quietly as possible. She couldn't remember if there were any obstructions that she needed to avoid.

There was.

Her head smacked against a steel girder. Mind spinning and tears flooding her face, she felt the outline of the hole in the tunnel wall. It was more like a crag, but that was no matter. With her senses of touch, hearing, and smell screaming at her, Bethany ducked down and squeezed in, dirtying everything in the process—hands, face, hair, clothes. She shuddered to think what unseen creepiness, living or not, might be in the hole with her. Dragging the last of her body out of sight of the tunnel, she pulled her knees to her chest and tucked herself back into the "make the bad guys go away" position. Someone looking directly into the hole couldn't miss her.

The tears flowed in earnest. They streaked across the grubby dustiness of her face onto her knees. Normally reserved, it was rare for Bethany to cry. Always clean, it was almost unheard of for her to have a grubby face. Crying *and* grubby? First time in her life.

The footsteps were at the intersection.

"Where are you, Bethany?"

A wave of fear and nausea washed over her. Even without her auditory gift, she would recognize that voice anywhere.

The small man.

She didn't want to think what his eyes would look like.

"You told me you'd be glad to talk to me later."

How did he know I'd be down here?

"I'm looking for two letters. Care to join me?"

Her eyes almost popped out of their sockets.

She clamped down on her teeth to stifle any sound.

How does he know about that?

Hot, angry tears dropped onto her knees. Silently, but in earnest, Bethany cried out to God from the gut. A simple, desperate prayer for safety.

Chapter 58

Little Girl

Thursday, July 31, 9:15 p.m.
The tunnels under Old Town, Wilson, CO

The dam broke.

Pent-up pressures related to her mom, her father's feelings about Jordan, *her* feelings about Jordan, the wide-open expanse of an unknown future, and the terrifying need for silence unleashed a flood of tears. Rolled up in a ball inside a hole in the wall of an underground catacomb, her hands covered her face but could not stop the flow. Saltwater streamed, freely but still unseen and unheard, through dust and dirt down the insides of her wrists and forearms.

The beam of a flashlight combed through the debris in the dead-end tunnel next to her. Through a blanket of fear, and with eyes blinded by tears, Bethany had the most difficult moment of her young life. For a dreadful two seconds, the beam rested half an inch from the outer sole of her left shoe, which had been bright white thirty minutes ago. She held her breath and tried with everything in her to keep the fear at bay and maintain total silence, even while tears pooled at the bottom of her forearms on the insides of her elbows.

The light, and the voice, moved on.

For a few seconds she could still hear the footsteps. She had to assume the small man had looked down the corridor, not seen anything of interest, and carried on with the search. Sloppy wet hands covered the area around her mouth as she gasped for breath while trying to muffle the sound. As quietly as she could, Bethany raised her head and leaned it back against the wall of the hole. She allowed herself to breathe. Her head pounded. Her heart raced.

She looked up to heaven, and Daddy's Girl let herself go. More tears flowed down the sides of her dirty face. This time they washed and cleansed and came with the familiar sense of God's presence. In the last several months He had drawn close to her as she clung to Him amidst all the uncertainties and pressures. Now, in the oppressive dark and stifling quarters of her underground refuge, Bethany felt a peace that made no sense.

Daddy was with her.

● ● ●

Bethany waited at least thirty minutes before she stirred. She felt so protected that, strange as it seemed, she almost didn't want to move. She even sensed that somehow God was hearing her prayers for her mom.

Time to get going.

She was hungry. She was dirty. And she felt a chill.

That's weird. There must be some airflow somewhere.

First, she had to try to find her phone. She squeezed her way out of the crag, stood up, and leaned against the wall.

It was still so dark.

Her eyes refused to connect with anything. She felt her way down the edge of the tunnel, being careful to avoid smacking the steel girder. She made her way back to the corner of the intersection where she had seen the beam of the flashlight. She oriented herself to the direction she had been facing when she threw her phone. Thank God Molencki had not seen the phone when he shined his light down this tunnel.

She prepared herself for a nasty job.

Fifteen minutes of back and forth, one side of the tunnel to the other on her hands and knees produced her phone—and the filthiest layer of dirt and grime that had ever covered her skin and clothes.

She laughed out loud.

It was a strange feeling. Her situation was still unresolved, but God was with her, and she was dirty. Head to toe, she could not believe how grubby she felt.

Turning on her phone, the battery was still at only 2%.

But she could see.

She knew it wouldn't last long, but for the moment, she could see. She grimaced at the section of dirt that she had just combed to find her phone. It looked like someone had raked it with their body—which, in fact, she had done.

She shuddered. "Oh, thank You, Daddy." The sides of the tunnel had slopes down from the walls that she hadn't noticed before. Besides the rubble she managed to not twist an ankle on, it was the only thing that had kept her from leaving a trail of dusty footsteps to the crag in the wall.

She walked over and shined her light into the hole, amazed that she had fit. She saw where she had leaned back. It was barely high enough. She was thankful that she had not hit her head again. The realization that she would soon be out of battery brought her back to reality. Even after the experience of God's presence, it was easy for fear to creep up on her because she didn't know how she was going to get out.

She gave a last look into the hole and noticed a curious thing. The wall that she had leaned back against had a small opening at the bottom.

Hmm.

That might have been where the draft had come from. But that didn't matter now. She had to get out of here. She switched off her phone so she could think without wasting precious battery life. She pulled her head out of the hole and stood up.

A thump.

Her phone hit the ground again inside the hole. She had thought her hands were free from the hole when she straightened, but they were not. The edge had knocked the phone loose, scratching the back of her hand in the process. Bethany grimaced and shook her head. Back to her knees, she prepared to dirty herself one more time.

Sticking her head back into the crag, Bethany felt around for her phone. It hadn't dropped in the immediate mouth of the hole so she reached in a bit further and assumed it would be in the area where she had been sitting.

On her knees this time, with her head at ground level, Bethany swept her right arm along the inside of the hole. Scrunching in further, she reached the area where the opening at the bottom of the rear wall had been, where she had leaned back before. She felt the hollowed-out area that she had noticed before but still didn't feel her phone. Left elbow on the ground Bethany rested for a moment and tried to think.

Is that light?

Unbelievably, her eyes picked up a glint of light. It was more like "less dark," but her eyes had been so starved to receive any bit of light that she could discern a lighter shade of darkness. Wriggling her way to where her head was under the opening, she looked hard. The reflection turned out to be the silver back of her phone about fifteen inches in front of her. It must have landed on its edge and rolled a bit.

What could it be reflecting?

After confirming that it was indeed her phone, Bethany held it out in front of her and fiddled with the angle of it to see if she could see any more light. She couldn't get any more, but there was no doubt she could make out a slight bit of less-than-pitch-blackness. Her arms were stretched out as far as they could.

This opening must go somewhere.

Bethany pulled her phone back to her, switched it on, and turned on the flashlight. Shining it down the opening she confirmed it did indeed go somewhere, but she couldn't tell where or how far it went. She looked again at her phone.

1%.

She switched it back off.

Lord, really?

Bethany had always identified with Jill in C.S. Lewis's *The Silver Chair.* She hated claustrophobic, tight places. When her dad had read it to her as a young girl, she had bristled at the thought of what Jill had to endure in the underworld. She was older now, but this was much worse. Unlike Jill, Bethany had no companions and no assurance of anything beyond a nasty trip down a tight crawl. If it ended in a dead end, she'd be forced to do it all backward.

The fact that she was already as dirty as she could be, and that the slight bit of light had to have a source, finally propelled her to do it. Bethany stowed her phone in her back pocket and squeezed in.

It was the second truly horrible moment in the last sixty minutes.

Smothered, scrunched, and struggling to draw a breath, Bethany battle-crawled for about twelve feet. Her head emerged from under the suffocating roof, and she could breathe. Not only that, she turned her head to the left, looked down an underground corridor, and saw—at last—a pale light.

She switched her phone back on and surveyed her surroundings. The tunnel looked similar to the others she had come from, with railway steel reinforcing the ceiling. Openings on the side walls had held oil lamps a century ago.

Where does that light come from?

Turning off her phone again, she picked her way along the corridor. Coming to the end, she looked around the corner into a chamber illuminated by the slightest bit of light.

Looking up, she saw the source.

Bethany switched on her phone again. Above her was the underside of a manhole cover with various rocks stuck into it in a definite pattern.

Crystals?

Moonlight came through, faint but distinct. She couldn't tell if the other side was inside a building or outside in the open, but it didn't matter. Bethany let out a long breath of relief. She still didn't know how she was going to get out, but the end was in sight.

Why have I not seen any more of these?

A fleeting thought went through her mind that the tunnels under Old Town were meant to be secretive so they didn't want evidence of them above ground. This is why they would have been lit with oil lamps.

I need to get out of here.

1% left on the battery. No time to muse. It was only ten o'clock, but it felt like ten lifetimes. She lifted her phone up to the underside of the manhole checking for cell service.

"Hah!" She said aloud.

One bar!

Good enough. Bethany typed out a text to Jordan and Gadg.

> **Help! Stuck under Old Town. Can see moonlight through a manhole cover with crystals.**

Bethany pushed the button to make sure she at least got one sent.

> **Don't think in immediate danger - but small man was here earlier**

Send.

> 1% battery. Crazy dark. I'll see if I can get any more about my location. Come quickly.

Send.

Risking blackout at any moment, she opened a tracking application after turning on GPS Services—a horrible battery hog. She knew the address information was irrelevant, being under Old Town, but if she could get the latitude/longitude coordinates to Gadg, he'd know how to find her. With all the GPS info on the screen she pushed the icon with the up-pointing-arrow to share the information.

She chose message instead of email. The contact list came up. She pushed on the O on the right side of the screen. Her hands shook and she missed. The P last names were in sight. Bethany could feel the time pressure of an imminent, full loss of battery.

Pearson, Allie.

She clicked on Allie's name and hit Send. A torturous five seconds went by as she waited. The coordinates reappeared. She repeated the steps, getting O this time. She clicked on O'Brien, Timothy "Gadg."

The screen went black.

History Lesson

Thursday, July 31, 9:25 p.m.
WDC2 headquarters, Wilson, CO

Jordan didn't feel they were in any real danger at this point. The problem was that they'd been caught trespassing on WDC2 property—the son of a police officer and the winner of the Senator's Internship. Now was not the time to be breaking the law.

Jordan hoped he could explain things to Mr. Carlyle.

Explain what? That his father was a murderer who built an empire on the backs of 20,000 suffering people?

If Tyler got away, this was a moot point.

The evidence was strong, and would vindicate Jordan's actions. Also, this trip to meet with Mr. Carlyle could lead to some much-needed information.

If Tyler didn't get away...

He didn't like where that was going so he forced his thoughts back to his surroundings. He and Gadg were escorted into a back entrance of what they could only assume was the executive office suite of WDC2 Headquarters. The man whose head Jordan had thrown the cigar box over looked like a five-foot nine-inch building of solid brick.

So why not just take us to the police?

Jordan could only conclude that, for now, it was in Mr. Carlyle's best interests to have a private meeting. Of course, Jordan and Gadg could demand to leave, but that could lead to police involvement and risk the internship, not to mention the negative press that would come down on Deputy O'Brien because of Gadg's role in this. Donald would be banking on that.

They walked down a large hall and into an elevator. The other of their escorts, who was about six-one and of a darker complexion, pushed the 4 button for the top floor. Jordan and Gadg stood next to each other at the back of the elevator. It was made of glass and looked out through the large open foyer of the main office onto the sprawling WDC2 campus.

"What are we looking at?" asked Jordan in the tone a gawking tourist would use with a guide. He used intentionally bad grammar, and, while gripping his phone in his hand, pointed out past the foyer. The men followed his finger to the front circular parking area outside the main doors. At the same time, Jordan used his other hand to tap Gadg on his front pocket where his phone created a bulge in the front of his jeans. After the tap, he placed his hand palm-up, indicating for Gadg to hand him his phone.

Gadg's face said that he understood the request but not the intent.

"That's the front entrance down past that loading circle," answered one of them.

"What's that third flag next to the US and State flags," pointed Gadg, trying to catch Jordan's drift.

With the eyes of their escorts looking forward, Jordan pulled his hand back and under the T-shirt that lay over his waist. He tucked his phone into the waistline of his jeans and straightened his T-shirt to cover it.

"The company logo," came the answer.

Gadg handed his phone to Jordan, who pointed with it at the campus just like he'd pointed at the flags. "I bet that's beautiful during the day," he said, making an obvious move to pull his hand back and put "his" phone in his pocket.

They exited the elevator into the fourth-floor foyer. Jordan pulled Gadg's phone out of his pocket, and held it in his closed hand. "May I use the restroom?" he asked, using Gadg's phone to point at the men's room.

"Give me your phone," answered the taller man.

Jordan handed over Gadg's phone and thanked him. Inside the restroom, Jordan chose the middle stall, pulled his own phone from his waistline, and tapped out a text to his dad.

> **URGENT, respond immediately. Did Tyler get away?**

Under his breath, Jordan said "C'mon, c'mon, c'mon," willing the answer to come quickly. To buy time, he increased his volume and launched into one of his debate speeches. "The ethics of living donor transplantation. In this speech we will explore whether it is ethical for a living person to donate an organ."

The smaller, stronger man walked in. "Hurry up," he barked.

"Yes, sir," said Jordan. He knew he had about one more minute as he continued with his opening speech. Shielded from view by the walls of the stall, he took his time going through the motions. Just as he was rebuckling his already-buckled belt, he felt the quick buzz-buzz of a text message. In one motion, he reached down to flush the toilet and reached into his waistline to pull out his phone one more time.

He saw the reply and his heart leaped.

> **Yes! Ask me later. I sent him to Deputy O'Brien, and then Grandpa and I had some business with Alex Jones. We went to check on you at the grange, but you were already gone. We're back at the house now.**

Way to go, Dad!

He must have been the reason for Tyler's escape.

A tremor wobbled across his mind. His dad's words rang in his head.

I sent him to Deputy O'Brien.

Not exactly the same thing as Deputy O'Brien *having* the evidence. Jordan shook his head. He couldn't worry about that now. He stashed his phone in the waistline of his pants as the sound of the toilet flush died away. He opened the stall door, walked to the sink, and washed his hands. He exited the door that was held open by his escort.

"Sorry about that, gentlemen," said Jordan. The leader turned to head down the hall. Jordan winked at Gadg with the slightest smirk and then asked the other security guy if he could have "his" phone back.

● ● ●

They were escorted into a spacious, plush office with a mahogany desk that was lit by a single desk lamp. Two huge windows faced the property that

Jordan had pointed to in the elevator. An enormous fireplace, held up with an arch that needed no mortar, stood to their left. Of course, being the last day of July, there was no fire.

On the other side of the desk, a high-backed leather chair faced away from them. Cigar smoke curled up from behind it. The chair spun around and revealed the face of Donald Carlyle smoking a fat cigar. Three comfortable chairs sat in front of the desk. They were not offered a seat.

"Hello, Jordan. It's good to see you again." Mr. Carlyle ground the last half of his cigar into an ashtray on the desk. "I have to say these circumstances are puzzling to me. What's all this fuss?"

"Hello, Mr. Carlyle. It's good to see you as well. What do you mean by fuss, sir?" Jordan tried to play it naive.

"I've been hearing reports of some young people snooping around my property and poking their noses into my company's business—very close to the 50th Anniversary Celebration, I might add. I'd like to know what's going on."

Jordan knew this was coming, but hadn't prepared to deal with it. "My dad and grandfather set up a treasure hunt for me. It's been crazy."

"A treasure hunt? That's neat. I wish my dad would have done that for me. So, tell me, did you find the treasure?"

Jordan narrowed his eyes a bit. He looked over at Gadg and smiled. "We did. I got a brand-new computer to take on the internship."

"Excellent. I'm sure your family would like to send you off with a *blessing*." Donald enunciated the last word.

Jordan stared back at him. Apparently, the CEO of the largest company in the region had access to plenty of information.

"So, did they hide any clues on WDC2 property?" Mr. Carlyle continued. "That's why you were poking around the grange, I assume?"

A small bead of sweat formed on Jordan's forehead. The dim light of the room made it imperceptible. He took a breath. "No sir, they didn't."

"I'm sorry to hear that, but I'm not surprised—especially since your ceremony was *two months ago*."

A patch of red crept up the side of Jordan's face. This shouldn't have been a surprise since he'd known they were being watched, but hearing it in such a stark manner made him feel exposed.

"Did you find any clues to anything else?" asked Mr. Carlyle.

"I'm not sure what you're talking about, sir."

Donald looked at Jordan and picked up the phone. "Don't play games with me, son. It's late and I'm tired. Do you want to have a conversation now, man-to-man, or would you like to have the same conversation at the police station? My next call would be to Senator Smith. I'm sure Matthew Harris would have a vested interest in that one. Is this the way you want to play it?"

Jordan sighed and shook his head. He felt like he was playing poker with unseen hole cards. A lose-lose situation for an attorney. Where was Tyler? Where was the evidence?

I'm either holding all the cards or none of them. He drew another shaky breath.

"Tell me what you were doing tonight," said Mr. Carlyle.

It was now or never. Time to play the hand. "Well, sir, I've been doing some research on my great-grandfather, William Nolan."

"That's a bit morbid, don't you think? Researching a murderer."

Jordan's pulse quickened a few beats as his jaw tightened.

Steady.

"We have reason to believe that the history of our town is different than commonly thought."

"Fascinating." Donald put down the phone. "Enlighten me."

"Mr. Carlyle, we believe that my great-grandfather may not have been the scoundrel he is thought to be."

"I see. And what does this have to do with my company?"

"William Nolan was an employee," Jordan played his cards carefully.

Donald raised an eyebrow.

Jordan couldn't tell if this was news to him or not.

"Employee of what? I assume you're talking about my company. However, I don't remember seeing his name in any of the WDC2 personnel files," said Mr. Carlyle.

"You wouldn't have, sir. He worked for *Carlyle Enterprises* before the name change." Looking Donald in the eyes, Jordan felt the slightest flicker of understanding pass between them.

Okay, he knows about Carlyle Enterprises. Jordan guessed the man had been about fifteen in 1964.

"I vaguely remember that name from my childhood," said Donald. "Though I'm still not sure what this has to do with me, as I didn't work there."

"Sir, with all due respect, you didn't exactly *invite* us here tonight. One of your men said that you would like to talk to us. I'm having trouble believing you don't know why we're here."

Donald almost hid the flicker deep in his eyes.

Jordan felt a pang of fear slice through him. With a flash of insight, he realized that, until this moment, he'd been thinking of Donald almost as a friend because of the man's warmth to him that day in the café.

"So, if William Nolan wasn't a scoundrel, what was he?"

"One of the brightest lights in our family," Jordan blurted.

"Assuming that's true, why kill himself?" asked Mr. Carlyle.

"He didn't," said Jordan.

Donald stared back at him. He flipped his fingers for Jordan to elaborate.

Jordan fought with himself on the inside and squirmed on the outside. Thoughts flew back and forth. He wasn't sure which cards he had left in his hand.

"William Nolan was a researcher," he said. "He and his colleague, Ray Clark, were commissioned to do research on a drug that Hampden Pharmaceuticals was about to bring to market."

"The drug that changed the world." Donald smiled and pointed at the wall.

Jordan looked up at the framed print that showed the magazine cover of Donald holding Amitolin, the familiar red and blue pill known as the Wonder Drug. The title said, "Big Shoes to Fill."

Jordan felt a rise of irritation as he read the tagline, "With the Man of the Century gone, can Donald Carlyle be WDC2's Man of the Hour?"

The "Man of the Century" had my great-grandfather murdered.

Jordan's tone came out low and sharp. "It changed the world all right. I'm not talking about Amitolin, however. Have you heard of a drug called XD?"

The eyes went dark and the smile vanished. Clearly this was news to Mr. Carlyle. Everybody connected with the medical industry knew about XD and wanted nothing to do with it. Three thousand stillborn deaths. Fifteen thousand worldwide cases of birth defects. Ongoing hereditary issues even to this day. XD, like Thalidomide, had become a byword for corporate greed and foolishness. Hampden Pharmaceuticals had received tremendous criticism for how they'd pushed XD to market and turned a blind eye toward an increasing number of negative reports about its side effects. Had it not been for the incredible sales of the Wonder Drug, Hampden would have gone bankrupt.

Whether he liked what he was hearing or not, Donald Carlyle was taking the conversation seriously at this point. XD being linked to his company was a terrible possibility. "How do you know this?"

Jordan fired a glance at Gadg, wishing for a lifeline. Gadg stood stone-still.

I sure hope the evidence is safe.

"We've been brushing up on our history," Jordan replied evasively.

"So you said," Donald's voice softened into a disarming tone. "So explain this: if William Nolan didn't kill himself, what happened?"

This conversation is out of control. Jordan looked for a way to back out, but all his cards were on the table. "He was murdered," he answered.

Donald was silent. He seemed to be distracted again by the print of the magazine cover on the wall. At last, he asked, "So, who killed him?"

"Some thugs," said Jordan, trying to sound casual.

"Thugs?" Donald looked at his security guys. "You mean hired guns?" He looked back at Jordan. "Who called the shots?"

"We don't know for sure."

Technically, that's true. We are only 99 percent positive.

Jordan took a breath. "Most likely someone high up in Carlyle Enterprises management."

"*Someone* high up?" asked Mr. Carlyle.

"Yes, sir."

The CEO looked thoughtful. Jordan knew that Donald's relationship with his father, Howard Carlyle, had been complicated.

"Okay," continued Donald, "let's suppose for a moment that *all* the records are wrong. Let's suppose William Nolan was *murdered.* Let's suppose the hit was ordered by *someone* high up in Carlyle Enterprises management. What, then, do you *suppose* was the reason?"

You're not as ready for DC as you think you are. How did you let the conversation get here? Jordan could only hope he'd made the right bets.

"The XD research threatened the Wonder Drug deal," he answered, deciding to go for sincerity. "Mr. Carlyle, Wilson Drug and Compounding Center was built on the cover-up of XD."

Donald Carlyle looked dumbstruck.

Could it be that he honestly didn't know?

Of course it could. Nobody knew this, with the possible exception of the mysterious informant known as R3. Jordan saw the wheels turning.

Mr. Carlyle looked as though he was reprocessing all he knew about his company and his father.

He really didn't know.

Nobody breathed.

Click.

The door behind them opened.

Chapter 60

Moment of Truth

Thursday, July 31, 9:50 p.m.
WDC2 headquarters, Wilson, CO

A short man with deep, black eyes walked through the door with another one of Donald's security men. He held a cigar box in his hand.

Oh no.

Jordan closed his eyes. Dread pressed down on his heart like a weighted vest.

Gadg shook his head.

The small man stepped around and set the cigar box down with its sides in perfect alignment with the edges of Donald's desk.

Jordan's mouth dropped open as he watched. He shot a glance over to Gadg.

Gadg returned it—there and gone in an instant. He knew.

This man was in my house.

Jordan stared straight ahead and put on his poker face.

The small man stepped back from the box and stood close—too close—to Mr. Carlyle. He didn't seem to care what Donald, or anybody else, thought. With almost imperceptible movements of his eyes he sized up the room and its occupants.

A flash of insight came to Jordan.

I wonder if he's looking for Bethany?

The small man caught something in Jordan's eyes and stared at him.

Jordan had never seen a look that carried so much warning. He turned away.

Mr. Carlyle unhooked the box clasp and opened the lid. The small man stood within a foot of him, crowding his space with little concern for how he felt about it.

Donald didn't like the man's proximity. Rolling his shoulders, he turned and whispered something into the man's ear.

"I don't think so, sir." His voice chilled Jordan as much as his eyes.

He's asking if there are any other copies.

Donald whispered again.

"No, he's fine. But he didn't get a chance to open it."

Tyler's okay. Jordan allowed himself a small sigh of relief.

With one more glance at the man twelve inches from him, Mr. Carlyle exhaled and retrieved the topmost document from the cigar box. Unfolding it, he read aloud,

Memorandum: R2-6
Date: April 27, 1964
To: Carlyle Enterprises Management

Subject: On the Side Effects of XD

Donald perused the rest of the document in silence. He then reached into the box and looked over a couple more documents, including the Master Plan.

Nobody moved.

If Jordan ever had the upper hand, it was gone now. Donald knew the truth in black and white. Jordan considered a bluff about having other copies, but decided on an earnest, truthful appeal. "Sir, as we've spoken about before, we both know what it's like to live in the shadow of an ancestor. Mr. Carlyle, you have no culpability in this matter. I urge you, please bring out the truth."

All eyes were on Donald. His gaze, however, was fixed on the Master Plan. He took his time. Reaching into a desk drawer, he withdrew a large cigar. He unwrapped the label that encircled its middle.

That looks familiar.

Using a gold-plated cutter, Donald sliced off the tip. One of his security men handed him a light as he took two more documents from the box and pulled a long draw from his cigar. The tip cast a glow that looked like a sunset on Donald's brow. He put several of the documents back into the box. Picking up the Master Plan again, he absently placed his lit cigar on the edge of the box as if it were an ashtray.

Jordan and Gadg exchanged a quick glance.

The moment of truth hung in the air like the smoke from Mr. Carlyle's last exhale. More smoke began to emanate from the cigar box.

Jordan's pulse sped up. When he could stand it no longer, he said, "Mr. Carlyle, your cigar."

Donald looked up from the Master Plan and replied, "Ah, yes."

Jordan breathed easier.

Donald folded the paper in half with a tight crease and then folded it in half again. He placed it back into the cigar box. He didn't seem to notice the lit cigar in the box.

Jordan gasped.

The Master Plan began to burn.

Jordan dove toward the desk. Two hands caught him from behind and gripped him like a vise.

As the contents of the cigar box began to burn in earnest, right on the mahogany desk, Donald Carlyle looked again at Jordan and Gadg. His eyes held a steel edge. "What were we talking about?"

The small man didn't move, but the slightest smile emerged on his face. Clearly, he approved of Donald's actions.

Unable to move, Jordan's eyes smoldered as he glared at Mr. Carlyle.

"You sure you're ready for Washington?" asked Donald. The veil of courtesy was gone. He motioned for one of his security personnel to take the cigar box and set it in the fireplace. "Make sure it finishes."

The man did as commanded. The contents took on an orange color. He planted himself in front of it.

Mr. Carlyle sat back. "This history lesson is over."

Jordan sucked in a breath. Donald's words and the savage grip on his shoulders brought a flash of memory. He could feel the kids holding him down as Matthew tortured him on the playground. His eyes went wild and white.

Donald dismissed it and continued, "All right. Let's get a few things cleared up. This meeting never happened, understand? No meeting. No trespassing. Jordan goes to Washington, Gadg helps his dad on the police force, and everybody lives happily ever after."

Jordan fought tears as his consciousness swam in a sea of red. He couldn't focus, and his chin trembled.

Gadg turned to Mr. Carlyle and spoke for the first time. "Yes, sir. We understand. Come on, Jordan. Let's go."

The only sound in the room was the crackle of the burning cigar box.

"Good," said Mr. Carlyle. He looked at the small man and back at Jordan. "We wouldn't want any unfortunate *accidents* to happen, now would we?"

"No, sir, we wouldn't," said Gadg.

Smoke twisted up from the cigar box. The iron grip released Jordan. He would have collapsed if Gadg had not been there to support him.

The eyes of the small man narrowed, but never left Jordan as Gadg helped him from the room.

● ● ●

"Jones," Donald looked up from his desk and gave an exasperated sigh. "What are you doing here?"

"Sir, they got away." Alex stepped into the office.

The others had left a few minutes after Jordan and Gadg, leaving Donald alone in the room. The air was thick with smoke. Two stubs and a bunch of ashes were all that was left in the ashtray. A bottle of scotch, one-third empty, sat next to a glass with a melting ice cube that looked as tired as Donald felt. He looked back down. Several photos and press clippings of his father, Howard, were spread before him. "No, they didn't. They just got away from *you.*"

"You got it, then?"

"Yes." Donald didn't bother to look up.

"What was it?"

"That's not the question you should be asking."

"Sir?"

He looked up. "Are you really that dense?"

Alex stood with a blank look.

"Okay, let me make it real simple. You're fired."

Where's Bethany?

Thursday, July 31, 10:20 p.m.
Jordan's room, Wilson, CO

Jordan plopped down on the floor beside his bed. He gritted his teeth and whisked away an angry tear. The evidence was gone. Donald Carlyle had betrayed him. Memories continued to assault him, and he was powerless to fight them off.

And William Nolan still stood condemned.

Kneeling beside his bed, the weight of failure pulled at him. He covered his face in his hands. The floodgates opened and Jordan Nolan cried.

Gadg was silent.

Minutes passed and Jordan regained his composure. He looked up at Gadg, who sat looking down at his phone. "Thanks, man. Sorry you had to see that."

"Why do you say that?" said Gadg. "I'm humbled by your trust. I felt like it was holy ground."

"Promise not to tell anybody?"

"I was thinking of calling Matthew," said Gadg.

Jordan gave a tired smile.

"All kidding aside," Gadg continued, "you ready to talk? Something urgent came up."

"What is it?" Something about Gadg's tone turned Jordan's face back to business.

"Look at this," Gadg showed him his phone. "I just saw it while you were …" He stopped. "It's on your phone as well."

Neither had checked their phones in a while. Jordan pulled his out and read the texts from Bethany. He wiped the sides of his face with his forearms. The red in his consciousness was gone and he straightened up. "Where is she?"

"Her phone must have run out of juice before she could send the location," said Gadg.

They turned sharply at an urgent knock on the window. Jordan cranked the handle around. The window opened sideways. "Allie! What are you doing?"

"Looking for Gadg."

"I'm here," said Gadg from Jordan's couch.

"I think something's wrong with Bethany," said Allie.

"We know it is," said Jordan.

"I knew it," Allie's face creased with concern. Fire kindled in her eyes. "Pull me up. We need to talk."

Jordan suppressed a smile. Good old Allie. She would want to be hoisted through a window rather than using the front door. "How about you come around front?"

A moment later, Allie stood in the room with them. She looked at Jordan. "You okay?" she asked. "You don't look so good."

"I'm fine," said Jordan. He didn't want to go down that road, so he said the first thing that came to mind. "Speaking of looking good, why are you all dressed up? Do I smell perfume?"

"None of your business," snipped Allie.

Gadg looked around the room, absently.

Jordan smirked.

"If you must know, I was on a date."

"Nice," said Jordan. "Who with?"

"Definitely none of your business. Where is she?"

Jordan's focus snapped back to the issue at hand. "We don't know. We received three texts in rapid succession. We think she might be trapped underground with no battery left on her phone."

Allie's face grew stern. "What are you talking about?"

Gadg handed her his phone.

Allie read through the three texts from Bethany. "That must be it," she said under her breath.

"What?" asked Jordan.

She reached into her purse and retrieved her phone. "This is why I came. I got a weird text from her tonight. Check this out—it may be what you need."

She held out her phone. "It looks like GPS coordinates or something."

"Let me see that," the boys grabbed for the phone in unison. They held it up next to Gadg's phone to read the messages as a continuous flow.

Gadg nodded.

"If these are for her location, I wonder why she sent them to you instead of us?" said Jordan.

"What difference does it make?" Allie fired back. "She's stuck underground!"

Jordan flushed. "You're right. I'm sorry. Stupid question."

"Can you read the grids to me?" Gadg launched an app on his phone.

Jordan read off the coordinates.

Thirty seconds later, Gadg said, "Whoa."

"What?" asked Allie.

"You're not going to believe where this is."

"Northeast?" asked Jordan.

Gadg nodded grimly.

"Northeast? What are you talking about?" she turned to Gadg and then glanced at Jordan.

Jordan looked at Gadg, assessing how much to say.

Allie caught his hesitation and her face tightened. She wheeled around, took two steps toward Jordan, and pushed her finger into his chest. "I've just about had it with you. Bethany is *trapped* underground. Tell me what I need to know this instant!"

Red flooded his mind for the second time that night as the memories launched another attack. He pushed her hand away, turned, and nearly stumbled over his desk chair. He leaned with both hands on the back of the chair and stared at his computer monitor.

"How dare you!" said Allie, almost breathing fire.

Gadg spoke softly. "Allie, listen." He stepped forward and laid his hand on her shoulder.

She turned to him with smoke coming out of her ears.

Gadg looked her in the eye, "Please trust me now as your old friend. You couldn't know this yet, but Jordan has just had, without question, the worst night of his life." He paused, lowering his voice. "The evidence to exonerate his great-grandfather is a pile of ashes in Donald Carlyle's fireplace."

Allie's expression disintegrated. She blinked, biting her lip, and looked away.

"To answer your question," Gadg went on, "Bethany received a cryptic message from a man with the code name of R3. We weren't sure how much you knew. This person told her to go underground and go northeast to find some info about why her mom is sick—and how it relates to the death of her great-grandfather, Ray. She's intrigued, but there's some danger. Jordan just wanted to keep you safe. We weren't sure it made sense to dump this on you. Sorry for the poor timing."

Allie looked at Gadg, eyes round. She stepped over to Jordan. "I'm sorry." She took a breath. "I had no idea. I know you want to find Bethany as badly as I do. Forgive me?"

Still leaning with one arm on the chair, Jordan reached out to give her a hug. He nodded without meeting her eyes as he wiped his face again. A few seconds later, he said, "So, where is she?"

"If this is right," Gadg replied, "the location is the abandoned mercantile building near the eastern end of Old Main Street."

Rescue and Records

Thursday, July 31, 10:45 p.m.
Under the abandoned mercantile, Wilson, CO

The darkness pressed in on Bethany from every side. The edgy quiet, broken only by subtle underground noises, seeped into her like a teabag in water.

Her only visible link to the outside world was the dim moonlight filtering through a few dusty crystals in a century-old manhole cover shrouded in debris. Her last text message, and the gift of God's presence, had left over an hour ago. Now it was a fight between the ears to keep from freaking out.

"Steady," she whispered to herself. Her eyes darted back and forth. She felt, as much as she saw, the tendrils of a darkness pulled straight from a poem by Edgar Allan Poe.

The small man could have been one of his characters.

Her thoughts drifted back to what he'd said while she hid.

How did he know about the letters?

She shivered. None of the possible answers were good.

What if he finds them?

An even worse thought assaulted her.

What if he finds me?

Her breath hissed through her teeth. She had to get out of there. Her rational mind said that she was fine. Gadg, Jordan, and Tyler knew she was down here somewhere.

The dark was unrelenting.

She drummed her fingers against her thigh and let out a long exhale.

Okay, I can do this.

Tiny feet scurried over the top of her shoe as whiskers and fur brushed across her ankle.

"AAAIIIEEEE!!!"

Bethany shattered the silence as she flung her foot and sent an unseen rodent flying into the blackness to her right. Rustling sounds came from a corner somewhere.

"AAAaaagghh!" Her hands shook wildly at her sides as she jumped and jumped and jumped. For the first time in her life, Bethany screamed out a prayer, "Daddy, send somebody NOW!"

● ● ●

Twelve minutes later, after sneaking through the back half of Nolan property and around several Old Town buildings, Jordan led Gadg and Allie through a doorway into a back room of one of the abandoned brick buildings that graced Old Town. Vertically, down the building's massive exterior side, light-colored bricks spelled out "MERCANTILE." This room, on the ground floor of the northeast corner, had two empty window openings and several holes in the ceiling. The moonlight gave the same eerie glow as it had in the grange earlier that evening.

I can't believe it's only been an hour and a half.

It felt more like a year since they'd found the evidence.

Holding up his phone, Gadg nodded to them. This was the place.

"Bethany?" Jordan spoke with a loud whisper. "You here?" He stomped on the wood floor.

"Jordan?" the faint sound of Bethany's voice came up from somewhere beneath them. It sounded weary, frightened, and beautiful. Relief flooded him.

"Talk some more," he said. "We need to pinpoint your location."

"The ethics of living donor transplantation," Bethany mimicked Jordan. "In this speech we will explore whether it is ethical for a living person to donate an organ."

Jordan's eyes misted as the emotions of the evening hit him afresh. Bethany's friendship was a bright spot on an otherwise horrible evening. He smiled.

Allie gave him an overdramatic wink that used half her face and all her mouth. She pointed at a pile of rubble in the corner of the room. "Over there."

Gadg smirked and shook his head.

They picked their way through the debris and cleared the area closest to the sound of Bethany's voice.

"Okay, Bethany, we got it," said Jordan.

She stopped speaking.

They scraped the dust from a round, patterned grate that resembled a manhole cover. It had a concentric, circular design with a few dull crystals inlaid upon it like a mosaic.

"Hold on, Bethany, I'm going for a crowbar." Jordan spun around to leave.

"Bring some rope," said Gadg.

Jordan jumped through the old doorway and disappeared.

● ● ●

With the flashlight on, Jordan dropped his phone down through the hole in the floor.

Bethany caught it and held it like someone dying of thirst would grasp a bottle of Gatorade. The darkness, though not complete, had borne down hard for a full hour on nerves overwrought by claustrophobia, uncertainty, and terror. Now, while Gadg figured out a way to secure the rope, the light from Jordan's phone and the knowledge that her friends were here gave her the courage to survey the hidden chamber.

Oh, thank You, Daddy.

After the last ninety minutes, Bethany gushed with thankfulness for the simple gift of light. She went back to study the crawl space. The tunnel appeared to dead-end a few feet beyond where she had emerged. There were no other entrances.

"What are you doing?" Allie spoke down into the chamber.

"Checking things out. I'll be right there," said Bethany.

She came back into the main chamber.

Could this be the "northeast" spoken of by R3?

Off to one side was an entrance that could have been her expected route.

No way R3 intended me to use the crawl space.

She looked around the chamber.

Are those shelves?

No doubt about it. In the far corner, which she had not visited yet, stood a dusty set of shelves.

One shelf held several books.

Old books.

They were records of copper-mining production. She could see the names of specific mines, dates, and amounts. The historical society would love this. The records seemed harmless enough. However, there was not much dust on them.

That's weird.

Was it possible she was in the location from the cryptic email? Were these meant for her?

She removed the books and saw something she hadn't noticed at first: a stack of magazines.

She scanned through them. Titles such as *Life, Time,* and *Newsweek.* Each seemed to have something to do with Wilson. One in particular caught her eye. 1967. *Time Magazine.* The all-black cover said "XD" in a huge, red font with a dripping, bloody slash through it.

Hmm.

"Let's get you out of there," Jordan spoke through the hole where the grate had been.

Bethany tied the rope around her waist and tucked the literature under one arm.

They hauled her up until she could hand off the books and magazines. Jordan then grabbed her by the wrist and pulled her up. She scrambled out and stood, covered from head to toe with grime.

Before he could gape or laugh, Bethany threw her arms around him in a fierce hug, covering him in dirt. "Thank you for coming," she mumbled into his shoulder.

Jordan stiffened as if unsure what to do with his arms.

Moonlight reflected the glint of approval off Allie's eyes along with a mischievous grin.

After a moment, Bethany felt Jordan's arms tighten around her. She surrendered to the hug and just let him hold her.

When the embrace ended, Bethany stepped back awkwardly. The hug had lasted longer than gratitude alone warranted. She coughed and hoped her blush was hidden under the layer of dirt that covered her skin. She turned to the others, "You guys are awesome! I can't thank you enough."

"You're welcome," said Gadg. He held the books and magazines.

Allie peeked at Jordan and then glanced at Bethany. "Yeah, you're welcome," she said with a twinkle.

Bethany narrowed her eyes.

"I must say," Jordan dusted himself off and looked back at Bethany, "I've never seen you like this."

Bethany looked down at herself and back up. She smiled a weary smile. "Yeah, long story."

"When I said it was going to be dark and creepy," said Jordan, "I meant *the woods*. I would never have let you brave *the catacombs* by yourself!"

The moonlight cast a shadow over Allie's smirk.

"In retrospect, I'm not sure it was the best idea," Bethany said in her most understated tone. "Let's get out of here. Obviously, I know what I need to do first." She felt the crust in her hair. "I'm glad my parents are out of town." She looked around. "Where's Tyler?"

Jordan's countenance fell.

Bethany's face switched to a layer of grime-encrusted concern. "What is it?"

Jordan looked away.

She glanced at Gadg.

"Bethany," he said, "the evidence is destroyed."

Chapter 63

Who Was Your Date?

Thursday, July 31, 11:30 p.m.
Nolan great room, Wilson, CO

Bethany's hug was the only reason Jordan hadn't given in to despair.

Seated around the Nolan great room, the group included Deputy O'Brien, Grandpa Walter, Johnny and Michelle, and the five young adults. The four had been able to get back home unseen, where his mom had helped Bethany get cleaned up and find some fresh clothes while they waited for an express wash on her filthy ones. Tyler had joined them as Gadg spread the old books and magazines across the coffee table in front of the couch.

As they compared stories, the weight of the situation settled onto the room. Bethany relayed her experience in the catacombs. Jordan and Gadg shared, in painful detail, their experience in Donald's office. Tyler looked at Walter and Johnny as he relived the exhilaration, followed by the devastation, of his escape and the subsequent loss of the evidence.

Deputy O'Brien listened, face grave, notepad in hand. A moment later he said, "Johnny, would you mind filling in what happened with Alex Jones?"

Johnny flushed. "Mark, this is not okay. How could we have known it would come to this?"

"Dear"—Michelle kept her voice even as she laid a hand on her husband's shoulder—"not now."

"I know." Johnny's ire dropped a notch. "I'm just concerned, that's all. This is huge." He turned to Jordan. "Did Donald Carlyle have his men detain you?"

"Yes," said Jordan. "Dad, you have to understand. We were caught trespassing on WDC2 property. I was concerned I might lose the internship. I was trying to keep it low-key. Besides, I thought Tyler had the evidence."

"I'm sorry, guys," said Tyler. "It was my bad."

"You don't have to apologize," said Jordan. "We saw *him* tonight."

"His voice is worse," said Bethany.

Jordan nodded. "I've heard it."

"Not underground, though." Bethany gulped.

Jordan gave her a sympathetic look as Deputy O'Brien took the floor. "The question is, how did he know *where* to intercept Tyler?"

"He came out of nowhere," said Tyler. "I had no idea he was there."

"This guy must have been doing some serious surveillance," said Johnny.

"That's what I'm getting at," said the deputy.

"There are only two options," said Gadg. "Either it was a total fluke, or he was directed there."

Jordan continued, "I'm going to guess it wasn't a fluke. If *that's* true, he must have been watching us or intercepted some communication from us."

"Watching us has two problems," said Gadg. "First, there was no way to have a signal on us while we were underground. Second, and more importantly, he was in place *before* Tyler got there. Assuming again that it's not a fluke, he had to have known Tyler would be coming back to the house. He must have intercepted some type of communication."

Bethany chimed in, "What communications went out from us tonight— especially after we found the evidence?"

"Didn't we send some texts? I remember talking in the back of the grange," said Tyler. "Check your phones."

"Jordan sent some texts to me tonight," said Johnny, pulling out his phone. "First, he told me about the evidence. I didn't know what he meant, but that's the reason Grandpa and I were out there when Alex was chasing Tyler."

Walter smiled. "Wish you could have seen it, Jordan."

Johnny nodded and continued, "The second text from Jordan, sometime after that, asked if Tyler got away. Unfortunately, at that point, I told him he had, and that he was headed to meet Deputy O'Brien. We didn't hear the truth until a good while later."

"I was totally freaked out," Tyler shuddered. "I went back to my room."

"He's small, right? Why didn't you fight him?" asked Allie.

Tyler grimaced.

"You would only ask that if you haven't seen him," said Bethany.

Jordan and Gadg both nodded.

"Who *is* this guy?" said Deputy O'Brien.

"His name is Isaac Molencki," said Bethany. "He's only about five feet tall, but I've never seen a more terrifying individual in my life."

A line creased across Michelle's forehead.

"Even Donald Carlyle seemed uncomfortable in his presence," said Gadg.

Deputy O'Brien jotted some notes.

"I'm sorry, Tyler," said Allie. "That wasn't fair. I seem to be making a lot of apologies tonight." She looked over at Jordan.

"This has gone way beyond the internship," said Johnny, looking at Jordan. "This is about your safety."

"I know," said Jordan. "We had no idea it was this big."

"Let's get back to the question at hand," said Deputy O'Brien. "What communications did you all engage in tonight?"

"I had some communication with you," Gadg replied. "You mentioned that we needed to get the physical evidence back to you."

Deputy O'Brien nodded.

"And I received a text from you, Bethany," said Allie.

"Yeah, I sent you a couple."

"It didn't make any sense. It was just some coordinates. Of course, Gadg was amazing in using them to locate you. We never understood why you sent them to me without any explanation."

"I didn't mean to," said Bethany. "I was treacherously low on battery and had to get the coordinates sent. My hands were shaking so bad I overshot O'Brien in my contacts and landed on Pearson. I had to make sure that at least one message got sent. I also tried to send it to Gadg, but my screen went black at that moment."

"Oh, honey," said Michelle.

"Yeah, she was quite grateful when Jordan pulled her up," said Allie.

Bethany pursed her lips.

"Allie came over right away," said Gadg, trying for a diversion.

"She didn't even have time to change after her date," said Jordan. He motioned to her outfit.

Allie frowned. She didn't like being upstaged.

"Oh, yeah," said Bethany. "How'd it go?"

Allie's face was a bit too bright. "It went well."

Deputy O'Brien opened his mouth to redirect the conversation. Bethany saved him the trouble. "You were probably out when I sent you the first text," she said.

"I had just been dropped off at the house," said Allie. "I jumped on a bike when I got your text. I had to get to Gadg because I felt something was wrong, but I couldn't make any sense of the numbers."

"Numbers?" Bethany frowned.

"The coordinates."

Deputy O'Brien looked up from his notepad. "Wait, are you ladies talking about the same thing?"

Bethany rested her chin on her knuckles and narrowed her eyes. "How many texts did you receive from me tonight?"

"One," said Allie. "The weird one with the GPS coordinates. Why?"

Bethany held out her phone. "Did you get a text that said Tyler was on his way back to the house with the evidence and to alert Deputy O'Brien if you saw him?"

"Nope." Allie grunted as she checked her phone.

"Maybe it didn't get through," Bethany said to Jordan. "We didn't have much of a signal."

"Both of ours got through," said Jordan to Gadg. "Is it possible for Bethany's phone to show a text got sent even if Allie's phone didn't receive it?"

"It's possible, but not likely," said Gadg. "Allie, can I see your phone?" She handed it to him. "What time did you send it, Bethany?" After she told him, Gadg spent several seconds fiddling with Allie's phone. "No sign of it here," he said, still looking down. "Wait," he squinted. "What's this?"

"What's what?" asked Allie.

"I only see the one text from Bethany in the 'Messages' app on your phone."

"That's what I thought," said Allie.

Gadg showed the phone to his dad. Jordan leaned over the back of the couch to see.

"Allie, I hate to put you on the spot like this," said Deputy O'Brien, "but why did you forward a picture of that text message in an email?"

"What are you talking about?"

Gadg handed the phone back to her.

Allie flipped a lock of hair around in circles as she processed the email. Her eyes widened, then narrowed, then smoldered as if molten lava had been poured into them.

Softly, Deputy O'Brien pressed, "Why did you send it?"

Allie's eyes blazed. "I didn't. A certain well-dressed 'gentleman,'"—she made air quotes—"asked to see pictures from my sister's wedding. He even said I looked beautiful."

"Are you saying you're not the only one who had your phone this evening?" asked the deputy.

"Yes, sir, that's what I'm saying." Her tears looked like they stung.

"Allie"—the deputy lowered his voice again—"who were you on a date with?"

Chapter 64

R3 Is Known

Thursday, July 31, 11:55 p.m.
Nolan great room, Wilson, CO

Allie choked out the answer through clenched teeth. "I was out with Matthew Harris."

Jordan stared down into his coffee mug. The news punched him in the gut.

A pall settled over the gathering. Sadness and anger, frustration and compassion blended together in a mood that, if it were a mixture of paints, would look like a weary, dark gray.

"So, Matthew Harris is the reason the small man knew to be here," said Tyler.

"I'm such a moron," said Allie.

Michelle sat down next to her and held her hand.

"It's not your fault," said Bethany. "There's no way you could have known."

"Next time I see him, he's gonna wish he hadn't done that," Allie seethed afresh.

"That still doesn't explain how Isaac Molencki knew about the catacombs," said Deputy O'Brien, "or how Matthew knew to contact him. This thing might be deeper than we think."

"We know it is, Dad," said Gadg. "We watched the evidence burn in Donald Carlyle's office."

Deputy O'Brien studied him. "Would you guys mind giving us a recap?"

Gadg looked at Jordan.

Jordan flipped his fingers in a lazy motion to proceed, though he wasn't sure what good it would do.

Gadg started from the beginning and laid it out, point by point. Johnny's face was pinched, holding back anger.

The gears in Deputy O'Brien's head turned fast as he looked between the pages of his copious notes.

Grandpa spoke up again. "Jordan"—he glanced at Johnny and then back—"for what it's worth, I'm proud of you. I know it changes nothing in this community, but you and your friends discovered the truth. Even if nobody believes it, you've made me proud to be a Nolan."

Johnny exhaled. "I agree, son. Please understand I'm not mad at you. I'm just upset. You guys were in danger tonight." He looked at his wife and then back at Jordan. "That said, I cannot tell you how impressed I am. You guys were thrown to the lions and you handled yourselves with poise. Well done." He continued, "I'd hate to be the defendant in a case you were prosecuting. You've got a bright future ahead of you, son. You're going to be an incredible attorney."

Jordan raised his eyes and blinked. He looked back and forth at the two men. "Thank you. It means a lot." He turned to his friends. "And thank you, too. You guys are the best." He shook his head as a wave of emotion crashed on him. "It's just not right. I'm a defense attorney and William Nolan still stands condemned. I failed." He looked back into his mug.

Walter and Johnny exchanged glances.

"*I* handled myself like a complete fool," said Allie.

"It's not your fault," replied Jordan without looking up. "I let Donald Carlyle get the best of me."

"Even if you did," said Tyler, "I still should've gotten away. Everything we needed was in that box. That R3 guy sure called it like it was. I don't know what Pandora's Box is, but that had to be it."

"This is much bigger than I imagined," said Deputy O'Brien, taking some more notes. "It has tentacles all over the place."

"What do we do?" asked Tyler.

"Nothing," said Jordan. "It's over."

"Who is R3?" asked Deputy O'Brien, looking up from his pad.

"No idea," said Bethany. "All we know is that he has contacted us a couple times to give us information and to warn us. He seems to know a lot."

"What's his game?" asked Walter.

"No clue," replied Jordan.

"Any idea what R3 stands for?" asked Bethany.

Jordan shook his head, gaze still downcast.

"Too bad Gadg's memory isn't admissible as evidence," said Allie. "He could probably get a conviction single-handedly."

"As much as I wish it to be different, that isn't enough," said Deputy O'Brien. "The physical evidence was crucial for any charges. I regret not being able to see it myself."

"Gadg could tell it all to you," said Tyler. "Couldn't you, Gadg? Tell him what one of the memos said."

"Not now." Gadg gave a dismissive wave of his hand.

"That's not a bad idea," said Deputy O'Brien. "Son, I know it's late and you guys are wrung out. But would you mind going through what you can remember?"

Jordan grimaced as he took a sip of coffee. He felt like a child trying to swallow a bite of canned spinach. *What difference does it make? The evidence is a pile of ashes.*

The deputy turned to a new page in his notebook. "We can't use it as evidence," he said, "but it's possible it could lead us to some other insight."

Gadg recounted the Master Plan, several pieces of evidence, and several internal Carlyle Enterprises memos that showed conclusively that the Wonder Drug had gone to market atop the cover-up of XD.

Tyler shook his head at Gadg's memory.

Jordan stirred from his listless state. His eyes perked up. "What did that last memo say?" He looked over at Gadg.

Gadg repeated it, "Memorandum: R2-6, Date: April 27, 1964, Subject: On the Side Effects of XD." He started into the text of the memo before Jordan interrupted him.

"Don't you find that strange?" asked Jordan.

The others looked puzzled.

"That date is three days *after* the night of their deaths," said Jordan.

"What does that mean?" asked Allie.

"It was post-dated," Bethany said, catching on. "They hadn't even given that memo to management yet. But why?"

"They were planning to go public the next week," said Gadg as his eyes brightened. "This was part of the body of evidence they intended to deliver suddenly, catching Howard Carlyle off guard."

Deputy O'Brien nodded his affirmation.

Jordan blurted, "Oh!" His eyes shot open.

"What?" several voices exclaimed.

His mouth hung open. "Duh." He nodded to himself. "I've got it."

"Got what?" asked Allie

"I know what R3 means."

Even Gadg looked surprised.

Jordan's eyes shone with fresh clarity. "Memorandum *R2*-6 was memo number six from William Nolan—the *second researcher* on the team."

Bethany piped up, "That means my great-grandfather must have been R1!"

"Does that mean that R3 was the third researcher on Ray and William's team?" asked Tyler.

"You got it," said Jordan.

"What do we do now?" asked Bethany.

"Officially"—Jordan looked at his dad—"we do nothing." He turned toward the deputy. "Right, sir?"

Deputy O'Brien nodded.

"Unofficially, and with extreme caution," Jordan said, lowering his voice to a whisper, "we go on a search for an old man."

PART THREE

The Promised Land

Dear William and Ray,

I turned 77 today. I'm "celebrating" alone. If you remember, we would have celebrated my 27th birthday that summer.

Today I'm writing from the sofa in a gorgeously furnished living room. I've told you about it before. The main area of this cabin could be on the cover of a magazine. Smoothly polished, hand-carved oak stairs, railings, furniture. Through three massive windows I can see the river flowing past. The beauty is striking.

I've owned it for several years.

I've enjoyed it for <u>none</u>.

How could I possibly enjoy it when everything around me has a touch of red.

Red.

I've tried to live a good life. I've tried to help people. Nothing works. Deep down, I know it's a sham. I'm just marking time.

This river cabin was paid for by the Man himself. Which means it was paid for with your blood and the blood of 20,000 others.

Happy Birthday, huh?

Chapter 65

A Walk Home

Friday, August 1, 9:30 a.m.
County road east and south of Nolan property, Wilson, CO

The morning sun that brought in the first day of August whispered a golden blessing onto the town of Wilson. While Gadg pushed the bike for Allie, Jordan walked with his friends on the East Road toward the Clark home.

"Jordan," said Allie, "please tell your mom thanks a million. Yesterday was the craziest day I can ever remember, and she was so gracious last night—putting us up in the guest room, getting me clothes to sleep in, stuff like that."

"Yeah," said Bethany. "I didn't want to go home last night, especially with just Allie and me at the house."

Allie nodded with a grimace.

Bethany continued, "I can't say I ever imagined I'd spend the night at the Nolan house."

Gadg chuckled.

"I can't imagine why," said Jordan. "What *are* you going to tell your dad?"

"I'm not sure yet," said Bethany as she rubbed a hand across her forehead, glancing away.

"You sure they won't be home?" said Jordan. "No offense, but I'm not in the mood to see him this morning."

"I'm sure," said Bethany. "They come back tomorrow. I got a text from him this morning. Mom is having a decent time of it, even though she is still wiped out. Dad is off to his meetings today with Jeffrey Kingston." Bethany's tone turned deadpan as she faced forward. "He asked me if I had a good day yesterday."

A couple seconds went by before Jordan smirked. "That's funny."

Bethany said, "Yeah, I thought so."

Allie put a fist up to her mouth to push down a smile and asked Bethany, "And what did you tell him?"

"I told him I have a great life and that it's good to be alive." She took a deep breath as if smelling fresh air for the first time.

Jordan's shoulders relaxed and he chuckled. "That is awesome," he said. Smiling, they rounded a corner onto Bethany's street. Jordan's upper arm bumped against her shoulder as they turned.

She didn't pull away. They walked side by side a few inches from each other.

Jordan sneaked a look at her.

She gave a tiny glance back at him.

Their eyes met for an instant, and they jerked their heads forward.

Jordan tried for nonchalant as he narrowed the space between them to an inch or two.

Looking past Gadg, Allie caught the exchange and let her lips curl into a smirk.

Jordan put his hands into his pockets to keep them from shaking and to dry his palms as discreetly as possible. As they walked up the driveway, he stopped and took it all in. "I don't think I've ever been in your house," he said.

"Well, I'd better give you the tour while I have the chance." Bethany smiled.

Allie raised an eyebrow.

Entering through the kitchen, Bethany showed the group around the house, even though Gadg had been there several times, and Allie lived there.

● ● ●

Jordan stared as if he gazed upon one of the Seven Wonders of the World. Never in his life had he expected to see the inside of Bethany's house.

"Well, guys, this completes the tour." Bethany waved her arm sideways with an open palm. "Welcome to my room."

Jordan stepped forward, followed by Gadg and Allie. The room had the look of someone who had been forced to grow up too soon. Functional efficiency with a subtle touch of beauty. Everything in its place, though Bethany did not have much in the way of things.

Sparse.

It was the only word that came to Jordan's mind. There just wasn't that much stuff. He scanned the room, trying to absorb as much of Bethany's personality as he could. He didn't know if he would ever have this chance again.

Allie dumped the plastic bag with her clothes from last night's date onto her bed. They became the only things out of place in the whole room. "Oh, look," Allie pointed, and her eyes glinted with mischief. "There's Bethany's diary."

Three pairs of eyes followed her finger.

Bethany did a double take. Her diary sat poised on the desk.

Unbidden, a spray of longing shot into Jordan's midsection. He turned his head quickly.

I wonder if I'm in it.

Steeling himself on the outside, he hoped no one saw what he was thinking.

The prospect of drama turned Allie into a loose cannon. Still amped up from watching Jordan and Bethany outside, she said, "Care to tell us what, or should I say *who*, is in it?"

Staring at the diary, Bethany furrowed her brow. "It's between me and God. It tells my thoughts, feelings, hopes, and fears—as well as many other things."

"Like when a hug lasts a little too long?" Allie suggested.

"Allie!" said Bethany as her cheeks went bright red.

Jordan stole a glance at the diary and then at Bethany. His insides burst into flames. A bit of red inched up the back of his neck. He forced his mind in a different direction.

The ethics of living donor transplantation...

"Oh, I'm sorry, I forgot," Allie continued with a twinkle, "you haven't had a chance to write about yesterday yet."

"Allie!" said Bethany, louder.

In this speech we will explore whether it is ethical for a living person to donate an organ...

Gadg stared at the diary and narrowed his gaze. "Allie, normally this might be hilarious, but we need to be serious."

"Oh, come on—don't you want to know what's in the diary, Gadgie-boy?" Allie tried to get a rise.

"Allie!" Bethany was aghast.

We must address a number of considerations in determining, not only the legal, but also the moral implications...

Gadg lowered his voice. "At another time this might be fun, but this is dreadfully serious."

Allie play-pouted and mellowed. "I'm just trying to put the obvious out on the table that two people need to stop acting like—"

"Allie, not now," Gadg interrupted.

Jordan looked at Gadg with wonder in his eyes. He was, perhaps, the only person on planet Earth who could put Allison Pearson in her place.

"Thank you," Bethany said. She gave a sideways frown to Allie and glanced back at Gadg.

He looked startled.

Her shoulders tightened. "Gadg, what is it?"

He faced the desk. Without turning his head, he looked up at Bethany at a curious angle that revealed mostly just the whites of his eyes. "Is that how you normally leave your diary—with the edges perfectly aligned with the sides of your desk?"

Jordan gaped. The hair on his arms stood on end.

Bethany's forehead creased. "No, it's not. In fact, I never leave it out. I stash it under my mattress." She shot an accusing look at Allie. "Did you put it there?"

Allie shook her head, mouth hanging open.

Bethany blinked. She looked at both Jordan and Gadg, catching their alarm. "What does this mean?"

Jordan swallowed. His stomach sunk to his toes. "It means Isaac Molencki was in your room."

Chapter 66

What's in the Diary?

Friday, August 1, 10:15 a.m.
Bethany's room, Wilson, CO

"Let me get this straight. The small man was *in here*?" Bethany recoiled in horror. Her chin quivered as she stared back at Jordan.

"Not just in your room," Jordan's voice was a whisper, "but reading your diary."

She wrapped her arms around her midsection. It felt like the walls had eyes and wanted to touch her with slimy hands. Realization came in a blinding flash.

That's how he knew about the two letters.

He saw my deepest secrets.

He knows how I feel about...

Pressing her lips together, her next inhalation made a whistling sound. She blinked back a stinging redness.

A vein on Jordan's neck pulsed. His eyes were soft, but anger smoldered deep inside them.

Revulsion welled up from within Bethany. For the second time in two days, she threw her arms around Jordan as tears spilled onto her cheeks. She shivered, pressing her head into his neck and shoulder. Her breath came in little gasps.

This time Jordan hugged back with a solid, unmoving strength.

"I c-can still hear his voice in my head," Bethany punched the words out between sniffs. Her face twisted as she relived the night before. "'Where are you, Bethany?'" Her voice morphed into a wail. She gripped Jordan like a life preserver as a fresh wave of disgust washed over her. She wriggled and contorted her back as if to shake a spider off without touching it.

He was silent, holding her.

There was no glint of approval in Allie's eyes this time. She was livid.

Even Gadg's jaw tightened as he surveyed the room, the diary, and the others.

Gradually, the trembling ceased. Bethany gave a couple last whimpering inhalations, and her breath slowed to a normal rhythm. She lifted her face from Jordan's shoulder, released her grip on him, and stood up straight. She blinked a few times and used both palms to wipe a swath of tears from her face. For good measure, she lifted each arm to brush shoulder and shirt across each eye. "I'm sorry."

Allie reached over and pulled her in for a hug.

●●●

Jordan stepped back to assess the situation. The diary sat smugly on the desk like a calling card—just like the old Bible had. He balled his hands into fists.

The horror in Bethany's face receded. She stepped back from Allie and wiped her palms across her eyes one more time, even though they were no longer wet. "Okay, I'm back."

Jordan spoke through clenched teeth. "I'm not. This is not okay. A CEO of a major corporation kidnaps us and destroys incriminating evidence. The creepiest guy ever, obviously hired by someone, breaks into your room and reads your diary." His voice rose in intensity. "Intimidated, threatened, stalked, and now violated. What's next?" His eyes blazed as he looked at the other three. "This ends here!"

The others looked like they were ready to salute. They'd never seen him like this. "So, what do we do?" asked Allie.

"We strike back," said Jordan. "It's time to go on the offensive."

"Starting with what?" asked Allie.

"Bethany's safety." Jordan turned to Gadg. "Is this something you could help with?"

Gadg looked around the room. "If you want, I'll put a camera up in that corner." He turned to Bethany. "You can engage it any time you leave, or even have it on while you're here. You just have to remember that you have a camera in your room."

"Ewww," Bethany grimaced.

"Oh, come on," chided Allie, "I thought your nickname was Gadg. Don't tell me that's the best you can do."

"It might be, on short notice," said Gadg. "I still have a lot to do for the celebration."

"Oh, that's right," said Bethany. "You're on the A/V, aren't you?"

"Yes, and it needs to work. Still, if you want, I'll get the camera installed today. You gonna tell your dad?"

"Probably," said Bethany. "Put it in. Make it turn on only if I engage it."

"You got it. I'll also put an app on your phone that pages me if you push any of its buttons three times in rapid succession."

"Thanks, Gadg, I owe you one."

"You're welcome. I'm going to tell my dad about this. I also think the rest of us need to go on full alert."

"I agree," Jordan nodded. "But with one caveat." He paused to get their attention. "We need to make sure we don't look like we're on full alert. Remember, as of yesterday, our opponents think this is over."

"That's true," said Gadg. "We know they're watching us—"

"You mean stalking," said Allie.

"Yes," conceded Gadg. "And since they are, we need to act like it's over and we're trying to get back to our lives."

"So, what then?" asked Allie.

"First," said Jordan, "we find out who R3 is. I've got some ideas. Second, we go after the two letters spoken of in R3's email to Bethany. I'm not sure how we're going to do that just yet. It's too risky at the moment. Third, since this is no longer just about what happened fifty years ago, we need to learn all we can about the current players and what they're up to."

The girls looked at each other and then at Gadg. He nodded for Jordan to continue. They were with him.

"Bethany"—Jordan kept his voice soft—"I don't mean to pry, but what could Molencki have learned from your diary?"

Bethany winced. "You mean besides my life story and some stuff that only God knows?"

Allie glared at Jordan.

"It's okay," said Bethany. She caught the look and put her hand on Allie's wrist. "It's a necessary question."

Allie pursed her lips, but sat back.

Bethany continued, "I mentioned in the diary that I thought you might attempt to use the tunnels to get under the grange." Fresh pain crossed her face. "I'm sorry."

"It's not your fault," said Jordan. "How could you have known somebody would break into your room, hunt down your diary, and read it?"

Bethany shuddered.

Gadg spoke up. "May I offer a theory?"

"Please do," said Bethany. "I'd like to know what's going on."

Gadg gave a thoughtful nod and began, "I'm guessing the small man learned about the catacombs from the diary and went looking for Bethany—or us—when he learned about the map from someone at the community meeting. He found out about the evidence from Matthew, who learned about it by reading Allie's text. I have no idea how those two are connected, but it appears that they are somehow. Putting all those pieces together puts the small man above ground getting the evidence from Tyler, underground looking for Bethany, and in Donald Carlyle's office a while later."

"He was everywhere," said Bethany.

Jordan continued, "He's got to have more than just Matthew working with him. I'm curious who is pulling the strings here."

"Mr. Carlyle?" offered Bethany. "You said Molencki brought the evidence to him."

Jordan gave a half shake of his head. "I'm not so sure. I mean, yes, you're right about the evidence, and he's obviously involved somehow. But"—Jordan paused and looked over at Gadg—"Molencki swaggered around the desk and planted himself next to Mr. Carlyle like he owned the joint."

Gadg nodded and looked back at the girls. "I agree. It was weird. Mr. Carlyle was kind of freaked out—in a high-powered, CEO sort of way, of course. He didn't seem like the boss."

"What are you saying?" asked Allie.

"I'm saying there could be another major player in this equation," said Jordan.

"Who?" asked Allie.

"That's what we need to find out." A sudden gleam shined on Jordan's face, and he turned to Allie. "Can I ask you a question?"

She narrowed her eyes. "I've seen that look before."

"What are you thinking about Matthew right now?"

Allie's face hardened. "The next time I see him he's going to wish he'd never met me."

Jordan let that linger and turned to look around the room as if he didn't have a care in the world. His tone turned disarming, almost offhanded, as he said, "Would you consider an alternate strategy?"

All three of them leveled gazes at him.

He looked up at the corner of the ceiling and drummed his fingers absently.

"What did you have in mind?" Allie crossed her arms.

"Something that would utilize your many gifts and require a high degree of skill." Jordan paused. "You'd get to play the starry-eyed ditz."

"If you say 'again,' I'll slap you," warned Allie.

"Actually"—Jordan turned serious—"you could play it any way you like. They started this war. It's time for us to get in the fight. Don't take this lightly, Allie. This is dangerous. It's not the time for a personal vendetta. What I'm asking for is an Oscar-level performance that convinces Matthew that you are smitten with him and clueless about anything meaningful while simultaneously *extracting information* from him."

"Ooh, I like it," Allie warmed to the idea. "What do you need to know?"

Jordan lowered his voice to a whisper. "We need to know who Isaac Molencki works for."

●●●

Turning down the offer of a ride, Jordan and Gadg walked the East Road back to the Nolan house after Allie and Bethany drove off in the Explorer that belonged to Bethany's dad. The only sound was sneakers on gravel as they were both lost in their thoughts.

"Gadgie-boy?" Jordan broke the silence.

"I don't want to hear it," said Gadg.

"And to think"—Jordan's smile lit up his face—"I was there."

"If you ever call me that"—Gadg shot him a look of playful warning—"you'll never own another device without a virus on it."

Jordan's eyes shone in the late morning sunshine. His sneakers made a soft crunch as he stared forward with a smirk.

Chapter 67

A Trip to Denver

Tuesday, August 5, 7:15 a.m.
Driving up the Interstate toward Denver, CO

As Gutless coasted down the gentle grade of I-25 into the dawning of a gorgeous Denver day, the road felt more like a tightrope than an interstate. Gadg and Tyler had commitments, so Jordan made the trip alone. A simple glance at the passenger seat filled him with warning.

Two phones—not one—rested on the seat.

Gadg had warned him that it was possible his real phone was tapped, and as a result, he had outfitted Jordan with a smartphone borrowed from his dad's stash of police toys. They would communicate only on a secure channel. Gadg had loaded Jordan's key apps, most of them cloud-based, onto the new phone. "This is your phone now," he had said. "Use your normal phone only for keeping up appearances."

Officially, Jordan was heading to Denver for his last meeting with Senator Smith before the internship.

Unofficially, he was on a reconnaissance mission.

First, he had to find out how thin the ice was that he was treading on after the trespassing debacle the other night. Second, and more dangerous, he needed to probe, with subtlety, to find out if Senator Smith was involved in this affair. Jordan had come home from his trip to DC to find that a secret known only to him and Gadg had been intercepted. The Grande bridge had been cordoned off with construction fencing, and the only time Jordan and

Gadg had discussed it was while Jordan was in the home of Senator Smith. Fortunately, the clue had not been under the bridge, but he couldn't escape the nagging feeling that the senator might somehow be tied into all this.

His list of enemies seemed to grow by the week. Matthew Harris, Alex Jones, Michael Clark, Donald Carlyle. Was it possible that Senator Smith, under all his charm and strength, was an antagonist as well?

He had to find out.

A sickening picture flashed across his mind as he realized he'd left one name off the list. A small, dangerous man stood next to Bethany's bed, taking his time to enjoy a read through her diary. Jordan could still feel Bethany's writhing as he held her, like she was trying to get slime off of herself. The sound of her beautiful voice twisting into a mimic of, "Where are you, Bethany?" brought bile to his throat.

He smacked the steering wheel, snatched up his new phone and launched a diary entry.

Current Issues

Okay, here's a brain dump of all the issues currently on the table:

The internship - do I still have it?

William Nolan's good name and the Nolan Stigma

The bizarre "summer school" accounting ledger that says William and Ray were murdered

The mystery man named R3 - now known to be the third researcher on the team in 1964

The cryptic message about two letters linking Ray's death to the health of Mrs. Clark

Hard evidence - now destroyed - of a deadly corporate cover-up

Possible links to a US Senator

The truth about Howard Carlyle - the one responsible for XD

Jordan paused before speaking his last thought.

> Bethany's safety and purity

He put down the phone just as he reached the concrete jungle of the Denver Tech Center.

"Lord," Jordan prayed with squinted eyes and one hand shielding the blinding orange of the rising sun, "You promised that Your faithfulness is unto all generations. Please protect us. Would you make a way for the truth to come out?"

A thought popped into his head.

"Oh, and one more thing, I'd really like to not lose the internship, if possible."

●●●

Jordan spent the rest of the trip meditating on the phrase "His faithfulness is unto all generations." At least he was calm. During the last few minutes of the drive and the finding of a parking space, he had made a conscious effort not to think about how angry he was with Howard and Donald Carlyle. As he walked the few blocks to the Capitol building he looked around with a smile.

What a beautiful city.

Many people, not from Colorado, did not know that Denver kept a wonderful secret.

Three hundred sunny days per year.

This particular Tuesday in August was a striking example. The city basked in the golden glow of morning sunshine.

DC will not have nearly as much sun—and when it does, it will be humid.

Bummer. Oh well. At least it was a long way from Wilson.

And a long way from Bethany.

And Gadg.

And Grandpa.

And my dad.

That was a new thought. He didn't have time for a diary entry, so he made a mental note to think about it later.

He looked up at the Capitol building. It was huge.

Jordan took a deep breath.

He found his way to the correct wing of the building, introduced himself to the receptionist, and waited out the remaining time until his appointment with Senator Smith.

Over the next few minutes, the excitement began to flow again. He recalled the awards ceremony.

"In second place ... Matthew Harris."

What a moment that had been. The last few weeks had so consumed him with the treasure hunt and the search for the evidence that he hadn't given much thought to the internship. He pulled out his new phone and smiled. Of course, Gadg had put the internship ticker on the main screen.

20 days, 0 hours, 5 minutes, 3 seconds
20 days, 0 hours, 5 minutes, 2 seconds
20 days, 0 hours, 5 minutes, 1 second

Jordan chuckled to himself at something he'd not previously noticed.

Another geek-point for Gadg.

Even on a thrown-together app like this he had made sure that 1 second was singular, not plural.

●●●

"Jordan"—Jeffrey Kingston walked into the outer office with an outstretched hand and a bright smile—"great to see you again."

"Thank you, sir, you too." Jordan stood up and shook his hand.

"Have a seat." Jeffrey gestured for Jordan to sit back down and then sat on a chair diagonal from him. "I only have a moment before your meeting with Senator Smith, but I needed to tell you something."

Uh-oh. Something about Jeffrey's tone brought foreboding. Jordan wondered if he was aware of the senator's possible association with Donald Carlyle.

"We've had some good conversations over the last couple months, haven't we?"

Jordan tried not to look wary. "Yes, sir, we have."

"Have you felt like it's been worth your time?"

"Oh, very much. I'm grateful for the time you've taken. I've learned a ton."

"That's great." Jeffrey's smile was still easy. "Do you feel like we are beginning to trust one another?"

"I hope so, sir."

"So, when were you going to tell me?" asked Jeffrey. His smile stayed on his face but left his eyes.

"Sir?"

"I've just been informed that you were caught *trespassing*."

The images of the evidence burning in the fireplace flashed into Jordan's mind. It took all he had to keep a lid on his emotions. "Yes, sir. May I ask how you found out?"

"I have eyes in a lot of places."

I bet you do. The question is, whose eyes?

"Jordan, we can*not* have this. The Senator's Internship is a privilege. It's not a free pass to do whatever you want."

"Yes, sir. It was a huge mistake. It won't happen again."

Jeffrey relaxed. "I'm glad to hear it." He lowered his voice. "You do understand the consequences if anything like this happens again, don't you?"

Jordan looked down at his shoes and nodded.

Chapter 68

Poker with Senator Smith

Tuesday, August 5, 8:00 a.m.
Senator Smith's office, Denver, CO

"The senator will see you now."

Jordan followed the receptionist into the large office that was Senator Smith's home away from DC.

"Welcome, Jordan." The senator's deep baritone resonated as he walked around his desk and extended his hand.

"Senator Smith," replied Jordan, attempting to hold his voice steady. "I must confess, I'm blown away to even be here."

"You've earned it, my boy," said the senator with such down-home ease that it calmed Jordan's nerves. "That was a prize fight you won that night in the Springs. Well done."

Jordan warmed with a mixture of pride, embarrassment, and gratitude.

Smith directed him to one corner of his spacious office. A homey set of three chairs sat in a half circle around a polished oak table. Jordan's eyes lit up as he noticed a coffee carafe surrounded by a porcelain creamer full of half-and-half, and two large Washington, DC mugs. There was no sweetener of any kind.

Jordan raised an eyebrow.

The senator nodded, a smile tugging at the corner of his mouth. "I do my homework," he said, motioning toward one of the chairs.

A chill ran over Jordan as the senator's words reminded him of his unofficial business.

Of course he would know of my love for coffee.

As he sat down, Jordan took a deep breath and tried to pretend the impossible—that this was just an ordinary conversation. As Senator Smith poured the coffee, then followed it with a surprisingly accurate complement of half-and-half, Jordan found his hands shaking as he reached for the mug. Wrapping both hands around it, mainly to steady them, his concern deepened as he noticed how hot the coffee was, and yet how well the mug kept the heat from his hands. It was just like the gift from his dad. Jordan forced a smile of thanks as he swallowed his first sip.

"Jackpot?" asked the senator.

A jolt seemed to shoot down from the mug through his fingers. "It's excellent," he said as he took another long sip to gather his composure. If not for the context, the question might seem friendly—but the familiarity with Jordan's life that it suggested, and the level of inquiry that the senator had undoubtedly authorized, reminded him how much power this man wielded.

Cordial small-talk took up the next two-thirds of the coffee in Jordan's mug. He had just started to relax again when the conversation took an unexpected turn.

"I've got a question for you, Jordan. Who is your hero?"

"My hero?" His eyes rounded with genuine surprise.

The senator's smile was disarming. "I like that question very much. A person's response tells me a lot about them."

The real answer—very politically incorrect—came in a flash.

William Nolan.

Jordan took another sip and offered a quick prayer for grace. Another realization hit him. This was an open door to pursue a line of discussion that could lead to some answers—if he was careful. It was time to step up to the table and probe the senator's involvement. "Do you want to know?" Jordan replied with a comfort level that surprised him. He was becoming a big believer in that prayer for grace.

The senator smiled. "With that look on your face, and the way you asked the question, how could I not want to know?"

Jordan nodded. "Well, sir, my hero is my great-grandfather, William Nolan."

Pause.

The senator's smile remained, but his eyes flickered.

Jordan studied him carefully. Yes, there it was.

He knows the story—at least, the official one.

"I must say," said the senator, "that is a most interesting answer—one that I didn't expect. May I ask why?"

Jordan took a deep breath. "Sir, I need to ask you a question first. Do you *really* want to know the answer?"

Senator Smith gave a look somewhere between wonder and concern. "That's the second time you've asked me that. Why might I *not* want to know?"

"Ignorance may not be bliss, but it does allow a certain wiggle room with respect to accountability. Wouldn't you agree?"

"I cannot remember a simple conversation that has intrigued me as much as this one," replied Senator Smith with a smile. "Yes, I want to know."

Careful.

It wasn't lost on Jordan that the senator was the honored speaker at the Wonder Drug 50th Anniversary Celebration in less than two weeks. He tightened his grip on the mug and continued, "William Nolan was the brightest light in our family for a few days. I would not be here if it hadn't been for him."

The senator narrowed his eyes.

Jordan put on his best poker face and tried to read the man seated across from him. This was either new information or he was involved with Donald Carlyle. Jordan couldn't tell which.

"Please go on." The senator threw the ante on the table and dared Jordan to play the hand.

Heart racing, Jordan anted up. "Sir, my great-grandfather implicated himself in a murder to save our family."

"Implicated himself?"

Jordan felt the thrill, and the warning, of the higher stakes. This was a game for big boys and Senator Smith had ushered him into a DC green room.

The senator placed another bet. "How does one implicate himself in a murder he did not commit?"

Jordan knew the man was fishing, but couldn't discern why. He had to play his next card. "By smearing blood and leaving articles of clothing at the scene."

The senator gave a patronizing grin as though he had seriously overestimated his opponent. He got up from his chair like a professional gambler leaving a game of Go Fish. "Really, Jordan?"

Something about the senator's manner flashed an image of Donald Carlyle sitting behind his desk while the evidence burned. It brushed the hair trigger of Jordan's taut emotions. Indignation, barely contained, flared hot. His nostrils widened. He had had just about enough of people maligning his hero.

"Do you really want it all?" Jordan ignored an internal warning and fired back with a mixture of cold professionalism and emotional heat that surprised both himself and Senator Smith.

The senator turned and sat back down. He might have given a hint of a smile.

Jordan's gut screamed as he threw down a dangerously high raise, "Sir, you asked, so here goes: Wilson Drug and Compounding Center was built on a cover-up related to the drug XD. William Nolan and Ray Clark were murdered because they were unwilling to keep quiet about the side effects. Howard Carlyle ordered them silenced because they threatened the Wonder Drug deal with Hampden Pharmaceuticals. My grandfather, Walter, survived only because William made it look like he had killed Ray, and therefore, it became in Howard Carlyle's best interest to leave Walter alone with the stigma. Just three days ago, Donald Carlyle was confronted with this, and I personally watched him incinerate the evidence in his office fireplace at WDC2 Headquarters. In case I'm not being clear, sir, let me state it in plain English: Howard Carlyle—Man of the Century—was a murderer. His son learned the truth and covered it up."

Senator Smith looked like a stone. No smile. No easy manner. No transparency. "You can prove this?" he asked.

Either the man was innocent, or he was assessing his own risk exposure. Just like real poker, Jordan would have to keep playing to find out. This man hadn't become a senator for nothing. "No sir, I cannot. Not yet, anyway. It all happened so fast. We were brought to Mr. Carlyle before we had time to make any copies. However"—Jordan lowered his voice and pushed all his chips in—"we didn't just stumble upon that evidence. We were *directed* there."

The senator raised an eyebrow.

Jordan leveled his gaze and waited. He had an ace in the hole and he knew it. *Yes, there's a living person who knows the truth.*

All the chips were on the table. The next thing out of the senator's mouth could give Jordan the information he needed.

Jeffrey Kingston appeared at the door.

The moment went up in smoke.

Senator Smith leaned back. "Ah, Jeffrey, you remember Jordan?" He said it more as a greeting than a question.

"Yes, sir," said Jeffrey. "We spoke this morning. How are you, Jordan?"

"I'm fine, Mr. Kingston," said Jordan, trying by sheer willpower to not make it a total lie.

"What can I do for you, Jeffrey?" asked the senator.

"I am sorry to bother you, sir. But it's time for our next meeting. Donald Carlyle is here."

Jordan stood up. A shaft of fear sliced through his stomach and threatened to take him out right then and there. He shook Senator Smith's hand, turned to leave, and wished the floor would open up and swallow him whole.

Homestead Offer

Tuesday, August 5, 8:30 a.m.
Office of Senator Smith, Denver, CO

As Jordan left the room, Senator Smith walked around his desk, put his hand on the back of his chair, and looked out the window across the city. He had scheduled the appointment with Jordan this morning because he could fit it in before he and Jeffrey met with Donald Carlyle. He had no idea that a young man, just months past voting age, would cause such a cascade of emotions. He had to scramble to get his mind ready for the next meeting. He couldn't believe the moxie that kid had shown. Yes, Jordan Nolan had a future in DC.

The senator's mind jumped to a horrible thought.

What if everything he said was true?

Smith gripped the back of his chair.

This could ruin everything.

He hadn't given anything away, but he'd played his cards too close to the vest to look squeaky clean. He wondered what Jordan thought of him.

His own future was the purpose of the meeting that was about to start. He had looked forward to it all week. Donald Carlyle hadn't come right out and said it, but Smith knew this meeting was a homestead offer. Jeffrey Kingston had done the legwork and reported back to him that he could write his own ticket as a career politician if he hitched his wagon to Mr. Carlyle and a group of high-powered Colorado businessmen. Informally, he had been riding along with that train for a while.

Another thought crept into the corner of his mind.

Is this the legacy I want?

He pushed it down as his chief of staff stepped back into the room with Donald.

"Good morning, Mr. Carlyle," said the senator as he spun from the window and moved to greet his guest. James Dakota Smith was not smooth like silk, but smooth in the manner of a polished, hand-carved piece of oak furniture in a mountain lodge. He mustered all he had to force Jordan's words, less than five minutes old, out of his head.

"Good morning, Senator," returned Donald Carlyle distractedly as he turned from watching Jordan leave the outer office. "Good kid, that young Mr. Nolan."

Jordan's words flashed across Senator Smith's mind like the world's fastest ticker tape.

Do you really want to know the answer?

"Yes, he is," was all he could manage.

Jeffrey eyed him.

"Of course, he's big man on campus back in Wilson this summer. Senator's Internship and all," said Donald. He shot a glance at Jeffrey. "We're real proud of him."

Jordan's words continued their assault.

We were brought to Mr. Carlyle before we had time to make any copies.

Senator Smith needed to tread carefully. "I'll bet he is. That's big news for a little town like Wilson."

"It is. Except for Johnny's college heroics, the Nolans have been persona non grata in Wilson for many years. Must be a nice change."

William Nolan was the brightest light in our family for a few days.

"I wonder why," said the senator innocently. "It seems like a long time to hold a grudge."

Only Jeffrey's eyes moved as he glanced at Donald Carlyle and back to his boss.

"Not that long for a semi-small town. There are people still alive who were directly affected."

"I suppose there are," said Senator Smith.

"Michael Clark, for example."

The senator turned to Jeffrey. "I know that name. Where do I know it from?"

"He's our emcee at the 50th Anniversary Celebration," replied Jeffrey. "You will have some conversations with him before then."

The senator nodded and turned back to Donald. "Michael Clark. He's not that old, is he?"

"Not quite sixty. It was his grandfather that was killed by William Nolan. Very unfortunate."

Sir, my great-grandfather implicated himself in a murder to save our family.

Senator Smith remained smooth.

Jeffrey's eyes narrowed ever so slightly.

"That is unfortunate," agreed the senator.

"It's still a fresh wound for some." Donald paused. "That's a part of what I wanted to talk to you about."

Senator Smith raised an eyebrow.

"James"—Mr. Carlyle leaned in, addressing him by his first name—"I need to bring you into my confidence."

"What is it, Donald?"

"WDC2 has a wonderful celebration coming up in less than two weeks."

Wilson Drug and Compounding Center was built on a cover-up related to the drug XD.

The senator only nodded.

Donald continued, "Well, Hampden Pharmaceuticals has offered to purchase WDC2."

This was not news to Senator Smith. Jeffrey had been keeping his finger on the pulse for him.

"This deal represents a significant influx of capital to the town of Wilson. The plan is to announce it right after your speech at the celebration. I'd hate to see anything jeopardize this."

"What are you suggesting, Donald?"

"Young Mr. Nolan has been stirring up some trouble around town this summer."

The senator glanced at Jeffrey.

"He was caught trespassing," said Jeffrey. "I just learned it myself, sir. I planned to tell you after this meeting."

"Trespassing?" Smith frowned.

"Yes, on WDC2 property," said Donald. "He's not a bad kid, but he's been poking his nose around in places that maybe he shouldn't."

"Why would he do that?"

"I had someone look into it. Apparently, there were some conspiracy theories from the early days regarding my father's leadership of WDC2."

Howard Carlyle ordered them silenced because they threatened the Wonder Drug deal with Hampden Pharmaceuticals.

"Conspiracy theories? Like what?"

"Jordan heard a theory that his great-grandfather wasn't actually a murderer, that the official police investigation was all wrong, and so on. Naturally, he would want to believe that."

"Naturally," agreed Smith. "Who wouldn't?"

"The bottom line is, I don't want any of these speculations or fears causing Hampden to get skittish."

Jeffrey studied his boss.

"What do you propose?" asked the senator.

"Well, you have two years left on this term. I know how much you love this state and how much you consider it a privilege to serve. I could see a mutually beneficial partnership between us for as long as you wish to remain in office. Furthermore, I and certain friends would find it advantageous to keep you around in different, and lucrative, capacities for many years to come. Your influence could expand dramatically."

So there it was.

Jordan's words broke in to the conversation like nails on a chalkboard inside the senator's mind.

I personally watched him incinerate the evidence in his office fireplace at WDC2 Headquarters.

Donald continued, "We've got too much to think about to be worried about chasing phantoms. That celebration—and the deal with Hampden—needs to come off without a hitch." He stood and turned to leave. "James, I'm willing to keep things quiet and let slide the trespassing charge if Jordan will keep his nose out of this. It's not my intention to make a mess here. If not, I may be forced to put you in an awkward situation. There's too much at stake." He walked to the door and turned back. "I know he wants that internship more than anything right now. Would you mind helping young Mr. Nolan understand why it is in his best interest to redirect his energies and focus on his upcoming time in Washington?"

● ● ●

As Donald left the office, Jeffrey closed the door. He walked over to the same window that Senator Smith stared out of a few minutes ago. "May I make an observation, sir?" Jeffrey directed his question to the gorgeous day outside.

Senator Smith straightened his shoulders. "Of course, Jeffrey, what's on your mind?"

"I watched that exchange closely." Jeffrey looked away from the window and back to his boss. "I would never tell you what to do. However, I would encourage you to be careful. This could be a good thing, being close to Donald Carlyle, but it might not be. As you know, I've been spending some time with him lately."

"And?"

"I'm still trying to get to know the real man."

"Do you suppose there's any truth to that conspiracy theory?" asked Smith.

"Probably not, but it isn't our business anyway, is it? Mr. Carlyle just made an ultimatum."

"Yes, he did."

"I spoke to Jordan before he came in to meet you," continued Jeffrey. "I told him that winning the internship doesn't give him a free pass to do whatever he wants. Then I warned him of the consequences if anything else like this happened. I think he got the point."

"Thank you," said the senator as he looked down at the mug Jordan had been holding earlier. "I want him to make it to DC. It means so much to him. I'd hate to have to take it away. In the meantime, what do you think about Donald and his offer?"

"He seems sincere, but I couldn't say for certain."

"Sometimes I hate politics," said Senator Smith.

"You wouldn't be a good leader if you didn't," said Jeffrey. "If you want my advice, I think you should go forward under the assumption that Donald Carlyle is sincere. However, if it would help, I think I can get in close and be your eyes and ears. Would you like me to do that?"

Senator Smith exhaled. "Yes, I would. As long as you're careful, I'd rest easier knowing someone I trust is on the case." As he reached for the carafe, Jordan's words hit him again.

We didn't just stumble upon that evidence.

Senator Smith looked back up. "Oh, and Jeffrey..."

"Yes?"

"See if you can find out anything about that conspiracy theory while you're at it."

"I will, sir." Jeffrey turned and walked out of the office, closing the door behind him.

The senator poured himself another mug of coffee and sat down in the chair opposite where Jordan had been. He played their conversation over in his mind.

One thing was certain. He could not choose to believe Jordan and also continue on his present course.

The question tormented him.

Do you really want to know?

His sip of coffee made the only sound in the room.

Chapter 70

The Search for R3

Tuesday, August 5, 10:25 a.m.
Driving west from Colorado Springs back to Wilson, CO

It took a lot of prayer and the first hour of his drive back from Denver to clear his thoughts. He slammed his hand down on top of the steering wheel.

What was I thinking?

Talking like that to a United States Senator. He only hoped it wasn't political suicide before his career even started. It might be.

I'm an idiot.

Two months ago he had convinced himself he was an unflappable, ice-cold trial lawyer in dark shades burying the opposition. Now, the realization came out of nowhere with total clarity. That image was a farce.

So who am I?

I am passionate.

I am emotional.

I speak too much.

I speak too quickly.

I can barely control myself.

Sometimes I can't even do that.

The internship hung by the slightest thread. Jeffrey Kingston had warned him to back off, and instead he had teed off on a United States Senator with an accusation that would sound crazy at best and like slander at worst.

Maybe I'm not cut out to be a lawyer.

The more he thought about it, Jordan saw his trip to Washington—his dream and his future—disappearing before the backdrop of Pikes Peak. Forty-five minutes of solid prayer, mixed with much self-chastising, kept him from despair and brought him an irrational feeling that things might not be as bad as he imagined.

I feel peace.

This made no sense.

Passing through Colorado Springs, he looked from the interstate and saw the large sanctuary of Purple Mountain Community Church. Nearly three months had passed since the night that had changed his life forever. It seemed more like three years.

Is this what Washington is like?

He'd be gray by the time he was thirty at this rate.

He exhaled. It was time to get back to business. Jordan spoke aloud to the inside of his truck, "What do I know?" He took a sip from a latte he'd gotten at a coffee shop as he entered town. He grimaced and looked at a paper cup with a plastic lid. "I know this coffee is grim." Maybe if his political career failed, he could open a coffee shop with Gadg—one that made good coffee.

"Okay, here goes. In 1964, R3 was a code name for the third researcher on the team at Carlyle Enterprises, which included Ray and William. I'm sure of it. Now I have to prove it."

He took another sip.

"No. You're missing the whole point, Jordan. What you need to do is *find* a man who has stayed hidden for fifty years, and then convince him to risk his reputation, and possibly his life, to tell a truth that powerful people don't want to hear. Worse still, this is your last hope."

Fresh urgency surged through him as he directed his gaze up Highway 24 toward the mountains. "Lord, would You make a way for the truth to come out?" He'd begun to read about the Holy Spirit making intercession for the saints according to the will of God. Jordan wondered if this might be that phenomenon. The prayer seemed to come from beyond him in some way he didn't understand. He reached for the new phone.

Who is R3?

Okay, so if he was a researcher at Carlyle Enterprises, who is he?

Male? Probably. Consistent with the Wilson workforce of that day.

In 1964, he would have been working age - no younger than 25

I get the sense, with no empirical evidence, that he is younger than William and Ray

William was about 37 in 1964

R3 age: 25 to 35? Let's go with that as a working supposition

That would make him 75 to 85 this year

Can we assume Wilson Colorado? Not totally, but we can start there

Ugh

That could still be dozens and dozens

He knows how to use email

He seems to have some serious intel at his disposal

It's time to hit the books again

As Jordan set the phone down on the seat next to him, it vibrated in his hand. He looked at the readout and snatched it up.

"How'd it go?" asked Gadg.

"I don't want to talk about it," said Jordan. "One of these days I'm going to learn to keep my mouth shut."

A pause. "Are you still going to Washington?"

"Maybe. Skin of my teeth. Jeffrey Kingston gave me a strong rebuke. He's holding the trespassing thing over my head. One more misstep and I'm done."

"Trespassing, huh? That's an interesting word for what I saw that night."

"I know, right? What could I say? A bunch of powerful adults around me are total liars? It's my word against theirs."

"Is the Senator involved?"

Jordan exhaled. "I don't know, Gadg. Something is not right—I can tell you that. He had a meeting with Donald Carlyle right after I left. I passed Mr. Carlyle in the outer office. He had the nerve to smile at me."

"Oh boy. What did you tell Senator Smith?"

"Nothing much. Only that Howard Carlyle was a murderer and that I watched his son destroy the evidence."

Gadg was quiet. Finally, he said, "The only way out of this mess is forward. I've got some information. Do you want to talk about it later?"

"No, I'm good. Give me what you've got."

"Isaac Molencki *is* his real name. Not sure why he's using it. He has many aliases. The mole. The small man. He's a former Army Ranger—barely met the height requirement. Breezed through the fitness requirements. Ran point on several special-ops missions. Medium-to-high-profile targets. All dead. Several years ago he went off the rails."

"What does he do now?"

"Do you really want to know?"

Gadg's tone caused an icy breeze to cross Jordan's heart. "Tell me."

"You understand this information wasn't exactly public domain."

"I wouldn't expect anything less. What do you know?"

"This could cost us more than the internship if we make the wrong mistake."

"Gadg, what do you know?"

"He's a contract killer."

Jordan went quiet. His face creased with concern. *He was in our house. He was in Bethany's room.* "Does your dad know?"

"Yeah, I told him."

"Any idea why Molencki went to the dark side?"

Gadg paused. "I don't know this for a fact, but I think I've pieced it together. Remember, this information could get us both killed."

"What is it?"

"It's not what—it's who. Her name is Elizabeth Sheridan."

Chapter 71

I Can't

Wednesday, August 6, 3:30 p.m.
Old Town Café, Wilson, CO

"May I?" asked Jordan.

Before Bethany could suppress it, something flashed on the inside. She only hoped it didn't register on her face. "Bonjour, Monsieur Nolan," said Bethany, adopting a French accent and nodding for him to take the seat across from her in the booth. She was on break at the diner and reading a book on her tablet. She still worked here a couple times a week, even with all the hours she was logging at the historical society.

"What are you reading?" Jordan asked.

She continued in her French accent. "*Les Misérables.*"

"Do you give all the characters their own accents?"

"Oui, Monsieur, but of course." Bethany then rattled off Jean Valjean as low and gravelly as her alto would take her, Monsieur Thénardier a flatted-seventh higher with a Machiavellian edge, and Fantine another fourth up from there with a melancholy ring that bordered on despair. The whole effect was an open, minor seventh chord that came across like a soundbite from an ad for a Broadway production.

Eyes shining, Jordan gave her a small shake of the head. "Wow."

Bethany grinned.

"May I ask you a question?" he asked.

Something in his tone pulled her back to plain old Colorado English. "You may." She set down her tablet and sat up a bit.

Jordan fidgeted with the salt shaker. Without looking up he asked, "What's your definition of 'going nowhere'?"

A hint of red inched up her cheek. She waited.

Jordan finally looked up.

Bethany's gaze could bore a hole through his face.

He turned away.

Oh, yeah. You better squirm. She chuckled.

He peeked at her as if sizing up whether it was safe.

Her expression had changed to a playful smirk. "Well, Mr. Nolan, what could possibly prompt that question?"

"Strictly rhetorical,"—his voice went British—"nothing behind it of course." He relaxed a bit.

"Of course," said Bethany. A few seconds passed. "Come on, out with it," she prodded.

"Well, let's just say there was a certain morning last May that I spent an inordinate amount of time at a buffet in Colorado Springs trying to find just the right pieces of bacon."

"You stinker!" Bethany kicked his leg under the table. "You were eavesdropping."

"The subject of the conversation, at that point anyway, concerned me closely, I'd say. I figured I had a right to hear it."

"You figured, huh?"

Jordan blushed and shook his head. "Not really. I just wanted to."

She smiled. An honest answer.

"I do seem to remember the word 'handsome' coming up in the conversation," he continued.

Now it was Bethany's turn to blush.

You sure did.

"Oh, you do, do you?" She was still calm as ever. "Then you may also remember the words 'grow up' in the same conversation?"

"Touché," replied Jordan.

The old clock on the side wall ticked a few times. The diner was empty of customers.

Bethany's face grew soft and serious. "Actually, Mr. Nolan, if I remember correctly"—she looked him straight in the eye—"I think the phrase was 'very handsome.'"

Jordan's mouth dropped open.

She paused, letting the words hang in elegant silence.

He stared.

Her midsection was in flames. Still rock steady on the outside, her head moved a fraction, but her eyes remained locked on his.

Tentatively, Jordan reached out and let his hand rest on top of hers.

She flinched, but didn't withdraw. It felt like a tiny down comforter covered the back of her hand. She smiled.

"So, Miss Clark"—Jordan put on a lighthearted attorney tone—"can you tell the court what 'going nowhere' means?"

Bethany glanced down at their hands and then up at his eyes. She was struck again by how handsome he was. "Why don't you tell me?" She spoke with a sincerity that communicated this was not the subject for a joke.

"Tell you?" his voice returned to raw Jordan.

"Yes. If you can't tell me, then you aren't ready for the answer."

Jordan paused. "May I make a guess?"

Bethany smiled. "That question is itself a sign of progress. You may."

He thought for a moment. "Even if I achieve all my dreams ... even if I become a US Senator ... even if I make it all the way to the UN ... if I don't have inward reality with God, if I don't have real *love*, I have nothing. I am going nowhere."

Her smile lit her whole face.

He gave her hand a slight squeeze.

More exquisite silence.

"Can I ask you another question?" Jordan paused to gather his thoughts.

Bethany reached with her other hand to scratch an itch under her chin. Her fingers came to rest on her necklace.

Oh, no.

She could feel the letters and hear her dad's voice in her head: *"Promise me you'll wait for my blessing?"*

Jordan didn't seem to notice anything different. "Do you still think I am?"

"Still think you're what?" asked Bethany, trying to hold it together.

"Going nowhere?"

Bethany looked away, wistfully. "No, I don't." Her voice sounded like a soft-rock eighties love ballad.

Jordan cocked his head and raised an eyebrow. "Is something wrong?"

"That just makes it all the harder," said Bethany without making eye contact.

"Makes what all the harder?"

Bethany just stared out the window as she continued to finger her necklace.

A glint of light reflected off the golden words. Jordan closed his eyes in a slow blink as he took her meaning.

Bethany looked back in time to see his Adam's apple move in response to a hard swallow.

"Really?" he finally asked, his voice no more than a whisper.

A knot twisted inside her. The fire from before had been reduced to smoldering ashes. "Oh, Jordan"—Bethany tore her hand away—"I can't." She grabbed her tablet and got up out of the booth.

His expression crumbled as his lips parted. He looked like a lost puppy given a bowl of food only to have it snatched away and followed up with a slap.

Way to go, Bethany. You just stuck a knife in him and turned it. She stole one more look at him, but couldn't meet his sad, gorgeous eyes. "I gotta go." She yanked her head forward and left without looking back.

Chapter 72

Miserable

Wednesday, August 6, 9:45 p.m.
Jordan's room, Wilson, CO

Jordan lay on his back and stared up at his bedroom ceiling. He couldn't sleep. He couldn't move. His insides felt like ground hamburger.

He replayed the conversation over and over in his mind.

The notes of Bethany's *Les Misérables* characters still rang like a songbird in his ears.

He could still feel the warmth of the back of her hand.

The look on her face when she had said "very handsome" was one of the greatest moments of his life.

A shaft of pain pierced his heart.

He could still see the light reflecting off gold-emblazoned words: "Daddy's Girl." Those two words may as well have been chiseled in stone, the meaning was so unchangeable.

Daddy's Girl would never be Jordan's Girl.

Mr. Clark would never go for it, and Bethany—the angel Jordan had loved since the age of eight—would never marry him without her father's blessing.

He turned his head. His gaze rested on his championship trophy. Even in the dim radiance cast by his bedside lamp, the inscription mocked him:

> **Forensic Communicators League**
> **2014 National Champion**
> **Individual Parliamentary Policy**
> **Jordan Nolan**

Nolan.

His jaw tightened.

I hate my name.

He looked away.

His eyes came to rest on a map of Washington, DC.

I've had it with Wilson.

It wouldn't be so bad if she just ignored him.

He looked at the red circle surrounding the building that housed the offices of Senator Smith.

"Actually, Mr. Nolan, if I remember correctly, I think the phrase was 'very handsome.'"

A fresh wave of pain slammed into his heart. His face tightened as the pain mixed with anger. Bethany knew what she was doing.

That was mean.

He turned from the map and rolled over onto to his stomach and buried his head in his hands. For several minutes he didn't move.

He turned onto his side and grabbed his phone. He launched the internship ticker, but it just mocked him. He shut it off and laid his head on his pillow. The ache was relentless. The arm that held his phone flopped lazily on the bed. He turned it toward his face and opened his Bible app.

Psalm 38.

The last verse was highlighted in a pleasant green. It didn't matter. He had no strength to read, pray, or do anything else at the moment. He lay there and faced the screen with vacant eyes.

At last, he focused on the passage: "Make haste to help me, O Lord my salvation."

His gaze remained on the words. As sleep took him, his phone slipped from his hand. His last semi-conscious thought was, "Yes, Lord."

Chapter 73

Friends

Thursday, August 7, 2:45 p.m.
Wilson County Historical Society Building, Wilson, CO

"May I?" Bethany asked.

Jordan didn't look up from his books at the back of the library.

"I've had a horrible night, Bethany." No subtext. No banter. No customary greeting her as Miss Clark.

Bethany wiped the corner of her eye. "Me, too."

Jordan looked up. As good as she looked, she didn't look good. He didn't care. "That was cruel."

"I should never have cracked open that door."

"*Cracked* open?"

Bethany's cheeks exploded in a red blush. She looked away. After a few seconds, she looked back.

Jordan drilled her with a piercing gaze.

She'd never been on the receiving end of a look like that from him. "All right. Threw open," she said, miserably.

Hearing the honest truth softened him one notch, but his voice still came out in a snip. "No, you shouldn't have."

Bethany rubbed the back of her neck. "I'm sorry, Jordan. I-"

"You wouldn't have gone there if you hadn't wanted to," Jordan interrupted.

"I know." Bethany used the same wistful tone he'd heard last night at the cafe. She met his eyes. "You're right, I wouldn't have."

Jordan tried to hold onto his anger, but desire won out. He looked away. "You're not helping," he said with the slightest touch of coyness in his tone. He almost smiled.

"Neither are you," she slugged him in the shoulder.

He perked up.

"Forgive me?" she asked.

"I'll think about it," he said, looking back down at his books with a smirk.

They were silent for a few seconds. She was still standing.

"So, where do we go from here?" he asked without looking up.

Bethany thought for a moment. "Friends?"

Jordan shook his head with his first smile in the conversation. He looked up at her. Using his fingers for air quotes, he said, "The 'just want to be friends' speech, huh?"

"Not really," her tone was playful again.

He cocked his head and narrowed his eyes waiting for her to elaborate.

"First, Mr. Nolan"—she broke into her polished British accent—"it's far too cliché."

He nodded. "And?"

Bethany leaned her arms on the desk and moved her face to within six inches of his. "And"—she lowered her voice—"it's not *true.*"

Jordan swallowed and looked back down at his books. "You're *really* not helping."

Chapter 74

The Two Letters

Thursday, August 14, 9:40 a.m.
Deck of the Historical Society Building, Wilson, CO

A few days later, Jordan was heads down again. He leaned back in the chair and smiled a grand smile.

Great-grandpa William would be proud.

Jordan was following in his footsteps. As best as he could tell from all the evidence, his very existence was owed to his great-grandfather's sacrifice.

Wow.

He leaned over the table that had become his favorite. The second floor of the library/historical building boasted a back deck that looked out over a large part of Wilson. It was a stunning view in the golden glow of a Colorado morning with nothing but blue sky overhead.

Jordan couldn't see it.

He sat with his back to the beauty. His view consisted of the windows that looked in on the upper floor of the library. He had only his computer open this time. No papers, no reference books, no articles. It was a hassle to try to accomplish all his research on his computer with only an occasional trip inside to look at a book, but with the altercation with Alex and the warning from Jeffrey, Jordan had to do his work under deep cover. Part of that cover was a software utility that Gadg had written for him. At the push of a button, Jordan could bring up a false screen with a few articles and websites that made it look like he was researching Washington, DC.

The real research felt like hand-to-hand combat.

His list of people that could be R3 had shrunk, but he had to look into each one individually. Gadg had provided some information—Jordan didn't ask where he'd gotten it—that cut the list down to maybe three dozen names.

When the weather permitted, Jordan preferred to research with his back to the railing on the far end of the outside deck. Besides letting him enjoy exquisite summer mornings, this gave him visibility to most of the library. Nobody could sneak up behind him.

Bethany didn't need to. "Hello, Mr. Nolan," she again adopted her most pronounced British accent.

In three words from Bethany, Jordan was spellbound. She sounded like a West End voice actress. The smallest flicker of a thought flashed across his mind. He could listen to that voice for the rest of his life.

Steady.

He looked up and smiled. "Hello, Miss Clark." His heart flitted like a teenage schoolboy. He stifled a chuckle as he remembered that, technically, that's what he was. He'd been thinking of himself as a lawyer and living in the adult world for so many months that he had almost forgotten his true age.

Bethany smiled back. She looked around the deck to see if anyone was within earshot. "Time travel again?" she asked.

"Of course, what else?" he spoke with relief at the chance to take his thoughts in a different direction.

"1964?"

"Khrushchev deposed, Johnson reelected, Beatlemania. Lot going on that year."

"Interesting things," Bethany smirked.

"Indeed," agreed Jordan. "Many interesting things. Some real pioneering going on in certain fields, such as *medicine.*"

Bethany leaned in a bit, lowered her voice, and dropped the English accent. "Any new insights?"

Keeping his voice low, he said, "Getting closer. I'm learning a lot more about Amitolin and XD. Thanks for letting me borrow the magazine." He reached into his backpack, pulled it out, and handed it back to her.

Receiving the magazine she set it on the table face down, hiding the huge XD on the cover. She looked out over the railing and surveyed Wilson. "Incredible view." She tried to hide the wistful tone. "What is your main focus now?"

"Check these out," he nodded at his computer. Bethany leaned over to examine a couple articles about XD, her shoulder an inch from his. Jordan could smell a trace of perfume. He backed his chair out to give her space and, at the same time, to distance himself from the torrent of desire that engulfed his insides.

Now at a safer distance, he tried to keep his voice even, "In answer to your question, I'm working on a couple things. First, I still want to identify R3, of course. It's a laborious process that I can only handle in small bites. I'm getting there, but there are still many possibilities." He clicked on a document he was working through.

Bethany's hands rested on the table as she leaned in front of his computer and looked over a long list of names with notes. "Yeah, that looks painful." She glanced over her shoulder at him. "What else?"

His voice lowered to a whisper. "I'm thinking of making another trip underground."

Her eyes got big. She stood up and grabbed a nearby chair. She planted herself in front of him and her voice took on an alarmed edge, even though it was in a whisper. "Jordan, you can't. The internship hangs by a thread already. One more thing happens, and you're stuck in Wilson. You're taking an awful risk even doing what you're doing."

"I know"—his voice softened—"but we have to find those two letters. We don't even know who wrote them, where they are, or what they're about. We must find out what's happening with your mom."

Bethany's hand shot up and covered her mouth. A mist sprayed into her eyes. She jerked her head away, stood up, and stumbled back a step. Her chair slid a few inches with an annoying metal-on-wood scrape. She looked over the side railing and saw the parking lot. Her dad's Explorer was parked near the end. Her face pinched. "Why does life have to be so unfair?"

Standing, he stepped toward her. "Oh Bethany, she's going to get better."

She turned back to him with eyes full of tears and longing. "That's not what I'm talking about."

His heart threatened to go into cardiac arrest. He wiped his hands down the sides of his shorts and tried to look anywhere but at her. He spun to the railing and leaned on his forearms. Staring straight ahead, he said in a breathy voice, "Is there any hope?"

She reached to put her hand on his forearm, but pulled back. With a tiny, aching gasp, she gritted her teeth and spun parallel to him. She leaned on the same railing and gave an equally empty stare toward the beautiful expanse in front of them.

A slight breeze came through the trees and mingled with the gentle sound of their breathing.

Leaning there, side by side, Jordan said, "I know you love your dad." His pulse had begun to steady. "I could never ask you to go against his wishes."

"Of course. That's why this is so awful."

He kept his gaze forward. "What do we do, Bethany?"

"I don't know." They didn't move for several minutes.

Finally, Jordan spun around, tore his heart away, and stepped back to his computer. Returning to the original subject, he asked, "Any news on your mom?"

"Not yet, but I've been thinking a lot about it." Bethany moved from the railing. "Especially the message from R3." She walked around the table and faced him with her back to the library windows. "Are you serious about going underground again?"

Jordan looked up from his computer. "Yes. Tell me again what the message said."

"Seek for two letters from the past; small number, don't you think? Yes, just two, written one after the other; link Ray Clark's death and what ails your mother. Many times, the truth lurks below the surface. If you need a hint, go underground and go northeast."

"Written one after the other," Jordan pondered. "Obviously, that suggests they were written or mailed close to the same time."

Bethany agreed with a nod.

"All you found were the books and magazines?" asked Jordan.

"Yes, but I'm not sure I was fully northeast. Remember, I made it into that room by accident."

"That's why I'd like to try again. I want to be sure."

"The risk is way too high. I can't ask you to do that."

He smiled at her and bounced his eyebrows up and down once. "You're not asking me to."

Bethany looked away. Fumbling with her hands she reached down and picked up the magazine. "I also appreciate you praying for us—for my mom."

"You're welcome. I seem to be getting some answers this summer."

Except on one request.

"Why would this be any different?" He said it as a statement.

"That means a lot to me, Jordan. My mom is way too young to be dealing with stuff like this."

"Your mom is a good bit younger than your dad, isn't she?"

"She is. By nine years." Bethany paused to reflect. "She'll be fifty this November. I want to have a big celebration, but with this looming over our heads, I'm not sure I should."

Jordan nodded with a thoughtful look and stared at Bethany's reflection in the glass of the library windows. He glanced down at his computer.

His head shot up.

He stared again at the window.

Bethany was taken aback. "You okay?"

The black cover of the magazine reflected off the glass in the morning sun. The blood red title that said "XD" peeked out from behind Bethany's arm. "Did you say she turns fifty this November?"

"Yes, why?"

"We don't need to go back underground."

Bethany's face grew serious, "What *are* you talking about?"

"Look in your hand," said Jordan. "You're holding the *two letters.*"

She held up the magazine. Blood red on black—the answer stared her in the face.

"Bethany, call your mom's doctor," Jordan spoke with an intensity that startled her. "I don't know exactly what it is, but the issue has to be hereditary."

She looked up at him, eyes wide.

"In 1964, your family lived in Wilson, and your mom was in the womb. It's a sure bet your grandmother was taking XD."

Dear William and Ray,

I wanted to be married. I really did. I wanted to share a life together. But, alas, that could never happen. I knew I could never be honest. What kind of relationship would that be?

You remember that I was on my way to being engaged that summer. I can still see her face as clear as yesterday. All I had to do was ask. Two people made for each other spending their lives apart.

She would have said yes.

Chapter 75

Made for Each Other

Thursday, August 14, 10:00 a.m.
Deck of the Historical Society Building, Wilson, CO

"May I speak to you?"

Jordan stiffened. At six-foot-four, Mr. Clark towered over him as he sat staring down at his computer. Bethany had just left a couple minutes ago. Jordan had been so engrossed in their discovery that he hadn't seen Mr. Clark approach.

So much for sitting where nobody can sneak up on me.

Jordan composed himself. "Sir?"

"I need to talk to you about something."

"Sure."

"Can you come to my office, please?"

Uh-oh.

Jordan grabbed his computer in one hand and his bag in the other and followed Mr. Clark into the building, down the steps to the first floor, and across the main commons area to his office.

Mr. Clark sat down in his chair and turned to face Jordan. "I noticed you've been spending some time with Bethany." He pulled his reading glasses from his shirt pocket and put them on.

So much for small talk.

"A little," said Jordan warily. "I was asking how her mother was doing."

"Thank you for your concern." The tone said otherwise. "How do you see your relationship with Bethany?"

"We're becoming friends."

"Friends?" Mr. Clark lowered his chin and peered over his glasses.

Jordan crossed his legs.

Take it easy.

With difficulty, he held his peace.

"I can see it in your eyes," said Mr. Clark.

"See what, sir?"

"An interest in more than friendship."

"Her eyes too, wouldn't you say?" said Jordan.

Mr. Clark's face grew stern. "Bethany's last name will never be Nolan."

What a jerk.

Bethany's father or not, Jordan took the gloves off. "Nolan is a *great* last name and I'm proud to have it."

Mr. Clark already had the gloves off. "The Nolan name is a cancer in this community," he fired back. "I won't have my daughter mixed up with it."

Jordan stashed his computer in his backpack. He zipped it shut with enough force to rip the pull tab off. He'd had enough of people throwing shade over his great-grandfather. "William Nolan was a *great* man. One day you'll see the truth." He flung the tab into a garbage can where it banged off the metal on the inside.

He might as well have slapped Mr. Clark in the face. With some effort, Mr. Clark spoke calmly, and the effect was an ice dagger from his mouth. "You might as well put it out of your mind. Bethany doesn't date casually, and there's no way I would let her marry *you*."

Jordan wheeled around and strode from the office. Trying to hold his humiliation at bay, he made a beeline for the exit. He cast a sideways glance at Bethany as she stood at the information desk.

Because she'd been working on something else, she was unaware of what had happened. Her face lit up when she saw Jordan.

He snapped his head forward as hot, angry tears spilled from the corners of his eyes. He burst through the front doors, vowing never to return.

● ● ●

The walls were paper thin. Like a death knell, Mr. Everett heard the final nail in the coffin from the adjacent office. "You might as well put it out of your mind. Bethany doesn't date casually, and there's no way I would let her marry *you*." He heard Jordan storm from the room.

Mr. Everett looked up at the ceiling. He squeezed his eyes shut, but tears forced themselves out anyway. He gripped fistfuls of white hair in both hands.

This is not right.

He should just forget it. Play it safe. The strategy had served him well for fifty years. Nice home. Comfortable retirement. River cabin. Peaceful life.

The problem was, it was a total lie. He had no peace. He hadn't had peace for fifty years.

This is not my problem.

His breath came in gasps as his chest heaved up and down. He fought with himself.

Two people made for each other are not going to be able to be together because of me.

Mr. Carlyle won't like it.

So what? Can I be a man just once in my life?

His soul was in agony.

I was one of two people made for each other. She would have said yes.

He slammed his already balled fists down on the sides of his chair.

That's it! This must stop NOW!

With hair disheveled and a face like a ghost, Robert Everett reached into his bottom desk drawer and pulled out an old tape recorder.

Chapter 76

End of Summer School

Thursday, August 14, 10:15 a.m.
Main Street, Wilson, CO

Jordan sat behind the wheel of his rusty and trusty companion, Gutless. It was so old, it still had a tape player.

He tilted his head toward the historical society building. He blinked back the raw sting in his eyes. Each thought of Mr. Clark's face drove a fresh dagger into his heart. His insides screamed at the injustice.

He reached for the ignition, paused, and pulled back. With his other hand, he grabbed the door handle and stumbled out onto the pavement.

As if in a drunken stupor, Jordan wandered around town. He sat. He stood. He walked. He stopped. He cried. He didn't try to cover it. He didn't pretend he was some high-powered, untouchable lawyer.

He let it hurt.

●●●

Ninety minutes later, when the pain had receded to a dull ache, Jordan opened the door again and slid behind the wheel. His keys were still in the ignition.

He closed his eyes for one more sigh and turned the key. The cassette player hissed with the unmistakable sounds of a tape playing.

That's weird.

Jordan never put actual tapes in the player. His only music was through an adapter that allowed him to pump the music from his phone through the stereo.

"Dear Jordan," an unrecognizable voice—as if someone were speaking through a pillow—filled the cab.

Jordan sat bolt upright. He rolled up the driver's window and rewound the tape to start over.

The voice came again. Indistinct. "Dear Jordan, I heard your meeting with Mr. Clark. Don't ask me how, but I did. You didn't deserve that."

The voice paused, "I have some information for you. It's dangerously confidential. Be extremely careful."

Jordan's eyes widened as he stared through the windshield.

"Meet me at two a.m. tomorrow morning at the location where a certain friend discovered some old books and magazines."

Jordan's mind whirled and shot back to Old Town. He knew where to go. The pieces fell into place and the conclusion came in a blinding flash.

This is R3,

"If you want, you can make the whole journey underground. Start at your cellar, make the first two right turns, go straight for a long stretch, and take the next two lefts. You'll find the room."

Jordan shuddered, a chill crawling over him. He'd decide tonight if he wanted to take that route.

"One more thing. Please come alone. Summer school's almost over. It's time to prep for the final exam."

Matthew and Allie — Part 2

Thursday, August 14, 5:25 p.m.
A few blocks from Chez La Fleur restaurant, Wilson, CO

Having convinced Matthew that she didn't want to go anywhere else, Allie said that she would meet him at the same restaurant they enjoyed on their first date.

Tyler pulled to the side of the road a few blocks from Chez La Fleur. "What do you know about this Molencki dude?" he asked.

"Not much," said Allie.

"Doesn't that concern you?"

"Of course." Distracted by her own smile in the mirror behind the passenger-side sun visor, Allie fluttered her eyelashes. She was dressed for a night on the town.

Tyler shook his head. "Allie, he's dangerous."

"I know." She made a clicking sound as she gave another smile to the mirror.

Tyler sighed. "Jordan asked me to remind you that this is not the time for a personal vendetta."

Allie made some different faces and never took her eyes off the mirror.

"You look great," said Tyler. "Why do you keep checking your makeup?"

She turned to him, rested her chin on her hand, and gave him a starry-eyed blink. "I'm not checking my makeup," she cranked up her brightest smile, let it fade to a hardened frown, and then warmed it back up. "I'm getting into character. Let's go."

●●●

An hour and a half later, Allie sat across from Matthew in the same cozy booth at Chez La Fleur and took dead aim with a continuous blast of full-throttle charm. She decided against starry-eyed ditz and instead went for intelligent, thoughtful, and interested. She kept the ditzy girl and several other characters in her back pocket should the situation warrant their use. A big meal and several shared tales later, she had the bait on the hook and prepared to cast.

"I must be boring you with all my stories." Allie laughed and waved a hand in front of her face.

"No more than I have to you," said Matthew, setting down his fork after polishing off a twenty-six-dollar lobster pavilion.

"Oh, not at all. It's fascinating. You've been hanging around some pretty high-powered guys lately." Allie was all smiles. "I mean, even more than usual, that is."

Matthew grinned. "Why do you say that?"

"WDC2 executives, attorneys, back-east reporters—you're looking the part these days."

Matthew leaned back with a satisfied expression.

Allie picked at the remnants of her meal. "Have you seen how many journalists have been in town for the celebration? It's crazy, but I'm loving it."

"Yes, I have. Wilson, Colorado, of all places. Who would have believed it?"

Allie leaned in and lowered her voice. "Can you keep a secret?"

"Of course."

Liar.

"Bethany had a conversation with an investigative journalist from DC. Talk about high-powered. He's the smallest guy she'd ever met, but he's clearly accustomed to walking the corridors of power."

A flash of surprise crossed Matthew's face. There and gone in an instant.

Here, fishy-fishy.

"What?" said Allie.

"Oh, nothing."

"Why the surprise? Do you know him?"

Matthew took the bait. "I might. What was his name?"

"Isaac something-or-other, I think."

He nodded. "I know him. His name is Isaac Molencki."

Allie launched into ditz-mode and gave a ticker-tape chatter with a higher pitch and no pauses. "Wow! Do you know him? That is so cool. I've always thought it would be amazing to be an investigative journalist. I'd love to meet him. I wasn't there when Bethany met him. He must have some fascinating stories! Any chance you could set up a meeting?" Allie panted.

"You okay?" Matthew raised an eyebrow.

"So sorry." She shook her head like she was chastising herself. Easing down her breathing, she toyed with the fish on the line. "Acting like this certainly won't help. I've just always wanted to be a journalist in a big city on the East Coast. I figure it would be good to talk to a real one, and you're just so well-connected."

"Well, maybe I could see what I could do."

"Really?" Allie dropped open her mouth. "You'd do that for me?"

"If I can." Matthew smiled.

Her face registered the flash of an idea. "Of course, he must work for someone awfully important. Perhaps we could meet him as well? Bethany might have seen him when she met Mr. Molencki." Allie poured on the charm as she put a fist to her forehead. "Oh, what was his name?"

"Jeffrey King—" Matthew caught himself. His eyes had a brief flicker of darkness.

Got you.

Allie's eyes lit up as she spread all her fingers on both hands and launched back to blabby-mode. "You know Jeffrey Kingston? Oh my goodness! I can't believe it! Do you know the senator, too? Wow, that's amazing! Could you please introduce me to him? Doh. How stupid of me. I'm acting like a groupie. But still, you know him? That's seriously cool. Oh, Matthew, I didn't realize you were *that* connected!" She panted again to finish the act as she pulled the fish off the hook.

Matthew looked stunned.

Allie covered her eyes with one hand. Her voice was calm again. "I've just made a complete fool of myself, haven't I?" She lifted the bottom of her hand and sneaked a peek up at him.

He shook his head with a collected smirk. "I didn't realize journalism was that important to you."

It's not. Just like my sister's wedding wasn't important to you.

"Well"—she wiped the corners of her mouth with a cloth napkin and slid back into charm-mode—"apart from my outrageous display of overeagerness, that was a wonderful meal. How about dessert?" Her smile radiated satisfaction.

"Certainly," said Matthew.

Jordan definitely owes me for this.

"Hey, I've got some more pictures from last summer. This time it's of the reception."

"Wonderful, I'd love to see them."

Yeah, I bet you would.

"Excuse me, I need to use the restroom," said Allie. "I'm trying out this new do." Allie fluffed the bottom of her hair just above her shoulders. "I need to compare it in the mirror to some photos I have on my phone. I'll send you an email while you wait, just to give you a taste."

"Excellent. I can't wait."

We'll see about that.

Allie turned down the hall toward the restrooms. She passed the ladies room without a glance, disappeared around another corner, and continued out the side door. She walked across the parking lot, opened the back door of Tyler's car, and got in.

"All right, step on it," she said as she slunk down below the level of the windows and crammed herself in the leg area between the front and back seats. She dug her phone out of her purse, opened up her email, and pushed Send.

As he drove off, Tyler reached his hand over the back of the seat and dropped his phone. "Jordan and Gadg on speaker," he said.

"You owe me an Oscar," Allie said into the phone.

"You got it?" Jordan's voice came through Tyler's phone.

"Yeah, I got it." Allie nodded to the air. "But you're not going to like it."

The phone went silent for a beat. "Okaaay," Jordan drew the word out, "let me hear it."

"Isaac Molencki was hired by Jeffrey Kingston."

It sounded to Allie like all the air was sucked from the other end of the line. "Unbelievable," Jordan finally said. "You better get back to your date with Matthew."

"No way. We just drove off. I couldn't stand to look at him for another minute. The snake."

The phone went silent for the third time.

"What?" said Allie.

"Nothing," said Jordan with obvious effort. "Great job, Allie. Consider yourself nominated."

● ● ●

Matthew waited at the table. A moment later, he saw the number one indicating that he had a new email. He lifted a breadstick to his mouth while he tapped a finger from his other hand on the email from Allie that said "Here you go..."

He froze. The breadstick stayed one inch from his mouth.

I know what you did last time.

Matthew's pulse quickened as he read and reread the email from Allie.

In case you're wondering, I prefer my dessert *cold.*

Matthew looked around to see if anybody was watching. He picked up the check as discreetly as he could. Allie would not be coming back to the table. Just as he started to feel sorry for himself, the realization slammed him.

This was a setup.

He ground his teeth.

Two can play at this game, Jordan.

He'd have to handle things carefully since he'd just spilled the beans, but he would get the information back to Mr. Kingston. The screws were about to tighten on Jordan's life.

Chapter 78

Holding Hands with the Devil

Thursday, August 14, 7:05 p.m.
Gadg's lair at the O'Brien home, Wilson, CO

"Oh, Gadg!" Jordan turned from the coffee bar and set two mugs on the Jetson's-style table in front of them. "I was afraid of that."

"Allie?" asked Gadg.

"Yes," said Jordan. He sat down, crossed one leg over the other, and sighed. "I knew it was a risk."

"This could be a serious problem," said Gadg.

"*Two* serious problems." Jordan took a sip of coffee that he didn't even taste. "Molencki will know that we know before the night is over."

"Which means Jeffrey Kingston will know as well."

Jordan made a whistling sound as he inhaled air through his teeth. "Hooboy," he said, reverting back to his Western Colorado roots, "we suspected this might go high up. But Jeffrey Kingston? This is serious."

Gadg nodded, deep in thought. "How long before you leave?"

"Don't you mean 'if I leave'?" said Jordan. He launched the internship ticker on his phone and showed it to Gadg.

10 days, 12 hours, 52 minutes, 29 seconds
10 days, 12 hours, 52 minutes, 28 seconds
10 days, 12 hours, 52 minutes, 27 seconds

"Wow, right around the corner. I don't know what to tell you. This whole situation is bizarre."

"Tell me about it." Jordan's face held a grim light. "Is it possible that this goes all the way to the senator?"

"Mr. Kingston is his right-hand man," said Gadg. "It's not only possible, it's likely. How much have you told him?"

"I don't even know how to process this," said Jordan, feeling numb. "Mr. Kingston is my mentor."

"I know. That's why I asked."

Jordan thought back over his last several conversations with Jeffrey. "I'm not sure. I don't think the subject of William has come up."

"That's good."

"No, it's not." Jordan grimaced, looking pale. "The subject hasn't come up with Mr. Kingston, but I dumped a truckload of it on Senator Smith the other day."

Gadg rubbed a palm across his face. "What in the world have we gotten ourselves into?"

Jordan leaned back in his chair. He spun his coffee mug on the table. "I don't know, Gadg. I feel like I'm holding hands with the devil."

Chapter 79

When Were You Planning on Telling Me?

**Thursday, August 14, 7:15 p.m.
Bethany's room, Wilson, CO**

Mr. Clark stepped into the doorway to her bedroom.

"Hi, Daddy," Bethany looked up from an entry she was creating in her diary and gave him a smile.

"Where's Allie?" his face was stern.

Bethany's smile faded. "I gave her the night off. She's out on a date."

"So, when were you planning on telling me?"

"Telling you what?" Bethany blinked.

"Don't give me that. You know what I'm talking about. When were you going to tell me about your feelings for Jordan Nolan?"

Bethany looked away and bit her lip. She squeezed her eyes shut. "You've been so busy this summer. I've been working up the courage to tell you—about a lot of things."

"A lot of things? Just what have you been doing?"

Her face paled.

"You know how I feel about this—about him," he continued.

"I'm seeing some incredible changes in him. He's becoming a wonderful young man."

"And just how would you be knowing that?"

"I can't believe you're treating me this way!" The tears came in earnest now.

"And I can't believe you would disregard my wishes like this."

Bethany wiped both eyes fiercely. "But Daddy, you don't understand."

"No, *you* don't understand. I don't want you to see him anymore, and that's final. If you continue to pursue a relationship with him, you'll do it going back on your promise to me and without my blessing." He wheeled around and strode away from the room.

Bethany buried her face in her open diary. Over the next half-hour, today's entry was washed into an illegible mixture of salt water and ink.

● ● ●

An hour later, Mr. Clark stood in the doorway to her bedroom for the second time that evening.

Bethany looked up at him.

He looked down at his socks. "May I come in?" he asked with the slightest peek up at her.

Bethany's face was a puffy mixture of red splotches and caked-on tears. She hadn't moved since he'd last seen her.

He walked over to her, got down on his knees, and put his big arms around her.

Her tears came again—fast and hot. She felt the strength of his chest as he held her close. She was so spent that he supported most of her weight with the hug. She felt like a life-size rag doll in his arms.

Several minutes later, he spoke. "I'm sorry, sweetheart. Regardless of how I may feel about Jordan, there is no excuse for my behavior toward you. I was out of line. Can you forgive me?"

"Daddy, you were horrible to *him* too." Bethany sobbed. "He's a dear friend. I I—" she stopped and buried her head in his shoulder.

Mr. Clark opened his mouth to speak. No words came. He tried a second time. Still nothing. He put his hand on her head and stroked her hair.

Chapter 80

Two Fires

Thursday, August 14, 11:35 p.m.
Senator Smith's bedroom, Denver, CO

His wife sleeping softly next to him, Senator Smith stared up at the ceiling. Saturday was the big day. Saturday was the day he could write his ticket. Saturday, his future in Colorado's Republican party was assured.

All he had to do was play it down the middle. Give the right speech, shake the right hands, smile the right smiles, and all would be well.

And yet ...

He couldn't shake the feeling that something was wrong.

He thought again about the meeting with Jordan Nolan in his office. Never in his political career, maybe never in his life, had he been spoken to like that. And by an eighteen-year-old kid! He couldn't believe the cheek that young man had shown. He should be angry, but there was something about young Mr. Nolan that gave him pause.

Stirrings from his past tried to push their way to the surface. His eyes traced the smeared popcorn pattern of his ceiling as he examined how he felt about his meeting with Jordan.

Was he annoyed? Certainly.

Was he offended? Somewhat.

Was he provoked? Possibly.

What was it?

Inspired.

That was it. The kid had passion—fire in his belly.

It was presumptuous and disrespectful, but Senator Smith loved what he saw. He saw himself. "No," he spoke aloud to the quiet bedroom. He didn't see himself. He saw a memory of himself—and his passion—from decades ago.

With a sigh he rolled over and stared at the wall. Thoughts of his younger days as an attorney—and crusader for justice—tumbled back into his mind.

Could I ever go back?

The answer scared him. Maybe he could. *If* he was willing to look a certain question straight in the face.

Is it possible that young Mr. Nolan is right?

He thought back to his last conversation with Donald Carlyle. If Smith had learned anything in his years as a lawyer and politician, such carefully crafted language could only mean one thing. Mr. Carlyle was hiding something.

Jordan's words came back to haunt him with new depth. *"Sir, I need to ask you a question first. Do you really want to know the answer?"*

What bothered him most was *his* answer.

I'm not sure.

• • •

Two hours later, Jordan's alarm jolted him awake at 1:30 a.m. A burning hot Scripture tormented his soul.

Love your enemies.

He stared up at the blackness of his ceiling as Matthew's face appeared in the recesses of his mind.

Not that again. Don't I have enough to worry about?

"Lord," he said aloud to the darkness, "I've been praying for him a good bit. I do want the best for him."

Crickets, literally, sounded outside.

Jordan's thoughts from the other day at Bethany's house came back to him.

What I'm asking for is an Oscar-level performance that convinces Matthew that you are smitten for him and clueless about anything meaningful, while simultaneously extracting information from him.

Jordan had thought himself clever. His friends looked like they'd thought he was clever. However, it didn't seem like God thought so at this ghastly hour.

"Okay, I know that doesn't sound like love. But, Lord, do You not remember what he did to us the other day? We lost the evidence because of him."

The verse was still fresh in his mind.

Love your enemies.

Jordan blasted back, "Lord, seriously? Matthew is working with a contract killer! Isaac Molencki is working for Jeffrey Kingston. I needed that information."

A thought came back at him like a boomerang.

"That's true," he blurted, "You could have gotten it to me some other way."

He turned over on his side to look away.

"No, I didn't ask You about it."

His chest tightened.

"I'm sorry. I was wrong to ask Allie to do what she did. That was not done in love."

A hint of insight sprang up in the form of a question.

What is Matthew's situation right now?

Jordan propped up on his elbow and shook his head. He stopped to think. "Is he in trouble?"

A few seconds passed.

"Sorry, that's a dumb question." Hanging around with Isaac Molencki could not be good.

"How did he get entangled with that guy?"

A strange memory hit him. Jordan flashed back to the first meeting with Jeffrey Kingston in the café.

"What's the currency of Washington, DC?"

He remembered the wobbly feeling that he had pushed down when Jeffrey asked to mentor him. The memory came back with fresh intensity. Several more thoughts tumbled into his mind. He didn't so much hear them as he just *knew*.

Matthew's in way over his head.

Jordan remembered the look on the small man's face in Mr. Carlyle's office. A shiver went through him.

These guys are bad news.

Jordan rolled to his stomach, leaned on his forearms, and prayed with all he had. "Lord, I don't know how to ask it right, but You've got to help Matthew. Please help him. He doesn't understand the fire he's playing with. Lord, I'm sorry. I ask for grace. And if You'd allow it, I ask for a chance to help him."

It didn't make any sense, but it seemed right.

Shaking his head again, he got up and reached for the stash of dark clothes under his bed. He didn't have to extract the information this time—it was offered to him by the mysterious R3. Two o'clock in the morning with a qualifier of *dangerously confidential*.

"Lord, please be with me. I have no idea what, or who, I'm going to find."

Chapter 81

R3 Comes Clean

Friday, August 15, 2:00 a.m.
Abandoned mercantile building, Old Town, Wilson, CO

A sense of spiritual darkness, amplified by something he couldn't nail down, crawled up Jordan's spine. He shuddered.

Honoring the invitation's warning about taking extreme care, he dressed in all black, with only the new phone in his pocket. He took a zigzagging way through the forest and then slunk up to the back door of the Old Town mercantile building. It added risk, but he couldn't stomach the thought of the underground trek through the catacombs, alone at two a.m.

Squeezing through a door that hung off its hinges, Jordan picked his way through the main floor to the northeast corner of the building. Moonlight shone again through the windows, long since empty of glass. The quiet was intense. Intense with something.

A soft scraping sound whispered behind him, sending a surge of adrenaline through his body. He whipped his head around. A piece of paper caught the wind and blew across the room. Jordan exhaled and tried to calm himself.

He reached the corner room and crept over to the round patterned grate where they'd found Bethany. He might have thought it odd that the grate was inside the building, had he not been studying the underground tunnel systems of the Intermountain states. Apparently it was quite normal.

He pulled out his phone, turned on the flashlight, and stuffed it back in his pocket, allowing a small light to escape from his black basketball shorts.

He unrolled a foldable escape ladder which he'd retrieved from his parents' bedroom. Using the same crowbar as before, Jordan removed the grate, put the escape ladder in place, and lowered himself down.

He hopped the last couple feet to the ground. Turning around, his heart almost jumped out of his throat. The dim light of his phone cast an eerie glow on an old man, seated in a chair with a book in his lap.

Mr. Everett.

Heart hammering, Jordan pulled out his phone and set it sideways on the shelf where Bethany had found the magazines. Light, just enough for this crazy encounter, pointed up at the ceiling.

Jordan looked down at the man. Mr. Everett's eyes were round, large, and glistening. A sheen of sweat reflected from his forehead. Jordan realized what had been punctuating the feeling of suffocation.

Terror.

It was like a noose tightening upon everything in its grip.

Jordan bent down on one knee and looked up at Mr. Everett. He reached out his hand and laid it on the old man's forearm. "I'm sorry, sir, if I have brought this on you."

Shaking, Robert Everett breathed heavily under the weight. "No. This is a long time in coming."

"Sir, are you R3?"

The old man closed his eyes and nodded.

Jordan patted Mr. Everett's forearm. "May I guess? You're risking your life to have this conversation?"

"That's true"—Mr. Everett opened his eyes again—"but it's way more than that."

Jordan swallowed.

"Fifty years ago," Mr. Everett continued, "I was the third researcher on a team with your great-grandfather and Ray Clark. My code name was R3. I was an ambitious, twenty-something hotshot—totally unprepared for the situation that was soon thrust on me. We were commissioned to research the effects of a drug called XD."

Jordan nodded. Nothing new there.

"Our findings began to alarm us, and Ray and William took their concerns to Howard Carlyle."

"Howard then told you, in no uncertain terms, to put a lid on it," replied Jordan.

"Yes. He was concerned—paranoid really—that this would threaten the Wonder Drug deal."

"That's the part I don't get," said Jordan. "The Wonder Drug deal and the XD research are two different things, seemingly unrelated."

"Not to Mr. Carlyle they weren't. I'll never know the exact reasoning, but it was crystal clear from the look in his eyes that our findings were unacceptable—never mind that they were true. Remember, Thalidomide was still fresh in everyone's mind. The hype surrounding XD was intense. Mr. Carlyle thought that Hampden Pharmaceuticals was nervous and would run away. Whatever the reason, things began to take an ugly turn. He started to threaten. How dare we endanger his big deal?"

"Is that when Plan A and Plan B emerged?" asked Jordan.

"Yes. All of sudden, I found myself in a swirl of danger. I remember thinking, 'I did not sign up for *this*.'"

Jordan's nod was deliberate—his eyes never left Mr. Everett's. "That must have been horrible."

"It was. Ray was brilliant from the beginning. He knew what was right and was prepared to do whatever it took. He began to play along with Howard Carlyle, all the while trying to garner enough evidence to go public swiftly. Your great-grandfather had a tremendous spiritual awakening in this crisis, and decided to join with Ray no matter what it cost. He was the one who came up with the different possible ways that Plan B could play out."

"And you?" asked Jordan.

"I was caught in a dilemma. On one hand, I was concerned about the suffering that we knew would come if XD went to market unchecked. On the other hand, I didn't want to die. I was afraid and didn't know what to do. I was playing along with William and Ray, but my heart was not in it." A bead of sweat formed on his temple.

"It's okay, sir," reassured Jordan.

"No, it's not," replied Mr. Everett, shaking now. "May I tell you why this meeting was so difficult for me?"

"Of course."

"Howard Carlyle offered me a deal. I betrayed William and Ray in exchange for a life of peace and comfort." Tears cascaded down Mr. Everett's cheeks. "I'm so sorry, Jordan. *I'm* the reason they're dead." Robert Everett buried his face in his hands and cried.

Jordan yanked his fist to his mouth and bit down hard on his index finger knuckle. He fought back shocked, angry tears as new information punched him in the gut. Right in front of him sat a man who deserved much of the blame for the plight of the Nolan family and the suffering of thousands of people.

Jordan looked away. Michael Clark's words sliced his heart open and poured salt into it.

There's no way I would let her marry you. Bethany would never be his— because of Robert Everett.

He pulled his hand back and balled his fists at his sides.

Your family's part in the story is like a black smear across an otherwise beautiful painting.

His jaw tightened. Red slammed his consciousness from all sides as he heard an eight-year-old Matthew Harris say to his friends, "Let's play 1964!"

"Yeah!" shouted the other boys.

Jordan's chest constricted as helpless rage squeezed his heart like a vise. He forced out a muted, but guttural, cry, clenching his eyes shut. A vein on his neck throbbed in the eerie darkness. He choked his breath down in tight gasps. Somehow, he managed to eke out a silent, desperate prayer through clenched teeth.

Lord, give me grace, now! He was dangerously close to punching an old man.

The answer came at once.

The red was blasted from his mind like a strong wind blowing out a cobweb. A wave of peace washed his soul as a vivid picture formed in his mind. This man in his late seventies had lived under constant fear of blackmail and a load of guilt and shame. The tension melted. Jordan's eyes became round and soft as he stared at the kind, old librarian, crying into his hands. Many, including himself, had suffered because of Mr. Everett's actions. He deserved what he had gotten. But something stirred within Jordan.

Something deeper than himself.

"Mr. Everett," a hint of a tear emerged in the corner of Jordan's eye as he said, "my great-grandfather was a terrible husband and father. I've read his testimony. You probably remember it. In his desperate hour, a promise from his distant past came back to his mind. He looked up to heaven and said, 'God, is it still true?' The still, small voice of God spoke back to him, saying, 'Yes, it's still true.' God turned him into the brightest light in our family's history."

Jordan felt as though the voice was not his own.

"My great-grandfather is my hero. But it's only because of the work of God in him." A boldness came over Jordan that made no sense in the context. "What about you? Will you receive God's forgiveness in Jesus? It's not too late."

Robert Everett had recovered his composure. He shook his head at Jordan through the blur of tears. "How could I?" He clutched a book with both hands and held it up. "Do you know what this is?"

"Yes, sir, I think I do. I'm guessing it's a ledger. Part of my summer school, wasn't it?"

"Yes." Mr. Everett's voice cracked. "It's my legacy—a memoir of cowardice. It's every person and issue I know about related to XD. I'm responsible for the suffering of thousands—including you, your family, and Bethany's mother."

Jordan wiped the emerging tears from his own face. He saw the horror of a life lived under the crushing weight of guilt. He guided Mr. Everett to set the book back in his lap and gently pried his fingers from the cover. Still holding his hands, he looked the old man straight in the eye and said, "That's true. You are responsible for some of it. But I'm going to offer you a deal. If I forgive you, will you accept God's forgiveness?"

A hint of longing fought for control against a lifetime of fear.

"Mr. Everett"—Jordan's words flowed with tender boldness—"the reason you reached out as R3, and the reason you agreed to this meeting, is because secretly, you long to be free. Now is the time. Lay down the guilt. Lay down the shame. Lay down the fear. Receive my forgiveness, and receive God's forgiveness. Receive His love. Receive His Son. Do it now."

Jordan was astonished at himself. His words carried the quiet, yet unmistakable authority of the Holy Spirit.

Mr. Everett appeared shell-shocked. All he could do was nod.

●●●

The same grace that had washed over Jordan rolled over Robert Everett. He entered a serene state where tears still flowed, but they were tears of genuine gratitude. Tears of unburdening.

Several minutes passed. Jordan's legs ached. He knelt before Mr. Everett and smiled a silent companionship.

The old man glowed with new freedom. Finally, when it had run its course, Robert Everett straightened.

"May I ask you a question?" Jordan stood.

"Of course, what is it?"

"Do you think the issue with Bethany's mother is related to XD?"

Mr. Everett's face went dead serious. "Absolutely."

"You think it's hereditary?"

"Yes."

"Is that what you meant when you said that the truth about her great-grandfather and her mom were related? The connection was XD."

The old man nodded.

"Two letters: X and D. Clever. That line about one being written after the other threw us off for a while."

Mr. Everett gave a grim smile. "I was still struggling with what to do. I couldn't make it too obvious."

Jordan changed the subject. "Sir, I want to vindicate my great-grandfather. The problem is, Gadg and I watched Donald Carlyle incinerate the evidence you led us to—the evidence left by William and Ray. We didn't even have time to make copies."

Mr. Everett's face darkened with a shadow of fear, but this time it didn't stay. He relaxed again and then grew resolute. "So he knows."

"Not only does he know," said Jordan, "I saw him *choose* to follow in his father's footsteps. He was confronted with the evidence. He lit it on fire himself. I'm sure you understand."

"I understand all too well," said Mr. Everett. He reached into his pocket and pulled out a solitary key. "Thanks to you, it's better late than never. I should have done this five decades ago." He handed the key to Jordan. "My river cabin." He pulled a piece of paper from the book and slipped it to him.

Jordan nodded again, looking over the directions.

"Inside the fireplace is a secret compartment. You'll find all the answers."

"Thank you, sir. I'll go about this time tomorrow."

Creak. The slightest sound somewhere up above.

A shiver of dread coursed through Jordan. His mind jumped to the worst. Could the small man be above them? Only the fact that God had been so near in the last few minutes kept him from freaking out.

Mr. Everett's eyes darted in multiple directions. His voice was barely above a whisper, "You need to go. You're not safe."

Jordan nodded and started back the way he'd come.

"You can't go back that way." Mr. Everett looked up at the ladder. "Go back the way I told you to come."

Jordan knew he could figure it out but didn't like the prospect. "You?"

"I know my way."

"What if something happens or it's not there?"

"Don't worry," said Mr. Everett. "I need to make a trip tomorrow."

"For what?"

"Jeffrey Kingston and Donald Carlyle are meeting in Denver with Hampden Pharmaceuticals. It's their last meeting with the senator before the celebration. They are meeting to get everything lined up for the announcement of Hampden's purchase of WDC2."

"What does that have to do with you?"

Mr. Everett smiled. "Plan B."

●●●

Alex hoped he was not too late. Watching Mr. Everett climb into Jordan's truck had alerted him that something was up. He had gone into full surveillance mode. Watching Jordan leave his house dressed in black at 1:50 a.m. removed any doubt. A sense of déjà vu came over him as he followed at a distance from the east side of Nolan property. There was no way Johnny could sneak up on him this time.

The old mercantile building was the destination.

A few minutes later, Alex peeked around the corner of a door to the back room and spotted the top of the escape ladder. He gave a satisfied nod. Jordan was back in the catacombs. Alex heard voices of a conversation in the room directly below.

He scowled.

He couldn't make out the words, and the hole was twenty feet from where he stood. The slightest noise might alert them to his presence. He hadn't come for business, he'd come for information. Quiet was the only answer.

He crept toward the hole at a painstakingly slow pace, using the utmost care for every single step. Ten minutes later, he squatted down just short of it and listened. The conversation had paused for some reason, but he could still hear occasional noises.

He heard Jordan start up again with, "May I ask you a question?"

Robert Everett responded. Interesting. So the librarian was involved.

Even more interesting, Donald Carlyle destroyed the evidence.

Wait.

He listened further. *There's another copy? Jordan's going to get it?*

His legs were on fire from the extended squat. As quietly as possible, he put his hand down on the dirty floor to take some of the weight off his burning legs. The floorboard creaked. He gritted his teeth. The voices from below dropped to a whisper. He could barely make them out. A moment later, the conversation ended, and both Jordan and Mr. Everett seemed to have left the room by another way. Alex concluded they must know their way through the catacombs.

He let himself down to a sitting position.

Jordan is going to get another copy of the evidence twenty-four hours from now.

Evidence that could implicate the Carlyle family.

Moonlight shone on the bottom half of his face, giving his smiling teeth a creepy, yellowish glow.

Perfect.

Two birds—the Nolan's and the Carlyle's—with one stone. Alex Jones had been played the fool for the last time. Tomorrow he would get his revenge. Two for one. Efficient.

● ● ●

Jordan found himself in an old office. He couldn't see any faces, but he knew he looked over the shoulder of power. The smell of cigar smoke permeated the room. Somehow, he knew that smell.

Jordan stood behind a man he didn't recognize and surveyed the desk over the man's shoulder. The man wielded a large pen in his hand. In the upper left corner of the desk, a memo spike stuck up with a razor sharp tip. Two pink slips had been pressed down over it.

While he watched, another man Jordan couldn't identify walked up and handed a third pink slip to the man at the desk. The paper looked old and weather-beaten. The man behind the desk signed it and stuck it on the memo spike.

Jordan shot up in bed. He'd been asleep for maybe an hour since returning from his meeting with R3. He pulled his breath in with difficulty. He tried to shake the disorientation as he struggled to get his heart rate down. The dream was still vivid and crystal clear in his mind. He didn't know if it meant anything, but if it did, it was not good.

● ● ●

Mr. Everett sat at his desk in his bedroom. He hadn't slept since he returned from his meeting with Jordan, but he didn't want to. Sitting up straight in his chair, as he'd been taught over sixty-five years ago, he basked in a peace that he had never felt before. With a bittersweet smile and a tear forming in his eye, he reached again for a pen and paper.

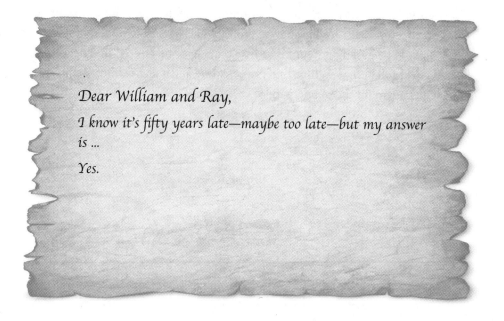

Dear William and Ray,

I know it's fifty years late—maybe too late—but my answer is ...

Yes.

Chapter 82

Plan B in Motion

Friday, August 15, 8:45 a.m.
Home of Robert Everett, Wilson, CO

Lit up with his biggest smile in decades, Robert Everett stepped from his front door into a stunning Friday morning in Western Colorado. Exhilaration flooded his being. He wasn't tired, even with his age and lack of sleep. Today was the biggest day of his life since that fateful night fifty years ago. The time had come. He pulled out his phone and forced his smile down to a grave frown. He felt so light and cheerful it was difficult, but he had to focus on the task at hand.

I've never been good at sales.

Jeffrey Kingston picked up on the third ring.

Mr. Everett had been in a few conversations with him this summer about the 50th Anniversary Celebration, so this phone call was not out of the ordinary. "Mr. Kingston, this is Robert Everett," he spoke into the phone and listened back. "I'm fine, sir. I'm calling because I have some information that may have direct bearing on the celebration. It appears to be something about WDC2 and a connection to the drug XD."

"You do realize we're in the final meetings with Hampden Pharmaceuticals and Mr. Carlyle today?" said Jeffrey.

"Yes, the timing is horrible, but I found something that appears to be evidence of some kind of cover-up. I thought it best to call you right away and arrange to get it to you. I'm planning to come to Denver as soon as possible, before your trip to Wilson. I'll explain it to the senator, and you three can decide what to do with it."

"Have you spoken with anyone else about this?"

"No, I haven't."

"Even the senator?"

"I thought it best to bring it to you first."

"Good thinking. He has many things on his mind right now. I'll prep him between meetings before you get here. Don't trust anyone else."

"I won't. I'll bring it personally."

"Mr. Everett, I appreciate this."

"Thank you, Mr. Kingston. I'll see you in a few hours. I plan to leave for Denver around ten o'clock." He cut the connection and smiled.

● ● ●

"Mr. Carlyle, this is Robert Everett." He paused to listen. "Yes, I know you're busy so I'll get right to the point. I just got off the phone with Jeffrey Kingston."

"Excuse me?" said Donald.

"Sir, you told me you wanted to know if anything could jeopardize the celebration. I found some stuff related to WDC2 and XD."

There was a long pause.

"I knew you'd be in Denver today, so I called Mr. Kingston to arrange to bring it to the senator while you're there."

"The celebration is tomorrow!" said Donald.

"Yes, sir. That's why I thought it best to bring it to you right away. With the celebration so close, I thought you'd know how to handle it."

"Have you spoken with the senator?"

"No, sir. You and Mr. Kingston are the only ones I've spoken to. He said he would brief the senator between meetings."

"That makes sense. When are you coming?"

"I'll be leaving about ten a.m. I'll see you soon." He set the phone down.

They think I'm a total idiot.

R3 smiled and looked up. Plan B was underway.

William, I hope you're proud of me.

It was time to tell his secret to the least likely person on planet earth.

Chapter 83

Tough Call

Friday, August 15, 9:30 a.m.
Jordan's truck, parked outside Old Town Café, Wilson, CO

Seated behind the steering wheel of Gutless, Jordan stared down at his phone. The number was already typed in. All he had to do was push the green button. He had put this off as long as he could, but if it was going to help, it was now or never. He drew in a noisy breath through pursed lips. He didn't want to think of what could happen to him—or Bethany—if the small man found out.

When Jordan had inquired how Gadg got the number, Gadg had replied, "Don't ask." Jordan didn't even know what city he was calling—only that it was back east.

He touched the button and lifted the phone to his ear.

A woman answered on the second ring. "Hello?" The voice was low and proper with a crisp accent.

"Is this Elizabeth Sheridan?"

"Who is this?"

"My name is Jordan Nolan. I'm calling from a little town in Colorado called Wilson."

"How did you get this number?" The voice snapped.

"A friend gave it to me."

"Listen, young man, I do not take calls from strangers. I am hanging up now."

"Ms. Sheridan, please," Jordan said quickly. "This is the riskiest phone call of my entire life. I wouldn't be calling if it wasn't a matter of life or death."

The phone was silent for a moment and a slightly less hostile voice came through. "I'm listening."

"Thank you. I don't know how to say this so I'll just get right to the point. Does the name Isaac Molencki mean anything to you?"

Dead silence.

Jordan thought he might have lost her. "Ms. Sheridan?"

"I'm here."

"Do you know him?"

"Never heard of him. I'm sorry."

"But-" Jordan stammered. "Why did you pause when I asked you the question?"

"I am very busy. Do you have any other questions?"

Jordan wracked his brain. This was not going well. He looked up.

Lord, help! Give me something, anything.

He opened his mouth with no idea what he would say. What came out shocked him. "Have you ever been in love?" He cringed and looked out the other window.

"I beg your pardon?" The tone dripped with upper-class, northeast offense. "What do you want, young man? I am extremely close to calling the police."

"No, please," Jordan responded. "Ms. Sheridan, I know I'm botching this call in every way possible. In fact, I can't believe you're still on the phone. I desperately need some answers about Isaac Molencki."

"Why?" Her tone still carried an undercurrent of suspicion.

"Let's just say it's important," said Jordan in a low, soft voice.

A few seconds later Elizabeth chuckled as if some insight came to her. "Maybe I should ask you the same question, even though it's clear you're still a youngster."

Jordan didn't say anything.

"What's her name?" asked Elizabeth.

Jordan sighed. He didn't want to do it, but this was his only chance at answers. "Her name is Bethany. She's the most special person on earth to me. She's being sta-"—he hesitated—"*watched* by Mr. Molencki."

It was Elizabeth's turn to sigh. She paused for a long moment. Her voice came back as if dredged from the past and thick with emotion, "All right. Yes, I knew him. Quite well."

Sensing she wasn't finished, Jordan waited.

"He and I dated for about eighteen months. We were very close."

Jordan proceeded with caution. "What is he like?"

"You mean besides being the ultimate soldier packed into a body less than five feet tall?"

Jordan rubbed his forehead. Although it didn't surprise him, this was terrible news. "Yes, besides that."

"Well, believe it or not, he's an exceptional wordsmith from all his training. Before email was so prevalent, we had the sweetest, most tender correspondence through an exchange of letters and poems. I have them to this day."

No wonder he wanted to read Bethany's diary.

Elizabeth continued, "We even had beautiful nicknames for each other. I almost married him."

"What happened?"

"I chickened out and took the safe road." She paused. "I chose another man."

Oh, no.

Jordan thought about the eyes of the small man. They were fearless to the point of a death wish. Now he knew why.

Elizabeth kept going. "I accepted a marriage proposal from a man named Charles. Isaac was devastated. He disappeared from my life. The last thing I heard from him was a note of condolence I received at my fiancé's funeral."

"His *funeral?*"

"Yes. He died in a car accident before we were married."

Accident?

The word popped into Jordan's head with a question mark behind it, but he dared not say it out loud. "Ms. Sheridan, I'm sorry. I didn't mean to cause you any grief."

She was silent.

"Did you ever reach out to Mr. Molencki?"

"I almost did."

Jordan heard the melancholy tone. "Forgive me for saying so, Ms. Sheridan, but it sounds like you miss him."

"I miss the man I once knew. I don't miss the man he's become."

"What kind of man is that?"

"I wish I had better news for you, Jordan Nolan, but if you or this young lady friend of yours are in his sights, you're in grave danger."

Jordan blew out a breath. "Does he have any weaknesses?"

"Besides an unimaginably horrible childhood full of abuse and neglect, he only has one—*me*."

Jordan could hear a bit of pride in the way she said it. Courage welled up within him. "Ms. Sheridan, I know I don't have the relational equity for this, but for the sake of my dear friend, I'm going to ask for an enormous favor. Is there anything you could give me that could help us?"

After a long moment, Elizabeth finally replied, "I don't know what good it'll do you, but if you need it, you can tell him that *Sheri-pie* misses going to the mailbox and finding a letter from him."

Chapter 84

Smell of Danger and Crispy Bacon

Friday, August 15, 10:05 a.m.
Old Town Café - Wilson, CO

"I am so ready to eat," said Tyler.

"You look like a pilot strapping himself into the cockpit. Take it easy," said Jordan as he sat down in the booth at the Old Town Café.

"No way, man. Five hard practices in four days and a good night's sleep? I'm ordering breakfast and lunch."

"They do a great brunch here," agreed Jordan.

"No, no, no," said Tyler quickly. "I'm ordering breakfast *and* lunch. Double bacon omelet that I'll slather with maple syrup. Pancakes that I'll load with fresh fruit on top. I'm trying to eat healthy. On the side, a large basket of waffle fries to connect breakfast with lunch."

"Yes, they're good," said Jordan.

"Gadg told me this was an Old Town Café special, worth trying because the particular type of cut increased the grease to potato quotient—whatever that means."

"Sounds like Gadg."

"Doesn't matter. I'll put a lake of ketchup in the basket just in case. Nothing worse than fries tasting too much like potatoes."

"Agreed," said Jordan. "You going to top it off with orange juice?" he asked.

"No chance. Large soda all the way." Tyler flashed a grand smile. "I ordered you coffee, of course."

Jordan nodded his thanks. "Speaking of Gadg, where is he?"

"Busy with the A/V for the celebration tomorrow."

Jordan zoned out—bags under his eyes.

"You should know that," said Tyler.

"I do," said Jordan. "I'm just tired. I've hardly seen him the last few days. He's been so busy. I saw him briefly yesterday. Speaking of which, guess who I met last night?"

"Who?"

Jordan lowered his voice to a whisper. "R3."

"What? No way. Where?"

"In the catacombs, where else?"

"Seriously, dude. That's amazing!" Tyler looked up at the ceiling. "Who is it?"

"This is strictly, life-threateningly, confidential." Jordan glanced around the café to make sure no one was within earshot. "I wouldn't tell you at all except that you've been in the guts of this with us."

Tyler bumped a fist against his heart. "That means a lot, Jordan. And I know that well enough. So, who is it?"

"Robert Everett."

Tyler blinked. Twice. "The librarian?"

"The same."

Tyler looked past Jordan to the library across the street, "Speaking of Mr. Everett, I've never seen him in suit and tie before. Is he going to a funeral?"

Jordan looked up just in time to see Mr. Everett leave the library, stash his briefcase in the backseat of his car, and get behind the wheel.

"So tell me about last night," said Tyler.

"It was déjà vu," said Jordan, refocusing. He spent the next few minutes relaying the story of his meeting with Mr. Everett.

"Do you think it was the small man?" asked Tyler when Jordan got to the part about the noise they'd heard.

"I can't be sure. We didn't stick around to find out."

"How'd you get back?"

Jordan gave one shake of his head. "The catacombs."

"Oh, boy."

"If I never have to go back down there again it'll be too soon. I'm getting tired of late-night outings." He decided not to mention that another was coming tonight.

Before Tyler could respond, the food arrived.

"Miss Kathy, please make sure you set it before him with the proper ceremony," said Jordan. "He's just come off four hard days of practice."

The waitress smiled and placed the plates on the table with reverence.

Tyler straightened up in his chair.

"You want anything besides coffee?" asked Kathy turning to Jordan.

"No, I'm good. Thanks. Where's-"

"She's not working this week." The waitress winked at Jordan. "Too much to do with the celebration."

Jordan smiled back as Tyler folded his hands and bowed his head. "You'd better go," he said to the waitress. "You might get hurt if you get between a football player and his food."

Kathy chuckled and returned to the counter. Another customer stepped up to pay his bill.

Picking up his fork, Tyler said, "Do you realize this will be the first bite I will have actually taken at the Old Town Café?"

"You still haven't eaten here?"

"No," said Tyler. "Thanks to you." His expression radiated satisfaction as he stared at a mammoth bite of bacon and egg from his omelet.

Jordan looked past him to the counter where the customer finished paying his bill. As Kathy pushed the drawer closed, the cash register made the old school "cha-ching" sound from the previous century. The man turned to leave, and Kathy picked the receipt off the counter and stuck it on a memo spike next to the register.

Jordan snapped out of any remaining tiredness and entered the present with a vengeance. The dream from last night blazed into his memory.

Most of Tyler's untried omelet bite dropped off his fork and into the whipped cream on his pancakes. "What?" he said, startled.

"Did you see him get into his car?" Jordan didn't wait for an answer. He was already up and out of the booth. "Dude, we're outta here. Mr. Everett is in great danger!" He grabbed Tyler by the upper arm and pulled him out of his seat. As they sped past the waitress, Jordan yelled over his shoulder that it was an emergency and he would pay for the meal soon.

● ● ●

Jordan had a bad feeling about this. Insight about the dream flooded him as he and Tyler ran out the door of the Old Town Café. Based on the conversation with Mr. Everett early this morning, he now had a hunch what the backup plan entailed.

Robert Everett was going to Denver to present the evidence to Senator Smith.

Jordan realized he'd never gotten a chance to tell Mr. Everett what he suspected about the senator—and what he *knew* about Jeffrey Kingston.

The dream nagged at him.

He'll never make it.

They left Gutless parked at the café and jumped into Tyler's car. "Maybe I'm overreacting," he said.

"I hope so," said Tyler. His face showed concern.

Jordan felt the vibration of a new text message. He fished his phone out of his pocket as Tyler pulled out of the parking lot onto Main Street. The message was from Bethany.

> Mr. Everett just slipped me a note as he walked past. I was busy with someone and just got a chance to open it. It reads, "Tell Jordan I've made two—and only two—phone calls this morning. One was to Jeffrey Kingston. The other was to Donald Carlyle. Tell him thanks for everything."

"What is it?" asked Tyler.

"I'll explain on the way," said Jordan, dread settling in his heart. "Go!"

Chapter 85

The End of Plan B

Friday, August 15, 11:05 a.m.
Highway 24, twenty miles east of Wilson, CO

Twenty miles outside of town, Jordan looked down the embankment at a car that had folded in on itself. The front was rammed up to the base of a tree. He shook his head and used the heel of his palm to brush away a tear.

Some time ago, Deputy O'Brien had arrived as the first authorized person on the scene. Now, two paramedics peeled back the body of Robert Everett from where it lay, slumped over the steering wheel. Two reporters circled the vehicle from a distance while snapping pictures. A third stood off to the side, talking into a camera from the local news.

Jordan looked down, kicking the dirt at his feet. Robert Everett had become dear to him in the space of one hour this morning. He couldn't believe it was not even noon yet and his new friend was gone. This morning's dream came back to him in force.

Any chance this was an accident?

The conclusion gripped his mind.

No way.

Two months ago, he'd thought that going on the Senator's Internship was serious business. This was an order of magnitude higher. Another good man had just been killed to perpetuate a fifty-year-old cover-up. Jordan brushed back another tear as his eyes dried and his jaw turned to iron.

This is not right.

Tonight he would settle this. Once and for all. Plan B may be dead, but Plan A was still on. He would avenge his new friend along with all the others.

He walked toward Deputy O'Brien's squad car. The deputy leaned into the front seat.

The news reporter spoke live into a microphone as the camera rolled, "Twenty miles outside the Wilson city limits, we are looking live at an unfortunate accident involving one of our beloved citizens. Longtime Wilson resident Robert Everett died tragically less than an hour ago..."

"Deputy O'Brien," said Jordan as he and Tyler walked up to the patrol car, "Can I speak to you for a moment?"

Deputy O'Brien had his head down, trying to do three things at once. "I'm kind of busy. What is it, Jordan?" he said without looking up.

Jordan spoke through the side of his mouth, "Did you recover a briefcase?"

"What briefcase?" the voice came out the door of the car as if from a tunnel.

"The one he had in his hand when he left the library this morning."

Deputy O'Brien climbed out and gave his attention to Jordan. "What are you talking about?"

"Tyler and I were in the café," said Jordan.

"Yeah," said Tyler. "I wondered where he was going dressed up in a suit and tie."

Jordan continued, "We saw him put his briefcase into the car and drive off. Look at how he's dressed."

Deputy O'Brien looked up as the paramedics placed the body in an unzipped body bag. The coroner had just arrived and was walking over to examine it. The deputy stroked his chin. "Guys, there was no briefcase in the car."

Tyler and Jordan exchanged glances.

Deputy O'Brien looked at each of them for a long moment as his face hardened. He turned and opened his mouth to speak to the whole group.

A flash of insight hit Jordan. The deputy was about to announce this as a crime scene. "Sir," he said in an intense whisper, "Don't say a word."

Annoyance shot across the deputy's face as he clamped down hard and swallowed what he was going to say. He turned to Jordan, eyes like flint.

"I'm sorry, sir," Jordan continued in a whisper. "I want to ask you to consider something before you say anything."

"And what's that?"

"Do you know why Mr. Everett was going to Denver?"

"No, I don't."

"He was taking evidence to the senator about WDC2's involvement with XD." Jordan lowered his voice even further. "Sir, Robert Everett was *R3*."

Deputy O'Brien lifted an eyebrow. He studied Jordan.

Jordan looked back, his face unflinching. He reached into his pocket, pulled out his phone, and showed the deputy his text message from Bethany.

The deputy stared at the text for a few seconds and then gave a slight nod. Looking up, his eyes darted back and forth across the scene as he reprocessed what had just happened. The wheels turned inside his head. When he spoke the annoyance was gone. "Thank you for stopping me."

"You agree?" asked Jordan.

"I do," nodded the deputy. His expression remained grim as he surveyed the coroner looking down at the body.

Tyler grimaced. "Um, what?"

Deputy O'Brien spoke under his breath, "At this point, it's better that the official report shows this to be an accident." He turned to Jordan and Tyler. "Watch yourselves. I'll be in touch."

Chapter 86

Playing with the Big Boys

Friday, August 15, 4:00 p.m.
Old Town Café, Wilson, CO

Jeffrey Kingston had asked for this meeting.

Gutless sat parked with the engine off, but Jordan still clutched the steering wheel. "Lord, you know I don't have a clue what Mr. Kingston knows or what he's thinking. I'm not sure I even want the internship if he's the point man. Bottom line," Jordan paused and looked at the café entrance, "I'm in way over my head on this one. Please give me strength."

Thirty seconds later, he pushed open the door to the café and scanned the room. At four p.m. there wasn't much to see.

Jeffrey Kingston caught his eye and waved him over.

Jordan walked up to the table and tried for casual.

"Thanks for meeting with me on such short notice." Jeffrey's ever-easy smile flashed as he stood and extended his hand.

"You're welcome, sir, and as always, thanks for meeting with me." Jordan shook hands and sat down.

Jeffrey looked him over. "Everything okay?" he asked.

Is it that obvious?

"I'm fine, sir. Thanks for asking. How are you?"

"Well, as you can guess, it's crazy at celebration headquarters. We are very busy. I just got out of a meeting with Mr. Clark."

Jordan looked away. The last thing Mr. Clark had said to him still carried a fresh sting.

Jeffrey's next words came out velvet smooth. "I'm sorry it didn't work out, Jordan. She's a good girl."

Oh my goodness! How much does he know?

He looked back at Jeffrey with wide eyes. The doors of his understanding flew open and slammed the pieces into place.

Bethany's diary. Allie's meal with Matthew. The small man. Michael Clark.

Jeffrey smiled a reminder of how connected he was.

Jordan took a long drink of water to buy time to send up a silent, urgent prayer for grace. Setting the glass down, he asked, "What can I do for you, sir?"

"Why did I get a call from Robert Everett today?"

This time Jordan reeled like he'd been hit with number two in a one-two punch. Four or five emotions fought for dominance. Shock won out.

"I'm sorry about what happened to him," Jeffrey said. He blinked, his eyes softening. "I spoke to him a few times. He seemed like a good man."

"He was," Jordan said.

"How well did you know him?" asked Jeffrey with a fresh keenness returning to his gaze.

Jordan thought back to early that morning. He could hardly believe it was still the same day.

Plan B is dead. My new friend is dead.

"Not well," he finally said. Jordan looked down at the napkin beneath the silverware. Red stood on the fringes of his consciousness, poised to crash into his mind at any moment and throw him into total vertigo. "Why are you asking me this, sir?"

Jeffrey leaned forward and engaged Jordan, eyeball to eyeball, across the table. "I thought I had made it clear to you how things work in Washington. What did I tell you?"

"You told me the currency of Washington, DC is allies," said Jordan.

"Did you learn nothing?" His tone had a sharp edge.

"Actually, it was excellent advice." Jordan's gut screamed out the risks, but he ignored it and stepped up to the plate to play some hardball. "It caused me to realize I don't want a power-hungry wolf as an ally."

Jeffrey drew back like Jordan slapped him in the face. All pretense at cordiality was gone in an instant. A savage glint reflected off his eyes. He waited a few awful seconds, leaned in close, and said, "You have no idea who you're dealing with."

Jordan stifled a gulp and forced himself to maintain eye contact. Fear shot through him. He stared at a ravenous face framed by a Washington power suit and tie. At any moment his rib cavity would be pried open and fangs would tear into his heart. He forced himself back into the conversation. "You were playing me. This was never about mentoring me. This was about making sure I didn't find the truth about William Nolan. With your spiel about allies, you're either in Donald's hip pocket, or worse, he's in yours."

Jeffrey turned deadly. "I will speak to the senator tonight. For starters, you can expect a call tomorrow morning rescinding the internship."

Jordan tried to steel himself. The man wasn't finished.

Jeffrey stood to leave. He reached down to set some bills on the table, cocked his head, and spoke in a soft yet menacing whisper. "*If* you keep your head down and *if* you keep your mouth shut, the internship might—just might—be the only thing you lose."

"Shall I set up an appointment with Isaac Molencki to get it over with?" asked Jordan.

Jeffrey's face registered the comment. Jordan's knowledge of his connection to Isaac Molencki was not news to him. He smiled. "Like I said, Jordan"—he paused as if he wielded an instrument of torture—"she's a good girl." He spun around and walked to the door.

● ● ●

"Goodbye, Donald."

After three phone calls, two of them to Mr. Carlyle, Senator Smith set his phone down on his office desk at the Capitol. He looked out the window as the sun's last rays ascended the final floors of Denver's tallest building.

Using the second of the three calls, he had just authorized Jeffrey Kingston to rescind the offer of the Senator's Internship to Jordan Nolan. Trespassing, coupled with a breaking and entering charge, right before the 50th Anniversary Celebration, was politically unacceptable. Donald Carlyle had forced his hand.

Or had he?

Once again, Jordan's words came, unbidden, into his mind.

"Do you really want to know?"

Staring at the small skyline, with the slime of Donald's words still echoing in his mind, the realization hit him squarely in the face.

He did want to know.

Regardless of whether Jordan's story was true, Senator Smith wanted to know the truth. Not only that, he wanted the freedom of answering only to the truth.

He caught his reflection in the glass. It looked perfect. Midfifties, fit, ruggedly handsome as ever.

But the eyes didn't lie.

Deep down, the real James Smith knew. He hadn't done anything overtly corrupt, but the fact that he was considering Donald Carlyle's homestead offer was proof he'd strayed from the sense of calling that had marked his leadership in the early days.

Leaning on the windowsill, he launched into a prayer of desperation—his first such prayer in years. "Dear God, I want to lead from a true heart again. Am I too far gone?"

His intercom came to life. "Mr. Senator?" said his secretary.

With a sigh, he turned to his desk and pushed the button on his phone, "Yes?"

"Michael Clark on line one for you."

Chapter 87

The Watchers and the Watched

Saturday, August 16, 1:10 a.m.
Forest behind the river cabin of Robert Everett,
three miles outside Wilson city limits

Jordan crept through the forest. It was disturbing enough in the daytime. At one o'clock in the morning, it felt like every shadow reached out to claw him down to the underworld.

He was dressed in a black T-shirt, black basketball shorts, black footies, and his black Ultimate Frisbee shoes. Gadg had provided the finishing touch earlier that day—a black cap that could have floated in a pool of ink without being seen. It was such a deep and dull black that it looked more like empty space than a solid object. When he asked Gadg if he could borrow a dark-colored cap, Gadg had given him a raised eyebrow and no questions. A couple hours later, Gadg passed it to him with a wink. Except for the hat and the fact that it was one a.m. in a forest, he looked like an athlete. However, it was one a.m. in a forest. He didn't want to think what he looked like.

It doesn't matter.

Either he found the evidence or he lost everything.

Robert Everett was dead.

Jeffrey Kingston was an open, dangerous enemy.

Isaac Molencki was *somewhere*.

Jordan's heart pounded as he leaned against a tree to listen and pray. Up ahead, he heard the slither of Wilson's Creek, which was more of a river, slipping past in its clear and foreboding beauty. He reiterated his prayer from his drive to Denver.

Lord, is there some way the truth can come out?

The different faces of Jeffrey Kingston in the café flashed across his mind. Jordan knew, beyond even a hint of doubt, that the senator's chief of staff had ordered the murder of a good man—on behalf of Donald Carlyle.

A flaming cauldron brewed in Jordan's stomach as he remembered why he wanted to be an attorney. He balled his hands into fists.

This was no longer just about exonerating two good men from the past. Jeffrey Kingston was a power-hungry animal in the senator's cabinet—who also threatened to harm the most special person on earth. Jordan had seen the look on his face when he spoke of her. He had no doubt Jeffrey would do it and not lose a wink of sleep. In addition, Donald Carlyle, a senior leader in the medical community, had egregiously violated even the most basic of medical ethics, for money and honor. Furthermore, Senator Smith himself might be a puppet or a stooge, or worse, a corrupt politician.

Jordan repeated his prayer, putting everything into it. "God, all things are possible with You. I ask You to help me make this right!"

Moonlight glinted off his eyes as he sneaked to the back door.

●●●

"Gadg," Bethany whispered sharply into her phone while Allie slept on the bed across the room.

"What is it, Bethany?" He didn't sound tired at all.

"I'm sorry to call so late. I just woke up with a start. My parents went to Denver because my dad had a last-minute meeting with Senator Smith. He said it was urgent. Allie's sawing logs on the other side of my room. I just ... I have a terrible feeling about Jordan."

Gadg was silent for a moment. "I'm watching him right now."

"What do you mean?" Bethany pictured him at the console of his trademark command center, talking to her through a Bluetooth headset.

"Earlier today, Jordan asked to borrow a black hat. I was suspicious. You remember those glasses I showed you in the café?"

"The ones you showed Jordan also? The ones with the hidden camera?"

"Yes, and microphone. I had a hat and shirt made as well."

"Jordan's wearing it?"

"The hat, yes. I can see and hear everything he's doing."

"That makes me feel so much better," said Bethany.

"Not me."

"What do you mean?"

"He's sneaking through the forest on his way to Mr. Everett's river cabin."

"At one a.m.? On the night before the celebration?"

"The morning of, you mean." Gadg sighed. "You know how he is."

"I do," Bethany gulped. Her tone was laced with anxiety. "Is your dad there?"

"He's at work," said Gadg. "I'll call him if there's trouble."

"Does Jordan know you're watching him?"

"I don't think so. It looks like he's dressed in all black. That can't be good. Do you want me to connect you so you can watch?"

"You can do that?"

"Yeah, you'll remotely connect to a server. You won't stream it to your computer."

"Whatever. Yes, please."

"You sure? If he does anything illegal, you might have to testify."

"Do you think he will?" Bethany asked in a wistful melancholy. She shook her head. "Never mind. I need to know what he's really like anyway if..." she trailed off.

"If..." Gadg continued her sentence. "If what?"

Bethany sensed a smile through the phone. "It doesn't matter. Just do it."

"Okay, click the link I send you. Type the password I'll give you over the phone." He spelled it out to her.

Bethany reached for an earpiece, put it in, and pulled up her laptop from the shelf next to her bed. Opening the lid, and then her email, she clicked on the link and typed in the password. "Ah! That's it." Bethany blurted. She could see Jordan as he picked his way through the trees. Allie stirred but did not wake. "What are those numbers on the screen?"

"GPS coordinates," this time his smile was obvious, even through the phone.

"Gadg, you're amazing. But this is freaking me out. This can't be good."

"I know," said Gadg. "Jordan told me his meeting with R3 last night went well. But..."

"... but then he ended up dead today." Bethany's voice cracked. "I loved that old man. I worked with him for a couple years. I can't believe he was R3. Do you think it was an accident?"

"No, I don't." Gadg spoke with an uncharacteristic anger. "Jordan doesn't either, which is why he's out at this crazy hour."

"What's that up ahead?" Bethany could see Jordan approaching a house.

"Like I said, that's Mr. Everett's river cabin."

On both screens, Jordan sneaked up to the back door. He drew a key from his pocket.

"How did he get that?" asked Bethany.

"I think Mr. Everett gave it to him."

"Then why would he go in the middle of the night dressed in black?"

"There's only one reason he would do this—evidence. I'm guessing Mr. Everett has something stashed up there. Maybe copies like we found before. Jordan's no dummy. He's not going to just waltz up there in broad daylight."

"He's going into the house."

"Bethany," Gadg's whisper was dead serious. "There's one more thing you should know." He paused.

"Gadg, what? You're scaring me."

"Jordan unmasked the wolf tonight. He told me about his meeting with Jeffrey Kingston."

"The senator's right-hand man?"

"You got it. Jordan basically called him a liar and a manipulator."

"To his face?" Bethany's voice rose in pitch.

"Yes. Mr. Kingston knows that Jordan knows about Isaac Molencki."

Bethany looked over and bit down on her lip. She squeezed her eyes shut to force back tears. Why did Allie have to get back at Matthew? She might as well have walked up to Mr. Kingston and said, "Excuse me, sir, did you know that we know what you're up to?"

"Did you say your parents are out?" asked Gadg.

Bethany heard the concern. "Yes, hold on." Ninety seconds later, she returned to the line with a "chk, chk" sound.

"Is that a shotgun?" asked Gadg. Allie rolled over but didn't wake.

"Of course," said Bethany. "This is western Colorado." She sat on her bed with her back to the wall below the camera. For easy reach, she set the gun, barrel up, in the corner. Her computer rested on her lap. Nobody could sneak up on her. "I don't want a repeat of the catacombs."

"I'd rather your parents were home or you were here," said Gadg. "Be careful with that."

"I will. I've been holding one of these things since I could hold a toothbrush."

● ● ●

Jordan made his way, by the dim light of his phone, toward the back door. Normally, the sound of the lazy river was a soothing balm. In this context, it sounded like a snake curling about a victim's neck. He pulled the key out of his pocket. His hands shook worse than at any tournament. He forced himself to breathe. Again.

Crick.

What was that?

He paused. His eyes darted and his ears strained. Past the side of the house, now maybe forty feet away, a bit of water lapped over a rock as the river flowed by. Not hearing anything more, he opened the back door. A beautiful, haunting mountain river cabin welcomed him.

Chapter 88

The Evidence: Round 2

Saturday, August 16, 1:20 a.m.
River cabin of Robert Everett, three miles outside Wilson city limits

Jordan tiptoed through the kitchen and made his way to the main room. Several large windows graced it from three directions. Moonlight reflected off the river and streamed in with such a ghostly luminescence that he didn't need to use his phone's flashlight or turn on any lights.

He shuddered. The sooner this was over, the better.

Looking around the room, he spotted the fireplace almost immediately. It stood proudly at the back, facing the river. But Jordan was not here to admire the view. He walked over to it and knelt down to look inside.

How ironic.

He had last seen the evidence in Donald Carlyle's office where it had met its end in a fireplace not unlike this one. Jordan reached up for the secret lever Mr. Everett had told him about. He pulled. On the right side of the fireplace, under the lip, a seam he had not noticed before suddenly appeared and popped out an inch toward him. Pulling on the newly exposed seam, he put his hands around a two foot by one foot portion of brick.

Adrenaline surged through him.

Could it be? Would this finally end?

The chamber opened up. Once again, the past came alive as Jordan reached in and pulled out a large, faded manila envelope stuffed half an inch thick with papers. He opened it briefly, confirmed it was much the same as what they found in the old cellar, and closed it by refolding the metal clasp.

"Bless you, Mr. Everett!" he said aloud.

Still facing the fireplace, Jordan straightened up.

"I was wondering when you'd show up." A gravelly voice behind him broke the silence.

● ● ●

"Oh no!" Bethany cried, almost losing the battle to keep it a whisper.

Gadg shot out of his chair. "Bethany, listen to me. You're going to have to be my eyes."

"What are you talking about?"

"I'll be back in a minute, stay on the line."

● ● ●

Jordan didn't even need to turn to know the voice. Fear shot through him. Standing up and turning around, he saw Alex Jones and two other men standing by the dining room table. The other two fanned out to triangulate Jordan with his back to the fireplace.

His insides screamed at the injustice. The sides of the yellow envelope crumpled under his grip.

"Zone defense this time," said Alex. "Do you want to do this the easy way or the hard way?"

Jordan reached into his pocket for his phone, pulled it to his mouth and spoke, "Start video recording. Say 'hello' to the camera, Alex." Jordan pointed the phone at him. "For the record, this is Alex Jones stealing evidence that Robert Everett promised to me."

The three closed in. At six feet away, Alex darted forward and slammed Jordan's arm down with an iron fist covered in a black leather glove. The phone clattered to the floor. With the other hand Alex snatched the envelope. One of the men clenched Jordan by the arms. The other picked up the phone.

"Stop the recording and delete it." Alex pulled at the fingers of his gloved hand, removed the glove and unclasped the envelope. "Interesting." He smiled at the contents and then stuffed them back into the envelope. He resealed it and put his glove back on.

The other man stopped the recording and pushed the trash icon.

"Let's take that with us," said Alex. "It might have some interesting information on it. Touch the screen every couple minutes to keep the phone from locking."

"Lock the screen," said Jordan. The phone Gadg had fitted him with had voice recognition software that allowed Jordan to execute commands by speaking.

The man holding the phone looked down at the screen. Only the password or Jordan's thumb would unlock it.

Alex glared. "You gonna put your thumb on this or am I gonna break it?"

Jordan gulped. Clearly Alex wasn't speaking of the phone.

The first man relaxed his grip on Jordan's right arm as the second held the phone in the palm of his hand for Jordan to unlock.

For a split second Jordan freed his right arm, grabbed the phone and snapped it like an Ultimate Frisbee disc into the rough brick surrounding the fireplace. Because Jordan thought smartphones looked more elegant without a case, he'd never used one. The phone smashed into a few pieces.

The first man gripped Jordan's shoulders as Alex slammed his fist into his stomach.

● ● ●

"They're beating him up!" Bethany gripped the sides of her laptop. Both cheeks were hot as tears emerged. "What do we do?"

Gadg had spent the last two minutes gathering what he might need— flashlight, another phone, and a few other assortments. Bethany could hear his steps.

● ● ●

Fear strangled Jordan with a violent choke hold. His insides flailed, even as his limbs were locked in place by strong hands. All the horror of the childhood playground rushed back in an adult version. Red assaulted his consciousness like pellets from a paintball gun. Not a hint of air remained in his body.

Gradually, and painfully, the oxygen returned. Jordan fought to stay coherent. With heaving breaths, he eked out a staggered sentence, "It automatically ... syncs with the cloud ... before a delete—as extra protection."

"You're bluffing," Alex retorted. "And even if you weren't, there's nothing recorded that is incriminating enough when this evidence is hidden away or destroyed."

Jordan looked away. It was true.

"Take that and get it to safety." Alex handed the envelope to his second associate. "We'll be along in a bit."

Jordan didn't like the implications of "in a bit." His face lost its remaining color as he watched the envelope, and his final chance for the truth to come out, walk toward the back door.

He blinked his eyes and shot up a silent prayer. Evidence or not, this might be the end for him. He didn't think the man was foolish enough to kill him, but he was seriously questioning the emotional stability of Alex Jones at this point.

Alex grabbed Jordan's jaw and snapped it forward so they were eye to eye. Jordan felt the kink in his neck.

"It's not your dad, so you'll have to do."

A quick jab from Alex exploded on Jordan's mouth. Every nerve on the bottom half of his face shrieked in complaint.

"That was about four out of ten," said Alex.

Boom. Another punch—harder this time—smashed him straight in the jaw. Jordan's head swirled. His knees buckled. Pain, confusion, and the color red splattered everywhere in his mind. He would have gone down if the first man hadn't held him up. Jordan's eyes went wide with terror as a question from Alex snapped him into the moment.

"Shall we take it up to seven or eight? Or maybe it's time for a little *accident* with the river?"

Chapter 89

River Cabin

Saturday, August 16, 1:27 a.m.
River cabin of Robert Everett, three miles outside Wilson city limits

"Alex is threatening an accident with the river," said Bethany, cupping the phone with her hand.

Gadg stopped, ran back to one of the shelves and grabbed a small canister. "I'm out of here. I'll call my dad on the way. I can be there in seven minutes."

Bethany heard the spew of gravel as Gadg raced out of his driveway.

● ● ●

Through a blur of pain, Jordan looked at his assailant. He knew Alex was a thug. He didn't know he was a killer. Jordan closed his eyes and sent another silent, urgent prayer heavenward.

Alex was poised when a silhouette came under the arch from the other room.

Isaac Molencki stood in the moonlight.

Alex and Jordan both looked at the envelope in his hand.

"What?" said Alex.

"I made him a deal," said the small man, nodding toward the man whom he'd stopped in the forest a moment ago. "Give me the envelope and live, or ..." He paused for a second and smiled. "He didn't even wait for the second option." Mr. Molencki set the envelope down on the dining room table. The corners of the table were rounded, but he still aligned the envelope perfectly with two of the sides. His eye caught Jordan's as understanding passed between them again. He gave a slight nod and then spoke to the man holding Jordan, "I'll give you the same deal I gave the other guy. Leave now and you can live."

The man looked at Alex.

Alex said to him, "You're not a coward, are you?"

"No, I'm not," said the man, "but I'm also not an idiot. Where have you been this summer? Do you know who you're dealing with? You're on your own."

He released Jordan, hurried to the back door, and disappeared into the forest.

Molencki spoke to Alex. "Jones, what are you doing here? Get away from him. You're way out of your league."

Alex's face turned crimson in the shadows of the dark room. He shoved Jordan toward the fireplace and squared around to face the small man. "You little runt. I'll show you who's out of his league."

Jordan stared with his mouth open as the smallest tic of Molencki's eye showed he had registered the comment. This would not end well for Alex.

Jones made the first move, and in an imperceptible blur, the small man spun Alex around and wrenched his arm from its socket.

Jordan cringed at the sound. He thought about making a break for it, but he would have to pass in front of Isaac. Besides that, his legs would not move, and his ribs were terribly bruised. A horrible tableau played out in front of him.

Alex went into shock. A few more punches and two kicks from Mr. Molencki left him facedown on the ground, unconscious. With hands quicker than sight, the small man pulled something from his pocket and bound Alex by his hands and feet. He finished it off with something covering his mouth and nose.

It took Jordan a moment to realize it was some kind of tape. He gaped as one more blow from Isaac caused the unconscious body of Alex Jones to convulse involuntarily before becoming still.

Jordan recoiled, realizing he had just witnessed a murder.

He stared blankly as Mr. Molencki took off both his own shoes and the shoes of Alex Jones. Understanding dawned on Jordan as the small man put on Alex's shoes, turned, and looked him straight in the eye.

Jordan was frozen in place, face white with an eerie glow from the moonlight.

I am going to die.

●●●

I need a miracle, Jordan cried within himself. *Please, God.*

Fear splashed the edges of his consciousness with a deep red. The one whom Elizabeth Sheridan had called "the ultimate soldier" took aim at him. In the center of his mind's eye, Jordan saw his options in deadly clarity.

Option 1: Run. Chance of escape: 0 percent.

Option 2: Fight. Chance of escape: 0 percent.

Option 3: Talk. Chance of escape: slightly better than 0 percent.

From out of nowhere, a bizarre thought hit him.

Stall him for five minutes and you'll live.

Jordan crinkled his nose.

Where did that come from?

Either it was God or it wasn't. He would know soon enough.

"Hello, Mr. Molencki." Jordan dropped his hands to his sides, palms open. "I'm not going to move since we both know that I am at your mercy."

"That's true," said the small man.

"Is there any chance you're going to let me live through this?"

"No. You know too much."

Jordan's eyes bulged. The moonlight made them look like a poster for a horror movie. Consecutive tremors wracked his body as his flight response screamed for him to run. Somehow he stayed put. With his conscious mind on tilt, something took over at a level below coherent thought. Jordan decided to play out the hand he'd been dealt. Even though it made no sense, he would try to stall the man for five minutes. He said, "I understand. May I ask you a question?"

Molencki didn't answer. He just stared at Jordan. All business.

Jordan took it as the only permission he would get. "Why do you work for Jeffrey Kingston?"

"I don't work *for* him. I work on *my* terms. He happens to pay well, and this is the current job."

Jordan played off a hunch. "Even if it's for the likes of Donald Carlyle?"

"You caught that, huh?"

"In his office I thought you made it obvious what you thought of him."

"He's an imbecile. However, he is my customer's client. I almost regret taking the job, but I never leave one unfinished."

"So they authorized this?"

"Of course."

"So this is what it takes, huh? Two murders? No, wait, I'm wrong. Counting Mr. Everett, it'll be three when you're done with me, won't it? Doesn't that bother you at all?"

Molencki didn't even blink. "You're stalling."

Jordan swallowed hard. Time slowed down. He was suddenly aware of how delightful the cabin smelled. Beautiful, polished wood surrounded him. Because of its proximity to the river, the air through a couple open windows carried a pleasant touch of humidity. A strange sense of calm descended on him as he remembered one more point of conversation.

"I don't have time for this." Isaac took a step forward.

Jordan played his last card. "Mr. Molencki, do you think *Elizabeth* would approve of this?"

Isaac stopped. His eyes burned like old coals in a fireplace. "You're grasping at straws."

"You sure?"

The small man didn't move.

"She has a beautiful voice, you know."

Isaac stared at him.

Jordan spoke softly, "She reminds me of Bethany."

"Oh really? Where did *you* hear it?"

"On the phone, of course. I wanted to find out a bit more about who was breaking into Bethany's bedroom."

Isaac raised an eyebrow.

"With the way you've been carrying on this summer..." Jordan trailed off. "*What?*"

Jordan played another hunch. "It's obvious. Bethany reminds you of Elizabeth."

"You're pretty sharp, Mr. Nolan."

"I hope it hasn't impaired your judgment or impacted your ability to do your job."

The same eye twitched like it had earlier.

"She said you were the ultimate soldier," the words flew out of Jordan's mouth.

Whew, that was close.

He could see the wheels turning. He wondered how far he could weave this tale. Of course, he might be dead in five minutes anyway. "She said she misses you."

"Now you're lying."

"Well, technically she said she misses the man she used to know. She doesn't miss the man you've become."

"You never spoke to her." Isaac gave his head an angry shake. "I can't believe I've even let you talk this long. You're totally making this up."

Jordan didn't stop. "Apparently you're quite the wordsmith."

"This conversation is over," said Isaac.

"Don't you want to hear the final thing she said to me?"

Isaac still didn't spring. Even though it betrayed all his training, he clearly *did* want to know.

Jordan waited as long as he could get away with and then told him the absolute truth, "She told me to tell you that *Sheri-pie* misses going to the mailbox and finding a letter from you."

Isaac's mouth dropped open. He doubted no more.

Jordan waited again and then went for broke with his wildest hunch. "She's like a hollow shell on the inside. If she had it to do over again, she would have chosen *you.*"

Isaac looked away, deep in thought.

Jordan stood motionless and defenseless. He was sure he'd made it five minutes. The situation didn't look much better. He softened his tone even more and tried to reel him in. "She sounded very *sincere.*"

The spell was blown away like a wisp of smoke. The small man's face twisted. His eyes snapped back into the moment and became white hot with fury.

A lance of fear shot through Jordan. Whatever he had said was the wrong thing. All pretense that he had been in control of the conversation was gone.

His face smashed into the floor as his hands were yanked behind his back and tied together. His feet followed. A grunt that tried to escape was stifled by a piece of tape gluing his lips shut. The small man yanked him to his feet, spun him around, and pointed him toward the river like a man facing a firing squad.

His time was up.

Chapter 90

The River

Saturday, August 16, 1:38 a.m.
River cabin of Robert Everett, three miles outside Wilson city limits

"Gadg, hurry!" Bethany yelled into the phone.

Allie jolted awake. "What is it?"

Bethany waved off her question.

Allie sprang up and jumped onto the loft bed with Bethany. The shotgun bounced and the barrel slid down the wall.

Bethany reached up and grabbed it before it pointed at them. "Watch it," she snapped. She set the gun back upright in the corner.

"What in the world?" said Allie.

"Be quiet!" Bethany pointed at the screen. She ripped the earpiece out of her ear and threw it aside. She pushed the button to switch her phone to speaker mode.

Allie scooted to the back wall and looked down over her shoulder.

They stared at the screen as the small man dragged Jordan out of the house onto the patio.

"Bethany, talk to me!" Gadg barked through the speaker. She'd never heard him use that tone before. "Tell me where!"

"Oh, I don't know." Bethany waved her hands, flustered. "I'm horrible at directions! They're on the patio. Going toward the river. Jordan's hands and feet are bound. I think his mouth is taped shut. Did you get hold of your dad?"

"No, I didn't," Gadg breathed hard. "I left a message. Told him it was urgent. Ouch!"

"You okay?"

"Tree branch in the face. Never mind! What does it say on the bottom right of the screen?"

Bethany read the coordinates. "I can see the river!" She looked up with a desperate appeal. "Daddy! Do something NOW!"

Allie screamed.

● ● ●

Jordan couldn't believe how strong this man was. Behind his back, the cords binding his hands sliced into his wrists without mercy. The cords around his ankles turned his two legs into one. He wanted to scream in pain, but the tape over his mouth might as well have welded his lips shut.

"Normally, I'd say there's nothing personal," said the small man as he half-lifted, half-pushed Jordan to the edge of the river, "but that wouldn't be true in your case."

Jordan's eyes grew wide with terror. His mind screamed red. His heart erupted in full-fledged panic. Not until this moment did he really think it would come to this. But he had watched what happened with Alex Jones.

I'm next.

The small man yanked off Jordan's hat and flipped his wrist so that it did a 360-degree spin and landed on the ground.

Jordan faced the water. Darkened by the forest around, it slithered like a huge serpent of black ink. The small man grabbed him by his bound wrists in one hand and the back of his T-shirt, by the neck, in the other. Without so much as a flinch, he flung Jordan into the river.

● ● ●

Thirty seconds passed and Isaac Molencki stood looking down over the bank. Satisfied that he would see him no more, Isaac turned his head at a sound from the direction of the driveway. "Gotta go." He gave one last look to the river. "Goodbye, Mr. Nolan."

The small man reached down and picked up the hat. They would find the body soon enough. He didn't need a hat floating down the river prematurely. He still had a bit of a mess to clean up. On his way past the patio table, he pulled the hat onto his head and strode into the house without looking back.

● ● ●

With his hands bound behind his back and his feet tied together, the water smashed into Jordan's face with a violent slap. He had no time to think about it as the cold hit him a moment later. Even in August, Colorado mountain rivers weren't much better than the North Atlantic.

Currents of panic consumed him as he sucked for air. All he got was a nose full of water and a mouth that tasted like tape.

Thrashing wildly, he snorted as hard as he could to force the water out of his nose. He managed to get most of it out, delaying the inevitable. He kicked his legs but had no control. All he could do was spin as the river dragged him downstream and down under.

He opened his eyes. He shut them. It made no difference. The darkness was total. So was the red. His whole mind swam in it.

He wrenched his arms and tried to pry the cords apart. Pain shot through his shoulders but the bonds didn't budge.

To top it off, vertigo added a cruel twist and took away all sense of direction. He knew he was deeper, but that was it.

All the scenes of helplessness in his life flashed through his memory in a crescendo to this moment. He screamed so hard his head felt like it would explode. The tape and the river tormented him with a silence that overwhelmed his scream and refused to allow even the slightest sound to escape.

The flowing water mocked his tears by whisking them away before they could hit his face.

He stopped moving.

Think!

He thought.

Besides the painful reminder that he was almost out of air, a horrible realization put the final nail in the coffin.

I'm out of options.

His arms and legs wilted as all the fight left him. The river wasn't particularly fast so he hadn't gone all that far. Somehow he knew that he had less than thirty seconds before it was over. The panic gave way to a nostalgic peace.

I guess this is it. God, I'm Yours if You'll have me. I'll see You soon.

From the depths he felt the sensation of tape being ripped off his lips.

That's strange. That should hurt.

Something plastic was jammed into his mouth as darkness took him.

Chapter 91

Getaways

Saturday, August 16, 1:48 a.m.
River cabin of Robert Everett, three miles outside Wilson city limits

Still wearing shoes two sizes too big and a hat that didn't belong to him, Isaac swept the main room with swift strokes that punched the broom in little bursts.

What an idiot.

The small man chided himself. How could he have been that unprofessional? The broom knocked against the legs of the dining chairs with an irritated thunk.

He never let someone go without making absolutely certain the job was done.

Never.

What were you thinking?

He had thrown Jordan Nolan in the river while still alive. He hadn't done anything like that since Elizabeth had dumped him for Charles. That was back when he still cared about making it look like an accident.

Young Mr. Nolan had done the unthinkable. He had talked his way into a chance, however small, of getting away.

Isaac looked back out the window at the water. He was worrying over nothing. The odds were slim that Jordan would survive.

"Idiot!" this time he said it out loud.

What had happened?

Jordan had struck the only chord that still played. He had caught the small man off his guard.

How could he have known?

Isaac slammed the broom back into the pantry where he'd found it.

"What difference does it make?" he said, mostly to shut himself up.

It didn't matter. The room had signs of a scuffle. The tracks leading to the water's edge belonged to Alex's shoes, and so would the tracks leading away from the house. At least for a while, the focus would be on Mr. Jones.

With his own shoes, the evidence, and the remains of Jordan's phone stashed in a skin-tight backpack molded to his frame, Isaac slung the limp form of Alex Jones over his shoulder and grunted. Thankfully, he kept himself in the same shape as when he was a Ranger.

Stepping back out into the cool night air, he pulled the side door shut with a gloved hand.

It was time to disappear.

It would be a strenuous walk, but Alex's own car, which Isaac had placed a GPS tracking device under, would provide the getaway. A separate car, which Isaac had purchased with cash from an online ad, awaited him in a nearby town. He would stash the hat, hide Alex's dead body in a place he'd scoped earlier that summer, and make his way back east with the evidence. He would be hundreds of miles from Wilson when the celebration started tomorrow.

● ● ●

Jordan woke as a blast of air filled his lungs. Gadg finished his mouth-to-mouth resuscitation and pulled away. Lying on his back, Jordan turned his head sideways and coughed up a spew of water between gasps. He coughed again. The plastic canister of air that had saved his life lay next to him.

Gadg pulled Jordan to a sitting position and pounded his back.

Jordan coughed once more. He looked upstream in the direction of Mr. Everett's cabin. His eyes widened in panic at the memory. Still soaked, water poured from everywhere on both of them.

Gadg grabbed him, pushed aside a slushy lock of hair from Jordan's forehead and held him with both arms. A pool of water formed between and around them.

Jordan's eyes were crazed—big, round, red, and alarmed. "Where is he?" He gasped, hyperventilating.

"Be still," Gadg whispered, still holding Jordan. He used one hand to pull his night vision goggles from the top of his head, empty the viewfinder of water, and place them down over his eyes. He scanned the area.

"I just saw a murder," Jordan gripped Gadg's forearm like a life preserver.

"Calm down, then we can talk," Gadg said. "Slow your breathing. You're getting too much air."

Jordan tried to settle, but his teeth chattered violently as the cold kept him shaking. Tears streamed from both eyes as the terror of the last few minutes assaulted him again. "I thought—that—was it," Jordan stabbed the words between involuntary sobs.

Gadg held him another moment and then pulled himself free. "We're too exposed," he said. He stood, grabbed Jordan under the arms, and drug him away from the bank into the forest. He didn't stop until they were at least fifty yards from the edge of the trees. Gadg propped him up against a large trunk, well out of sight.

Jordan leaned back and breathed hard.

Kneeling down in front of him, Gadg took his hand. "Be still," he commanded in a sharp whisper this time. He peeked his head around the tree. Hearing nothing from the other side of the river, Gadg lifted the goggles to the top of his head and turned back to Jordan.

Jordan's chest heaved as he calmed down. His lips were deep blue in a small bit of moonlight that shone through the trees. "Isaac Molencki just killed Mr. Jones."

"I know," said Gadg.

"How?" asked Jordan, disoriented. The dots refused to connect.

Gadg grabbed his face and pointed it directly at his own. "You were wearing my hat. Remember the glasses I showed you?"

Jordan's eyes widened again—this time from surprise. "You got that on tape?"

Gadg reached into his pocket, pulled out his phone, and pushed a button. Looking up at Jordan, he said, "You did. Whatever you looked at is what we saw."

"We?"

"Yes, Bethany had to be my eyes after I left the house."

"Bethany was?" Jordan almost smiled. "Even with her sense of directions?"

Gadg pushed the earpiece harder into his ear and chuckled.

"What?" asked Jordan.

"She says she heard that," said Gadg.

"She's on the line? How did that survive the river?"

"Toys," said Gadg. "It's one my dad gave me. The whole thing, including the earpieces, is waterproof. I lost the call, of course, when I dove into the river. I just called her back."

"May I talk to her?"

Gadg pulled off the neck ring that connected to the two earbuds. He handed it over to Jordan and pulled his night vision goggles back on. He got up and walked a few feet closer to the river. Like a sentry, he scanned the bank up and down.

Jordan stretched the neck ring over his head, and his shoulders screamed in protest. "Ouch!" he said as he set it on the back of his neck and popped one earpiece into his ear.

"Jordan!" Bethany yelled into his ear. Her sigh was audible and full of relief. "Thank God you're alive. It's so good to hear your voice."

Jordan's heart melted despite his shivering. The tears began again in earnest. "Bethany," he blubbed her name out and broke down. All the horror of the last half-hour poured out like the water that had drained off his body. He buried his face in his hands and sobbed.

Bethany's voice floated through the earpiece like a songbird. The words of the old hymn washed over him as she sang, "Whenever I am tempted, whenever clouds arise; When songs give place to sighing, when hope within me dies; I draw closer to Him, from care He sets me free. His eye is on the sparrow, and I know He watches me; His eye is on the sparrow, and I know He watches me."

Jordan's body relaxed as a flood of peace settled over his soul. He found himself able to speak. "I can't thank you enough."

"We're so glad you're safe."

"We?"

"Yes, Allie and me. She's here."

"I'm going to kill you when you get back," said Allie from a distance. "You scared me to death."

Jordan smirked as he could almost see Bethany shake her head.

Gadg stepped back around a tree and knelt. "We need to get you some medical care. Residual water in the lungs can still be dangerous."

"Did you hear that, Bethany?" asked Jordan. "We've got to get to the ER. We'll call you..." He stopped and spoke with a sudden clarity. "No, that's wrong." He turned his head, "Gadg, get ready to call your dad. Bethany"—he pressed his fingers into the earpiece as if trying to make it easier for her to hear him—"for now, I want you and Allie to pretend you know nothing about this. Do you understand? Absolutely nothing."

"Yes, I understand. So does Allie."

"Okay, we'll be in touch. We need to talk this through."

"Jordan, I-" she paused.

"Bethany, what?"

"I'm glad you're safe."

A warm current flowed through his insides. He really wanted to hear whatever she was going to say before she stopped.

"Thank you again. I owe my life to you and Gadg. We'll talk soon." He hung up and handed the phone back to Gadg.

"You ready?" asked Gadg.

Jordan gave him a funny look. A tear came and a smile spread on his face. He reached out and wrapped Gadg in a hug that reminded him of Grandpa Walter. "Yes. Thanks for everything."

Chapter 92

Secret Visitor

Saturday, August 16, 3:15 a.m.
Room next to Gadg's lair in the O'Brien home, Wilson, CO

"Dad, it's me."

"Jordan, it's three a.m. Are you okay?" Johnny's voice went on instant alert.

"Yes, I'm okay, barely."

"What are you talking about?"

"Remember that conversation we had this morning about how things have been heating up?"

"Yes." Johnny's tone was wary.

"Everything went ballistic tonight."

"What happened?"

Jordan heard his mother wake up at the sound. "Johnny, what's going on?"

"It's Jordan," he said to Michelle. "I don't know yet, but it's serious."

"Dad, listen to me. Alex Jones was murdered tonight. I was nearly killed myself." Jordan left out as much detail as he could.

"What?" Jordan heard both his mom and dad. She was listening in close to the phone.

"I don't have time to explain right now. I'm putting you on speaker. Here's Deputy O'Brien." Jordan held the phone between himself and Gadg's dad.

"Johnny," said the deputy.

"Mark, talk to me, what's going on?"

"Isaac Molencki killed Alex Jones tonight. Jordan is lucky to be alive."

A pause.

"I know this is a shock in the middle of the night. Things have gotten very bad, very quickly. You can thank God that Jordan is alive at all. He's safe. I've got a paramedic and a former Denver cop who I trust with my life with him now."

"Paramedic? What happened?"

"I'll give you the full story later. Suffice it to say that Jordan almost drowned. We're watching him closely. Residual water in the lungs can be life-threatening for a couple days."

"Nearly drowned? What in the world?"

"It's still dangerous and up in the air. There are a lot of loose ends right now. I need you and Michelle to do something for me."

"What's that?"

"First, ensure your family is safe. Get the other kids into your room with you and get a shotgun or something. Contact your dad as well."

"Mark!" Michelle sounded frantic next to Johnny's ear. "You're scaring me!"

"I know, I'm sorry. You got that, Johnny?"

"Yes, I got it."

"I need you both to act like this conversation never happened. I need you to wake up tomorrow morning and act as if Jordan is missing."

"As if we'll sleep now," said Michelle.

"It doesn't matter." Deputy O'Brien was all business. "What's important is that you need to call the station tomorrow morning and report a missing person. Tell them Jordan never came home last night."

"Are you serious?" Johnny asked.

"Totally serious. Alex Jones is dead. There are things in motion that are going to hit this community hard, one way or the other."

"Okay," Johnny said and blew out a hard breath. "I got it. We'll do it."

"Thanks, friend, we'll be in touch."

●●●

"Bethany!"

"What is it, Gadg?" The intensity of his tone alarmed her.

"You asleep?"

"Not after that," she said. "Truth be told, I wasn't anyway. I'm too keyed up. What's going on?"

"I just spoke to my dad," said Gadg. "We don't think it's a good idea for you two to be alone in that house tonight. Jordan's here with a paramedic and a trusted friend who's an ex-cop. My dad is coming to fetch you."

"Gadg, I've got the shotgun right here."

"I'm not going to argue with you. Be ready in seven minutes." Three tones came from her phone and the screen read, "Call Ended."

● ● ●

An hour later, Bethany stood before the door to Jordan's makeshift hospital room. "May I?" She asked the former cop who stood guarding the door.

"He's sleeping hard, miss. From what I've heard, it sounds like exhaustion along with some strong painkillers. He won't be up for a few hours. The doc is monitoring his heart rate from the other room. He comes in regularly to check on him."

"I understand, sir. But Jordan's a dear friend. I'd like to pray for him."

An almost undetectable smirk touched the corner of the cop's mouth. He opened his hand and swung his arm toward the door. "Be my guest."

Bethany entered the room and shut the door behind her. She looked around. The room was saved from total darkness by a small desk lamp in the corner. There were no windows because Deputy O'Brien wanted Jordan in a high-security area after what had happened. Jordan slept soundly in the hospital bed, sitting up at an incline.

Bethany crossed the room and stood behind him. Tentatively, she reached down and rested both hands on either side of the hospital gown covering his shoulders. "Daddy," she looked up and whispered a prayer, "he's been through so much this summer." A tear came into her eye. "I thought I'd l—" she stopped. "We almost lost him today," she corrected. Another tear, this time for keeps, tumbled out and pushed the first one and itself down her cheek. "Thank You so much for Your mercy. I feel horrible about Mr. Jones." She looked back down at the top of Jordan's head. "But thank You for sparing this one."

A tiny snore escaped Jordan's lips. The combination of fatigue and medicine had indeed taken him, and he was dead to the world—so asleep that he didn't recognize Bethany's delicate touch on his shoulders.

She bent down to whisper near his ear, so quietly she could barely hear it herself. "I couldn't sleep. I'm going to have to get to celebration headquarters early today so you won't see me. Deputy O'Brien told us to pretend you're missing."

She pulled back a bit to see if he would awaken.

Satisfied, she leaned in again. "The truth is, I'm mad at you, Mr. Nolan. Don't you ever do that again." A second line of tears rolled over a crease of concern just under her eye and cascaded down the other cheek. "You almost ripped my heart out tonight."

Jordan stirred and shifted to lean his head the other direction.

She pulled back just in time.

He was too far gone to come close to waking.

She switched sides and spoke just behind his other ear. "If I haven't already made it obvious, I don't think you're 'going nowhere' anymore."

Her voice became almost inaudible. "I don't know how it could happen, because God's going to have to move a mountain ..." she said, closing her eyes in silent petition, "... but if somehow He does," she opened them again and whispered into his ear, "I want you to know that I'm all yours."

She raised up, lifted her hands from his shoulders, and turned toward the door. Before she could take a step, she looked both ways. Smiling, she bent back down and planted a gentle kiss on his cheek. As she pulled away, a bit of moisture from her tear-dampened face stayed behind and reflected off Jordan's cheek in the dim light.

She straightened, wiped away her tears, and stole away as if she'd never been there.

Chapter 93

Death of a Dream

Saturday, August 16, 2:30 p.m.
Room next to Gadg's lair in the O'Brien home, Wilson, CO

Still in the room next to Gadg's command center in the O'Brien basement, Jordan had slept well into the afternoon.

As instructed, Johnny had called the police department to report that Jordan didn't come home. Jordan, Gadg, and Deputy O'Brien had decided last night that their enemies might not look closely if they thought Jordan was dead. Also, the authorities would have minimal resources to search for a missing person on the busiest day Wilson had seen in years.

Bethany and Allie had left early with Deputy O'Brien to go to celebration headquarters. The deputy had circled back to the Nolan house to speak with Johnny about his son's disappearance.

Because of Gadg's techno-lair, the O'Brien household rivaled Fort Knox for security. The paramedic friend of Deputy O'Brien kept regular tabs on Jordan, and the ex-cop guarding the door would have allowed an enemy into the room only over his dead body. Jordan was safe and comfortable—in a physical sense.

In every other way, the blows just kept pounding him. Jordan let out a long breath as he pinched his lips together. He ran a hand through his hair.

His laptop sat open in front of him, courtesy of Deputy O'Brien picking it up from the Nolan home. Jordan, because of his tech savvy, was able to receive all his emails, text messages, and voicemails through his computer now that his new phone had been destroyed and his old phone had been shut off last week.

He sighed.

Why did I bother?

He stared at an email from Jeffrey Kingston letting him know that Senator Smith had revoked the internship. A follow-up voicemail, like salt in the wound, confirmed it. Even though he had known it was coming, it still hurt. Mr. Kingston had kept the July 31st trespassing, and breaking and entering charges as an ace in the hole.

Jordan reached for the old Bible, also brought by Deputy O'Brien, which sat on the table next to the bed. He opened and reread the blessing from William Nolan to Grandpa Walter. He turned to the front and read again the blessing from the old patriarch, which called on God's faithfulness to Nolan posterity. Flipping to Psalm 119, Jordan confirmed verse 90 was indeed still written there. He hadn't imagined it. In the old King James it read: "Thy faithfulness is unto all generations." He kept his eyes fixed on the verse, hoping its truth would somehow bring a whisper of comfort to the turmoil in his heart.

Nothing happened.

Setting the Bible aside, he moved on to a news article that stated Robert Everett was pronounced dead in a tragic car accident.

This one cut even deeper.

Jordan balled his hands into fists, pulled them up to his forehead and squeezed his eyes shut. Robert Everett was dead—and there was nothing accidental about it. He couldn't shake the feeling that he was somehow responsible.

A reminder about the Wonder Drug 50th Anniversary Celebration popped up on his screen. Today they would hail Donald Carlyle and his father as modern-day heroes. They would not honor William Nolan. He was still a murderer.

The truth, even if known only by a few, was exactly opposite. The hospital gown, which lay over his bare upper body and gym shorts, made him feel even more helpless. He had given all he had, and it was not enough.

He wondered if Bethany had been right.

Maybe I really am going nowhere.

This summer, it had seemed otherwise. He'd felt so alive. His childhood faith had been renewed, and answered prayers came right and left. A passion for justice—especially for his great-grandfather's name—had erupted inside him. He had connected with his family—even his dad.

What happened?

His computer indicated that he had a new text message. Jordan reached for the touchpad with his left hand and opened it.

> **Like I said, this isn't over until you're on the plane. Here's how you spell it: W-A-S-H-I-N-G-T-O-N. See you in a year if I don't get offered a full-time position. ~ Sincerely, Matthew.**

He slapped the screen shut and threw it aside.

Images cascaded through his mind one after another. The smug, easy face of Jeffrey Kingston in the café as he declared war on Jordan and threatened Bethany; Donald Carlyle's condescending look as the evidence burned in the cigar box on his desk; the sideways landscape of trees and rocks as Alex Jones slammed him to the ground on the East ridge; the overwhelming blur of terror as Wilson's Creek rushed up to meet his unprotected face as he was tossed over the bank.

He thought of Bethany's shaking hands as she realized that Mr. Molencki had sneaked into her room and read her diary. The incredulous face of Senator Smith that said he did not buy Jordan's story about William Nolan; the crisp movement of Mr. Clark's mocking lips as he spat the words, "Your family's part in the story is like a black smear across an otherwise beautiful painting"; the terse prose of the article in front of him regarding Mr. Everett's death.

Staring at Matthew's text, now branded into his mind, something snapped.

Jordan gripped the bed sheet with both hands and wrung it like a wet towel. He threw it off, pushed himself from the bed, and shouted, "THIS IS WRONG!"

Still wearing his black shorts, Jordan ripped the hospital gown off and threw it on the bed. He yanked his black T-shirt from the chair next to him. He stuffed his feet into his now-dry socks and crammed them into his athletic shoes. Except for the missing hat and the addition of a few new bruises on his face, he looked like he had last night. He grabbed one of Gadg's old caps from a tech conference and pulled it over his head.

The paramedic and former cop burst into the room and said in tandem, "Are you okay?"

Jordan snatched his gown, wadded it up, and threw it to the paramedic. "Other than the fact that I've had it up to here"—he put his hand just under his chin—"I'm fine!"

He stepped up to the two men. "Excuse me, gentlemen." Jordan pushed past them and walked out.

Chapter 94

The Celebration

Saturday, August 16, 5:55 p.m.
Wilson County Fairgrounds, Wilson, CO

From her perch in the front row, Bethany scanned the crowd. She recalled the only other time that so many thousands had crowded into the Wilson County Fairgrounds—a couple years ago, when a rodeo association had hosted a national event in Wilson. The entire area, especially anything related to hospitality, had been bursting at the seams.

She sat at the far end of the front row with the rest of the committee and several others who had helped with the celebration. The senator's speech would begin shortly. Her dad would continue as the master of ceremonies and provide the introduction.

She looked toward the platform and tried to mask her disgust. Donald Carlyle looked like a kid in a candy store as he shook hands with Senator Smith and some of the gentlemen from Hampden Pharmaceuticals. Because of her position on the committee, she was privy to the forthcoming announcement that WDC2 would indeed be sold to the drug empire.

She spotted Matthew Harris, which was no surprise after she learned that he was taking Jordan's place in the Senator's Internship. He stood next to Jeffrey Kingston. A wave of nausea, revulsion, and fury swelled over her. Donald and Jeffrey had authorized the deaths of both Jordan and Mr. Jones, and now they stood smiling near the stage. She looked away.

She remembered how tired she was from last night. She focused on her dad, who smiled with them. Though it disgusted her to see him in proximity with those men, it had been good to see him this morning. He had held her so close that she had detected a shift in something. She couldn't figure out what. She remembered how much she admired that man. Of course, that thought brought the immediate memory of another man that she loved, one she could not have. She closed her eyes and sighed again.

Her phone vibrated inside her pocket. She pulled it out and saw a text from Gadg.

> CONFIDENTIAL: He's here. He's wearing dark sunglasses and one of my computer caps is pulled far down over his forehead. But it's him. Same black outfit as last night. Keep it low profile. Remember, some people here would not be happy to learn that he's alive. He's leaning against the third large pine tree east of the cotton candy booth. (That's *right (not left)* if you're facing the booth.) :-)

Bethany shook her head. Her sense of direction had become a running joke. She texted back her thanks, glanced toward her dad, and slipped away to find Jordan.

A moment later, Michael Clark was back at the podium. "Dear friends," he began, "in a moment, I will welcome to the stage our very own United States Senator, James Dakota Smith."

Walking around the outskirts, Bethany looked over the sea of people. The crowd seemed to be in a festive mood after several hours of food, drink, and celebration. It spilled over into a rousing applause for Senator Smith.

"Truly, this is a day for celebration," continued Mr. Clark. "The Wonder Drug has contributed greatly to the well-being of millions of lives."

Once again, a joyful buzz rippled through the audience. Mr. Clark waited for it die down.

"No one likes to be a downer at an event such as this, but even in the midst of our celebration, we have some sadness."

The crowd hushed. Bethany looked forward. Her dad was now quite small at the podium. She looked up at one of the many screens that had been erected for the event.

From the screen, she watched her dad say, "Yesterday, one of our beloved citizens—and a dear friend of mine—died in a car accident. Many of you know Robert Everett, a longtime fixture at the library and records office. He was a quiet man who was always willing to help. Let us take a moment of silence to honor his memory."

A wave of sadness washed over the crowd, as the message was new for some and a reopened wound for others. Many of the people there had known and liked Mr. Everett.

A minute later, Mr. Clark continued, "As a memorial, we have a video we'd like to play. After the video, I will invite Senator Smith to the stage."

Michael Clark stepped away from the podium as Gadg pushed the play button. The face of Robert Everett filled one huge screen and several smaller screens scattered throughout the fairgrounds. The video contained no music, and the background looked like a plain room. Bethany recognized it as the horrible-looking wall of her dad's office.

● ● ●

Donald Carlyle narrowed his eyes. He searched the face of Michael Clark. What was this? A chill swept over him despite the warm August day. His jaw tightened. This was not on the program.

Chapter 95

The Truth Comes Out

Saturday, August 16, 6:00 p.m.
Wilson County Fairgrounds, Wilson, CO

Still leaning against the tree, Jordan pulled his sunglasses down and pinched the bridge of his nose with one hand. He clenched his other fist. His friend was gone. The reminder of his death—and all that was behind it—hit him again like a punch to the stomach.

"Dear citizens of Wilson," Robert began. Jordan pushed his sunglasses back into place and looked up at the screen.

"My name is Robert Everett. Most of you know me from my service in the library and records office these many years. In 1964, at twenty-six years old, I was a researcher and scientist at Carlyle Enterprises Incorporated, which was later to become Wilson Drug and Compounding Center. At that time, Carlyle Enterprises was both a drug *and* research company. I was part of a team of three researchers which included Raymond Clark and William Nolan. We reported directly to one of the most senior executives.

"My code name was R3, in reference to my role as the third researcher to join the group. In early 1964, our team was commissioned to test a drug called XD which was soon to be released by the major drug company, Hampden Pharmaceuticals. Around the same time, Carlyle Enterprises and Hampden were also involved in negotiations that would allow Hampden to purchase and license another drug called Amitolin, later known as the Wonder Drug. It was developed by Carlyle Enterprises and would provide an enormous boost of capital, along with huge financial increase to the Carlyle executives. During the first quarter of 1964, our research began to reveal that XD had some damaging side effects. We grew from concerned to alarmed."

Jordan stared at the screen, transfixed. His mind raced through his late-night meeting with Mr. Everett. He smiled and reprocessed the events of the last twenty-four hours.

My assumptions were totally wrong.

The video, dull by any technical standard, continued to captivate the crowd. "We began to share these concerns with our boss. You must understand that XD, much like Thalidomide, had tremendous hype in those days. People couldn't—or wouldn't—believe that there might be something fundamentally wrong with it. Our boss told us to go back and do the tests again. During this process, it became obvious that he was attempting to stall the research.

"I couldn't understand why. Our lead researcher, Ray Clark, figured it out. He reasoned that the XD research, especially if the findings were negative, could jeopardize the Wonder Drug deal. We pretended to play along and began to do our real work in secret. Our boss found out what we were doing and let us know, in no uncertain terms, that our findings were unacceptable. He could be an extremely persuasive individual. He put before us a choice: falsify the research and go along with him, or persist in what we were doing at the risk of our lives and the lives of our families."

● ● ●

Thousands watched in wonder, staring at the screen with open mouths. Donald Carlyle's neck flamed red. He clamped down on his already tight jaw. Everything was unraveling before his eyes. He looked toward the stage at the senator, but the senator was looking up at the large screen at the rear of the stage.

● ● ●

A thrill shot through Jordan's frame and blew away all the anger and mourning and weariness of a moment ago. A time machine had whisked him back fifty years as the past came alive. He was watching a reprise of his great-grandfather lived out on the screen. Robert Everett, with his own new twist, was making good on Plan B.

● ● ●

"I remember that day like it was yesterday," Everett's voice on the video continued, "I knew they were coming for us. I was single, and my family was back east, so I wasn't concerned for their safety. I was concerned for my own. On the other hand, Ray and William each faced a horrible, personal crisis because of the threat to their families.

"Ray was amazing. He was convinced we had to do what was right, regardless of the cost. William experienced a sudden and dramatic personal transformation, which I didn't understand at the time. He decided to follow Ray's lead, even if it meant his own death.

"I pretended to agree with them. At that time, William thought up and proposed two plans—we called them Plan A and Plan B. Plan A was a strategy to accumulate sufficient evidence to go public suddenly. William reasoned we would be safe because the resulting media swirl would bring much scrutiny on the company. Plan B, which would only be instituted if Plan A failed, was a desperate attempt to save their families, even though William was estranged from his wife and son at that point.

"Plan B had various options. The goal was to find a way that would ensure it was in the best interest of our boss and his cohorts to leave the Clark and Nolan families alone. At this time, our boss gave us an ultimatum. Falsify the research or be killed, along with our families. He gave us twenty-four hours to decide."

● ● ●

Up to this point, Jordan had never fully believed that the families—not just the three researchers themselves—were in mortal danger if the men didn't go along with the XD cover-up. Jeffrey Kingston's smile from yesterday's meeting at the café flashed into Jordan's mind and fanned Mr. Everett's statements into red-hot reality.

"Like I said, Jordan, she's a good girl." Jeffrey's last words hissed again in his ear and pressed the truth of the past threat onto his heart like a branding iron.

Jordan shuddered, refocusing on the screen. Mr. Everett's story, and the Nolan family story, struck him with the new vitality of fresh belief.

● ● ●

"The boss removed our access to the lab, and most of our research findings, until we decided. That night, Ray and William broke into Carlyle Enterprises headquarters just before midnight and split up to gather the rest of what we needed. It was then that fear overtook me."

Robert's eyes misted on the screen. He squeezed them shut. "I betrayed my friends."

Robert Everett wept openly in front of the camera. The video played for several seconds while he gathered himself enough to continue. "I went to the boss and tipped him off. This resulted in a forest chase that caused the death of Ray Clark. William used that opportunity, as the last and worst option from Plan B, to implicate himself in Ray's murder. He smeared Ray's blood on his clothes and left his bloodied hat at the scene of Ray's death. William himself was killed a couple hours later in his apartment. It was made to look like a suicide. Few knew what had happened. Even the men who murdered William were just hired guns and didn't know what was actually going on.

"Only two people knew the truth.

"The resulting investigation implicated William Nolan in the murder of Ray Clark and closed the case. Hampden Pharmaceuticals was contacted with the unfortunate news of a quarrel between employees that had resulted in both of their deaths. Of course, that was a total fabrication. They were told that no issues related to XD had been raised and were politely asked if Hampden, under these difficult circumstances, would let us out of the research contract.

"Having no idea about what was really happening, they graciously agreed. I was transferred to a different department, and the research arm of Carlyle Enterprises was disbanded. The name of the company was changed to Wilson Drug and Compounding Center—purportedly to commemorate the closing of the Wonder Drug deal. The real reason was to bury the truth.

"XD went to market. The result was more than fifteen thousand worldwide cases of stillborn deaths, birth defects, and many other harmful side effects. I have lived fifty years under a load of guilt.

"I am truly grateful for the wonderful benefits from Amitolin. Unfortunately, these benefits were built on top of a cover-up that caused the deaths of Ray and William, and the suffering of many thousands around the world. Two sets of evidence to substantiate these claims have been handed over to Jordan Nolan and Michael Clark."

●●●

Jordan's heart nearly burst out of his chest. He tipped his face upwards as if the rain of heaven poured down on him. He stood, mouth open, dumbfounded as he stared at the screen. Never in a million years would he have seen this coming.

Michael Clark—the least likely person in the whole world—had the evidence.

Jordan pushed down the thought that followed. He couldn't let himself go there. Not yet, anyway.

● ● ●

Tears flowed down both sides of Bethany's cheeks as she gazed in wonder at the screen. Her heart swelled as she sent a silent prayer of thanksgiving up to her Heavenly Father.

My dad has the evidence!

Joy shot through her whole being. She dismissed the next thought that came to her. It was too wonderful to even entertain.

● ● ●

Mr. Everett drew his statement to a close: "I can never atone for the suffering that my cowardice has caused. I sincerely ask for forgiveness from the Clark and Nolan families, the town of Wilson, and from anyone who has suffered, directly or indirectly, from the effects of XD.

"My hope from this video, and the supporting evidence, is to clear the air once and for all. William Nolan was a good man. I was a coward, and my boss, the high-ranking executive, was a power-hungry man who stopped at nothing to further his interests."

Robert paused and spoke into the camera, "That man, our boss at Carlyle Enterprises and the man who really deserves the blame for XD, was none other than Howard Carlyle."

● ● ●

The crowd sucked in a collective breath that charged the atmosphere like the moment after the tossing of a hand grenade. The entire place erupted in one united gasp.

Thousands of people gaped and struggled to realign all they'd previously believed.

Jordan beamed.

He had never been prouder in his whole life. Mr. Everett, a man who had lived in cowering fear for fifty years, had just told the world the truth.

A thought came out of nowhere.

Mr. Everett is with Me.

Jordan basked as though the smile of God shined down on him. Standing at the rear of the huge crowd, his thoughts went back to the catacombs where he had offered his own forgiveness and encouraged Mr. Everett to receive God's. Now watching Mr. Everett do the unthinkable, a surge of adrenaline shot through his body. He could take on the world at this moment.

Mr. Kingston and Mr. Carlyle had better hope he didn't get a microphone in his hand anytime soon.

Chapter 96

Plan B Lives

Saturday, August 16, 6:05 p.m.
Wilson County Fairgrounds, Wilson, CO

"There you are." A voice like an evening melody snapped Jordan back to the present.

Emotional mayhem was everywhere as people struggled to make sense of the new information. But here was the voice of one who understood what this moment really meant. He pulled off his shades and faced her.

Bethany's smile vanished. A crease of concern spread across her forehead. She reached out and gently touched the bruises on his jaw.

He nodded.

"I watched the whole thing," she said. Her fingers trailed up three inches as she rested the palm of her hand on his cheek. Her eyes released the worry and radiated a new message just for him.

A warmth arose from his belly. He didn't want to move. He stared and let the moment linger. Eventually, he felt like he should say something. "What are you doing here?" he blundered. He sighed and looked away.

She laughed, unfazed. "I'm fetching you, of course." She pulled her hand away and put it behind her back like it would be safer there. She whistled a doot-te-do and gave a little swing dance in place.

His mind shot back to her conversation with Allie in the hotel cafe at Nationals.

Speaking of fetching, how about that debate final?

He pushed the thought aside and moved his mouth to protest, but before he could say anything she grabbed him by the hand and pulled him forward.

● ● ●

Donald leaned over to whisper in Jeffrey's ear. "This is a disaster. Do something!"

"Hold it together," Jeffrey whispered back. "Isaac Molencki called this morning and assured me that both Alex and Jordan were taken care of. There is nothing that can implicate us. The evidence is about the past, not the present. Your father's name is ruined, and you'll have to deal with the fallout, but you will be fine. You might even come through this looking good, if you play your cards right."

Donald straightened. A glimmer lit up his eyes. Jeffrey was right. It would be a bumpy ride, but he would make it through this. Not only that, he was out from under the shadow of his father. He did his best to look grave and contrite. He would be the leader who would have to navigate poor WDC2 through the investigation into the misdeeds of his father. He forced down a smile and looked back at the stage.

● ● ●

Bethany refused to let Jordan stay where he was. She dragged him through the outskirts of the crowd toward the stage. Fumbling with his free hand, he put his sunglasses back on.

The senator took the podium amidst the chaos. Many had lived in Wilson their whole lives and had never heard even a whisper of this.

"Dear friends," the senator boomed over the rising din and quieted the crowd with the force of his voice reverberating through the loudspeakers. He waited for silence. "I know this comes as a shock to many of you. Howard Carlyle was a beloved figure in this county and this state. Indeed, I considered him a good friend. Also, The Wonder Drug has provided great benefit to untold numbers of people. We must never lose sight of that."

As she wormed her way around to the far left side of the front, Bethany pointed at a television camera and whispered in his ear, "One of the networks."

"However," continued Senator Smith, drawing out the word, "we must acknowledge the truth. The Wonder Drug deal rode on the back of the XD cover-up. Falsified research, the murders of two of our citizens, and thousands of suffering victims were the result. Ladies and gentlemen, I have not only seen the evidence spoken of in the video by Robert Everett, but I have had several legal and forensic experts examine it to make sure that it is genuine. I can say with certainty that it is. You might wonder how I came into possession of this evidence."

Jordan pulled his hat down further, doing his best to stay unseen. Even as they sat down on the far edge of the front row, Bethany did not release his hand.

"Earlier this summer," the senator continued, "Jordan Nolan brought this information to my attention. At the time, he said he did not have the evidence to prove it, but he was passionate in his belief that William Nolan was innocent. Today, I am here to tell you that it is true. Ray Clark, William's mentor and the senior researcher on the team, stood as an unwavering figure from beginning to end. William experienced a radical change and followed in Ray's footsteps by giving his life for his family and those who would suffer from XD."

Jordan saw Bethany peek out of the corner of her eye as he forced down a smile that tried to take over his whole face.

"Citizens, you need to know that acquiring this evidence was not easy. Because of the ongoing investigation I will not mention any names. However, there are several suspects related to multiple criminal incidents, including the death of Robert Everett. In addition," Senator Smith took a breath, "the police have received reports that both Alex Jones and Jordan Nolan are missing."

Surprise rippled through the crowd again.

Jordan leaned in closer to Bethany, trying to stay hidden behind her ear. It wasn't that difficult. All eyes were glued to the senator.

"Mr. Everett knew that this evidence could put him in great danger. He could have gone straight to the police. Ironically, he had his own Plan B that no one knew about except himself. Mr. Clark, will you join me back on the platform?"

● ● ●

Donald swallowed down a slight tremor. He didn't like the sound of this Plan B, but he reminded himself that Michael Clark possessed evidence from 1964, not now. He forced himself to take a long, slow breath.

● ● ●

Seated behind the men from Hampden Pharmaceuticals, Matthew craned his neck as covertly as he could. He stared at Jeffrey Kingston.

Who is this guy?

Matthew digested what he had just heard. It was true that he hated Jordan with a passion, but he didn't think he wanted him dead.

Jordan is missing. Was that Jeffrey's doing?

He thought back to the moment when he'd stepped into the limousine and met Isaac Molencki.

He shuddered and looked away.

What have I gotten myself into?

● ● ●

Still wearing his lapel microphone, Mr. Clark joined the senator at the podium.

Heart beating too fast, Bethany looked up from the far edge of the front row. She could feel Jordan's tight breaths on the back of her left ear. They sat on the opposite side of the WDC2 and Hampden Pharmaceuticals group.

"Ladies and gentlemen," Mr. Clark spoke, "as you can imagine, an event like this celebration requires a tremendous amount of coordination. In a role such as mine, the last thing anyone wants is a big surprise the day before it starts."

He took a quick drink from a water bottle.

"Yesterday morning at nine a.m., Robert Everett came into my office and dropped a bomb into my lap. He told me the story you just heard, showed me the evidence, and handed me a letter from my grandfather, Raymond Clark, that he was supposed to have delivered to me fifty years ago. Mr. Everett told me of his own role on that fateful night. Not only did he betray William and Ray, but he never delivered the letter—until yesterday. It was the most beautiful letter I've ever seen.

"Robert then told me he was going on a trip to Denver, and that it was a decoy. He had made two phone calls—to whom, like the senator—I will not divulge any names yet. The purpose of the two calls—and the decoy—was twofold. First, he wanted to draw out some people he suspected. Second, he had to keep anything from happening to him before he got a chance to talk to me. Basically, it was to buy him an uninterrupted hour with no suspicion. During that hour, after he told me the story, we made that video in my office.

He left at about ten a.m. He knew, somehow, that he would not make it to Denver. He told me the names in case any foul play was suspected. I tried to dissuade him from going, but he was resolute."

Bethany sat next to Jordan and rested her hand on top of his. She felt like a child reaching into the cookie jar as tingles shot from her fingers to her elbow. Her mind shouted for her to pull her hand back. Her heart was standing on the counter with chocolate on her face.

Mr. Clark glanced over, did a double take, and sized up the situation in an instant.

Busted.

She gave a sheepish grin as Jordan squirmed next to her. She felt him look down under the weight of her father's gaze. A second later, Mr. Clark gave her a wink.

A current of electricity surged through her. Her mouth dropped open. Was she allowed to have a cookie?

An almost imperceptible grin pushed on the corner of her father's mouth as he refocused on the audience and continued. "Robert told me that his trip to Denver was a diversion and bait, and that his conversation with me was Plan B. He said I was the most unlikely person to do anything in support of Jordan Nolan, and therefore nobody would suspect anything if he spoke to me before leaving for Denver."

Mr. Clark looked again in Bethany's direction. "Isn't that right, Jordan?"

Chapter 97

Unleashed

Saturday, August 16, 6:12 p.m.
Wilson County Fairgrounds, Wilson, CO

The crowd gasped again.

Bethany tightened her grip around Jordan's hand. Heat shot up the back of his neck as hundreds of pairs of eyes, including Mr. Carlyle's, snapped toward him. The camera wheeled around and zoomed in. He wanted the ground to open up and swallow him.

Mr. Clark singled him out, "Jordan, Mr. Everett mentioned that he gave you a copy of the evidence. I assumed from that statement that you already had it. I had no idea that you were going by yourself in the middle of the night to retrieve it. I'm sorry for your suffering. Would you care to join me on the platform?"

●●●

Donald reeled and worked his mouth as if gnawing on an invisible cigar. His mind flew through the possibilities. If Jordan was alive, and Isaac Molencki said he was dead...

He glanced at Jeffrey.

Mr. Kingston's gaze was hard as stone. Muscles on his neck tightened.

Bile rose up in Donald's throat. His face paled. He had never seen anything like this on Jeffrey's countenance.

Jordan Nolan was alive.

This changed everything.

● ● ●

Jordan froze like a pinball machine on tilt. A smiling Mr. Clark was inviting him to the stage.

Bethany gave a final squeeze and let go of his hand.

The quiet of the stunned crowd was so intense that he could hear the soft whir of the television camera as it zoomed in on him. He stood up like a zombie and turned his head in slow motion toward the podium.

Mr. Clark extended an upraised palm toward him.

Bethany reached with one hand to pull off his sunglasses. She placed the other hand on the small of his back and pushed gently.

He started forward, ascended the side steps, and walked across the platform in a daze.

"I'm guessing you didn't expect this," said Mr. Clark. "Ladies and gentlemen," he addressed the large crowd, "please welcome Jordan Nolan to the stage."

The applause was a tentative mix of relief, welcome, and suspicion. Several from the WDC2 group fumed. The men from Hampden Pharmaceuticals exchanged irritated glances. This was supposed to be their day in the sun.

Mr. Clark ignored both groups, waited for the applause to die down, and said, "I've made no secret of my animosity toward the Nolan family. Jordan in particular has taken the brunt of my anger. Therefore, I want to publicly apologize to him, to his father, and to the whole Nolan family." He faced Jordan again. "I've treated you horribly, and most of it was old resentment for something that your great-grandfather didn't even do." Mr. Clark offered his hand. "Please forgive me, Jordan. It looks like you were right. William Nolan was indeed a hero."

Jordan looked down at Mr. Clark's outstretched arm and then back up into his eyes. The gentle press of Bethany's hand still warmed his lower back. His cheeks brightened. A smile broke out on his face. He reached out and shook the hand that was offered.

Michael walked two steps to the podium. Picking up a handheld microphone meant for Donald Carlyle, he stepped back to Jordan and said, "Now that your great-grandfather has been exonerated, would you like to say a few words?"

Mr. Clark didn't wait for an answer. He handed over the microphone and stepped back a few paces next to Senator Smith. As the smooth metal pressed into Jordan's palm, he spotted Jeffrey Kingston. His brain fog was blown away like a puff of smoke. Everything came into sharp focus.

Jeffrey glanced at Bethany, who still stood. Turning back to Jordan, he smiled and mouthed the words, "She's a good girl."

The silent message hit Jordan below the belt. If he said anything against Mr. Kingston or Mr. Carlyle, Bethany was next on Isaac Molencki's list.

Jordan's T-shirt felt like a noose. He was standing before a crowd of thousands wearing an old technology cap and gym shorts he had slept in.

He was unprepared, bruised, and bone-weary. His thoughts refused to become coherent. Enemies glared up at him from twenty feet away. He looked straight down and saw he was dressed in all black. The horror of last night rushed into his memory like the river that had smashed into his face. Panic stabbed him once again.

Heat rushed into his eyes as he looked up into the sea of faces. Many were confused, some were hostile. A few seconds ticked by and the crowd became anxious.

I don't belong in Washington.

He closed his eyes in a slow blink.

Why am I here?

Out of nowhere the shrill, piercing sound of feedback screamed from the speakers. People everywhere covered their ears. Mercifully, the sound died down.

Jordan's eyes snapped open. Thirty rows back, in the center of the crowd, a figure stood up in the sound booth.

Gadg.

Jordan exhaled and shook his head with a weary smile.

His best friend gave a fist pump.

Jordan's heart downshifted and made it halfway to calm.

He took in a deep breath and looked over at Bethany. Her luminous gaze, proprietary in the extreme, reached into his chest and grabbed his heart like she owned it with a title deed. Molten lava erupted in his belly. He blushed and turned away—right into the grip of Senator Smith.

The senator grabbed him by the shoulders, looked him straight in the eye and smiled. Jordan couldn't believe how strong the man was. He saw a light on the senator's face that he hadn't seen before. A strange thought hit him.

No more lies.

He was looking into the face of one who had a clean heart.

"You can do this," said the senator. "Tell them." He stepped back.

A sense of coming home—of belonging right here at this moment—descended on Jordan like a blanket from heaven. All five fingers tightened on the microphone as he straightened his back and said, "Yes, sir."

Fire came into Jordan's eyes as he wheeled around and faced the front. He was back in the arena. The microphone made him feel like a gladiator holding a bloody sword as he fastened his gaze on two men in the front row.

"Hello, Mr. Kingston. Hello, Mr. Carlyle. Are you surprised to see me?" Jordan didn't wait for an answer. "I'm here to finish what Ray Clark and my great-grandfather started."

He addressed the men in suits who stood next to them. "Dear leaders of Hampden Pharmaceuticals, you've already heard the truth of what happened in the past. Let me tell you about the present. I'm aware of the ongoing investigation that caused Mr. Clark and Senator Smith to speak in such guarded language. You'll forgive me, gentlemen, if I'm less politically correct, but it's only been a few hours since my best friend fished me from the bottom of Wilson's Creek with tape over my mouth and my arms and legs bound."

Several of the Hampden executives looked at each other.

"My question to you today is this: do you really want to enter into a business or political relationship with the two men standing beside you?"

Jeffrey Kingston's eyes flashed a message that he would kill Jordan—and Bethany—if he got the chance. Donald looked as though he'd seen a ghost.

Jordan unleashed a torrent. "I've had enough of cover-ups. The truth is that Jeffrey Kingston and Donald Carlyle have conspired to do whatever it takes—including murder—to make sure this deal goes through. Alex Jones isn't missing—he's dead."

Jordan looked at Donald and Jeffrey. "You wanted to hush it up. I'm going to say it to the world."

● ● ●

Looking past Jordan, Bethany saw her dad glance at the senator as if to ask if he should go and put an end to this. The tiniest head shake from the senator stopped him.

● ● ●

Jordan raised his voice to the crowd. "The police are examining a video where Isaac Molencki, a professional hit man hired by Mr. Kingston on behalf of Mr. Carlyle, killed Alex Jones in cold blood and then tied me up and threw me in the river."

He looked again at Jeffrey. "Yes, they have it on tape, Mr. Kingston. You should have been more careful who you *allied* yourself with, *sir*." He practically spat the last word.

A vein on Jeffrey's neck pulsed. Hatred shot out of his eyes as if to burn a hole through Jordan's forehead.

Jordan smirked. Raising his head to the huge crowd, he continued, "If it wasn't for the grace of God and two dear friends, I would be dead right now."

He looked back at the two men. "You can try to paint this as slander, but the closer people look, the more they will find you both at the heart of this mess. I defy anyone to try. Both of your names are spoken by Isaac Molencki on the murder tape from this morning."

"Gentlemen," Jordan spoke again to the Hampden executives as his face hardened into steel, "take care what you do. I've never seen such a gross breach of public trust and medical ethics as that perpetrated by Jeffrey Kingston and Donald Carlyle."

Jordan glared down at the two men. "You're finished."

He dropped the microphone onto the podium and walked off.

● ● ●

Still seated a few rows back from the men whom Jordan had just accused of murder on National TV, Matthew stared in shock. Thoughts assaulted his mind as Senator Smith stepped up to the podium.

My uncle is dead.

Mr. Kingston lied to me.

Mr. Molencki lied to me.

I could lose the internship again.

I'm in serious trouble.

The senator took it upon himself to close the proceedings. "Friends," he addressed the audience, "there is not much more to be said. Obviously, there are some legal matters to be attended to. Please allow me, as a representative of the state of Colorado, to say how sorry I am to those affected by the drug XD. Hampden Pharmaceuticals has repeatedly apologized for bringing XD to market and has paid out millions of dollars in aid to the victims." He looked down at the men in suits. "It is not my intent to cast any more negative light on Hampden. The purpose of my apology is for the state of Colorado, and this area specifically, to take responsibility for the role we played in the tragedy of XD. If this cover-up had not happened, it is possible that much suffering may have been avoided."

Matthew thought back to yesterday.

How could Molencki have known where to be?

He tried to push the thought aside. Three different times he had seen his uncle Alex keeping a close eye on Jordan from a distance. When Molencki had called him later that day, Matthew had made an offhanded comment to that effect.

My uncle is dead.

Before he could finish his train of thought, the senator turned to see if Jordan was still on the stage. He located him standing next to Bethany and said, "I would also like to extend my thanks to Jordan Nolan, who first brought this to my attention. He was relentless in his pursuit of the truth." Looking straight at Jordan, the senator said, "I look forward to spending a year with you on the Senator's Internship. Please accept my apologies for what has happened. I have some housecleaning to do." He looked down at his chief of staff.

Matthew gripped the plastic on the sides of his chair. Mr. Kingston, his supposed advocate, stood and made his way toward the exit.

Gadg's words came back and slapped him in the face.

You're 0 for 2 against him when it's really counted.

He bit down hard and ground his teeth. Now he was 0 for 3. He had sent the text to Jordan only on Mr. Kingston's promise that he was going to talk to the senator next week. Jeffrey Kingston would not be convincing the senator of anything, now or any time in the future.

A trail of sweat slid from his neck to the middle of his back. He gripped harder, trying to hold it together. Not only had Jordan beaten him again, but there was a link, however small, between him and the death of his uncle. He looked over at his enemy, shining in the praise of the senator with Bethany's hand tucked under and wrapped around his upper arm.

Everything bad that's ever happened to me is because of him.

A toxic mix of fear, self-pity, and hatred sprayed into his heart. He would get back at Jordan if it took all he had.

Senator Smith's booming voice interrupted Matthew's internal tirade: "In closing," he spoke to the crowd, "I want to reiterate that Amitolin has been a great gift to the human race. Many citizens of Wilson gave their best to bring us the Wonder Drug with no knowledge of the XD research cover-up. Please hold your heads high for that contribution. You have nothing of which to be ashamed. Good night."

Chapter 98

A Dream Re-Reprised

Tuesday, August 19, 6:45 a.m.
Jordan's room, Wilson, CO

Jordan shot awake. Images filled his mind in living color. If it had been anyone else he would not have believed it.

The same dream.

Three times.

It had been a while since the second time, and so much had happened that he had almost forgotten about it. Now wide awake, the word "Wilson" was etched on a bridge and burned into his mind's eye. He could still feel the texture of the wood against his fingers when he picked up the quill pen. It had a feathered end and looked like it was used for calligraphy. He saw himself, with dramatic flair, signing away his life savings to purchase the bridge. His smile spread wide across his face as a sense of joy overwhelmed him. He blinked a few times to ensure he was awake. Yanking himself out of bed, he turned to the mirror.

His face didn't lie.

Radiant joy.

Another idea, one that he'd been having for a couple days now, rushed back into his head and covered his mind like a warm blanket. He looked away from the mirror.

The weirdest thought of his life flashed back from a few days ago.

Stall him for five minutes and you'll live.

What had happened? Had the Holy Spirit spoken to him then? Jordan reflected on the events. He had stalled a professional hit man. And he had lived.

This new thought was horrible, but it wasn't *that* bad.

Maybe it's God again.

He sneaked a peek at his reflection. The joy from the dream still lingered. He squared up and looked himself in the eye. Lifting his head toward the ceiling he prayed, "Lord, I'll do it. If You'll help me again, I'll go tonight."

He sat down on his bed and looked at the alarm clock he had dug out of Grandpa's attic. He shook his head and laughed. He still had not replaced the destroyed phone from the weekend, and they had decided to disconnect and decommission his "keeping up appearances" phone last week. He smiled at how low tech he was at the moment. It didn't matter. The work to be done was not technical in nature.

6:50 a.m.

Almost nine o'clock in Washington.

He walked into the great room, grabbed the old cordless phone that he never used, and walked back into his room. Seated on his bed, he reached onto his nightstand, unfolded a piece of paper, and stared at a phone number he had written down last weekend. He never thought he would use it.

The joy from the dream was just enough to counteract his trembling hands. He pushed the buttons and raised the phone to his ear.

When the answering machine picked up he said, "Hello Senator Smith, it's Jordan Nolan..."

Chapter 99

Love Your Enemies

Tuesday, August 19, 7:15 p.m.
Office of Matthew Harris's father, Wilson, CO

At least three times, Jordan almost turned back. This made no sense at all. It was raw obedience.

He stopped on plush, purple carpet outside the open interior door of the downtown office. He had to catch his breath, even though he wasn't winded. The name on the glass read, Trenton Harris, President.

Jordan's chest felt like he'd been hit with a bat. According to Gadg, Matthew was there alone.

Jordan stepped around the door.

Matthew sat at his father's large desk staring down at the Wilson Press newspaper. Eyes glazed, he looked more like he was zoning out. The headline said, *Hampden Pulls the Plug.*

Jordan didn't wait for an invitation. Knees buckling, he forced himself forward.

Matthew looked up as Jordan approached his desk. "How dare you come down here?" demanded Matthew savagely as his gaze sharpened into full clarity and rage.

Jordan blinked one more prayer for grace. He had no idea it would be this difficult. "I've come to apologize, Matthew. I'm sorry for being such a jerk."

"Oh, sure," scoffed Matthew. "Now that you're in, and I'm out. Talk is cheap. Get out of here."

Mathew's words stabbed him in the heart. He took a deep breath. "I care about you, Matthew." He cringed. It sounded idiotic as it left his mouth.

Hate smoldered in Matthew's eyes.

"I spoke to Senator Smith today," Jordan said quickly. "He knows about Jeffrey Kingston—what he did to both of us."

"Do you want me to throw you out? If I never see you again, it will be too soon. Now, leave!"

"I'm sorry to hear that," said Jordan, taking a deep breath, "because I asked Senator Smith if you could have his wild-card pick."

"What?" Matthew's mouth cracked open. Anger still held the upper hand in his eyes, but the rest of his face was a picture of confusion.

"Two things," Jordan continued. "First, the senator's most recent wild-card pick backed out. Second, he doesn't want our only experience of Washington to be through the lens of a treacherous chief of staff. He plans to mentor *both* of us, personally."

"What are you saying?" Matthew tried to keep up the bluster, but the fight was gone.

"I'm saying it could be a long year if you still hate me." Jordan smiled and set a plane ticket on the desk. "Pack your bags, Matthew. We leave on Monday."

Chapter 100

Two Families

Friday, August 22, 5:20 p.m.
Clark home, Wilson, CO

The room was full and the party festive. With the one exception of the nagging unknown about the health of Bethany's mom, it felt as though the weight of decades had been lifted from the Clark and Nolan families. Gadg and Jordan sat next to each other on the couch in the Clark's family room. Jordan had only been in the home one other time—when the four of them discovered that the small man had been reading Bethany's diary. Allie, Tyler, and Bethany all sat opposite them in a semi-circle around the coffee table, which was strewn with the paper-plate remains of Deputy O'Brien's Kansas City barbecue.

"This is the reason I could never be a vegetarian," said Tyler. Sauce covered not just his mouth, but most of his face. He smiled like he couldn't care less what anybody thought.

Jordan offered a fist bump and then spoke in a softer tone to Bethany. "Any news on your mom?"

"She had another round of tests this week," said Bethany. "My dad's been waiting by the phone. Even though it's almost the weekend, we understand from the medical center that we could get a call as early as today. Learning that my grandmother was on XD gave them a new path to explore. Thanks to you."

"You're welcome," Jordan smiled.

Allie's eyes went back and forth, and her mouth curled in the slightest hint of a grin.

Deputy O'Brien approached the group wearing his grill master outfit, complete with a frayed apron and four-inch-high roadkill trucker cap.

Gadg looked like it hurt him to be related.

Jordan laughed out loud. Shaking his head, he said, "Deputy O'Brien, how could you wear that hat? Just looking at it makes me feel like someone just shared a bad pun."

The deputy's face lit up. "For exactly that reason. You sure you don't want to borrow it?"

Jordan laughed and then his face turned grave. "Speaking of borrowing hats"—he looked first at Gadg and then back up at the deputy—"I never properly thanked you both." His lip gave a quiver as the memory of that night haunted him afresh. He put his arm around Gadg's shoulder and gave him a squeeze. He then got up and faced Deputy O'Brien. Offering his hand, he looked up into his eyes. "Sir," Jordan said, suppressing a smirk, "I'm trying to thank you. You must take that hat off."

The deputy shook his hand and then pulled him in for a hug, leaving his hat in place. "We're just glad you're safe." Letting go, he said, "By the way, how did it go with Matthew? Gadg told me you were going to see him."

Jordan blinked twice to clear the mist. "Amazing. Better than I had hoped for. It was one of the hardest things I've ever had to do, but the Holy Spirit helped me. It was incredible to see the softening in Matthew's heart. I wouldn't be surprised if we become friends someday."

"Well done, Mr. Nolan," said Bethany in her polished British accent. Her eyes gave a reprise of their performance at the celebration.

Jordan looked away so as not to melt on the spot.

For once, Allie missed the exchange. Her voice came out laced with anger. "I can't believe you asked the senator to let *him* go with you, after what he did."

"Allie, I was wrong in what I asked you to do," said Jordan, back on steady ground. "The Lord convicted me that Matthew was in way over his head."

"Good," said Allie. "He deserves it."

"No," Deputy O'Brien took off his hat. "Jordan's right. This is still serious, for all of us, including Matthew. Senator Smith fired Jeffrey Kingston, but Isaac Molencki is still at-large." He turned toward Bethany. "Your dad showed us the full video that Robert Everett made in his office last week. On the tape, Mr. Everett said that he had made two phone calls before coming to visit your dad. Guess who?"

"Jeffrey Kingston and Isaac Molencki?" Allie jumped in.

The deputy shook his head. "You're halfway there—Jeffrey Kingston and Donald Carlyle."

Gadg picked up the story, "On the tape, Mr. Everett said that if anything happened to him, and any foul play was suspected, those were the only two people he contacted."

Deputy O'Brien faced Jordan. "The river cabin video is even more damaging. Mr. Molencki admits to being hired by Jeffrey Kingston on behalf of Donald Carlyle. In addition, the hat was on his head for a while after he threw you in the river. That tape led us to the vehicle and, ultimately, the body of Alex Jones. It's too bad Molencki took off the hat before he changed cars. They might have caught him."

"Is anybody going to jail?" asked Allie.

"Perhaps," said Deputy O'Brien, looking at the others. "The evidence is strong, but you can bet there will be some high-powered attorneys coming to Colorado in the next few weeks. All of us may have to testify before it's over."

Gadg continued, "It would help a lot if someone could catch Molencki. Even the FBI is after him now. I doubt they will, though."

"Why is that?" asked Allie.

Deputy O'Brien jumped back in, "His intelligence is matched only by his training, experience, and utter lack of regard for human life. He's an extremely dangerous individual. In all my years of law enforcement"—the deputy took a tight breath—"I've never faced anyone like him. I hate to say it, but I'm amazed, Jordan, that you lived through that night."

Jordan gulped.

A sense of sobriety blanketed the group.

"It was a miracle, pure and simple," he said.

"Wouldn't he be long gone by now?" asked Tyler.

Bethany gave a quick glance to Jordan.

His eyes narrowed at her. "You don't think so," said Jordan, more as a statement than a question. "Why?"

"I don't know," said Bethany. "Just a feeling, I guess. Like he said on the video, he never leaves a job unfinished."

Deputy O'Brien nodded. "I wish I had better news. But think about it, guys"—he looked each of them in the eye before continuing—"in all of Isaac Molencki's career, no one has ever beaten him. He won't forget this."

"So, what do we do?" asked Tyler.

"We trust God with all our hearts, and we live with heightened vigilance. This is part of the life of a law enforcement officer."

"Even with someone at the level of the small man after you?" asked Jordan.

"No," agreed the deputy. "Not usually at that level."

Jordan nodded. He had hoped to leave this summer behind and get on with his life.

"In other news," said Gadg, "Donald Carlyle has been forced to resign at WDC2 by the board of directors. He and Jeffrey Kingston are both being charged with second-degree murder."

Jordan's face lit up at the memory of Jeffrey Kingston. "Thank you, Gadg." He breathed out so deeply that the whole group heard him. His smile radiated contentment as if he'd just taken a sip from a jackpot cup.

The others looked at him as if he'd just departed from reality.

"Don't you get it?" He looked back in turn. "This is why it's worth it—even if we have to watch our backs for the rest of our lives."

"Why?" asked Allie.

He gave a fist pump. *"Justice."*

● ● ●

Deputy O'Brien had left to scrub the grill down. "Let's talk about something else," said Bethany.

"It happened again," said Jordan.

All four looked at him.

"What?" asked Tyler.

"The dream," Jordan replied.

Gadg shook his head in amazement. "The same one? You didn't tell me."

"Yes, sorry about that. It came with even more clarity this time."

"You had the same dream twice?" asked Allie.

"Three times," corrected Gadg. He looked over at Jordan for confirmation. Jordan nodded.

"When?" asked Tyler.

"Earlier this week, before I went to speak with Matthew."

Bethany looked at Jordan with furrowed eyebrows. "You had the same dream three times?"

"I know it sounds crazy, but yes."

"Do you mind if I ask what it was about?" asked Bethany.

"I was standing before a bridge that had the word 'Wilson' written across the top in huge letters. I had a feather quill pen in my hand, and I signed over my life savings—which I understood to be a significant amount—to purchase the bridge. Once I had bought it, I had a stronger sense of joy than I've ever had in my entire life."

"How much do you have in savings?" asked Allie.

"Not much," laughed Jordan.

Bethany didn't laugh. Her eyebrows still pinched together, her gaze never left his.

From the other end of the living room, Mr. Clark clapped his hands and addressed the whole gathering. "Dear family and friends," he spoke like he was on stage again, "in the grand scheme of things, this is a small get-together. However, in the Clark and Nolan families, this day is historic. I want to say publicly we are extending the hand of friendship to the Nolan family."

Applause went up from all around the packed room.

"Johnny," Mr. Clark said, "would you join me here for a moment?"

Jordan's dad weaved through the chairs and tables to stand with Michael.

Mr. Clark continued, "Welcome to our home. I want to ask you to forgive me for how I have treated you and your family. Even if the original story of William Nolan had been true, it was no excuse for the years of bitterness." He paused as he struggled for words. "I'm sorry. If you are willing, I'd like to go forward as friends. I now know that our grandfathers, Ray and William, wouldn't have it any other way."

Johnny Nolan reached out his right hand and Michael Clark shook it.

A flame blazed in Jordan's heart even as he tried not to look her direction. He knew what this could mean.

Wilson's Bridge

Friday, August 22, 5:40 p.m.
Clark home, Wilson, CO

Mr. Clark faced the group again. "For those of you who wish to participate"—he had regained full strength in his voice—"we have a 'getting to know you' game we'd like to play. Kind of strange since we've lived in the same town for years, but I think you all understand." He smiled. "Do you have your phones?"

A chorus of yes answers.

"No," Jordan reached into his pocket and pulled out his plane ticket to Washington.

"Is that a *paper* ticket I see?" asked Mr. Clark. "When do you leave?"

"If I had my phone, I could tell you exactly," said Jordan. "What's it say, bro?"

Gadg was already looking it up. Since he had written the code, he kept a copy of the Internship Ticker on his own phone. "Two days, fourteen hours, eighteen minutes and forty-six seconds."

"Monday, eight a.m." said Jordan. He sneaked a fraction of a glance toward Bethany. "After all that's happened, I can't believe it's finally here."

"Do you still want to go?" asked Michelle.

"Absolutely," said Jordan, a little too quickly. "After what I saw in Senator Smith last weekend, I can't wait."

Allie glanced at Bethany.

Bethany wasn't playing her cards. She held to a tight poker face.

Mr. Clark looked at Johnny and then Michelle.

Michelle gave her son a twinkly-eyed, overdramatized frown.

"It's only a year, Mom," said Jordan.

Michelle turned her frown into a pout that even Allie would be proud of. Jordan smiled at her.

"So, what's up with your phone?" asked Mr. Clark, moving the conversation back toward the game.

"Let's just say it's no longer a coordinated whole," replied Jordan. "It introduced itself to a brick fireplace at an excessively high speed." The mood was far too festive to think about who now had the pieces to it. "All the king's horses and all the king's men told me to get a new one, but I've not had a chance yet. To tell the truth, I've not been in a hurry to do so."

"Welcome to the old school," smiled Mr. Clark as he turned to Johnny with a nod.

Johnny nodded back and said, "Isn't it wonderful? I just learned about this cool new technology called email."

The young adults groaned.

"The game is called '*So, You Think You Know Your Friends?*'" Mr. Clark spoke to the whole group. "Here's how you play. The game will pose a multi-part question that has one player as the best answer. One point for guessing the correct person and a second point for the closest answer to the second part of the question. It's easy. Let's just start and you'll get it right away. This flip-chart here will have a table of the players, the questions, and the answers. Bethany, will you facilitate?"

Bethany got up, shaking her head. "Sure, Daddy," she said with a touch of snarkiness. The excellence of her penmanship, and the pleasantness of her voice earned her a number of such opportunities.

"Who's in?" asked Mr. Clark.

Several people, including the young adults and Mrs. Clark, decided to participate.

Mr. Clark looked at his wife. "You sure you're up for this, honey?"

Pamela nodded from her chair, "Yes, I don't feel horrible today."

Mr. Clark looked down at her. The small pursing of his lips communicated months of tender agony. He spoke to the group, "I'm going to just watch. I'm still hoping for a phone call."

Bethany wrote a list of players' names down the left side of the flip-chart. She drew a card from the deck. "First question, which player was born the furthest distance from our present location and how many miles away was it?"

After a bit, Bethany wrote down the answers as people shouted them out.

Gadg nudged Jordan on the leg and motioned with his head as Mr. Clark exited into another room with his phone glued to his ear.

"The doctor?" whispered Jordan.

"Probably," said Gadg.

Bethany was busy writing and had not noticed. "Okay," she said. "Looks like we've got votes for Deputy O'Brien and Tyler."

"Too many of us born in Wilson," said Jordan as he put on his hick voice. "If you'd asked who was born closest to the old waterin' hole you'd have a more interestin' question."

Bethany frowned him down.

Jordan tipped an imaginary cowboy hat, "Ma'am," he said with a drawl.

She grimaced and turned to the rest of the group. "So, who is it?"

"Portland is farther away than Spokane. It's my dad," said Gadg.

"Yep," said Deputy O'Brien. "1,200 miles from here."

"1,208," corrected Gadg. "Weren't you born at Providence Hospital?"

Deputy O'Brien smiled a mix of pride and competitive irritation at being one-upped by his son. "Yes, I was."

Jordan gave Gadg a fist pump. "Geek point."

Allie whispered with a twinkle, "Way to go, *Gadgie-boy*."

Tyler turned his head toward Gadg with eyes wide and mouth dropped open. "Dude, Gadgie-boy?"

"I don't want to hear it," Gadg said.

Bethany took the floor back. "That makes two points for Gadg, and one point for about five others. Next question." She paused. "Ooh, this is interesting. Who has the rarest blood type and what is it?"

"Who knows their blood type?" asked Tyler.

"I do," said Jordan. "Just had the physical for Washington a few weeks ago."

"I do, too," said Mrs. Clark. "All too well."

"Okay, everybody has one minute," said Bethany. "Go." A couple minutes later she had written the first three guesses onto the flip-chart. "Mom?" she asked as she got to Mrs. Clark's name on the list.

"I think it's me," said Mrs. Clark. "B-Positive. Not the rarest, but pretty rare."

"Seriously, Mrs. Clark?" said Jordan, speaking out of turn and looking over at her. "I thought *I* had it in the bag. B-Positive for me as well. Nine percent of the population."

She nodded. Her face said that if she never heard about blood again for the rest of her life, it would be too soon.

"How do you know all this?" Tyler asked Jordan as Bethany wrote in their answers.

"How else?" Allie stood up, adjusted an imaginary tie, and belted out her best Jordan impersonation, "The ethics of living donor transplantation. In this speech, we will explore whether it is ethical for a living person to donate an organ."

Several people groaned again.

"She's right," said Jordan, looking at Gadg. "It's all we did for a year."

Gadg nodded grimly. "Hours and hours. But I'm afraid neither of you is even close. B-Negative right here—1.7 percent of the population. I bet you didn't even know that one, Dad," Gadg looked at Deputy O'Brien.

"Actually, I did," Deputy O'Brien said with a wink. "Bethany, put my answer down as Gadg with B-Negative." He held up his phone to the group as if he needed to defend himself against a charge of cheating. "I'm paid to know much about many things."

A laugh from the room. Bethany wrote down both of the answers.

"*I* didn't know that," said Jordan. "Apparently, I didn't pay close enough attention."

"You were a lot more concerned with Matthew," said Gadg.

"*And* Bethany," Allie whispered into Tyler's ear, just loud enough for Jordan to hear.

Tyler bit his lip.

"What'd you say, Allie?" said Jordan. His stomach flipped once.

"Oh, nothing," she gave a devious grin. "Carry on." She flipped her fingers in the 'keep going' motion.

Bethany gave her a suspicious eye. She continued, "We're going to miss you, Jordan, but we're not going to miss debates about medical reform."

Nods all around. Vigorous nods from Jordan's parents.

"I couldn't agree more." He made his voice sound exhausted.

Bethany pulled everybody back to the game with, "Anybody else? Looks like Gadg, to nobody's surprise, is off to a good start with four points after only two questions."

● ● ●

Jordan got up to take a quick trip to the restroom. He scooped his plane ticket off the coffee table and headed toward the hall. He stopped when Mr. Clark came into the room from the other direction.

Mr. Clark still held his phone as he walked up to Pamela, knelt down and whispered in her ear.

Jordan saw them talk back and forth for a moment. Her last statement was punctuated with a nod.

Mr. Clark stood up, walked toward Bethany, and turned to address the group. "Dear friends"—his tone was so heavy that the room quieted immediately—"that was the medical center. I have some good news and some bad news. The good news is that they now have a name for what's ailing my dear wife."

Several people looked at each other and turned back to Mr. Clark.

"Unbelievably," he continued, "it's called Wilson's Disease."

Jordan did a sharp double take with Gadg.

Mr. Clark noticed it. "You know about this, Jordan?"

"Some," Jordan replied. "The disease comes from excess copper accumulation in an organ—especially the liver."

"That's correct. Sometimes it can be difficult to diagnose"—Mr. Clark paused for a beat—"as in this case. You're not going to believe where they think it comes from."

Everyone was all ears.

"Wilson's Disease can be hereditary. Thanks to Jordan, the current working theory is that this was inherited from Pamela's mother as a side effect of her use of XD while Pamela was still in the womb."

The room took in a collective breath. Several deflated sighs followed.

"What's the bad news?" asked Deputy O'Brien.

"The bad news is that Pamela's liver is failing," replied Mr. Clark. "The disease has been latent for most of her life, but it has accelerated in the last few weeks." He squeezed his face tight to fight back the rising emotion. Taking a deep breath, he continued, "She wants me to share this with you to ask for earnest prayer for a solution. It looks as though we'll have to sell this place and move to Colorado Springs or even Denver. We're going to need to begin dialysis right away."

More pinched looks and sighs from around the room.

"Thankfully, there is dialysis," said Bethany, trying to keep it bright. "I'd rather have mom around on dialysis, than not around at all." She rushed over to her mom's chair and hugged her tight. Bethany's tears wet both their cheeks.

Mr. Clark looked at his wife before continuing.

She nodded to him around Bethany's hair.

He waited a long moment. This time a tear did form in the corner of his eye. "Unfortunately, that's not the way it works."

Arms still around her mom, Bethany looked up at him imploringly.

"Liver dialysis isn't like kidney dialysis." Mr. Clark softened his tone. "You can't continue it indefinitely. It serves only as a bridge to a transplant."

Jordan put his forearm on the wall to steady himself. The earth's rotation slowed and all his senses became heightened to an ethereal, other-worldness. He could hear the smallest of sounds and see the tiniest sights. He felt he could take way more sensory input and not be overloaded. If he spoke it would be like listening to someone else's voice.

He looked over at Gadg. Then Tyler. Then Allie. Then Bethany.

The texture in the paint on the wall felt dappled on his forearm. The smoothness of the paper ticket felt like the soft edges of a child's security blanket.

Mr. Clark knelt with his arms around his wife and daughter.

Jordan noticed the flip-chart just behind them. He closed his eyes and breathed a prayer for grace. Time slowed even more. Mr. Clark's words echoed in his ears.

Wilson's disease.

Bridge to a transplant.

His dream rushed back in 3-D. His final speech at nationals blazed into his mind with new understanding. Bethany's fluid script on the flip-chart may as well have read two plus two, the answer was so obvious.

Wilson's Bridge.

He looked down at the ticket in his hand. The airport letters mocked him. Would it be his life or Bethany's mother's? Reality mingled with his dream as, somehow, his heart and the plane ticket became one with each other. He closed his eyes, put his other hand on the ticket and gritted his teeth.

He looked up to heaven and ripped it in half.

An earthquake tore open his insides. All he'd worked for—all he'd lived for—was swallowed up and taken down with wave after wave of aftershocks.

The internship was history. He might never leave Wilson.

Taking a deep breath, he stood up straight. Focused, subdued conversations told him all that had happened was between him and God. Squaring his shoulders, he walked two paces to the outside edge of the group and raised his voice to address Mr. Clark. "You're not going to need to move."

Bethany looked up at him.

Mr. Clark caught up a half second later as some conversations trailed off. "What did you say?"

"I said," Jordan felt grace coming out in the strength of his voice, "you're not going to need to sell your home and move."

Everybody in the room heard it this time. All eyes looked at him.

Mr. Clark asked, "Why? Do you have half a million dollars?"

Jordan's eyes shined. "No, I don't, but I do have B-Positive blood."

Chapter 102

Letter to a Killer

Wednesday, August 27, 10:00 p.m.
Bethany's room, Wilson, CO

Isaac Molencki never left unfinished business.

With the heat turned up right now, he would have to wait. But the time would come.

Having disposed of the body of Alex Jones, he had switched cars two more times and taken himself way off the grid as soon as he saw a replay of Jordan's speech. Solitude pommeled him for a full week as he cursed his own carelessness.

How could he have been so stupid?

First, to let the young man talk his way out of a certain death, and second, to let him get the whole thing on tape.

Unthinkable.

Isaac now had to live under deep cover, and his customers, Jeffrey and Donald, might go to prison because he—one of the most feared hit men on the east coast—had botched a job.

He squeezed his gloved hand. Oh yes, this was far from over.

Now, a few days later, he had circled back to make one last house call. He would head east after this to let some time pass—and to plan.

With both the Clark and Nolan families staying in Denver for Mrs. Clark's liver transplant, this was so easy it didn't even count. He opened the back door and strolled through the house to Bethany's bedroom.

It looked different this time.

Last time it was still in the golden hour before twilight. Now it was night. A pleasant reading lamp cast the only light in the room.

Interesting. Why would she leave a light on if she was going out of town?

He walked up to the bed, reached under the mattress and fished for Bethany's diary. Coming up empty, he turned to scan the room. There was the desk, the other bed that Allison Pearson slept in, a pile of clothes, and the nightstand. He turned away and his gaze snapped back. The only other object on the nightstand was a book.

And not just any book.

Bethany's diary, sitting perfectly aligned with the sides of the table, stared up at him. His eyes narrowed and focused on it.

Strange that it would be there—and even more strange that it would look like that. Perfectly parallel to the sides of the table.

Almost like she knew he was coming.

He walked over and picked it up with his gloved hand. Starting where he'd left off last time, he sped through Bethany's accounts of the last month.

He smiled at the thought that certain people would pay for this. He never left a debt unpaid. He turned the page to the last entry and his heart nearly stopped.

Dear Mr. Molencki,

Allow me to welcome you to my diary. I knew you'd be coming, and we were supposed to have a conversation anyway, so this will have to do. I give you my full permission to read it—again. You might be curious as to why I haven't called the cops. Several reasons:

1. That would make it more interesting for you. I'm guessing you love a challenge, and the town of Wilson has been too easy for you. I have no desire to make this into a game.

2. You're too good for that. I know I don't have any real protection from you in that way.

3. We'll be at the hospital for a few days so I know we're not in immediate danger—unless you did a bomb or something—which is not your style.

4. This room has already been wired so we are at least getting this on tape. Wave to the camera in the Northeast corner. Hi!

"Wow," he spoke aloud to the corner of the room. "I'm impressed, Bethany. You know me better than most." He put his head back down and continued reading with a smirk on his face.

I should feel threatened, violated, or just plain angry. However, at this point, guess what I feel for you?

Compassion.

I know you're a killer, and I know that I'll probably be on your list at some point, if I'm not already. However, I also know something about you that most do not. The real reason I've not called the cops is the same reason Daniel (in the Bible) had the guts to tell the captain of the king's guard to stop killing the wise men—which was in direct disobedience to the king.

I know a secret.

My heavenly Daddy, who kept me hidden from you in the catacombs, has shown me a picture of a little boy, maybe three or four years old. This boy has been alone in his house for two days and is covered in dirt and his own waste as a result of trying to scrounge an old biscuit behind the oven in order to get something to eat. His mother, who has been out on a drug binge, comes home. She screams at him and beats him because of how he looks and smells ...

He slammed the book shut so hard a plaque on the wall fell to the floor. A mist, followed by icy venom, sprayed into his eyes. His face twisted into a helpless rage. He threw the book as hard as he could and smashed it into the wall over her bed.

"This isn't over, Bethany. You may not want a game, but you just got one."

He ground out the words through facial muscles so tight that they threatened to break his own jaw. He turned to the window and kicked the bottom sash with such force that wood and glass exploded onto the pine straw just outside her bedroom. The small man stepped through what used to be her window and disappeared into the night.

Chapter 103

Grandpa and Jordan

Thursday, September 25, 8:30 a.m.
Outside Nolan guest house, Wilson, CO

Setting aside his cane, Jordan grunted, groaned, and eased himself down onto the bench that looked toward the back of Nolan property. Running his fingers along the hand-carved wood transported him back four months to when he'd opened a letter in this very spot and set off a chain reaction. The town of Wilson would never be the same.

Grandpa Walter stood over the bench holding two mugs of steaming brew. "I never would have guessed you'd have a cane before I did," said Grandpa.

"I'm hoping this isn't a permanent fixture, but at least I'm up and around." Jordan chuckled and then winced as he adjusted his position.

"Barely, I'd say," said Grandpa. He handed Jordan his Washington, DC mug and sat down next to him.

Jordan stared down as his thoughts took him to the Washington Monument itself.

"Any regrets?" said Grandpa.

Jordan shook his head once. "Not really." He took a sip from his mug, and his face lit up. "Grandpa, I can't believe it. This is one of the best cups of coffee I've ever had."

Grandpa's face radiated joy. "I've learned a secret."

"You have?"

"Yep, I learned that if I want to make an excellent cup of coffee, I need to do one thing."

"What's that?" Jordan leaned closer even though it brought a small grimace.

Grandpa got a twinkle in his eye. "I call Gadg." He pointed to a window in the Nolan guest house where Gadg peeked around the curtain and waved.

Jordan rolled his eyes and threw back his head. Forgetting his condition for a moment, he laughed out loud. Pain reminded him instantly, and he blurted "oh" and "ouch" in between the breaths of his laugh. To make it worse, some coffee spilled over the rim of his mug onto his hand. Another "ouch" and another sharp reminder of the state of his bandaged midsection made the affair rather comical. By the time he got the mug set down he was panting.

Grandpa pressed his lips together as he tried not to smile. He almost succeeded.

"That doesn't help," said Jordan, groaning through a chuckle.

Grandpa let a moment go by and stared toward Old Town. "How do you do a liver transplant if you only have *one*?"

"Think of it like a starfish that can grow appendages back. The human liver can regenerate itself. I only had to give part of it."

"Incredible," said Grandpa. "I'm guessing they don't use a wrench for that procedure."

"No, they don't," said Jordan, controlling his smile this time.

"So, what's next?"

"I'm not sure. I'm just taking it a day at a time at this point," Jordan also looked toward Old Town. "Guess what we're doing tomorrow?"

"What's that?"

"We've been invited to a meal at the Clark home."

Grandpa turned his head toward Jordan in amazement. "Who would've believed it?" He looked up to the sky. "His faithfulness is unto all generations indeed."

"Yeah, it is," said Jordan. His gaze drifted to the Old Mercantile, and his memory landed on a hug that lasted just a little too long.

Chapter 104

Two Doors Swing Open

**Friday, September 26, 6:15 p.m.
Clark home, Wilson, CO**

"I gotta go," said Tyler. This was the only weekend in September that he didn't have a Friday night game.

"Where are you going?" asked Jordan. Gadg, Bethany, and Allie looked at Tyler as he pulled open the front door.

"Out," said Tyler, turning back to him.

"What do you mean out?"

"Just out."

"Can we go with you?"

"There's no way I'm taking you with me."

"Ouch," said Jordan in mock seriousness, "After all we've been through, where could you possibly want to go without us?"

"You really want to know?"

The other four exchanged curious glances and looked back at Tyler.

"I'm going to drive to town. I'm going to get out of my car and walk into Old Town Café. I'm going to sit down and take my time looking over the menu. I'm going to order way too much food. I'm going to wait patiently for them to bring it while remembering all we've been through this summer. I'm going to smother everything in condiments that make you sick to think about them. I'm going to pray a heartfelt blessing over the meal. I'm going to take a deep breath, and I'm going to eat, not just look at, a huge hamburger." Tyler smiled at them. "You're not invited." He pushed open the screen door without a look back.

● ● ●

Returning from the restroom, Jordan peeked around the corner and reflected on the spot where his life had changed.

Would you trade it?

He scanned faces all around—subdued but joyful. A massive burden had been lifted from the Clark family. As he lingered for another moment, a smile spread across his face. Leaning on his cane, he hobbled over to the chair where Mrs. Clark was resting.

When she saw him, both eyes watered, and she put her hand over her mouth. A portion of his liver and all of his dream had given her life back to her. Not able to speak, she reached out her other hand to receive his.

Jordan waited several seconds. When she had put the finishing touches on her composure, he asked, "How are you, Mrs. Clark?"

"I'm still sore, but I'm feeling better than I have in months." She fanned herself to waive off a fresh bout of tears. "How can I ever thank you?"

"By never mentioning it again," Jordan said. He glanced up and saw Bethany over Mrs. Clark's shoulder.

She turned away. The back of her hand brushed across the side of her face.

"But you gave up the internship," Mrs. Clark persisted, oblivious to her daughter.

"I've never felt happier," he countered. "I'd do it again—in a heartbeat."

Mrs. Clark closed her eyes and squeezed his hand again.

A knock on the front door turned their attention elsewhere. Straightening, Jordan didn't think much of it. It was, after all, a party.

One minute later, two of the least expected people on earth entered the room.

"Senator Smith!" Jordan blurted.

James Dakota Smith himself stood before the gathering.

"Hello, Jordan. How are you feeling?" He offered his hand. Even in the close quarters of the Clark family room his voice carried the authority of one born to lead.

"Sir," Jordan said with a narrowly avoided squeak, "like Mrs. Clark, I'm still tired and sore, but I feel better than I have for a good while. Thank you for asking."

"Young man, I'm here to thank *you*."

Jordan just stood there, leaning on his cane. A fold of skin appeared on his forehead as his eyebrows bunched toward each other.

"But first," Senator Smith addressed the whole gathering, "you all know Matthew Harris..."

A chorus of greetings.

The senator continued, "Matthew has something he wants to say."

"Jordan," said Matthew taking the floor with his voice, "first, I want to apologize. For everything."

Jordan's eyes widened as he pressed two fingers into his neck as if checking for a pulse.

Matthew laughed. "Didn't expect that, did you?"

Jordan's mouth hadn't made it all the way to a smile, but it was on its way. "Is Allie here?"

"I'm here," said Allie, looking up from a conversation in the corner. Her voice carried a razor blade edge.

"I'm extremely sorry. What I did, and why I did it, was inexcusable."

A glint of steel reflected off her eyes. She gave a wary nod.

"Also"—Matthew looked back to Jordan—"I want to thank you for what you've done for me. This is the opportunity of a lifetime, and even though I'm working harder than I ever have,"—he looked over at Senator Smith—"I'm having a blast. I love DC."

Jordan forced back a stinging redness in his eyes. His mouth pinched up and a cloud darkened his face.

Matthew swallowed hard. A small patch of crimson crept up his neck.

The room quieted.

Jordan looked down as Matthew stood there awkwardly.

From deep within, the still small voice came unbidden and unwanted.

Love him.

Jordan countered with the slightest shake of his head—imperceptible to everyone, except maybe Gadg.

Lord, I already did. This is too much.

No, it's not. Trust Me.

Jordan still hadn't raised his head.

Lord, it hurts.

I know. Trust Me.

Jordan blinked and looked up at Matthew. He stepped forward by teeth-gritting faith and said, "That's great, Matthew."

Matthew held out his hand.

Jordan's handshake was flabby.

Come on Jordan. Give Me more. I went all in for you.

A searing lance pierced his heart. He had given it up before, but it wasn't until this moment that the dream had truly died. Jordan straightened his back, strengthened his grip, and smiled as big as he could muster. "I'm happy for you. You're welcome."

The room broke out in a spontaneous burst of applause.

Senator Smith let the moment conclude with a satisfied nod and took the floor back. "Jordan, you said earlier that you feel better."

"Yes, sir, a little," said Jordan.

"Thanks to you," the senator continued, "I feel lighter than I have in years. I have been much too cozy with the money people. No more. I'm leading again from a true heart and a sense of calling. And"—the senator paused to give a big mountain man smile—"I have joy again. I can't thank you enough."

Jordan gaped. He opened his mouth to speak, but nothing came out.

"How would you like to come to Washington?" asked the senator.

"I'd love to," he said, finally finding his voice. "But I'm afraid I've still got a good bit of healing to do. I'll have missed too much of the internship to make it worthwhile."

"Son," Senator Smith put his hand on Jordan's shoulder, "you don't need an internship. I know what you're made of. I'm here to offer you a *job*."

Jordan's eyes bulged and his heart took off in a sprint. In a breath, the entire internship journey flooded back—wanting it, winning it, losing it, getting it back, giving it up. His mouth snapped shut. Wonder filled his gaze.

Senator Smith laughed. "I understand how you feel. This is a paid position with paid schooling: undergrad and grad. I want you on my team. Pray about it and let me know."

"Yes, sir, I will." The words came with such force that no one in the room doubted what the answer would be. Jordan shook the senator's hand once more. "Thank you, sir."

Senator Smith gave a definitive nod and turned to leave. Matthew followed him as people returned to their conversations.

Jordan stared until the front door shut. An enormous smile radiated from his face. He turned from the door and his eyes landed on Bethany.

A tear ran down her cheek. She caught his eye and looked away.

Jordan's smile vanished. A sharp pain stabbed him in the chest. He took a few steps forward to plant himself in front of her. "Can we talk?"

"I guess," she said.

He grabbed her gently by the hand and led her into the hall. He spun to face her. "Bethany, what is it?"

She ran the base of her hand across the side of her face. "I'm sorry, it's nothing. Congratulations." Her voice sounded like Bette Midler's rendition of "The Rose."

Jordan's heart ripped open on the spot. His face looked like an eight-year-old who'd wet his pants and tried to stay strong as the whole third grade class laughed at him.

"Oh, Jordan," tears seeped out of both her eyes. She reached up to put a hand on his face, pulled it back, and wheeled around toward the bathroom door. Stepping in, she pulled it shut behind her. The fan turned on immediately.

Jordan stood dumbfounded and exposed as Mr. Clark said from behind him, "Can I talk to you for a moment?"

●●●

Jordan had not yet met Mr. Clark's gaze when he sat down in a chair at the kitchen table.

When he finally did look up, his eyes were so red and puffy that Mr. Clark was taken aback. "What's wrong, Jordan?"

"I don't know, sir." Jordan shook his head. "As soon as the senator left the room, Bethany freaked out. Her congratulations sounded like a funeral dirge. She locked herself in the bathroom."

Mr. Clark let out a slow breath, smiled and nodded. "She doesn't want you to leave."

"Excuse me?" Jordan stared blankly.

"She's never opened her heart to anyone," Mr. Clark continued. "Until now."

"I'm sorry, sir." Jordan blushed and turned away. Old memories launched a fresh assault.

"No, don't say that." Mr. Clark softened. "The reason I wanted to talk to you was to reiterate, to you personally, how sorry I am."

"Mr. Clark, please, you don't need to go there again."

"Look at me, Jordan. I don't know if you understand the depth of what you've done for us. You've given us our lives back. I've never seen such an incredible display of character." Mr. Clark pinched his nose and squeezed his eyes to keep them from flowing. "I want you to know that I completely retract what I said to you before. I'm not sure how ready Bethany is, what her answer would be, or even if you want to ask. However, for my part, not only do you have my full blessing, but I can't think of *anyone* I would rather give my daughter's hand to. It would be an honor to have you as a son-in-law."

Chapter 105

Going Somewhere

Saturday, September 27, 6:45 p.m.
Wilson Park, Wilson, CO

It was nearing the end of an unseasonably warm, late September day. Taking his time and leaning occasionally on his cane, Jordan decided to take a longer route to town. In the wake of all that had happened, and the forced slowdown of his recovery, he was learning to appreciate the rugged beauty of his hometown. Fifteen minutes before sunset, the temperature still lingered above seventy degrees. The sun cast long shadows and a radiating glow that blanketed a thousand objects all around him.

What an incredible day.

Jordan still had significant walking to do as part of his physical therapy, and for the first time in his life, he enjoyed it.

Beautiful enough to take the long way to town?

Jordan laughed to himself.

Of course not.

He looked toward the bridge that spanned Wilson Creek. He had learned from Mr. Clark that Bethany was spending the late afternoon at Wilson Park enjoying a book and the gorgeous weather. Seated on a bench near the bridge, her legs were crossed with one swinging gently over the other. Her tablet rested in her hand.

A mist of desire sprayed across his midsection.

Easy, Jordan.

Bethany had not looked up. He leaned against a tree to collect himself. He reached for his phone and pulled up the Bible app to remind himself of the promises. His hand shook so badly he could scarcely read it. The last time he saw her she had shut a door in his face.

Get a grip, man.

He took a deep breath and let it out slowly.

Lord, once again, I ask You for grace. I really need it right now.

He stuffed the phone back in his pocket leaving his hand there with it. He approached the bench as if he was passing by on his way to town. Technically, he *was* on his way to town. Leaning on a cane with shaking hands, Jordan didn't think he could pull off *suave* so he at least hoped to look nonchalant.

At fifteen feet away, Bethany looked up. Her smile said it all. Today was a new day.

Jordan could tell she was a bit sheepish from her outburst last night. "Hello, Bethany." He gave a smile of his own and skipped past any discussion of the bathroom door incident. "Amazing day, isn't it?"

She looked around and took it in afresh. Closing her eyes, she breathed deeply and answered with a satisfied nod. She opened them again, looked down at the cane in his hand and then past the bridge to the town of Wilson where any of the stores might be his destination. Without taking her eyes from the town she asked, "Are you going somewhere?"

The residue of his prayer still lingered. He chuckled.

Bethany gazed off into the distance.

He thought back to her conversation with Allie in the hotel café. He stretched out the words and said resolutely, "Yes, I am."

Turning back to him, Bethany hadn't clued in to the subtext. She waited for him to elaborate.

Jordan locked eyes with her and let the words hang in the air.

In the few seconds that followed, Bethany's understanding rose from predawn, to dawn, to bright morning. The full meaning of what he was saying manifested in her warm, knowing smirk.

Seconds passed in beautiful silence. Jordan gazed deeper. Bethany opened her eyes slightly and cocked her head.

Now or never.

He leaned down and extended his right hand to her. "Would you like to go with me, Miss Clark?"

Steady as the bench without a hint of shaking, his upturned hand beckoned.

She looked up at him. Her eyes were round, searching, and vulnerable.

Never releasing his gaze, she set her tablet to the side, got up without taking his hand, and threw her arms around him in a hug that said she was all-in.

Jordan ignored the wince. He had to drop his cane from his left hand and pull in his right hand to hug back. Flames ignited in his belly and overpowered the pain in his side. When the embrace ended, the setting sun wrapped a gilded glow around their faces, now six inches apart. Another beautiful silence followed.

"Yes, I would, Mr. Nolan," Bethany finally answered.

Jordan savored the sound.

Am I going to get to hear that voice for the rest of my life?

His memory shot back to the first time they ever spoke. A tear emerged.

Her eyes rounded again, this time with concern. "You okay?"

Another tear pooled in the other eye. "Do you remember our first conversation? Way back when we were eight-year-olds?"

She bit her lip through a compressed smile and nodded.

"Did I ever tell you how much that meant to me?"

Bethany rested her palm on his cheek. With her other hand she wiped away his tears. "Only with your eyes—nearly every time you've looked at me for the last ten years."

"Was it that obvious?"

"Only to me."

He laughed.

"What?" her smile changed to a smirk as she pulled her hand back.

"I'm still a debater at heart," Jordan replied. "I'm having a debate with myself about whether to kiss you or not."

Bethany put her index finger over his mouth and leaned in close to his ear.

A spray of fire shot into his stomach as she lowered her voice to a whisper and breathed, "Just wait."

Acknowledgments

To God the Father, Jesus my beloved, and the wonderful Holy Spirit. It would be an understatement to say this work would not exist without You. I've so enjoyed our fellowship throughout this process. It goes without saying that the rest of this beautiful list would be nothing without Your grace. Thank You for everything. May it be to Your glory.

The number of people that God has blessed me with—those that have made a material contribution to this work—humbles and astounds me.

Without a doubt, the MVP goes to a rockstar young editor and story consultant named Emily Morgan. (Find her at www.thisincandescentlife.com.) I cannot overstate her contribution. Emily, your mix of encouragement and constructive feedback helped give me the courage to tackle draft two and to not settle for something I was less than happy with. Huge thanks! It's going to be fun to watch where the Lord takes you on this journey. You truly have a gift.

Right up there with her is Tommy Sargent, who has invested countless hours in the audiobook, trailers, and music. It's been such a delight to work with you.

To my dad, Phil Sargent, and my daughter, Hannah "Sal" Sargent, for being my story buddies and sounding boards in the grit and grind of the day by day over the last few years. Nate: you get an honorable mention on this too. We can't go anywhere without listening to an audiobook.

To David Blair: for your friendship and your annoyingly good feedback. To Elijah Pyles: for some helpful words of wisdom, especially in the painful, early parts of the project. To some wonderful beta readers for your insightful help: Robin Grattet, Zach, Jason, and Leonard. Thank you so much.

To Shane Williams: for being a great friend and kindred spirit. Iceland here we come! To Gary Wiens for your friendship, spiritual fathering, and the real-life inspiration for the "God, I'm not ready to die" prayer from John Philip Nolan.

To "the Bitlings"—you know who you are. That was a fun year-and-a-half.

To Emily Lusk: for giving me permission to honor "Gutless." I've had a lot of fun with that truck in this story. To Sam Sargent: for the inspiration for the "jackpot cup."

Special thanks to Ted Dekker, Kevin Kaiser, and Erin Healy of The Creative Way. Beyond exaggeration, your material inputs are too numerous to list. Your fingerprints are all over this work.

To Jerry Jenkins: thanks for teaching me to "just say it," to "omit needless words," and to "resist the urge to explain." Thanks also for showing me that the writing life can be done on an ironing board after 9 p.m.

To Phill and Nancy Erickson and your wonderful kids. You guys are an unspeakably great gift to the Sargent family. Same goes for Angus, Kathy, JB and Aubree Meadows. Destined to do life together! To Kevin and Janell Lusk and family. We love you guys!

Special thanks to Scott and Lauri Lane and your beautiful family. Thanks for your great friendship and always pointing us to Jesus.

To the Hirsch family: great friends and fellow pilgrims on this journey of story and life. Thanks for your encouragement, support, and godly example for many years. And to our great friends Dave and Tabby Webb and family. God bless you guys.

To Doug Tjaden and family: for help fleshing out the wide receiver stuff and for being such a great friend and sounding board.

To my friends on the Systems Team at Compassion International: Thanks for being real life geeks in the most affectionate sense of the word. Thanks for putting up with the craziness of my life in 2017/2018 while we landed this thing. Click your heels three times and say, 'There's no place like code."

To Stephen Kendrick: for putting the "we pray about everything" concept into my heart as a storyteller.

To K.M. Weiland: for helping this writer become an author. Many excellent posts at www.helpingwritersbecomeauthors.com. Thank you.

To Bryan and Jeanna Helgesen and Kevin McHugh: for your enthusiastic support and wise counsel in the early days.

To Davis Bunn: I've read so many of your stories, multiple times, that your voice is woven into the DNA of my voice. Thank you for teaching me what quality, devout fiction sounds like. You'll forgive me if it's over-the-top, but I put a direct, three-line tribute to you in the novel: "The wrench was a giant affair. With a practiced flip of his one good arm, the business end slapped into Walter's massive palm. Another spin, like a cowboy with a six-shooter, returned the handle to his grip and put a smile on his face."

To Brian Bird and John Fornof: for encouragement and support during the grind of the third quarter of this journey. Brian, thanks for sharing your insight that God showed you about Him being a writer, too.

To Terri Blackstock: for showing the way to write wholesome, gritty stories that are "lovingly dedicated to the Nazarene." And to Frank Peretti: for great Christian fiction (I particularly loved "Illusion"), and for one of my favorite sermons of all time. (Search YouTube for "Frank Peretti The Chair" for a tour-de-force of humor and edification.) Also, I borrowed a technique that you used in "The Oath"—that of the creepy, past writings at the beginning of the early chapters. It was so helpful in this particular story.

To Leonard and Maggie Carabellos: for opening your hearts and making me a part of the team at CaryAnn Productions, even before I was ready.

To Mike Bickle: A true spiritual father and a great gift to me as a person. Thanks for teaching me about the heart of God and living before the Judgment Seat.

To my fantastic audiobook team: Tommy Sargent, Leonard Carabellos, Danny Sargent, Zach Webb, Katherine Koplin, Runner Francisco, Caresse Hassoldt, Steve Vaughan, Sean Bateman, Paul Allen, Paul Cooke, Dave Webb, Kevin Lusk, Jeex Barlau, Phil "Papa" Sargent, Justin Schluessler, Maddy Wewel, Ben Bradbury, Sammy Sargent, Jeanette Williams, Emma Sargent, Caramia Sommers, Nate, Sarah, Ellie and others who may not be on the team as of the writing of this. It was so much fun to work with you!

A special shout-out to Zach Webb and Jackson "Jeex" Barlau for their insightful and enthusiastic help. And to Steve Vaughan for his eager participation, willing assistance, and use of his equipment. I loved working with you.

To Tom Khazoyan and Jess Stainbrook for some key counsel, friendship, and support of my boys in the early days. Your input was invaluable in setting me on the right trajectory. Same goes for Clyde Taber—thanks for locking me into 10,000 hours and the Rule of 3 at such an early stage of the journey. (One down, at least two to go, Clyde!)

To Shawn Sikkema: A great friend, spiritual father, and fellow visionary who believed when it was still a long way off. By the way, I'm lifting weights. To David Sorteberg: A dear friend and brother. Thanks for listening all along the way.

To Laura Hackett Park: for the music to enter the fictive bubble. I'm still "caught up in the Fellowship."

To Karen Pickering and the rest of the team at Book Villages. Thanks for being patient with a newbie. It's been a pleasure to work with you. To Doug and Darla for a significant housecleaning effort on this thing. Doug, thank you for teaching me the role of an editor. To Jeff and Lisa for your illustrative gifts and for putting up with "authors" (insert shake of Jeff's head).

To Ryan Opfer for being a good friend and helping us get going with the audio equipment. I'm not sure we would have started without that initial push.

To Sarah Sargent, my wonderful eleven-year-old daughter, who saved me from an embarrassing blunder. Great eyes, kiddo!

To Katherine Vandersluis for "loaning" me the old bibles that kicked this whole story into gear. (I still need to get them back to you :)) Say hi to Rolland for me. It was great meeting you guys.

To Dave Arnold, Paul McCusker and so many others at Focus on the Family Radio Theatre. Hundreds of hours of Narnia, Father Gilbert, and Adventures in Odyssey have continually exposed me to great storytelling.

To my dear kids: Danny, Joey, Sammy, Hannah, Tommy, Emma, Nate, Sarah, Ellie, and Mikey. For believing, supporting and going with me on this journey. I love you all dearly. You know you're becoming a story family when your *six*-year-old says, "You know what, dad? Darth Vader is a really good antagonist." Looking forward to many more years and many more stories if the Lord wills.

To my beautiful wife, soulmate and best friend, Erica. I know this has been a frog-in-the-pot for some years now, but you've been a faithful, trusting supporter of me that whole time. I so look forward to the next twenty-five years with you. My heart is yours, babe. Middle age is awesome! #withallofmyheartistilldo

Excerpt from
Generations 2: The DC Gambit

Love *Is Still the* Key

Still staring at the Washington Monument, Jordan sat down on the bench. He ran a hand along the faded wood. Delightful memories.

Thank You, God. I don't deserve this.

The email app on his phone had a "1" next to it. A touch of OCD usually compelled him to triage his Inbox down to zero. The day and the memories lingered—almost to the point of letting go of his compulsion.

Almost.

Jordan tapped. His heart jumped.

My dearest Jordan,

Seeing the first line, he leaned back on the bench and settled in for a slow read.

Next June couldn't get here soon enough.

He read through the letter. It encouraged him to rise to the level of Senator Smith's belief in him and to look forward to their life together. A few Scriptures about love wove tastefully through it. Even in an email, Bethany wrapped the words like cords around his heart and prepared to pull them tight.

His eyes lingered as he allowed himself to move to the end of the message.

Never forget: I'm your beloved always and forever,
Bethany

A warm glow filled his chest, and his smile lit up the park in front of the Monument.

P.S. Love is still the key.

What?

His heart lurched from peaceful to third gear in an instant. His face turned grim as his eyes darted back and forth over the letter again.

Four Scriptures about love.

This cannot be an accident.

Jordan counted aloud as he traced the words of each verse with his finger. He stopped each time he reached the word "love." Last year, in an old family Bible, his great-grandfather had used this technique to hide a clue that rewrote the history of his hometown. William Nolan, condemned thief and murderer, had been exonerated.

Maybe it's another of her playful games.

He shook his head. *Maybe.*

1-2-3-4-5-6-7-8. "**H**." He counted on his fingers like a schoolboy—too much in a hurry to worry about doing it the cool way with his phone and his voice. He moved down to the next scripture.

1-2-3-4-5. "**E**."

Next scripture.

He counted to twelve. "**L**." He didn't like where this was going.

Last scripture.

He counted to sixteen. "**P**."

His heart accelerated to fourth gear.

How can this be?

Jordan launched the voice diary on his phone.

What's going on?

There's no way this is an accident

What are the clues?
1. Bethany would never use "Love is still the key" on accident
2. Couple that with four Scriptures that just happen to have the word "love" in them
3. Combine that with the word position numbers spelling H-E-L-P

So, Bethany needs help
What am I thinking? BETHANY NEEDS HELP!!!

Slow down. Breathe. Think.

She just got to New York—what, maybe, three weeks ago?
Why would she need help?
Why not just call and ask for help?
Why so cryptic?

● ● ●

Bethany looked down at her phone as yet another tear slipped from her eye and trickled down her face. Locked in the bathroom, as much as possible away from prying eyes and listening ears, Bethany contemplated the hardest decision of her life.

Seven missed calls.

She thumbed through her photos. One of them, from last month, particularly captured the memory. Jordan stood behind her, leaning on the railing of Wilson's bridge, with one arm wrapped around her just under her chin. His other hand held her selfie stick and camera. Both of Bethany's hands came up from below and gripped his forearm as her knuckles cradled her radiantly smiling face. The late summer sun gilded them and reflected a twinkle off her ring finger.

She pulled the phone to her forehead while the tears flowed freely—again. *I can't believe I'm even considering this.*

With her other hand, she picked up her diary. It fell open to the same page she was on three days ago. She had walked into her dorm room and *knew*, in a blinding flash of dread, that her life was about to change. Her diary had sat on her desk and mocked her. Perfectly positioned, with both sides aligned to the edges of the desk, it may as well have been a calling card. She couldn't keep her hand from trembling as she reached for it.

Not again.

Now sitting alone in the bathroom, three days later, she read it one more time—willing it to change.

> Hello, Bethany,
>
> Did you miss me?
>
> It's been a long time, I know. But not long enough for me to forget.
>
> I never forget.
>
> That was pretty clever what you did. I'm impressed. Nobody ever scores a point against me.
>
> But you did.
>
> An eighteen-year-old girl—now nineteen.
>
> Even worse, that fiancé of yours scored several. I've never failed on a job in my life. Until I met Jordan Nolan. Now I'm a fugitive. An event that unprecedented deserves an extra special response, wouldn't you say? Besides staying hidden, I've spent a year planning this.
>
> Here's how it's going to play out: You do exactly as I say and the story might, just might, have a happy ending for some of the people you love. If you say a word about this, or if you run back home, several people you care about will have early exits from the story.
>
> It starts with him.
>
> Not only did he do the unthinkable in getting away from me, but he reminds me of someone who robbed me of the only one that I ever loved. Therefore, I'm going to rob him of the one he loves.

If you want him to live, you will break off the relationship.
You have three days.

Fifteen minutes later, she cried the last drop. More would come, but that was for another day. Time was up.

Bethany heard the voices of her classmates in the common area. She used her whole hand to wipe the tears from her cheeks. She reached up and turned on the fan. Because of the age of the building, the fan—like many other things—hadn't been modernized. It carried plenty of volume.

I must do it.

Under her breath, so quietly it could be heard only by herself and God, Bethany put all she had into the prayer. She still addressed God in the same way she had done as an eight-year-old.

"Daddy, You know what's at stake. I need You like I've never needed You before."

She looked down at the photo one more time and gripped her phone tighter.

"You did the miracle and brought us together. You know I'm all his and no one else's. Please don't let this be the end. In Jesus' name. Amen."

Bethany stood up and wiped her eyes. She flushed the toilet even though she hadn't used it. Walking to the sink, she looked at herself in the mirror. Not good enough. She washed her face. Still not good enough. She opened her purse and reapplied her makeup.

Okay, that's passable.

She took the ring off her finger and buried it deep into a pocket in her purse. Then she turned from the mirror, steeled herself, and walked out into the common area to wait for call number eight.

Three days and eight phone calls later, he finally got a hold of her.

"Hello," Bethany's normally melodic voice sounded flat. Music or other voices could be heard in the background. She must be in her dormitory at the academy.

"Bethany!" said Jordan.

"You've got a lot of nerve calling me, Mr. Nolan." Bethany's tone was acrid.

Jordan gripped the edge of his kitchen table to keep from falling over.

What in the world?

"How dare you call me after what you've done?" she continued.

Jordan had never heard her speak with such venom to anybody—especially not him. There was no more noise in the background. Whatever voices had been speaking were probably listening with jaws dropped.

"What have I done?" Jordan brushed back a tear.

"I can't believe you would even ask that."

Never in a million years would he have expected this.

"Bethany, are you okay?"

"No, I am *not* okay."

More silence.

"Listen, Jordan; I gotta go."

"Bethany, wait. What about us?"

"US?"

She bit his head off through the phone.

"I'm gonna need some time. Don't contact me for a while. In fact, it's over."

Her words lanced his heart open.

"In a relationship," Bethany paused, "*Love* is still the key." She almost spat the words. "Don't contact me again until you figure out what that means."

Future Generations

What's next?

Dear Reader,

Allow me to welcome you to my diary. I hope you've enjoyed our story. The gang and I have enjoyed the ride immensely. You might be wondering what's next:

1. Did you like the story? Jordan and I (and especially Allie) would really appreciate it if you would leave us a review and tell your friends. We'd love to see how our lives unfold, and your support can help make that possible. Gadg might even like it too, but he would never say so.

2. Generations: The Audiobook. Due out in late 2018/early 2019. This is a full-cast, dramatized, mostly unabridged, audiobook of the story you've just read. Join Jordan and company as some very talented actors and actresses bring us to life. Dear Reader, I know you must do dishes, work out, travel, commute and do many other things. Wouldn't you rather do them while listening to a story? Download us at amazon.com and possibly some other channels. Coming soon to a device near you.

3. Generations 2: The DC Gambit. What happens to the gang a year later? What about the job with Senator Smith? Do Jordan and I finally get to kiss? What about Isaac Molencki's threat? I wonder what would happen to Gadg if Allie really wasn't out of his league? Whatever happened to Jeffrey Kingston? I don't even know what a "gambit" is, so I'll let Jordan give you some details below.

4. Generationsthestory.com: Check out news, updates, backstory, behind-the-scenes and more at the official website. You might even hear from us, the characters, personally.

Well, dear friends, it's been a wonderful journey so far. We trust it's been a blessing for you, and we hope to see you again soon.

Sincerely,
Bethany

Notes on Generations 2: The DC Gambit

What might a reader want to know about Generations 2?

First, what's a gambit?
In chess, it refers to an opening sacrifice of material to gain in some other way—such as a stronger position. Its broader definition is a device or action that entails a calculated risk to gain an advantage.
Second, what's the story about?
Remember the end of Generations 1? Several people were unhappy with us. Guess what? A year later, they're not much happier with us. What does that mean? Trouble—and a lot of it.

Questions:
What would happen if Gadg had a life and death battle of wits with one of the best hackers in the world? How could two people maintain a relationship if one of the most feared hitmen was bent on destroying it and them? What if I got an insider's view of politics in the swirl of a DC power grab?

Summary:
Generations 2: The DC Gambit is a high-stakes, plot-twisting mystery filled with danger, romance, deception and redemption. Readers should check out generationsthestory.com for updates.